Dedicated to
Anthony Edward Mathew,
1945-2005

Montag Press
ISBN:978-1-940233-22-2
Cover art © 2015 Daniel Serra
Jacket and book design © 2015 Rick Febré
Author photo © 2015 Jonathan Jewell

Montag Press Team:
Project Editor – Charlie Franco
Managing Director – Charlie Franco

A Montag Press Book
www.montagpress.com
Montag Press
1066 47th Ave. Unit #9
Oakland CA 94601 USA

Montag Press, the burning book with the hatchet cover, the skewed word mark and the portrayal of the long-suffering fireman mascot are trademarks of Montag Press.

Printed & Digitally Originated in the United States of America
10 9 8 7 6 5 4 3 2 1

DAVID MATHEW

O MY DAYS

MONTAG

there the waves were storied with his deeds

Herman Melville, *Moby Dick*

DAVID MATHEW

O MY
DAYS

contents

PART ONE:
Are You Listening?

One.

No one kicks off in the Cookery class. Kicking off in Cookery means the class is cancelled, and for some of us it's the only good meal of the week. So there are consequences. Naturally enough, the D responsible gets a battering later on. That stands to reason. But far worse than getting twisted up is the cold shoulder the brother receives for the duration of the Cookery ban. Some rudeboys can't handle that at all. They can't stand not being spoken to; can't stand the pantomime reactions, the dilated nostrils, that suggest a bad aroma has wafted over. Anyone busted? the D will hear.

Roller really should have known better. The Gov goes for the bell, and he moves fast for someone so hench; I feel the air whip past my ears. I turn. And Roller's got Meaney in a headlock; he's pounding the brother's head with a rolling pin. No expression on his face. No build-up to the incident, no bickering, no beef. It's like someone's flipped a switch. It happens from time to time, but not in the Cookery class.

There's blood on the rolling pin by the time the screws arrive, a couple of seconds later. We're all shouting, *Allow it, bruv, Allow it, cuz,* but Roller keeps on rolling. Doesn't hear us. Doesn't hear how desperate we are not to lose our bangers 'n' mash or our chicken terrine every week. Even doing the fucking theory worksheets is worth it if it means a Wednesday apple crumble or cauliflower cheese.

Allow it, blood! I'm screaming.

Just as quickly as it began, it ends. Roller loses interest and starts blinking away some tears. He releases Meaney. Brother falls to the floor in a jellyfish heap. There's blood on his face like a Balaclava. Roller looks confused, even as the screws start to twist him up. They are surprised that he doesn't fight back. We all are. The screws don't like it; they're not used to passivity or playing possum. Their confusion lends them energy and malice. What would normally have waited until 'an unfortunate accident' during Sosh or after the evening meal is executed, there and then. They twist him up something different. So much so that the Gov is going again for the panic bell — to stop this new scuff.

It doesn't happen. Activity ceases. There are two broken bruvs on the Cookery Room floor; six inmates looking stunned — I count myself among this number, and if I don't look stunned I certainly feel it; a hush in the air, of dust settling, maybe; and a dreadful smell tickling the hairs in my nostrils. My bacon's burning, my eggs are turning brown; how the fuck has that happened in a hot minute? It's going weird.

O my days! someone says.

Then the fun starts again. Food is burning in three or four frying pans; an oven is belching out dense burps of smoke. The fire alarm squeals. The screws' radios begin bleating—and then comes the bit that makes Ray, the Cookery Gov, pale visibly—like he's just been shanked—and that guy's old school and he's been in the army.

Simultaneously the two screws lean down, one over Roller and one over Meaney; and do you know what? It's horrifying. In the smoke, the pong and the din, do you know what? Those screws *lips* the co-Ds.

Swear down. Mouth-to-mouth kisses. They lips the brothers and the scuff re-commences, and no one knows what to do. Ray's veiny thumb-pad hits the bell. We should dust, I'm thinking; we should get the fuck into the corridor. They'll come in charging. The afternoon's flavour has changed; I've never tasted it before. I don't know if I like it or I don't.

Someone sighs. O my days! the cuz breathes.

O my days! someone answers. O my days!

Two.

Man! When man get to Big Man Jail, well, man! That when man know man blessed, rudeboy. Man know it and man allow it.

It's Ostrich talking. We call him Ostrich because of the length of his bird. He's a lifer. Murder. A Johnny-99, full stretch. Chair leg to cranium.

Man, he is mumbling on.

Me? My bird is five years. Wounding with Intent. It could've been worse. I say, Why, Ostrich-man? Big Man Jail tough. This is sick.

This ain't sick, Ostrich contends. This is explosive.

Twos on that, I add, hoping to change the CD. I'm referring to the burn that he's pinching—oddly—between third and fourth fingers. He hands me the cigarette. I drag. Hand it back.

Ostrich is still in happy-clappy land, in his head. Me own duvet. Me own cloze, he says. Me this. Me that.

Twenty-four seven bang-up, I say.

That noise, rudeboy.

We're outside, although it's cold. Why not? You live in a box, you want to be unwrapped, time to time. There in our grey sweats, with our burns. And I'm longing for Canteen, Friday morning. I've earned well this month and I should be eligible for a new pack of burn and a bash mag.

What you make-a this morning? I ask Ostrich. Cookery, in-nit. That time ting. It was put on peculiar.

Man? says Ostrich. Like I don't even know. Are you listening? I'm listening.

Time went long. Yeah. Difficult.

Allow it, cuz. Time went devious innit. Allow it *again*.

Who that? asks Ostrich.

I look up. And here he comes, five foot and a squirt of shit, and he's in He-Man pyjamas—blue and yellow—for trying to escape from the previous jail. Three-man escort, fully-armed. I'm impressed, blood.

He's a fish. Name of Dott, I tell Ostrich. Tell you more if you twos me on a burn. If not, ask the chaplain on Friday. I'm going back in to play pool.

He the fish? Ostrich goes on. Thought he be a hench moth-erfucker.

He's the size of a poodle.

It's at moments such as these that you start to get a grip on how the screws, the Ed.U Govs, the Health Care staff and others form an opinion about the collective psyche of the members of a non-voluntary club such as ours. Because Ostrich says, *That* squirt? Fourteen women?

Lifed off, I tell him.

Man, Ostrich says disgusted. Man shoulda known bet-ter than to stop at four, man, he says. Man knew man was only breaking cherry.

I accept the offer of his tiny burn. What you mean? I ask cautiously.

There's three man no man know about, rudeboy, Ostrich tells me.

And I guess that's where it all begins.

Three.

Seven-thirty in the a.m. and I'm awake a long time before I need to be. I bash one out, using whatever porn I haven't lent out in return for burn or for a favour, and I sit at my desk with my beads in my hands. I pray. I contemplate the day: Thursday.

I'm looking forward to next Tuesday in the same way that I always do, and it seems like a distance, blood. But it's a mark. Tuesday is the day I get to meet the new fish in the pond, traditionally: unless they are deemed unsuitable for interaction with other prisoners (for whatever reason; for protection for them or for us), or unsuitable for interaction with the staff. There are some I don't get to meet as they're immediately strapped into Health Care, into Suicide Watch, into Maximum Segregation ('going down block') or the worst of the worse: to the Puppydog Wing. If I have to, I'll talk about that at a later date. I haven't had my breakfast yet and my stomach is still queasy from yesterday and from a bad sleep on what sometimes feels like a bed of rusty nails. Feeling sick, I wait for unlock.

The screws make no attempt to take you by surprise. That's what happens at some of the remand centres I've known: they creep to a certain lucky someone's door. They flip back the peep slot. Catch you bashing, you're falling down a flight of stairs sometime. Me, I'm staring at the metal door and waiting first for the movement of heavy feet, and then the club on the frame. Quite often they don't even bother to open the slot.

Alfreth?

Gov! I answer.

You showering this morning, son?

No, sir!

Fine, son. Get ready for Movements.

Yes, sir!

Just to explain, I tend to save up my shower entitlement for the weekend. I'm not one of those filthy bruvs who can't be arsed. I queue for my cereal. I take it back to my cell. Then I queue to dispose of the rubbish: the carton and the small pot of milk with a postage-stamp sized rectangle of cellophane over the top. It's another day in Paradise. I listen to some Death Rap as I munch. Then it's time to Move. At eight-thirty the doors of us fortunate to have a prison job, or a class to amble over to, or Gym, snap open, and it's off to work we go. For me it's the tiny Library. I work in the prison Library. And as I'm released from the Wing at nine, along with the rest of us, I cross the exercise yard, then the yard between D and E Wings—acknowledging the *Wogwun*s and the back slaps, shoulder crashes and reminders of favours of half a dozen yoots on the way, all the while thinking: Can't wait to meet Dott next Tuesday.

Tuesday being the day the new boys get their thorough Library induction. The morning is as charged as a hotwired engine. Screws know it; cons know it; in about a hot minute I'm going to understand that the civilian staff from the County Library Service know it too. There's scarcely a lip not flapping with rumour: about yesterday's events, in the Cookery class.

Wuppan? I'm asked.

Is it true yat?

Dunno, is all I can answer. I've started to doubt my own eyes. But there are facts—and I do mean facts, blood—that can't be denied. Such as: Roller and Meaney are down block, awaiting their Friday adjudication (loss of TV and Canteen privileges, is my guess; and a nice long solitary stay in a six by six, on a mattress with no bedsprings beneath it); and the fact that the screws in question in the incident—not on my Wing so I don't know their names—have been sent home, pending a full investigation.

The Education block smells of bad vegetables, as ever. It's into the holding area, and then through the heavy green gates, up the stairs. The Library is as big as a lounge.

Morning, Alfreth, I'm given.

Morning, Miss.

I make my way round to the business side of the counter, trying not to meet the eyes of the stranger standing next to Miss. Sit. Boot up the old PC.

Alfreth? says Miss Patterson. This is Miss Thistle.

All three of us stand up in unison.

All right, Miss? I say.

To my surprise she extends a hand for me to shake. Not only is she not, therefore, prison staff, or even civilian staff (whose hand you won't touch either, and believe me I've tried), but she is something else. Another step removed. But a hand's a hand, right? I take the opportunity: the first female flesh I've encountered in two years, four months and seventeen days. With hindsight, I grip it, I think. I'm confused. It's like stepping on the moon or curtain-working an alien.

Miss Thistle is here from a university, says Miss Patterson.

Is it?

Yes. Miss Thistle can probably explain better than I can. Miss Thistle?

Yes.

And Alfreth? says Miss Patterson.

My eyes sweep from the one woman's to her considerably older counterpart's. And I answer, Yes, Miss?

Please let go of Miss Thistle's hand, Alfreth.

Sorry.

So, I'm a D—I'm a Defendant—in a crime, for once, that I haven't even contemplated. Sod's Law if I get an extra 28 days on my sentence. Miss Thistle is more of a Miss Rose, looks-wise. To be frank, she's still not buff, but beggars can't be choosers. All of the pretty screws—certainly on Wings A to E—are chompers and refuse to take my mild attempts at flirting seriously. I let go of Miss Thistle's hand. Sit down. Chat-time, is it? Seems so.

Tell me, Alfreth. That's a Derbyshire name, isn't it?

I nod my head as the other two women take to their twirly, expensive chairs.

Innit, is all I'm happy to offer them.

It is indeed. A town, I think, says Miss Thistle. Maybe a village.

I nod my head, thinking: lose nothing by making conversation.

Me old boy's family from up that way, back in the day, like. Never seen it, cuz.

Alfreth, Miss Patterson warns. Do not refer to our visitor as cuz.

I swivel away to see my screen booted up. I type in the Library Staff password. I've heard enough, I almost say, but refrain from doing so in fear for the loss of the left-arm bicep Redband that speaks of my trustworthiness, compliance, and which has landed me the job in the first place.

Better get wriggling, I offer.

Miss Thistle is only making conversation, Alfreth, says Miss Patterson.

Angela, it's okay.

Angela.

I turn to the two women again, aware of a breach of protocol.

Patterson is too. But it's Thistle, blatantly trying to cover her tracks, who speaks next.

I can see that Alfreth wasn't aware of that, Miss Patterson, she says. I apologise.

Although I can't see any immediate mileage in knowing the Library Manager's Christian name, it is good to see that Patterson thinks I might be able to use the information. But who is going to care?

That's quite all right, Miss Thistle, the old girl states.

Alfreth is an Enhanced Level prisoner and as such has had to be trusted. So that's what I'm going to do right now, Alfreth. I'm going to trust you.

Thanks, I tell her.

Because I'll know where the information came from if it gets around, won't I? she bangs on, point made but needing to be re-made.

You will, I tell her. Shall I get on with the orders?

I don't want Patterson—and that's Angela to her friends—or Thistle—first name unknown—to understand that I'm curious to learn why someone from outside has been allowed into the Library on the business side of the desk. In all my days I've never heard of it happening. Even the local councillors and politicians and other who-gives-a-fuck bigwigs who sometimes visit, they stay where they're put. Swear down. As I start to tear open this week's orders—mainly TV guides, a few bodybuilding mags, a periodical on trainspotting of all things (for one of the four-eyed wankers on Puppydog), a bit of bog-standard bash—Miss Thistle rolls her chair a half-metre closer to me. There is something she wants to say. Or needs to. I can smell her perfume, and it's like a fresh drop of the disgusting hooch that Naylor on C Wing used to brew, before he was shipped out to Big Man Jail. The impact, I mean. Thistle's perfume was sweet; Naylor's hooch smelt like an enema. But they both go to the back of your head, no messing—one-way delivery. It's the first perfume I've smelt in *time*.

Do I call you Alfreth? Miss Thistle asks. Or would you prefer I used your first name?

Angela starts typing away.

No one's ever asked me this before.

You don't know my first name, I inform her, perhaps a bit harshly.

Your first name is William, she says, immediately scoring a point. She's done some research on who—it seems—she's to be working with.

No one calls me William, I answer. Usually it's Billy.

Then Billy it is. Billy, I'll be working here for the next little while, on a placement. Do you know what a placement is, Billy?

Don't play me for a cunt, I want to tell her; but instead I nod my head. It's where you're working for someone else and you're getting an inside.

Kind of. I work for the university. She leans forward slightly and puts her elbows on her knees. Good job that although she might not have been told about forename procedures, she's at least been informed about dress code. The beige-coloured top she wears beneath her light-grey trouser suit is a polo-neck.

She's not worried about being in a prison and that's strange.

I'm writing about the Young Offender experience as part of my PhD in Adult Basic Skills Education, she goes on. I want to know all about the learning pathway for Young Offenders. Not the facts, she adds quickly, in a voice that leaks out bare disgust, that I can get from any number of reports. Not the stats. The experience.

I'm with you, I reply. You want a guinea pig.

Well, not exactly.

You want a snitch, Miss Thistle, is what you want.

Alfreth, warns Patterson in her deepest voice.

I don't snitch, I tell her categorically; but I'm thinking different things entirely. I'm thinking *three* different things entirely. I'm thinking: *One.* If you're interested in the so-called learning pathway, then why are you sitting with someone who's passed all his exams and not in a motherfucking classroom? *Two.* A letter to the Governor. Not an Education Gov, but *the* Gov: the Governor of the jail, Glazer, who I'm assuming has okayed this malarkey. The letter about my confusion, and which I'm already penning in my head. The one that reads and goes along the lines of:

> *Dear Bumberclutt,*
> *What the fuck do you think you're doing letting this woman into a maximum security prison, arsehole? Are you trying to mash her or something?*
>
> *Love,*
> *Billy Alfreth.*

And *three*. The sense—the feeling that I can't much describe and even less explain—that something is wrong here. Something is missing. I am certain, right now, that Miss Thistle is lying to me.

Billy, no, she continues, I don't require a snitch. I require a mind.

Excuse me?

Someone with intelligence, who knows the workings of the Education Department inside out.

I stop tearing my way into the magazine bundle.

Still sounds like a snitch to me, Miss Thistle, I answer politely.

Call me Kate, she answers—no doubt to Angie's disapproval—but in such a way that I know I've just been played.

As Ostrich might say, *Man fall in love for lesser ting*.

Four.

Tango One to Papa Alpha. Request permission to send Redband Alfreth from Education Block One to A Wing, over.

The screw talking is nearing retirement but he's okay. Worn at the belt, his radio tweets and I hear: *Permission granted, over*. So

I'm on my way, on the first leg of today's deliveries, carrying my luminous yellow satchel of TV guides and other periodicals. The rain is coming down and I'm only in my sweats. By the time I get to the A Wing gate I'm frozen and sopping wet. I'm let in. Then it's onwards. *Albert Three to Papa Alpha. Request permission to send Redband Alfreth from Albert to Bernard, over.* So it goes. *Permission granted, over.*

At least I don't have to shovel shit all day with the Gardening Crew. But the rain is like nothing I've ever known, up here. You get used to the cameras following your every move; you get used to the constant threat of violence (accepted and doled out); yet I still haven't got used to the weather. Swear down it rains harder up here, up in the hills. I can't wait for Sosh. I don't expect to find any answers to anything, but if I can at least find the way to pose the right questions I'll be happy.

Lunch is manure in a bun.

Five.

Segregation Unit, I'm told. Tooty suite.

I don't correct him. You don't correct Screw Jones, unless you happen to have two weeks left to live and you're aiming for a story that will live on longer than your own mortal bollocks do.

What's the charge against me, sir?

Fuck off. You saw it. Join the line.

Thank you, sir.

It's nearly ten o'clock, and I've long since feared my way past the point of rational self-delusion. I'm not called for the Library, so I'm going to be called for something else—and I know what the something else is. Adjudication.

Down block, bruv.

But what can I say? It's a fight in the Cookery Room. Roller and Meaney go batshit and start the process. In come in the screws. Mashed if I'm going to mention the kissing.

They're waiting for me. I go straight in. Jones is behind me and I walk the long, long corridor that leads to the Adjudication Court, where Governor Glazer will be waiting with his hang-dog smile and his halitosis. The room is, as ever, the colour of tar-flecked phlegm. I take my seat at the bolted-down table and place my hands on the surface, knowing the drill. Look up to see Glazer looking down from his throne.

Do you know why you're here, Alfreth? he asks.

Yes, sir.

Good. And what have you got to say?

It's a twist-up, innit. Two yoots, two screws.

That's not what I'm getting at and you know it.

I shrug my shoulders. Can't explain it is it, I answer truth-fully.

Were you aware of any conflict beforehand?

No, sir.

Were you aware of anything, Alfreth?

No, sir. Shit went long of a sudden. Hot minute, yat.

And you understand the results of your being found out to be lying? Grazer adds, like the bloodclot he is.

I understand, sir, I reply.

Loss of Enhanced. Loss of Redband. Loss of privileges.

Sir? I say, I don't know dick. Much a revelation to me as to you.

I sincerely doubt that, Glazer answers. Dismissed.

I haven't even been asked to confirm my name and pris-on number. There's no doubt about it: this has shitted them up ghost-style.

I said *dismissed*.

Thank you, sir, I mutter.

But there's no way I can fail to notice the woman sitting in the witness stand, as all new employees are entitled—or forced—to do, to scratch their heads about the Adjudication proceedings.

It's Kate Thistle.

Six.

Kate Thistle is thirty-nine years old. I know because I asked her. She could have lied but she didn't. Or so I'm assuming. Are you listening, though? I'm not sure I'm doing the right thing.

Like, she asks me, *Do you regret your crime?* and I'm like *rah. Allow it.*

And she's like, *Tell me. If you want to.* And I'm like, *Nappin, Miss.*

You won't think she's thirty-nine by the looks of her, mind. She looks twenty-six, and I *would*. In my head, I already have.

It's immaterial. I say to Ostrich, Man alive. I can't wait till the weekend.

It *is* the weekend, he replies.

No, man. I mean tomorrow night. Saturday.

Why, what's so explosive about Saturday night, man?

Playing Shelley at pool, innit. Three burn stake.

Ostrich whistles. Who knows about this?

You, me and him, I answer. I can trust you with this, can't I, Ostrich?

Sure, man. Man lips as sealed as a lady panda poom-poom. But be careful, innit. They catch you gambling again, man lose his Enhanced.

I know. But he challenged me. I can't let it get around that man challenged me and I didn't do nothing about it. Be worse than when he stole that CD and I didn't fight him to get it back.

That different. Everyone know you couldn't fight him on that occasion. You just had your job. You fight, you lose it. Ostrich shrugs. You might lose. Just contemplate the ifs, innit.

I won't lose to that fucking squirrel.

Just contemplate, man.

For a second I do so. And I arrive at the conclusion, which I voice, that losing is no biggie: it's failing to respond to a duel, in this place, that's the biggie. When that starts getting around, God knows what'll occur.

Screw Jones gets his radioed orders. In the exercise yard, in the gloom, under the impotent floodlights, he responds with a barked out command:

Okay, fellas. Everyone in. Time for night-night.

We get to our feet. We are all dressed in grey. We are already in our pyjamas, but we'll have to get out of them to turn in. Some of us will stay up all night. Some will pray; some will play—the X-Box, the PlayStation; some will read and improve their minds; some will bash their bongos until nothing comes out but water. But we're all the same. That's what this place does. That's its job. To neutralize us.

I've timed it to perfection, I think. I've timed it so that Ostrich and I have less than two minutes between the yard and our adjacent cells on the ones. I've waited two days to say what I'm about to say, but the time has been important; I've needed the time in order to firm up the deal with Shelley: the same one that I've just lied to Ostrich about. Two minutes. Less than that now, as we enter the disinfected atmosphere and start our climb up the first set of metal stairs.

Ostrich-man? I say. Are you listening, though? I'm risking a lot so I keep my voice down.

I'm listening.

What I win tomorrow, man, yeah?

Yeah? he says cautiously. He knows he might be in as much trouble—for conspiratorial silence, for duplicity—as I am if it becomes known that he is aware of my gambling pact with Shelley.

It's yours, Ostrich, I whisper. Three burn.

At the top of the flight of stairs we turn left and he looks into my eyes, his bloodshot orbits neatly framing two pupils shaped like question marks.

If you tell me about the others you killed, I tell him. Three burn.

I enter my cell, drop down to my knees for prayers. The door closes and the night begins.

My *life* begins.

Seven.

I mean that. Night time brings on the truth and the spray that dissolves all of the glue that I need to use in order to hold my day together. My dreams are like balm, like salvation. My dreams are vivid. My dreams give me clues about how best to go on and how I've royally messed up. But there's a life I enter— briefly—before I even touch my dreams. That place between prayer and coma. You're not quite awake but you're not quite asleep either. Jerked this way and that, you're a puppet at the whim and the beck and call of the stronger forces in your head. I like that feeling. That drifting, dozing feeling. I feel at home there. In one dream I take it all back. In one dream I swim back to Bricky—or Brixton if we're still on formal-names terms—and I do it all in reverse. Take my pen-knife from his arm, watch him un-punch my beak, and slur my way backwards through my demand for cash. The film stops. Then it starts the right way again, but this time my co-Ds and I are not mugging; we're giving him directions to the museum or something. We're helping. I like that dream. Most of my dreams I like, in fact, even the bad ones. Even the ones where I'm climbing a hill and I keep falling down, sliding down to the foot; or being chased by an animal; or trying to lift something that squishes me. Because they're not real, the dreams, and reality is the worst horror when you can't control it or understand it. Dreams are oases. I lie about my dreams when I have my monthly psychiatric report. It's nice, if not vital, to have something to myself. Something not in the notes that will wriggle their way into my Parole Report. Not that I'm going to get parole; I'm not stupid. I did it. I pleaded guilty. And I did it for money.

She asks me how I'm feeling and I say sick. What's wrong with you? she'll ask. And I'll say nothing, man, I'm sick. Sick good. Yeah, blood, I'll answer—as though she hasn't heard it before. And then I'll realise I'm just a case study number and she's forgotten me since last time; and what's worse is that I haven't even charged up enough respect for her to consult the notes that she made at the previous meeting.

Your dreams, she'll sometimes ask. Tell me about them.

And that's where I lie. I tell a fib. Because it doesn't matter much if I do or if I don't and if there's one more thing that unites all of us here, it's the element of needing something to call our own.

I name an actress or a pop star. I tell her she's sucking my dick. She records the information with a penciled smile, because it's what's expected. I tell her I come on her breasts. She writes it down. I wonder, parenthetically, what she feels when she interviews the nonces and ponces on Puppydog Wing, where the questions are presumably an equivalent. What does a four- eyes dream of? I know there's a yoot on Puppy who raped a puppy. What colour are that cunt's dreams? A colour I don't understand and whose flavour I don't like. Oh. Oh, and he happened to rape his sister and his mum as well. Nice guy. I'll send a Christmas card.

When I deliver the magazines to Puppydog, I always wish for a few more extra minutes than I get when I go to all of the other Wings. A few more minutes with which to light up some kind of firebrand and burn the dirty fuckers in their customised homes. The perverts.

Anyway. Where was I? Where was I, in the night?

Her name is also Kate, by the way. Kate Wollington. But her accent is foreign and she married into the surname, is my guess, like someone marrying into a family business. My psychologist, I mean. Married or not, we still call her Miss. Off the top of my head, I can't think of anyone called Mrs.

Won't happen to me. The marrying bit, I mean. I'm tired, yat.

Sometimes the Night Screw opens the flap and I pretend to be asleep. It's a way of warding the cunts off, no pun intended. *Umleitung*. It's a German word, meaning diversion, that I learned doing my German GCSE, here on the in. I got a B. Accent poor but delivery clear. Swear down. Can't wait to see how my German GCSE will help me on the out. When I hit road, as Ostrich might say. A boon, no doubt. My tongue is in my cheek like a pestle and mortar. What am I warding them off from? From my freedom.

Only free when you're asleep, in this place.

I miss my mum. I miss her resembling a Rottweiller chewing a chilli, but most of all I miss her laughing and gassing and giving it a good time innit. I miss her arms, I miss her smile. I don't miss my dad. I never knew him. Not many of us miss our dads.

I'm going to sleep.

Eight.

I'm going to dream.

This bastard's my favourite. I'm a pulse of electricity, I think, without weight and without physical form. I'm dusting large: here, there, yay under the stair. No wanker can stop me yat. And I approach the wire mesh surrounding the Wing; I sail through it. I approach the thirty-foot walls; I sail through 'em. Not over them, is it, but through 'em. It's beautiful. It's my vindication.

For what precisely, I don't know. Because I did it.

Sometimes I dream I didn't, but I did. He wouldn't give me his wallet. I stabbed him quickly, three times in the right arm. Five years. High on drink and bare sniff at the time. But as ever, when I think about that night, I get the memory mangled with another, in which I am being attacked. I am fighting for my own life. It's what I've said all along. I can't shake free of the idea.

It's Saturday morning, and I pray in my crackers, bare-chested.

Always feels like a new beginning, does a Saturday. I'm there in nothing but tattoos, boxers and beads. It's the closest thing to peace I get, some weeks, outside night-time.

Short-lived.

Door opens. Screws Jarvis and Jones. I'm thinking: twist- up.

On your feet, Alfreth, says Jarvis. Middle-aged; red nose of the hardened drinker I want to be and would have been.

What's the charge, sir? I ask. It's the middle of the night.

No charge, says Jarvis. Just come out of your pad.

I'm still thinking twist-up. But any road, I move. Time what? Two-thirty? What choice do I fucking have?

Jarvis says, Piss test.

I can't help myself. I say, I'm sorry.

And Jones says, You *will* be fucking sorry, cunt, if you refuse.

I'm not refusing, sir, I say. I'm just confused. It's the night. Squat.

I'm horrified. Here? I ask. On the landing?

Just do as you're told, says Jarvis.

I will, sir, I reply, not knowing where any of this has come from—and confused that the parcel has been delivered to my own door. Done nothing wrong, I keep reminding myself— nothing at all. It's the early hours and everyone is asleep. Or if not asleep, then at least banged up. It'll do.

I'll do it, sir, I say; and I drop to my haunches. No problem.

Jones says, You'd better be fucking certain there's no problem, cunt.

There's none, sir. You wanted a piss test.

Say I did.

I'm starting to believe that I've offended Jones without knowing it, such is his unregulatedly violent approach to me and my life. Done dick.

Where's the piss pot? I ask.

Squat.

For the first time I notice that Screw Jones has on the gloves. Open up and say ahh, the cunt gives me. And in he goes. Two fingers. No remorse. It's happened before, but never in the middle of the night.

A mobile phone? A key of C? What the hell are they looking for? They rummage, right there, until they're satisfied that I haven't secreted the Crown Jewels inside my rectum.

And then I say: You done? Are you done? Now it's my turn, sir. I demand the right to piss in your bottle. Please produce it. And I do mean toot-suite. I want my clear piss on your record. Sir.

You cunt, says Jones.

I'm not doing anything wrong, I inform him. Where's your bottle, please? My voice is even and don't-give-a-monkey's. Please, sir, I add.

Or what, you little shit? Jones asks.

Or tomorrow morning, I tell him, I'll be requesting the G-11 form. And I'll fill the fucker in, sir. The one about abuse. The one that will put on the record, quite clearly, that you and

Officer Jarvis raped me this evening. Good night, sir. And whatever you're looking for, I hope you find it elsewhere. Not in me.

You cheese-eater, says Jones, quite obviously rattled. But I close my own door on his words.

I've even taken that power away from him.

Nine.

What you do is, you learn indifference. You learn a new way of dealing with stimulus, and that new way is thought of as indifference. Like talking *rah*. Like talking *yat*. Hear the bruvs, for example, talking rap. Sure: they're animated—as animated as when they're giving the bullshit about 'rolling with the nines'— nine millimetre pistols—or 'mashing poom-poom'—banging skirt—but it's just a dive, it's a way, it's a method. Avoiding time. Means jack. Means zero. I don't go down that avenue. Got my eyes wide open. Call it a failing if you will, but that's me. Like me or loathe me.

Half of the bloods spouting about burglary, anyway, are in for rape. Fact as fact can be. Check the papers. Check the records. Check their sperm counts and get ready for the scum to hit the roof. I assure you. I drop one, when he first come in and me too. We arrive together. It's got to be done for the sake of authenticity. Not that I am personally trying to be a leader or a warrior; but it's good to have something to call your own, to call your calling card— and that something can be a matter that you know about someone else. Hence my arrangement with Ostrich. Who is watching, by the way, as we queue for our cereals. Who is trying to converse with me, but I'm staying a few lads ahead of him in the line. Whose eyes on my neck are like paper-cuts.

I collect my gruel and stamp back to my pad. I blow my nose in the sink and try my roughage with my plastic spoon. It makes me sick to the gut. There is too much static in my head.

You learn indifference. And you learn the feeling of being re-garded as indifferent and that every day will be indifferent—o my days!—and it's like an Indian summer has obliterated a half-year of grey astral slime. Too much has happened too quickly in the last couple of twenty-fours for things to be natural, but it takes a bit longer—and a long chat with Dott—to convince me of the same.

The day passes like a piece of vinyl slowly melting on a dashboard. I pray and play. I watch the afternoon film—some piece of nonsense about evacuees during the Second—and I use up some of my phone privileges on a wasted phone call in time for Valentine's Day, with Julie. What do you say when you said it all last week—and the week before that—and yada yada? You've said it, and saying it again doesn't mean it gets cancelled from the memory of the one you said it too.

How's Patrice? I ask Julie.

She's relieved to have something else to speak about, other than ennui, regimes and the famous Dellacote ducks that strut around from pond to pond inside our compound. She's heard it all before, after all. The ducks that hardened, so-called *career criminals* change their stride to avoid.

(The one bruv who ever kicked one of the ducks, about a year ago, was hospitalised within the hour. The ambulance ar-rived and drove him down the hill to the waiting hamlet. Taking instant umbrage, two yoots from the Bricklaying course saw it happen and it resulted in violence: four stitches to the cuz's head. You don't fuck with the ducks. Word went around.)

I go to the swimming pool and I don't share a single word with Ostrich. We splash with our floats, learning front-crawl; we say nothing.

He wants to. And I know that. Then suddenly it's time for lunch. It's dreck in a kebab skin.

How's Patrice? I ask.

Her back teeth are giving her the arsehole, Julie tells me. She's had something that felt like it was turning into whooping cough but didn't.

What are you wearing?

Is that the end of our conversation about our daughter? she asks.

No. But what are you wearing?

Jeans.

What else?

Nothing else, she replies.

Where is she?

Upstairs. With the babysitter. He's putting her down.

He? I shout.

Screw Trover—one of the weekend brigade—turns to fight me with his eyes. I turn my back on him and cuddle up closer to the phone's armour.

The fuck you mean he? I demand.

Alfreth! Screw Trover warns.

I lower my voice. Who is he?

She waits, and the gap in the conversation is like the time it takes for a planet to re-form after cosmic detonation, yat.

She says, Bailey.

And who's Bailey? I persist.

Time like a gulped breath. Release, please!

Julie says, She needed help. She sounds desperate. Your mum thought it was a good idea as well, innit. She needs a father figure, Billy. Someone to look up to ain't in jail. Someone older.

She's made an enemy, I answer.

I hang up the phone. Deep down I'm satisfied and aggrieved at the same time, but I am pleased to have my suspicions confirmed. It's easier.

Ten.

It's six o'clock in the p.m. Our meals run like trains on a track. The sticky toffee pudding for a dessert is like brandy. I wait. I clean my mouth and tastebuds with wash. I wait some more. I have heard the story of the fight for first place on the pool table: the one that results in the tip of a pool cue up the nose and destroying a left eye. My approach will be more civilized. The guy wears a patch on the out. Three burn stand before me and knowing a new truth. Seems important. Seems vital.

Come on then, Alfreth. I'll bust you open. I'll show you what time it is.

Fat chance, I tell him while I'm chalking my cue.

I start the game with Shelley, knowing that he knows nothing of where his booty—should I win—will be headed; and caring little more either. Roller and Meaney are still down block, but the screws in question, the rumour in the wind has it blown, are coming back on Monday. I know what I saw. Now I need to know why I saw it. First off, I have a game of pool to win. I need to know.

Part Two:
Chicken Escalations

One.

Boxing mags are forbidden, but God knows why. Miss Patterson won't tell me and neither will anyone else. Maybe I should drop the question on Miss Thistle. I can explain that they'll expand my learning pathway and that no one ever became the world heavyweight champion by scanning a piece of paper. The works of principle-level, high-security Man Jail prisoners are also forbidden, but those of lesser-known criminals are hunky-dory. What up? I'm doing my rounds in the rain, as per the norm. Papa Alpha-ing from one warm Wing to the next with my invisible chaperone and a trail-blaze known only to a swarm of rotating cameras. I'm doing my job, rudeboy.

Then I get to the Puppydog Wing. I'm admitted in. I enter the Main Office and chat with some guy called Walsh, who wears the pips on his shoulder of a Senior Officer, and who informs me that I'm late and that the Puppydogs will one day have their way. I've done nothing wrong. So I tell the O.G.—the old guy—I inform that old bastard peculiar—that it's none of my responsibility as to when I'm freed from the Library to distribute. It's obvious. I fear a decent twisting-up after that, but the cunt is just busting chuckles. I feel like a total cheese. Want to bend him over.

Can I get on, sir? I ask.

Hold your horses, son. You know the drill. What you got?

I go through the inventory of what and for whom.

That's quite a lot, Walsh acknowledges. You'd better get wriggling. But before you go, Alfreth.

Internally I give a sigh. I'm waiting for the so-called joke he always tells. It makes him smile; it gives him something to think about all morning, no doubt. But hey. It's all part of my sentence. It's probably on my tariff sheet: along with all the training courses that I have had to go on—the Better Father courses (as far as I know, I'm a good enough father), the Being Assertive courses (I'm assertive enough, rudeboy, I've got an off-switch, sure, but I know when to get loud and deep when the time is right), and the Money Management courses (I've got eighty-five grand in the bank, cuz, for when I'm on the out; I've got bare peas and I don't need any advice about money management)—I'm sure it's written in small print somewhere that I have to take madness from screws.

Is it? I give him grudgingly.

How is Treat lifeing you? he asks again, one more time, thinking he's the belle of the ball, no doubt. But as usual, I'm ready for it. Been here for bare time, right, and it's easy as pie now.

I'm not a lifer, I answer.

I ignore the reference to Screw Treat. A more mis-nomered piece of skin-waste I've never seen still or had the disadvantage to engage in conversation.

Allow it, sir, taking the piss, I tell Walsh.

I'll allow it when you're dead. Start your rounds.

Sometimes, to be fair, he's okay, just sarcastic, but this must be his time of the month; he's a shade more hostile than I'm comfortable with. I sense a sudden wave of anger towards me. I don't like it. It's similar to the feeling that I sometimes get when I'm on the out and I've had a busy night—jacking cars, maybe—and

I've wound down with hooch and a few nooses of badly-cut sniff. The sense of guilt I feel when I wake up the next day. Because I know I've got my faults, and most of them I can live with; but I've never got used to a sense of guilt. I hate it. Especially when I've done nothing wrong. Seeing Mum in her dressing-gown and pink slippers, knowing she knows I know she knows that I've been up to no good in the small hours, but she doesn't know what. Knowing she's waiting for a phone call or a visit from the feds. Knowing she loves me but would rather I moved out. Knowing that her attempts at getting me ready for school are a way of shielding herself from the reality that her son—her only son—is a tearaway tyke and wondering where she went right with her two daughters, who eat their toast in their uniforms and proffer no backchat, and where she went wrong with me.

I hoist up the sack of publications. It's as heavy as lead and it keeps me fit. Delivering is better than a class at the Gym. Outside Cell 3 on the twos I plonk a copy of *New Scientist*. I slap the metal flap, either to wake the brother up or to interrupt him doing something I don't want to see. There is his laminated I.D. card of name, prison number, and the photograph that must be replaced by the screws, within twenty-four hours, in the event of a cuz changing his hairstyle, or shaving off a beard, or getting a tattoo on his scalp. It's Schyler; I don't know the yoot. But he's one of the yoots on Puppydog that are not there because of their sex crimes. It's something petty like serial robbery but if I scratch my brain cells I can recall something about there being some beef on road with a bruv named Pewter, on B Wing. Schyler's a Puppy for his own protection.

Still on the twos landing I take the opportunity to peek through the window into the common room. The sight of the common room on the twos always soothes me. Beyond the barred gate and metal door, inside, they've got a trio of metre-high cages, each containing a tropical bird of some description: a noisy car crash of colour in an atmosphere of grey and beige. God knows I wouldn't want to have my pad on this landing, but I like to watch the birds for a few seconds—even to hear them squawk and holler. It probably smells like a zoo in there—and I hate that smell—but I like seeing the birds move from perch to perch, wishing that something equivalent could be introduced to some of the other Wings. Or at least mine. The cages are cleaned out and the birds are looked after by the prisoners. I wouldn't want that responsibility, but it would be nice to have birds around. I lobbied the Governor once for such a privilege—before I understood that he doesn't give a fuck about what I want and that I should silence my pen. I'm nearly at the stairs, about to ascend, when I hear:

Hey, Library!

Shamefully I take my time—it's a rare and gravy moment of power; I'm walking, they're banged up—but I go to the cell that has called out to me. Open the flap and say, Wogwun, cuz.

You finished on the twos?

Yeah, bruv.

Where's me TV guide innit?

Not in me sack, rudeboy.

Fuck that. I paid innit, he protests, reasonably enough.

I don't know what to say, man; I'm just the paperboy. Make a complaint, is all I can think of to advise him—in the sense that it's what I would do in a similar situation.

Elevate the motherfucker innit, I add.

Yeah, right, he says, turns his back on me and returns to his bed.

Sorry, man, I tell him. I'll ask when I get back.

Safe, Library.

I close the flap.

As I move up the stairs to the threes my heart starts beating a little bit faster. The new boy, Dott, is on the threes, and I have something to push under his cell door. It occurs to me to wonder how he's placed his order so fast but it's on my list and I will honour my duty to dispatch. I take a good hard look at Dott's photograph: at the mugshot of Ronald Dott. He's got the sort of baby face that you have to learn to respect—even to fear. You get to our age with no wrinkles, no lines, it's not down to genetics. It's down to you don't give a fuck. Nothing's scarred you, blood. Nothing's guilted you out. You're capable of anything. Bust into the equation the fact that man's been convicted of raping four-teen women and mutilating half of the same, and you're looking at one deep rudeboy. I bang on his flap. I open it up.

TV guide, innit.

Safe, cuz, he calls from the sink.

I've interrupted him shaving his chest. Feeling somewhat disappointed, I push the publication under his pad door. I'd ex-pected something different. I'm just about to close the flap when he turns to me. He has eyes like the Indian Ocean, blood, even through the reinforced glass. Piercing, is it.

What happened to the two screws in the Cookery Room? he asks.

How do you mean? I reply, thinking: News moves swift.

Suspended. Compassionate. Fired, he elaborates.

I'm not willing to give too much away. When you do it's like one of them anorexic chicks must feel while throwing up: you've lost your nourishment. You feel weak. I tell him that I don't even know and he returns his attention to the mirror be-hind the mesh that is supposed to stop the suicides breaking it to use as a vein-slitter but doesn't.

He says to me, offhandedly, Would you keep me posted?

It's like I've been on an alcoholic bender and I'm sweating

out all of the poison.

What's in it for me? I demand.

He returns his gaze to the window that he's not supposed to see much through. But I get the impression he sees me widescreen plasma.

I can treat you in so many ways, Alfreth, he answers.

I'm chilled to my fucking atoms. Guy creeps me.

Is that a perv threat, Dott? I shout, aware that I've got about two more seconds before the cameras pick this up—that I've been at Dott's cell for too long and that we're doing more than chatting shit—but I'm all but trembling.

It's not a perv threat, Billy. It's a promise. A good one.

I slam shut the flap. Rattled. Continue to make my way to the stairs.

Hey, Library!

The address is very welcome. I want something to do that's routine, even if it's a complaint about a paper that hasn't been delivered.

Jesus Christ. It's Downe. Downe and Dirty, as he's known to his enemies. Maybe to his friends as well, if he has any.

Wogwun.

Open the flap, cuz. Thanks. That Dott, yeah? he whispers.

Yeah, man, I say.

Maybe you could arrange for someone to bang him up regular.

My eyebrows pinch together.

What makes you think I have those resources? I ask him, genuinely confused.

I don't know. It's the word.

Mildly flattered that my reputation for organisation— albeit long since relinquished now that I've earned my Redband— has rippled the waters.

I ask him, And why would I want to do that anyway?

Downe's reply is unequivocal and non-confusing. He freaks us all out.

This from a yoot who used a cocktail of shampoo and lighter fuel to toast a baby within an inch of its life, just because it had the wrong eye colour.

A pouch of burn, man, Downe continues in a whisper that only just penetrates the glass. His words shock me.

A pinch ain't much, man, I seek to clarify.

A pouch, cuz. A packet.

In all my time inside I have never known of a stake so high. Remarking that I'll think about it, I close his flap—there are footfalls on the stairs below me, screws approaching—and I'm marshalling my reasons for dawdling. I'm badly shaken by the wager's proposal. I'm badly shaken by the fact that Dott knows not only my surname—impressive enough after a few days of incarceration—but my first name as well. But I'm shaken much more by the following interaction. My feet on the stairs, the bag on my back.

Yo, Billy! calls Dott.

Fuck you! I call over my shoulder.

I heard your whispers, Billy! he shouts. Give my love to Kate!

Two.

I been looking at me penis for the best part of three hours, says Ostrich.

Tell me more, I say. It's Sosh Time: therefore we're chatting shit.

And I can't understand the conundrum of the egg and the chicken.

There's a beat of silence. Until Carewith—a quite new

yoot in from Chelmsford for bad behaviour—says what we've all been feeling.

The fuck that got to do with your dick, dude?

Ostrich says, Nothing. Just two ting happen same time. Me multi-tasking innit. Man looking at the chap and thinking about life, yat.

And what conclusions did you draw, Ostrich-man? I ask.

Ostrich stretches his neck and rotates his head: clearing the clicks. Man don't know innit. The fucking chicken lay the egg, right? But what made the fucking chicken, right? Y'nar. It's a fucking astronaut shit situation.

Roper is a div kid with learning difficulties, and he's slow to catch on to *The Teletubbies*, let alone psychological rah.

And how your dick figure?

There no dick, man! Ostrich shouts. Just a piece- together, innit.

To which Carewith adds, Man know all about fucking chicken, yat.

As we've got another twenty minutes, and the pool tables are already and always occupied, I bite the bullet and ride the noise and say:

Chicken wogwun?

But Roper isn't finished—it's his way. He still wants to talk about the notification he's received about a Sunday visit.

I want to know, he mutters absently, who's coming to chat me.

Shut up, man, Roper-man, Carewith offers, equally as ab-sently.

At least the seconds are passing. It's a way of killing time.

One day, yeah? says Carewith. I'm teefing bare poultry from the supermarket, innit. It's me and my ting. My girl Aleisha. Not me babymamma, another ting. And we're up there at the hot chicken shit. The counter, yeah? And she's like, rah, I don't feel well innit.

Your girl says it? I want to confirm.

Yeah. But she's faking it, rudeboy. She giving it the hand to the head, right? I don't feel good. I need to sit down.

We all start to laugh.

Making sure the chicken chick's clocking her. Getting her nice and worried, yeah? She virtually be having a cardio innit.

I remember in Felts, I dashed a yoghurt in a yoot's face, says Roper.

Ostrich says, Shut it, Ropes-man. Allow it.

Carewith is smiling broad. Then she fall down innit, he continues. So what the chicken chick gonna go? He raises his hands: case considered and case closed. Leave her position, of course. Offer assistance, rudeboy.

That Miss Simpson ting, Roper carries on, following the line of his own internal logic—his own gingerbread trail. He's talking about a screw on his Wing. She's something I'd *move to* on the outside.

We're not talking about that, guy, I tell Roper, impatiently. So shut your beak. What we say has got nothing to do with your life.

You make me shut it, Roper says, his features yokelly and not to be trusted.

He resembles the Cowardly Lion from *The Wizard of Oz*. Such fear as he inspires is diluted with sadness. You can't help but feel sorry for the cunt, regardless of what he's done. Or who he's hurt. Arson is not a man's game anyway.

I'll scoop you out, motherfucker, I inform him.

Give him the stare that I've learned from Dott, although I'd never concede my sources. And I doubt that mine is one tenth as fucking chilling as that bruv's.

Carewith is squirreling in a store of impatience. In an instant he stands up and says, Rudeboy, yat. You wanna tell me my story, rah? Yah?

No, man, says Roper.

Then rope up your lips, char. Allow it. Me taking piss.

Roper nods. No allow, man. He raises his hands. Swear down, blood.

You fucking dickhead, I add.

Roper strokes me with the look that I've granted as worthless. It means nothing, cuz.

And you're speaking to me, rudeboy? he asks.

I'm cool. I wave the yoot away. He's not important.

Carewith is eager to carry on, which is an underlying theme. What he says next is, and he says it with impatience on his taste-buds, *Are you listening?* And while she's doing that, I'm dusting behind the counter with my sports bag. Filled that up with chicken, rudeboy. Made a split for the doors.

All of us laugh like latrines.

What happened to your ting? Ostrich wants to know.

Carewith shrugs his sloping shoulders. Made a miracle recovery innit. Met me back in me yard an hour later.

But Roper won't let it go. He called me dumpling, he mutters.

Who does, blood? I want to know.

You're not listening. This is Carewith again, eager to carry on with his tale, now that he's obtained an audience.

Okay, blood, says Roper, finally seeing the light. As I may have intimated, he's a nice yoot and that, but not exactly management material, if you follow my drift. It takes him a while. Now he farts. Loudly.

Ostrich is not best pleased at this turn of events. Frowning, I would expect, in the same way he did when he busted the cranium of that cheese-eater in Canning Town, he now says, How are you gonna do that, man? Respect it, you filthy cunt. He brushes the foul air away from his face.

I can feel things tensing up. And this is in Sosh Time: when everything is supposed to be a gulped breath of freedom. On the surface, at least. Carewith is getting cross at not being able to finish his chicken anecdote; Ostrich is also pissed—and both of them are on at Roper. Not that the boy needs any help. What Roper lacks in intellectual faculties, he makes up with with speed of fist and a bulldog's aggression. I once heard a yoot name of Welling (long since left the establishment) give someone else a précis of Roper's talent.

Man, man say, man move from Chelmsford innit, because man love fighting too much. He put it on passionate, cuz. Had a fight with bare man. Make a statement innit. He have a madness with man? Man go down. No more beef. No more street beef. Bang beak. No more shit. Allow it, blood. He pauses his rant. Man, he adds after a couple of seconds, man must have done some *stupidity*.

So I'm not exactly overly arsed about Roper's predicament right now. But I don't want Sosh to be abandoned in a riot of arriving screws. Too much of that I've seen in the Cookery class, recently still.

What happens next? I say to Carewith. Anything for an easy life.

It's later. Couple of days later, and we're chatting shit, he tells his adoring public, blazing a zoot.

I miss that, man. I miss zoot, says Roper.

My guess is that he's about to get his head busted open.

But Carewith simply says, Yeah—and says it fondly. Then we get the fucking giggles, right, and we get the munchies. And my ting says, Why don't we get some chicken? And I'm like, rah, Can't, babe, innit; spent all my peas on zoot.

Carewith's whip is off the road, due to some issues concerning no peas to fill up the tank; and the local petrol stations have all become wise to his habit of flashing his Blockbuster Video card from the pumps as a way of attempting to convince them he has the funds to pay—before driving off. They see him coming and they turn off the pumps from the counter. So what's a poor boy to do? Man uses a selection of kitchen tools to break into the sideboard, where he knows that the neighbour in the yard next door has had his keys stored for the duration of his holiday in the South of France. Carewith's mum has volunteered to feed the three cats. Carewith and his girlfriend hop into the neighbour's enhanced whip and head down to the BetterSave to lick some chicken.

Problem is, says Carewith, I'm high on zoot. Man catches me.

He is wrestled to the floor by the shop's security baboon. Word has gone round the ends and every shop in the area has been shown some grainy CCTV footage about the chicken-licker of old Canning Town. The worst is yet to come. Bruv's girl, when she's nabbed, denies even knowing him still. And that is serious betrayal. Until his mum comes home, Carewith does his seven hours in the cell, sweating out the marijuana. Then he's released on bail (the matter of the stolen car is yet to come) and he takes the bus over to gritty Ilford. Where he finds his ting and batters her blue.

So that's my madness, Carewith concludes, fondly rolling an indulgent second burn. It's all about the little becoming the big, innit?

Chicken escalations, says Roper, oddly reading the mood correctly for once—and even nodding his head in what appears to be genuine sympathy. There is a silence. It is as rare as it is uncomfortable. Sosh is nearly over.

It all starts with a chicken, Carewith adds, unable to believe his dark fortune, his hard-done-by-ness.

I wish I had thought of chicken escalations.

So what comes first, the chicken or the egg?

No man ever done bird because of an egg. The chicken comes first.

I've heard enough. I have to collect some winnings from Shelley.

Those twenty minutes go quick time, I say, standing up for a stretch.

Three.

Kate Wollington knows all about how to keep a man hungry. She's someone I'd move to on the outside, anyway. In here—in this poom-poom drought—I would sell my yard and give up my savings, for the chance just to wank on her shadow. Not that she's buff, particularly; but your standards change. You realise how lucky you are that a woman is willing to share floor-space. You get tired of bash. You get tired of late night Channel Five. I don't know why I've been called away from the Library. I'm in the Meetings Room, next to the dentist's surgery. Dressed head to toe in black, as usual, she enters the room and the screw ups and leaves, with the promise that he'll be right outside the door. Kate checks that I'm wearing my Redband—as though failure to do so would signify a dramatic descent on the graph of my trustworthiness. She seems appeased and she straightens her skirt as she sits down. Polo-neck sweater.

And how are you today, Alfreth? she asks as she skims her clipboard. There I am, in small typed print: my life, my crime. It's the only one that I was caught for—that wounding—and it's in there like punctuation.

What can I say? I'm top of the tree.

Really?

Yeah. Miss, a question, yeah, I add swiftly.

Go on.

I choose my words carefully, and what I say is: Why do we have to carry on with this, Miss? Mean, I've given you all I've got, innit.

It's part of your tariff, Alfreth, Miss Wollington informs me.

I know that. But my question is why, Miss?

She shrugs the cute shoulders that slope so definitely that her bra straps keep falling down beneath her top. And I should know: I've studied her often enough over the time in her presence. I sense her helplessness.

It's part of your tariff, she repeats, unable to elaborate.

Now is the time for me to consider that she, in her way, is as trapped as I am. It's just that the bars have a different colour. No one wants to be here. Not the yoots; not the staff. Not even the ducks, most likely. I'll ask Ostrich to have a word with the latter to confirm. Dumb thought. But it leads me right back to Dott's door. Suddenly I get the impression—chilled cold as it is by the conversation that follows—that Dott, with his weird ways and weirder manner, can talk to the animals.

Sensing no possibility of escape, I say: Okay. I'll ride it.

Any objection to my turning on the tape recorder?

Do I ever?

No. But I thought it a professional courtesy to offer, as ever.

I nod my head. Courtesy acknowledged, I say to Kate. Fire away.

Okay. She reads her notes. She doesn't glance up. Do you ever think about your past? she asks me with a straight face.

Question knocks the wind from my sail. Swear down we've done this bare times.

I say, Nope. I exhale. I want to go back to my pad, I almost add.

Why not? she wants to know.

Ain't got one innit.

She tries to appeal to my sense of reason but I'm fed up and pissed and I want to get back to my pillow.

Well, everybody's got a past, she says.

Not me.

Call me bolshy. I can't help myself sometimes. And she's the psychologist; let her pick the bones from my temper. Let her diagnose me. Miss Wollington abandons that line of inquiry for the time being. I watch her scribble something out and something down. For the first time I understand she's a smoker. Never noticed it before. And you never know what is going to be important to retrieve in Dellacotte. When she sighs out her sensation of impotence, there's a smell of tobacco riding the surface aroma of strong coffee and peppermints.

Do you think about your crime then? she asks.

How many more times? I want to ask but I hold my tongue.

Nope.

Why not?

I copy her shrug. I can do nothing else. Virgin, I tell her.

Excuse me, Alfreth?

Consult your previous minutes, Miss, I say. I'm innocent innit.

Now this is a horse she can jump on. The judge didn't seem to think so, she replies.

Well, the judge doesn't have three yoots on bare sniff trying to kick his eyes out. You listening?

Yes, I'm listening, she interrupts.

I'm smiling now. It's not, I say, it's not like a question, man. Yeah, I'm smiling, right, but it's in spite of myself, as they say. I don't like it that she's broken my armour. Been far too much of that noise of late.

I'd rather you didn't call me *man*, Miss Wollington informs me.

Sorry, Miss.

Kate is fine. Ms Wollington is fine.

It's a bit like having my fur roughly fondled; it's like what I remember of my old boy—my only memory of him, in fact. No — That's not the case. There are a couple of things I recall. I know that I sat on his lap and coloured in the tattoos on his forearms with a blue biro. I know how important I felt when I was sent out to the kitchen to fetch another bottle of beer. And I can remember the bloody nose he got from Mum—the vase in the face—when he refused to leave the flat and kept saying that he'd done nothing wrong. I remember. Is this my first memory of fear?

It's the first time that Miss Wollington has given me permission to use her forename, although it's common knowledge. I've never used it before. Nothing more do I offer than a nod of the head, saying: message received; let's not talk about it anymore. But Kate wants to.

I notice you ask it a lot, she says.

Ask what?

Are you listening though? It's as if you're frightened of losing your interlocutor's attention. Would that be fair?

The fuck? I shout. I ain't frightened!

Concerned, then.

I'm getting pissed. I'm getting vex, blood, I tell her.

To which she smiles; it's a comforting sight of back molar black bits and lumpy fillings: it convinces me once and for all that behind the shield of that clipboard and the notes on my case, she's anything but invulnerable. It's a nervous laugh and I'm only a few seconds from seeing her nervous once again. But for the moment it's me who's on the back foot.

There's really no need, she informs me. And please—I hate

blood.

Considering my possible replies, I wait. And then I add: I wanna go back to my pad.

I'm afraid the hour isn't up yet, Billy. . .

Fuck the hour, fam! I ain't your puppy, Miss Wollington. Allow it.

She has solidified; she's a fossil. I'm trying to help, she tells me, her voice as patient as it's been hard trained to be, her accent as mild but pretty as ever: like good perfume, ah, the perfume of her voice, man. I like it sweet.

Where you from? I ask her, calming down but betraying myself by revealing a curiosity—a long held-back question—to someone holding a pen. She's not used to being asked much. Her business is on the other side of the counter: it is she who takes the hard cash of my conscience. But if she's an emotional salesgirl what's she's vending? What's in it for me, this transaction? Oh yeah, I've got it. She sells me guilt.

She adjusts her glasses and fidgets for a fraction of a second that she doesn't think I'll notice.

Why do you ask?

Conversation, rah, I tell Kate. Shrugging my shoulders.

We were already taking part in a conversation, she tells me, consulting the pages in front of her, thumbing the bull-clip.

Feeling cocky because I've made her squirm, I lean forward.

Don't remember that, I reply. I do not quite fully recall, Miss, I'm having a conversation.

My breath is a little bit nifty but I'm coming up out of this good.

Kate smiles. Good girl that she is, she has come to understand the power of a well-meant compromise. She places the clipboard on her desk, to her left; she smoothes the skirt out over her legs again, her fingernails perfect and as purple and shiny as a plum.

From what used to be called Czechoslovakia, she answers, when I was a girl. When I was your age.

How old are you now? I ask.

Never you mind! she answers, still smiling—and quite possibly smiling because I haven't asked the obvious question of *What's it called now?*

I'm not sure I'm winning and I'm not certain that she isn't reading me. What I do know is, she's not expecting something so personal.

My turn, she says, whipping the matador's cape. You've referred, in the past, to the fact that three men attacked you, she says.

Fact is right, I tell her. But it's the same old song, and she knows it, swear down. As fully as she knows that I'll now be staring at her chest until she grows uncomfortable.

Despite the fact the assault was filmed on CCTV.

She is growing vex herself. She says, Billy. Billy, are you listening?

I'm listening, I can't resist saying.

Then listen to this. There was only one man there, Billy. One man.

I refuse this line, as I've refused it from day one. Three men, I tell her straight. I was attacked by three men. And when I discuss this, I even manage to confuse myself— routinely. I have been in a situation where three men attack me, I know I have; but I can't recall the incidentals. What they've got me on is an attack I made on a guy who shares my first name.

Billy, I've seen the film, she tries.

Yeah, me too. But it's three men, I repeat. *Uno, dos, tres*, innit?

Kate Wollington nods her head and removes her spectacles in order to give them a clean on the fabric of a silk scarf that she has slung down over the spine of a metal radiator. The process takes less than a minute. It's like a ballet, but in miniature. It's something like poetry. And then the bombshell.

Can I change the subject? she asks.

Feel free.

She waits. She is picking at her words with the choosy lack of charm of a fussy eater—like some of us do actually eat when we first get here. Until we realise that it's all shit and that shit food is better than no food.

What did you talk to Dott about? she asks.

In truth, I feel sick. The news has spread too quickly.

How do you know I spoke to Dott? I ask her. More importantly, I think, what business is it of yours?

The conclusion I jump to is not a tricky leap. Either Kate Thistle has asked her to ask me; or Kate Thistle has mentioned that I'll be delivering a publication to Dott (at the staff canteen, perhaps) and Kate Wollington is firing off on her own pursuit; or Kate Thistle has gained her own version of events from Dott himself, and she's using Miss Wollington to verify the facts. The suppositions point firmly to an identical solution. One that has crossed my mind more than once, and has left bare footprints. Kate Thistle is a fed. Kate Thistle is Billy Blue-Light. Kate Thistle is a copper. Here to keep tabs on the raping piece of shit name of Dott. And I can buy that. The part I can't buy is precisely why.

Four.

So what do you wanna know? Ostrich asks.

About the others still, I tell him. The ones you squash up.

We are eating our baguettes during Sosh. It's the nearest we get to going out for dinner: saving our baguettes for an hour until we're unlocked. If we're unlocked. So tonight Mr Ostrich is my dinner date. We're an item.

O my days!

Sure I'm busting chuckles, but swear down, blood, it's nice to eat together, rudeboy. It's amazing the things you miss. While it might not be an Indian meal with a nice glass of beer, it's pleasant to watch the muscles pulse on Ostrich's left temple— as he chews, as he swallows. As he prepares himself to honour his side of the bargain. I watch his deep eyes: they're searching for something in the noisy distance. No one is bothering us. We must appear too serious to be disturbed. It's crisis talks.

You know when you have to do something, Ostrich intones, regardless of the consequences innit.

I nod my head.

We're all here for precisely that reason, I tell him.

Ostrich shakes his head. Nar, man. I ain't talking about normal crime madness.

He is fingering what's left of his baguette; he is like a child mashing up play-dough. The action speaks of distraction and inner pain. It makes me feel like a waste to hurt a friend, but a deal's a deal. Man needs the knowledge. Man's thirsty for that knowledge.

So what are you chatting? I ask.

Ostrich sighs. The salami we've just munched comes out in a flow of garlicky bad breath.

We're criminals, blood.

Allow it.

But are you listening, though? We made choices, blood. We took chances, we do what we have to do. We gamble.

Allow it, I repeat.

But we didn't have to do it. We might have come into some beef. We might've, fucking, lost some face, rudeboy. Name be mud innit. But we didn't have to do it, bruv.

Swear down, I tell him.

Then imagine a situation, yeah — a ting where you know the consequences are gonna be deep, blood. But you have to do it innit. There's not like there's no freewill about the madness, he says, sighing again.

I tell Ostrich that I'm puzzled. Then I come across the only logical response. Are you talking about a family ting? I ask.

Yeah yeah. A straight down, confrontation, mad astronaut shit family ting. Ostrich laughs. But this is lips-is-sealed, right?

I'm surprised you have to ask, I answer.

Check it. Ostrich nods his head. He holds out his left knuckle; I tap it with my own. Matter closed.

It was a ting with my Mumsy innit. Gets herself a new man, right? And he all right! She has a few before him. The sniff he gives is dismissive, disdainful. Just there to take up space, bruv.

I laugh.

To make up the numbers, the quota, he continues.

Some, rah, some exclusive pricks innit.

I hear you, man, I'm listening. Sounds familiar, bruv.

But he's not giving me stodge about staying out too late. You've got to go to school: all that. You're disappointing me. Allow it, man! Those other wastes, boy, they try too hard, rudeboy. This Anthony guy was okay. He tosses the remains of his baguette to the floor: a sign of disgust rather than of satiation. He's on a roll, ha ha. Check the chuckles, blood.

I still don't know where this is going. Journeys through the dark are only swish if you know the destination like the skin on your dick. I'm getting busy.

Man was even preparing his Father's Day present, blood. I'm there, out at all hours, jacking cars and licking stereos for some peas to buy man a nice present. Show my respect innit. I go to bare trouble, rudeboy. I buy man a nice set of matching cufflinks and a duster ring. Cost me bare peas, blood! And what does the waste do? Man leave my Mumsy. On Father's Day!

So what did you do?

Well, Mumsy's ruined, rudeboy. Obliterated, says Ostrich, so I'm in the market for buying up a nine-millimetre strap and going over to his yard and putting a hole in his heart.

Allow it.

But Mumsy's no, no, don't do it, Maxwell innit. Why not? I know where to sell the motherfucker's present. Get man some peas. And I know where to buy a strap. Friend of a friend, bruv. Not in my ends but I know where man live; it won't take long. Man can get it in a hot minute. So I'm all for dusting over and showing the waste what time it is.

I'm nodding my head. This stands to reason: I myself have seen the need, back in the day, to teach a paramour or two of my mother's a lesson. It's what a good son does. Because a good son is the man of the house, and a good son hates seeing his mum bust a tear. It's not right.

I'm with you, cuz, I tell Ostrich, aware that Sosh time is spinning fast.

So man dust over to man's yard. Somewhere in Stepney, yat. Man driving enhanced two-litre whip in them day.

With a strap?

Nar, man. Just going over to polish the man's face, blood. Seeing my Mumsy on the vodka at ten in the morning. She's fucked. Gives man a toot on the mobile. Don't do it, Maxwell— I'm begging you, innit. And I'm like, rah. Why, Mum? And she does it: she drops her fucking bombshell.

I haven't seen it coming.

He's your dad, Maxwell. Anthony motherfucker is my *blood*, rudeboy.

O my days! I say.

Yeah, man. My own dad leave my own mum on fucking

Father's Day, Ostrich informs me. It beggar belief innit. He is shaking his head.

Are you going to pick that up, Thomas?

Our attention is drawn to Screw Jones, who has approached with the stealth of a viper. For a fraction of a second neither of us know what the troublesome piece of lamb manure is referring to, and Ostrich even says: Pick what up, sir? Genuinely confused.

That piece of bread.

The abandoned baguette; our sustenance until the buttered toast in the morning. And we're growing boys. Sorry, sir, says Ostrich, doing as he's told.

Point made, Jones strolls away.

Ostrich rolls his head in a figure eight to get rid of the clicks. Enhanced though we might be, we're not privileged to the sort of personal, tension-relieving massages that I used to like, back on the out.

So you punched him out?

Eventually. But I find out, says Ostrich, what the game is first. And I find out that Father's Day. He busts a chuckle. Is not exclusive to me.

Meaning what exact?

Man has other yoots. Man ring his bell and he's there, giving it the lemon. Shit didn't work out. Sorry, son, rah. I say, Anthony? You're my dad and it Father's Day and I want to give you a fucking present. What's that, son? he ask. Bam! Give the waste five knuckles to the chin. Cunt drops, rudeboy. But who's there? Babymamma number two, with her yoot. And babymamma, fucking, number three—who just happen to be cousins—and I'm rah. What's a man to do? I go in knowing and there's no way of going out not, innit.

You killed the babymammas? I ask.

Nar, man. Point I'm making is, I have no choice. This was

family, cuz. Ignoring it is not an option. I know I'm gonna be-devil a good day for two chicks who've done nothing to me. Man know this, rudeboy. But man can't help it.

That journey through the blackness has not finished. Not by a mile.

Because he hasn't left me once, man, Ostrich says slowly, in a different voice from the one that he usually uses, but twice. That's fear. That's fear of me, blood. It's suddenly got nothing to do with Mumsy. It's me.

The picture is clearing. He hit his head on the way down, didn't he?

Yeah, man. The little table with the phone on it, Ostrich answers. A chance in a fucking million. Damage his neurons in-nit. Cunt die. I kill my dad.

That's a tough call, I remark.

I ain't finished, rudeboy. I dust that shit. Man dust the fuck out of that place. Babymamma's not seen shit. I'm a free man. Conscience excepted.

Allow it.

Man not know that man's new dad has siblings, innit.

Unexpectedly, Ostrich starts nibbling at the baguette. It's a way of wasting time.

Uncles. They come to my ends, then to my yard. An explo-sive situation, I'm all but certain you'll agree.

That cheap meat in Ostrich's baguette is like nose poison. But this is newsworthy. If Ostrich has managed to wipe out the alpha male line of a perfectly respectable family, where is the bulletin?

I had to do some mad shit, rudeboy. Kept myself to myself but the truth was as known as riding a fucking bike innit. I had some strangers to leave out in the cold. Or they were going to the feds. Man know it was wrong. Man weak, I reckon. I squash out three man. Happy Father's Day, blood.

The third one you got caught, I wanted to know.

That's the deal, Ostrich tells me.

Swear down trust? I ask.

Swear down trust, he says.

I don't know why but I think that Ostrich is lying. One minute he's bemoaning the fact that he's only done whatnot and would have enjoyed doing more; the next he's being criminally restricted.

Is Ostrich responsible or is he not? This is all getting peculiar.

Five.

As predicted, the Cookery class is cancelled. We're kept banged up. In protest, Cawthorn and Williamson start simultaneous fires. Unplanned synchronicity, but that's the funny way of this place sometimes. Smoke like a bad dream. I'm getting emphysema innit. I have a pray and then a bash. I hoist myself up to the window and hang from the bars, in order to watch the Garden Party—sorry, the Estates Party—doing their thing, cleaning up duck crap and chopping back hedges. I watch a few members of the Education Department having roll-ups outside the block door. I watch a few of the screws scuttle by, doing whatever the fuck they do when they're not tormenting us. I'm bored as a man can be. The screws involved in the lipsing incident in the Cookery Room are Sinclair and Mews. And I find myself struggling to remember their faces.

Yo, Alfreth! someone calls.

I'm at the window anyway so I do what I don't usually do. I answer.

Wogwun.

You got burn?

It's my next-door, Jarvis. Inside for three for handbag theft and computer fraud. What used to be called a granny- basher, before the market expanded to teenage girl victims and foreigners carrying change in a sack while delivering pizza in oversized boxes to boardrooms and the slums. He's nearly a millionaire but will it cheer him up? Will it fuck.

I've got burn. A pinch or two; no more than a prison ration. So I say, almost honestly, No, man. Give it away innit.

Who to?

Ostrich.

Turn the music down, man. Can hardly hear you, bruv!

Sorry.

The decibelage and rap carnage deteriorates to no more than a whining jet engine sort of level.

Twos on what you've got, still, Jarvis says, for my ham baguette.

He's bargaining on a straight exchange: nothing ventured, nothing gained; and no one's the loser, let the buyer beware, not to mention, waste not want not, fair exchange is no robbery and other long-tried and abandoned petty bullshit philosophies. What he's hoping for is for a swing: a highly risky—block-visit-likely—enterprise that extols the virtues of comrades sharing, and which involves tying a named object of booty inside a knapsack made from the end of your bed sheets. Then you dangle the sheet and the prize out your window and start swinging the noose for enough momentum for it to carry up to the window, either of your own next-door, or—if you're particularly famished of self-destructive impulses—on a double-length twine to the pad beyond that. At the best of times I don't care too much for that noise.

I tell him: No deal. I'm on a diet, cuz.

There's nothing of you, fam! he protests, evidently eager

for a smoke. Desperate, in fact. In protest, the volume of his music rises up—like a flood.

I return to my thoughts. Having lost my weekly extra meal—the meal that I would have cooked personally and might not have burned; the one that Jarvis would have known I've been deprived of (he's picked his moment well)—I am obviously starving. It's psychological, no doubt; but it's curdled my stomach lining and I'm livid with Roller and Meaney. Who are returning to their respective Wings this afternoon. God help them. Time passes, and I'm viewing an afternoon movie about the American Civil War, when to my surprise the heavy key turns in the lock. It's a screw name of Wayne.

Stop wanking, Alfreth, he tells me, and put your jacket on.

I'm not, sir. What's happening?

A visit, is all he wants to reply.

But visits don't happen on a Wednesday. Even someone as new to the prison as Dott—especially Dott—knows that visits are Friday, Saturday and Sunday. Nonetheless, I pull on my denim coat and brush my hair quickly.

A shower might have been nice, I say to Wayne. Who's coming to link?

Wayne frowns his doughy face. How the fuck should I know? he says.

Thus it is that I'm led from my pad, past the Servery, and through the opened gate and outside door. The air is as cold as a Puppydog crime. Leaves from the trees are shifting this way and yonder. I can smell the duck pond on the gale: the birds themselves and the fresh cement of the Bricks Department's refurbishment—the one I have yet to see and might never will. Expectantly I turn right, towards the Visits Hall—near the main gate. But I'm corrected in my assumption.

Over there, says Screw Wayne.

Towards what? The laundry? The recycling depot? The Estates Party changing rooms? Then it hits me: I am being taken to the Education block. It's Kate Thistle who wants to see me.

Six.

In my time I have heard a host of opinions about where it is hardest to live. Ilford is gritty. Acton is bare road shit beef, blood. Tyneside is full of maniacs who will carve you up for the price of a kebab. Roads is nuts, cuz. That's the common consensus.

I'd invite any one of the roads gangsters to sniff one day inside the fucking dump that is Dellacotte Young Offenders.

Allow it.

I have witnessed attempted murders: inside. I have witnessed rapes: inside. I have witnessed four kidnapping attempts: inside. None of this I saw on the out. It doesn't happen if you don't chat it. Here we live with the paradox of possibility and no possibility.

I'm weak with hunger but the sickness I feel can sense a release, one way or the other. I enter the Education block with bare sweat busting. A classroom is as frightening as a tenement. But not the Cookery Room, which is where I am headed, as it turns out.

Seven.

Later on in the interview, I am yet again asked to repeat what I saw. In front of Roller and Meaney, each in cuffs, and the screws in question—and even in front of the prison governor (a rare and no doubt post-prandial appearance)—I am asked to repeat myself. Leaving out the bad bits, I do so. Kate Thistle is also present. As is Kate Wollington. A boy called Cello is also there. He was one of the lads in the class itself, and he's so-named because of his low notes. No one can work out how he makes a living, selling at such reasonable prices.

Cello says, Nothing happening, innit.

I'm not so sure. But I don't know the equation either.

Governor Mannidge says to Roller and Meaney: What made you do it?—as if their behaviour has been controlled by freak weather conditions or by additives in their yoghurts. The words that Dott used come back to me. As do the words of Ostrich, from a few months earlier. At the time we're working together in the Education Department, Ostrich as a Cleaning Orderly and me as an Induction Redband. Which means that I'm there to run errands, like photocopying chores and donkey-work carting, for the Education Manager; and Ostrich comes to empty the classrooms' bins and occasionally hoover the filthy carpets.

One day he chats: Has man heard the word?

What word? I ask him.

We've got, like, ten seconds before the Gov adds something like, That's enough, Maxwell, and throws him out of the room and locks himself (and me) in again with the lads.

Mobile found, he whispers.

Who the yoot?

Some yoot on Honeymoon Wing, Ostrich tells me.

He's referring to H Wing, in which some of the pads are co-occupied: two random strangers sharing a twelve-by-twelve and one khazi, with the only space available being vertically. Sky-walking. You want to get out of each other's faces, you climb on to the top bunk and you try to forget about the floor for a while—at least until the sweats subside like a summer storm. It's not pretty. But what is? Unless you're a Mr and Mrs Smith, of course. So named—and excuse the digression—on account of the fact that it's like they have checked into a fucking motel. They've got it sick. Not only are they co-Ds from road, they're actually a couple. Pearce and Trent. One vast and one man tiny:

sexual partners. And yes, it does make a man sick to the stomach. I wish I could hate them but Pearce (the senior partner) is okay. I don't know Trent from a boil on my bum. He has never attended Education as he already has four A Levels and is never called up.

You don't mean Mr and Mrs Smith? I wish to clarify.

Nar, man. Some other yoot. Keep the phone secluded up his arse on a piece of cord, innit, Ostrich answers. For four *munt*.

O my days!

Allow it, blood. Apparently, man's screams could be heard from A Wing to the motherfucking Bricks Workshop.

When what?

When man, says Ostrich, tell him to squat, and then man see the cord and give it a playful yank. Like giving birth, rudeboy, through your rectum.

Heinous.

Allow it. But imagine. He spits a guffaw. If it's Mr and Mrs Smith. Mrs Smith is behind him, reminding fam what fucking time it is, and then the phone goes off inside blood's intestine.

We laugh.

Is that for you? I bust a chuckle.

Tell the motherfucker I'm busy, Ostrich elaborates.

He's bumping his purple against technology, I tell him.

Leave the room, Ostrich is told.

It's the same as now—in the Cookery Room: something is being hidden. I don't like it. Something small inside something larger. A case of chicken escalations, once again. Shit always starts midget. Then expands. I'm not laughing now. I am terrified. I am risking a lot.

Getting up to leave the room, I turn to Kate Thistle. How well do you know Dott on F Wing? I ask, and with effort I keep my gaze on her face.

She retains her composure. I don't know what you mean.

With respect, Miss, I think you do. He certainly knows you.

Governor Mannidge pipes in: What the fuck has that got to do with this, Alfreth? He is perched on the room's one stool, for the old guy teacher.

I tell him that I'm not entirely certain. This is not chatting shit.

Questions will follow, Alfreth, Mannidge informs me.

Indeed they will, sir, I tell him. Such as why this interview has been conducted in a classroom and not in your Adjudication Suite. Which does not exactly fill me with confidence, sir.

Watch it, Alfreth.

But I'm in my full flow, four-cylinder.

What I'd really like to know is, why the change of location? If this is a disciplinary, sir, then please discipline me. Even if I've done nothing wrong. And if it's not, please inform me of what precisely is going on. Is that fair, sir?

I expect a comment along the lines of what a cheeky swine I've been.

Mannidge says, Fair enough, Alfreth. And then I'm led back to my pad.

Eight.

Morning, Billy.

Kate Thistle acts as if nothing but ghosts and ash have passed her way. The dislike I feel for her and for this reason is intense. Fuckable bitch or not.

Good morning, Kate, I return. Any more interviews for me?

The Library Manager looks up from the wishing well of her computer screen. Her smile is of a sated state. She is relieved that we're not getting on. Intrigued by what I mean by *interview*. The remark goes unmentioned. I am sent, with my fluorescent sack, on my Wing duties. I am calmly aware of Dott's TV guide inside the sack. You don't do it in order but sooner or later you get to Puppydog Wing. And Dott's cell. I'm just about to push the publication under his door, when I hear:

Open the flap, Alfreth.

Though distinctly repelled to the notion of a direct command, I grudgingly do so. I give him a *Wogwun* and I try to slake my fears. The pussy is shaving his oxters in front of me.

What time is it? Dott asks.

About ten. Blood, you could stop doing that for thirty seconds, yat.

Yeah I could. It's ten-fourteen, he says, still looking into the mirror. And thirty-two, thirty-three, thirty-four seconds. He has not consulted a clock.

Then why'd you fucking ask me, dickhead?

It's like the song says, he replies. I'm just checking you out. I'm just making sure. The raised eyebrow that he now offers me is like an arrow. It goes through the flap-glass and straight into my eyes.

What fucking song, cunt?

Before your time, he tells me. It was in the 70s. Billy Joel, Billy Alfreth. With which he turns back to the mirror and raises his left arm.

Dickhead, I repeat. I slam shut the metal flap.

The previous night I watched a documentary about wildlife. An alligator swallowed a baby deer. Right now, he's the alligator. I'm the deer, I feel.

Oh, Alfreth, he calls out.

What do you want? I ask. Against my better instincts, I open up the flap. He is there: eyes to the glass. It disturbs me something peculiar.

A message, he says, for Kate Thistle. If you don't mind relaying it on my behalf. Just tell her: Don't try it. She's nowhere near as smart as she thinks and I've left smarter women than her in a city car park. Bleeding from internal injuries and wondering what the hell they've done to deserve me.

Ignoring the puffed-up hubris, I reply: Try what?

Those silly mind games. They won't work.

I'll tell her, I confirm. If you tell me what you mean.

She knows what I mean. Ask her; you might get lucky enough for a response. Alfreth, do you know that a bee can only sting once—then it dies.

I'm thrown off-balance by the question. I've heard something of that nature, I answer.

Unlucky for some, no? he says. Wasps get greedy. I frown and ask him what he's been smoking.

I'm the wasp, Billy. You're the bee.

I wait for a second, churning that one over, like a cow chewing grass. And then he drops what is to be another bombshell.

Forget about alligators and deer, he tells me, and turns away.

I'm shaking so much—that noisy kind of shaking that makes you forget where you are for a few seconds—that I don't hear Screw Jones mount the stairs to this landing. He has to say my name a second time before I hear him.

Stop talking to your boyfriend. It's time for his afternoon wank.

Yes, sir.

I heard that, sir, Dott shouts. The closing of the flap clips his voice off.

How has the man read my mind?

What are you doing? Jones asks. Proposing marriage or summing? Get the fuck down those stairs and on your way.

Yes, sir, I reply.

Little queer that you are, Jones adds, fishing for an argument.

Yes, sir, is all that I'll give him.

For the next two weeks I don't see Dott. He is down block for a punishment: he has damaged Jones's left cheekbone with his toilet seat.

Nine.

I dream about Dott. We are sailing some endless waters. Up ahead, squalls; there are sharks in the water and octopi waving for attention. I have on a pirate's hat. I am the captain of a voyage that feels like pain, and I am carrying a cutlass and I'm chewing tobacco. The waters drain away. We are sailing through the graveyard that rumour has it exists to the south end of Dellacotte Young Offenders. As the ship ploughs the land, the ghosts of the prisoners who were hanged here rise up like gusts of mist and genie-smelling wraiths. The ghosts start dancing. In the dream, Dott is the ship. It's even called The Little Dot.

When I wake up I don't want my cereal. I ask to go to Health Care but I'm told to put up and shut up. Not even the sweat on my body is convincing. Further dreams follow—increasingly horrific—for the next fourteen days or so. I serve bird in the sub-jail of my own fevered imagination. The riven ground now offers up, not ghosts, but the rotten remains of the hanged themselves. In reality those dead will be pale as a nun's tits; in my dreams they hug their own flesh to their brown bones like mugging victims clutching their handbags and purses. Or their knife wounds. The dead walk towards me. The dead steal parcels of loose skin and muscle from each other. The dead meet me for a pow-wow in the Cookery Room.

Why have you found me? I ask in one dream. Why are you here?

Because, answers one, the bone of his jaw quickly slipping away from the remainder of his skull, like an O.G. sucking back a set of dentures, we don't want to be in the ground anymore. We've done our time.

Part Three:
A Million Years of Bee-Stings

One.

Ostrich is waxing lyrical, once again, about the benefits of Big Man Jail.

None of this bullshit, he is saying, about once-a-week Sosh, bloodfam. He is irate. Man a big man? Sosh automatic, blood. Swear down.

It's still a prison, bruv, I inform him—as though the cunt's an imbecile.

My mind is on other things—on Dott, specifically—but I'm drifting. At first I notice that Ostrich hasn't noticed that I'm noticing something other than his overused opinion on the relative benefits of YOIs and Big Man Jails. I don't know what it is, but I want to talk to Dott.

Allow it. But none of this softly-softly magic. Regular Visits.

Though I'm not entirely sure what Ostrich means by 'softly-softly magic'—there's not much suppressed around here, and for sure nothing softly—I nod my head in agreement. I want to return to my pad and think quietly. Ostrich is having none of it. Regular Gym, regular Cookery Class. It's a privilege you earn, whether you want it or not, on becoming friends with a yoot in a prison: the privilege of compulsory ear-lending. To leave Ostrich now is a sin, now that he's on a roll. Nevertheless. Change the CD, I'm thinking.

It's back on, I tell him. As of a.s.a.p.

This brightens the man's mood. Allow it, fam, he says.

You see the new yoot? The what's-his-name, Marris. On Induction now innit.

It disturbs me slightly that I've been so preoccupied that I have all but overlooked the arrival of a new prisoner. I'm aware of the background, vaguely, but that's about it. Even the name rings unfamiliar.

What he get? I ask Ostrich.

Eighteen do nine.

This sounds harsh. You're dropping that on me? I want to confirm.

Swear down, blood. Already tired of the subject, Ostrich spits out a slimy string of snot; he's getting a cold. But fuck him. Man's a waste.

It's a most peculiar evening. It's only now, this evening, when everything seems chaotic—like a ball of random shoelaces being violently unpicked, with yoots dusting from one pocket, one clique, one landing, to the next—that I realise Association Time is usually much more structured. Disregarding the occasional fireworks, of course. Forgetting the sporadic pool cue to cranium scenarios. For no reason at all, or at least for no reason that's immediately obvious, I find myself thinking of swallows in flight. Is it swallows? The ones that seem to go haywire in the air—go nuts—but you don't worry too much (or at all) because they all know the codes and the map. The same as in a beehive. The same as in a wasps' nest. We all have a role and a function—and a price. But bees can only sting once, Dott reminds me, and wasps can bang and bang in their papery home.

I've finished rolling a burn. Bust me a lighter, I say to Ostrich.

He's smiling. Hustle me harder, he replies.

Please bust me a lighter.

Spoken like a true gentleman innit.

For a few seconds we pull on our burns, probably both relieved that a comfortable silence has settled between us. We're getting more like an old married couple every day—a marriage that has lasted four or five decades. Forty years of food on the table at six. Forty years of finishing each other's sentences. Forty years of slippers and milky drinks and early nights. Becoming comfy is not such a good thing, still. Screws notice that shit and they don't like it. In order to avoid getting shipped out to a different Wing—one of us—we're going to have to engineer some beef pretty soon. Among ourselves. Maybe even a swing, still. Man comfortable, way it goes; man don't want to move pad. So only a war of words will convince the screws that we're not exactly knitting woollen booties for our children's children, yat. We're not ready for the shared grave. For they like to keep us tense: tension they can monitor on paper; they can control. Happiness, not. We've discussed this. One day, with malice aforethought but no malice intended, one or other of us is going to accuse the other of something. In good grace we'll take the nickings and the time spent down block. We'll each lose a few points on our Wing files—I might even lose my Redband, but only briefly: fights are dick, everyone knows it—but we'll be able to share Sosh for a good while longer. I'm tempted to swing him right now, when he says:

The news ain't out. What happen to Roller and Meaney?

I sizzle out my burn in the wet sand in the ashtrays provided. Down to Basic, I tell Ostrich. No TV. No fucking visits. Depriving man of rights, innit.

They had it coming, Ostrich tells me dismissively.

What do you mean? It was beef, blood.

We all do it. From time to time, he expands.

It's as though he's been reading my mind.

The news is out that the fight started over a shared colander that both men wanted at the same time. And it don't explain the kissing.

Straight, I concede.

No one is speaking to Roller and Meaney, of course; they'll be spending a further few days minimum going through the cold turkey of conversation withdrawal. The overall opinion seems to be that Meaney has come off worst due to Roller's unprovoked attack and is already sporting a bruise like a sunset on his left orbit. To balance things out, and for fairness in the light of the fact that Cookery has been cancelled—although not for as long as anyone imagined it would be—Roller has found himself some new abrasions to trace with his fingertips in the small hours: left temple, lower jaw. Perhaps I'm desperate, perhaps I'm dumb, but I decide to allow Ostrich into the inner sanctums of some of my thoughts about Dott.

That yoot the new fish. What do you really know?

The question foxes the man. Has time gone all twisted? he asks. Don't man just have this conversation?

Not Marris. I mean Dott.

Okay, he says slowly. What do you need to know?

I've only got what I read in the papers.

Well, same here, rudeboy. Why does man wanna know?

My face, I suppose, is contorted with confusion.

There's a lot of damage out for the cuz, I say to Ostrich. On Puppydog. I want to know why.

Ostrich laughs. Just possibly because of his crimes? he asks.

Nar. More serious than that, blood. Not beef on road. Not the crime—we're talking Puppydog Wing, fuck's sake; they're all eligible for electrocution, cuz. Nar. It's something else, something local.

Man have no idea, says Ostrich, and even less inclination to find out.

Allow it.

You can't force a man to have an interest in something, but you can't force him not to either. We all need a hobby. And knowing it's going to make me seem perverse but I'm going to be the only one who wants to speak to Roller, to Meaney; and the only one who wants to speak to Dott.

Assaulting Ostrich might be a solution to two problems.

Two.

So what's the word about me, Billy?

The question is aimed at my back: I am stacking the shelves marked Quick Reads—the bowdlerized versions of the classics, for the div kids with learning impediments.

The word, Miss? I call over my shoulder.

Yes, Billy, the word. I've been here a good few weeks now. And I know how you fellows talk among yourselves… What's so funny?'

Miss, I ain't heard *fellows* in time. I pretend to take an inordinate interest the diet-down version of *David Copperfield*.

That can't be true. The guards say it every day, Kate Thistle replies.

With a smile on my face I turn to her. She is sitting behind the desk, her fingers poised on the keyboard.

One, Miss: it's officers and not guards. And two: they say *fellas* and not *fellows*. Say fellows in here and you're likely to be mocked at the very least.

Thanks for the tip, Kate replies.

If nothing else, she is gracious enough in defeat—even if the victory is hardly worth mentioning, if not for the conversation that follows. I see some mileage from her question.

Trade down, I suggest.

The relay of rapid blinks that she offers implies a quick-lit fuse of thought and repercussion. But we've already established something of a wary understanding; we have started to engage in conversations when Miss Patterson is out of the room, as she is right now, on a comfort break. Like boyfriend and girlfriend caught in coochy-coo conversation by teacher, we close our mouths when the door handle turns: therefore we have a secret. Therefore we have a bond.

What are you proposing? Kate asks.

I will tell you, I say carefully, slowly, holding the rest of the Quick Reads in front of my chest like a shield. Might be I look like confidence itself, but there's an echo in my chest that sounds like an Electrolux. I'll tell you what man saying about you, Miss— if you tell me why you're studying Dott.

She's not shocked; she's not offended. Worse still, she's not confused. Up until the very last syllable I've been hoping— somehow—that I've got it all wrong; wishing for a puzzled expression.

You first, she says.

I tell her straight: We think you're a fed.

And that's when the Library door opens. In walks Miss Patterson, snapping shut the conversation between me and Kate. It's like being caught red-handed. For a second that copper is banging on my yard again. And Mum's screaming: *It wasn't him. It wunt my boy. Please don't take him away.* My sisters are standing behind Mumsy. *He's a good boy*, Mum's shouting. And I can't believe I've been caught; I can't believe my mother's defence, despite what I've done.

So angry am I at this interruption, this torn circumstance, that I spit the first thing that comes to mind.

I'm just filling up the shelves, Miss, I say—too quickly.

That look of perplexity I hoped for on Kate's face, is here

now on Miss Patterson's features. I can see that, Alfreth, she tells me. She turns to Kate and asks her if everything is all right. Phoney smile follows. If we ever had it in the first place, I get the impression that we have just lost the Librarian's trust. It creates a certain sense of irreparable loss. But then, life's full of disappointments. Innit?

Three.

The disappointment lasts for most of the morning. Then it's time for me to take the Library Pass to Classroom 1, to begin the slow process of letting one prisoner into the Library at a time. It's one of the I.T. classes; the Gov is John, and he turns to me as I knock on the door and look through the wire- meshed glass. He straightens up from one yoot's screen and walks over, unleashing his keys from the pouch and he lets me in. I have taken a risk—a huge risk. Beneath the laminated A4-sized pass is a tiny scrap of paper I'm holding to the plastic, like a magician secreting a playing card. But the paper is much smaller than that, folded down to the size of a pill. I am gambling that Roller, who is nearest to the door, will take the usual scrummage to be first out of the room seriously. It's my only shot. Once I've given up control of the pass it will shuttle back and forth until nobody in Classroom 1 wants it any more. Then I will take it to Classroom 2.

Me, Gov! Roller shouts, standing up and pushing his chair back a metre on its wheels. Our eyes meet. It's not friendly. It's an urgent understanding. It's a battleground stasis.

Wogwun, Alfreth, Roller mutters, discerning what John has not seen: that I'm holding the pass very tightly and in an awkward way.

It's wet, blood, I tell Roller.

John does not know that this means nothing at all. I hope Roller will understand that I'm trying to talk in a code that only the two of us can bust. Watched by the Education Landing Officers, we walk in silence back to the Library, with Roller now in possession of the pass and of my note.

I enter the Library but Roller says to the screw, Before I go in, sir, would you mind just unlocking the toilet. I've been drinking a lot of water.

The screw stands up. Don't get any drops on that Library Pass, I hear him say as the door closes slowly on its fire-hinge.

Before we hear the toilet flush, carrying away its flotsam of one discarded piece of paper, I fancy that I hear other things. I hear Roller unfolding the note; I even hear Roller reading my words—*What REALLY happened?*—and I imagine him sitting there, and I can hear the swish of his hair as he shakes his head.

You're all sweaty, Alfreth, Miss Patterson informs me.

Sorry, Miss. Think I've caught a cold from Jarvis. My next door.

All sympathy, of course, she ignores what I say and instructs me to boot up the machines at the end of the room that teach driving test theory. We're expecting a couple of bookings in half an hour and the PCs have been experiencing some technical problems.

I couldn't give a fuck about driving test theory. I'm just waiting for the pass to arrive back at the Library so I can take it to Room 2, passing 1 on the way. Though I'm not sure if Roller is smart enough to give me my answer. My pessimism is unfounded. After the I.T. class has finished ordering mags, renewing books and browsing atlases, I stroll slowly along the corridor—even more slowly as I approach the window to Room 1. Roller sees me coming and very quickly he uses his mouse to click onto another file that he has obviously prepared behind Gov John's back. He highlights the miniscule font on the screen and clicks it up to size 48—massive—so I can read it from outside. He has twisted the monitor slightly towards me, and it's a good job I'm a swift reader, man, because he's typed more than I expected.

It was like time stopped man—I went DEAD—and there was some-one else in my head, I could feel him there but I could not get him out—he tells me he can make my time go faster, he's got a way, and he shows me he can control people's minds, some people, and he makes me fuck Meaney up bad, and I don't want to, yoot done nothing, you know what's up Alfreth, man I'm scared, then he makes them screws kiss us, he's evil.

Move on, Alfreth! the screw calls from his desk.

Yes, sir.

My teeth are chattering; my skin is raw. But I am happy.

Four.

Visits! We all look forward to Visits! Unless your visitor has specifically indicated that today's the day, you don't have any idea of who you're going to meet in the Visits Room, near B. I'm praying with my beads when Screw Oates tells me. Pull on the denim. Make a good impression yat. Could be Mumsy. But it's unlikely. She always phones first to arrange a visit. (Leave a message for me to use my credit to call back.) So it's one of my boys! Yay! No. It's my babymamma Julie, and our daughter Patrice. It's like a Christmas visit; it's like a birthday. Oh fuck, I realize. . .

Happy Birthday, darling, I say to Patrice.

I haven't shaved; I haven't even deodorised properly. It's my little girl's special day and it's slipped my mind. What sort of father am I?

You could have brought a card, Billy, says Julie.

And you might have noticed that I don't have a free range, I answer sarcastically, of the ordinary person's shopping facilities.

Fine. You made one on the computer last year.

Not allowed anymore, I lie, innit.

Well, why not?

Some yoot send out coded escape messages.

This part is true. The problem was discovered when some-one came to comprehend that at the age of nineteen it's unlikely that one boy can have seventeen daughters.

Patrice is taking turns between gurgling and sulking. The Visits Room is packed—because it's the weekend. More people have time to exercise their guilty consciences at the weekend. Ju-lie has returned from the tuck shop with the most chocolate that I'm allowed to receive: five bars. I have never once mentioned that I hate the stuff.

I need a favour, I tell her. I need some books sent in.

Julie frowns. You work in a Library, Billy; just order them, she says.

They won't let me have 'em.

Then they'll never get past Reception.

Just listen. Are you listening?

Julie huffs. I'm not a fucking gangster, Billy. Don't do that line with me.

Ignoring her, I add: The people in Reception are dicks. Don't know what the fuck they're doing. Call it a distance learn-ing gig. Call it anything you want. I'm asking you for a favour, not a kidney. It's just a couple of books.

I turn to the nearest screw. Don't know his name.

Gov! Permission to kiss my girlfriend, sir.

Granted.

Hadn't you better ask permission from me, too? Julie asks as I lean across the table.

Our lips meet and open wide; I use my tongue to push into Julie's mouth the wish-list I have written, inside the saliva-proof prophylactic of a folded-over piece of paracetamol casing. As usual, Julie hides it on the left side of her mouth, near the back, where a molar is compacted and there's a bit of space.

You could say something like: that was nice, Julie. I miss you, Julie. I'm kissing you because I want to, Julie, as well as I have to. Anything would do. I'm easily pleased, Billy.

Sorry. I'm distracted.

So I see. And by the way, how exactly am I supposed to pay for these books? They's expensive, you know, Julie wises me.

I know, I know. Am I chatting shit with you, woman? Getting vex now.

Speak English, Billy, Julie says wearily. She picks up Patrice and gently settles our little girl onto her lap; the girl squirms. That movement makes me winsome.

I calm down. Take the money out of my account, I tell Julie slowly—releasing a clot of invisible steam through my teeth.

Can't innit, I'm told. She averts her eyes.

Why not? Why not, Julie?

All gone, Julie answers.

Excuse me? I can eventually say.

Once upon a time, boys and girls, I was doused in petrol. The assailant ignited matches, one after the other, until I agreed that he had permission to take my wallet. *Just take it!* I screamed as the next match got closer. You feel chilled to the bone. It's how I feel at this precise moment.

Julie. I left eighty-five-fucking-grand in my current account, I say. What are you chatting me, it's all gone? Before I get angry. Angrier.

I've been meaning to tell you, Billy.

Tell me now.

It was Bailey. She sounds relieved to be made to tell the tale. To make it past tense. She won't look at me—she looks at the top of Patrice's head—but there is light in her voice; there is light on her brow. He stole your card details. This she says almost proudly. Said he'd invest it wisely.

I can't help myself. *Eighty-five grand's worth of details!* I scream.

I stand up; the chair behind me is bolted to the floor and won't move. Suddenly the thought of requiring Ostrich to further my ambitions seems dumb: I have all the inspiration that I need right here. The violent motion of spanking Julie across the face makes me fall to the side. I have lost my balance. Wanting to hit her again, I am instead hit. And not once. Without knowing what I'm doing, I have moved a step closer to Dott.

Five.

It's a few days earlier that I stumble upon the idea of the books. I am chatting breeze with Carewith—he of the rationed intelligence—because breeze is all you *can* talk with the brere. Most of the time you can't even chat shit with the brother: chatting shit at least contains a nugget of sense or wisdom on occasion. But Carewith's engine has long since run out of petrol: too much skunk, on road, too many cocktails of medicinal alcohol and cider. So we're chatting breeze: worthless air. Something about weekend breakfasts. When Carewith moves his lip and suddenly releases, not breeze, not shit, but reality. All of a sudden man chats me point blank: it hits me between the eyes.

I was having a chat with that screw from the Cookery Class, he says.

Why? I interrupt him immediately.

He shrugs. Something to do innit. Wanted to hear his side of the story.

His side, I tell Carewith, is pure bullshit. They're denying all knowledge of it. And blood, they ain't fucking around with any teasing still.

I heard. Dusty Palestinian yoot, Carewith says, confirming the rumour. Said yoot bust a chuckle with said screw in good humour; said screw bust a knuckle on said yoot's left femur. Yoot went down. The message? No jokes. The subject is serious.

Turns out we're from the same ends, Carewith tells me.

It's breeze. But sometimes a breeze contains dirt.

Big deal, I say.

Them's bad boy ends, blood.

So?

So how does a man from our ends end up as a fucking screw of all things? Most mans' ambition from our ends is not getting blazed with a nine-fucking-millimetre, cuz.

It's no more than a mild coincidence, but what Carewith says next makes the skin on the top of my head chill and tingle; it's as though I've torn the caul and been reborn once again.

Be it heard, cuz. The same ends as Meaney, as it happens.

The remark is throwaway; the irony is that Carewith accepts it as breeze but it's this simple statement that puts the rat among the pigs.

I don't know what root in the forest I've stumbled upon but I understand instinctively—or so I think—that it's the root to a very big, gnarly old oak.

Roller's from the south coast, I argue.

As the ignorant do when they are adamant about a fact, Carewith contends the point passionately: his brief argument back to me is almost hostile, in fact.

Grew up on the south coast. Spent five years in my ends.

Crime has neighbourhoods. It's not the other way around. Crime is the landlord and a neighbourhood pays crime's taxes and monthly protection. Crime replaces the lightbulbs in the streetlamps—but first crime smashes them out. Crime paints the fences a uniform council colour—but first crime slashes the metal with thickly penned graffiti. Crime closes down libraries. It was crime that chose me. I didn't choose crime. Because I lived in crime's neighbourhood; I lived in crime's ends. The same ends as Roller.

When Association Time ends I am delighted and frightened to be returned to my pad. I wait for the stereos to start competing for decibelage and then I know that I am as safe from interruption for the night as it's possible to be. The line of thought I follow is like a whip, like a heart line.

It can't be a coincidence, can it? I'm starting to sweat.

I've heard in the past—much as I dislike referring to the past—about such phenomena as mass hysteria and mass misdirection. And I think, there at my table, with my hair gels and unnecessarily stockpiled toothpastes (the market's dead for toiletries) that these phenomena are what we're visiting. He's *planted* something, has Dott; I simply don't know what yet. Or why. And there are other concerns pertaining. History says it all. You can convince an entire nation to believe in a murderous campaign: that's a fact. It's been proven. You can ask a lifeline to believe that it's okay to delve for riches through the vaults of the under-valued. Not one motherfucker will raise an eyebrow, and you know it. How do you persuade the innocent that left is right? By mass hypnosis, I reckon; by mass hysteria, mass compulsion. Irrespective of my feelings about having been manipulated, I am certain that there was something in the air that we responded to and applauded.

Thanking the Lord for the female menopause—the one that causes Miss Patterson to take such frequent toilet breaks—I use my computer and my few stolen minutes to research a portfolio of books on the subject. No longer do I flirt with Kate Thistle. She thinks she has done something to hurt me, but hey—you have to treat them mean to keep them keen. She wants to know what I'm doing but I refuse to tell her. By not forcing the issue, which she can certainly do, she makes me even more suspicious of her intentions. But I'm not scared of Miss Thistle anymore; it is strange that I ever was.

Six.

I'm approaching his cell in the Segregation Unit.

Thank you for coming to see me, darling! Dott shouts.

And I know that if I flip back his flap he'll be there. Teeth or eyes to the meshed glass. I don't even tell Dott to fuck off. Flanked on either side by my superstar minders, I continue to walk to my designated cell. I'm pulsing with anger and fear; but I have no intention of showing it to anyone. With good grace I will accept my Seg cell: its bucket, its mattress. And I will promise my advisers that I have learned my lessons and it won't happen again. I will be a good boy. I will show anyone who wants to know that I've learned my lesson. And in secret I will plot my revenge.

But Dott isn't finished. Fancy seeing you here! he calls. And: Do you fancy going out tonight? he calls.

Motherfucker, I whisper.

The screw to my right agrees. Shut the fuck up, Dott! he shouts, and the taunts cease immediately. But I can feel him laughing behind the steel. When my cell is unlocked I say to the officers: I'm sorry, sir. And then again, turning slightly: I'm sorry, sir.

For what?

For having to listen to that from Dott, I say. It was for my benefit.

The screw to my left—Peterson, I think his name is— regards my admission as a sign of something possible in the future.

You two cunts got beef? he asks me and squashes up his face. Beef will entail a rethinking of my sleeping arrangements.

I shake my head. Nothing serious, I tell him, hoping for it to be so.

Only the night, I think, or the following nights, will say for sure.

The door opens. I have seen inside a Segregation Unit cell on more than one occasion, on business, on my travels as a Library Redband. But viewing through a flap does not prepare you for the narrowness of the room, nor the low ceiling, the hum of the empty pot in the left far corner. Not since I arrived at Dellacotte have I experienced such a sensation of dread. I am wringing wet and starving and poor, let's not forget. The sort of poverty that most people live with every day—I'm with you brothers.

My cell is two away from Dott's. The previous inhabitant has made his escape by creating a noose from a pillowcase and getting transferred to the Psychiatric Wing of a prison forty miles away. His name is Henry. I won't see him again, and I wonder if anyone is thinking in similar terms about me. The door closes. The chunky clunk of a heavy lock. I lie down on a mattress that smells of sweat and semen; I plump the pillow against the cold brick wall. There is nothing to do. That is why it's called Seg.

Night brings a different collection of noises. I'm used to music, the blur of late-night TV, and hollered conversations from cell to cell. I am not used to the wailing and the moaning of the yoots on this Wing. The pain; the endeavour. Never in my life have I heard young men suffering so. I'm trying to ride it; I'm trying to blow ignorant. It's not easy.

How has Dott done it? What he's done is create a system of mass hypnosis and hallucination, so that at the beck and call of the bruv's finger—or a signal of some kind—my cuzzes do what the fuck he wants them to. And I can live with that. I have heard more far-fetched: the yoot in the burka and the face-veil, pretending to be a Muslim matriarch and holding up the Post Office; the yoot whose dad works in an agency for security guards, getting a job and robbing a Woolworth's depot of nine grand's worth of kids' clothing. It's not the audacity that stymies me; it's the not knowing that breaks my heart. I can't wait any longer. In the middle of the night I call his name.

Dott refuses to answer. I call again and the night-screw (face unknown, name unknown) bangs on my door and tells me to can it immediately. I leave it an hour before calling Dott's name again. It's four a.m. He doesn't answer in words but in an action that makes me jump. He has created a swing-line from his bed sheet, using a roll of toilet paper as a weight. Like a raven the package thumps at my window. I get up off the floor and open the slits. The night air is chilly, blood. Dressed in nothing more than boxers and perspiration, I await his second swing. It comes but I miss it; I cannot reach out far enough. Increasingly riskily, awaiting another thump on the door, it's not till the fourteenth swing, my right arm by now raw from friction with the slits, that I manage to take hold of what Dott is sending me. Stuffed inside the toilet roll is a pillowcase. I pull it out.

There are clichés aplenty in the books to which my job allows me easy access—clichés about fear and about wanting. Especially fear. So what is my heart like? A drum? A thunderstorm? It's beating so fast that I cannot hear anything else as I squint at the pillowcase. It's marked with something dark but the light is too poor to be able to see for sure what it is. Turning on my lamp will illuminate a tiny light on the power board in the office and a screw will come along, wondering why I'm awake so early; all I can do is hold the pillowcase up to the slits, and then wondering how Dott has managed to smuggle a pen into the block, I rely on a different sense. I sniff the pillowcase. Blood. I will later find out that Dott has written his message to me with blood from the sole of his left foot, using a short sewing needle that he has secreted in the flesh behind his right shin. Drop by drop. Stitching blood-stain to bloodstain, for my benefit. The letter must have taken the better part of an evening: little wonder that he has been quiet.

He has been working.

But I can't read it! I have to wait until first light at 5:47 before I get any relief from the biting frustration I'm feeling. But I still can't read it properly. My new next-door is a Czech lad named Jacob. I don't know if that's his first name or his family name, but he clearly believes he owns the Seg Block, the cunt. At 5.50—rise and shine!—he shouts for attention; it's almost as though he knows something is going on that he wants to ruin, but he's probably been sleeping. He rings the night bell. Footfalls on polished tiles, the screws come running. Jacob is on suicide watch and he's attempted before, bare times. It will be a matter of seconds before they arrive. It's in those seconds that I realise Jacob has given me my reason for turning on my light; other inmates will be doing the same, protesting against their sudden alarm call. If the screws are with Jacob, they can't be with me. Thank you, cuz, I'm thinking as I light up the room.

Seven.

I'm faced with a series of worries and dilemmas. In no particular order. Before I face Number One Governor at the Adjudication I am sweating in my cell, fearful of losing my Redband and my Enhanced status. Lose those and it's no Library job for me. In a few days' time I will enter the small court of law at the end of the Seg corridor, limbs trembling, eye sockets twitching no doubt through lack of sleep.

Take a seat, Alfreth, the Governor will tell me without looking up from his paperwork. Hands on the desk. You know the routine.

Yes, sir. But no, sir, I will want to protest. I don't.

The desk faces his; there's a space of two metres between the two facades. In addition to me and the Governor, there are officers to my sides in case I make a sudden violent movement;

there's the officer who will read the charge, and the officer who will give the eye witness statement.

Second worry is Julie won't get me my books.

Third worry is, if I lose Enhanced, my mail will get read in both directions—and I need to send a letter to some of the boys I roll with. I need my money back from this fucking Bailey waste—and I need to offer him a reminder, via the medium of non-verbal communication, that I am not to be fucked with. The money gets returned (this itself a sub-concern: how far can I trust my own boys not to spend the rewards?); and he stays away from my ting and my daughter. In return, once his bruises heal, he has given back to him the full use of his limbs and the only visible memories will be the shank scars on his torso, every one of them a tale to tell, a tale that was told.

My fourth worry is what Dott wrote in blood on the pillowcase.

And my fifth—and most pressing immediately—is how I'm going to get rid of the fucking thing. Flimsy prison-issue pillowcase it might be, but it's still a pillowcase. I can't dash it out the window—it'll get found and I'll get blamed. Not even the Della-cotte winds, up here in the hills, are going to move a pillowcase far once it's snuggled up nicely to the tulips in the flowerbed. And I can't eat it.

I'm tempted to wrap it inside my towel for when I'm allowed a shower, but then what? The single shower down block is checked before and after every rinse, just in case someone leaves something— a sewing needle, for example—for someone else to use. (I wonder if Dott has dashed the needle out the window. It's the sort of thing he can easily hide in his mattress, after all. What's he thinking?)

The answer to the pillowcase conundrum arrives, as so many solutions do in this place, when I am moving my bowels into the fire brigade red plastic bucket. I have heard from other lads that when you're down block, it's best to time your bowel movements for just after breakfast. You don't want to eat your cereals with a container of shit in the corner of the cell. But I can't wait. My body clock is out of sync from so little shut-eye. I must be quick. Clenching my batty cheeks, I knock-knee my way back to the mattress. The pillowcase is under it. I complete my defecation into its open maw, a sense of self- disgust rising within myself. As best I can, I flatten down the waste and replace the loaded linen beneath the mattress. I wipe myself clean and dry. What the screw will see in the bucket, if he's one of the sick govs who look, is a small amount of prison-issue shit, battleship grey, bulked up with too much paper.

Slop out, I'm told in due course. When I empty the bucket into the chute there is no comment. And when I empty the bucket, eventually, containing the shit-soiled pillowcase— its whiteness stained darker—with my faeces and a load of bumwad, I hope there will no comment either.

I have been allowed one roll-on deodorant for my stay here in Hell's Hotel. I apply a layer of it to the pillowcase, to ease any smell that might start wafting. It's as close a procedure to feeding a pet as I've ever known. I don't recall having a pet in the flat when I was a boy. Not allowed.

At the Adjudication I plead guilty. Hot on the heels of my belief that I have no choice but to do so is the thought that I am still innocent until.

Allow it.

It's to your advantage, Alfreth, I'm told, that the assailant refuses to make any kind of statement at all. What did you pay her?

Eighty-five fucking grand, I want to say. Good old Julie. I nod my head; it's a sympathetic, humble gesture.

So I have no choice, he adds, but to hold you here pending further psychiatric reports. I want to be sure, Alfreth, clean record or not.

My backside rises now from the plastic seat.

Sit down, Alfreth, I am told.

I deep-breathe to regain my composure.

Sir. I've never been in trouble before. I'm going legit.

I'd like to believe that, Alfreth, the Governor tells me.

It's true, sir. I'm going to be an accountant.

Is that so?

Yes, sir, it's so. It's true, it's actual. Everything is satisfactual.

Less of it, Alfreth.

Sorry, sir. I glance up at Kate Wollington. She's there as my *compadre*. I don't know why, but you learn to ride it. I can't stand that smirk on her face though still. Or the thought that she'll be reporting back to Kate Thistle. I wish her dead. At this moment. Swear down.

Alfreth. As this has been your first serious charge since you entered this institution, I am willing to offer you the benefit of the doubt. The tone is weary, icy. You may keep your Enhanced status.

Thank you, sir. May I ask you a question, sir?

The question has him wrongfooted and distracted. He thinks he's done me a favour but he says, Go ahead, Alfreth.

Sir, why is Miss Wollington present here today? I don't look at her. I want to exclude her from the inquiry.

She'll be writing your psychiatric assessment, Alfreth.

I understand that, sir.

Don't stand up.

I'm not about to, sir. I just thought I'd mention that this is highly irregular and I would like a reason. Most psych reports go on the evidence of the court report and I'm curious why Kate Wollington is here right now.

Yeah, Charlie, I know her first name. I know yours too. I have painted him into a corner and he knows it.

He betrays a sign of weakness by asking: Are you taking the piss out of me, Alfreth?'

No, sir. Quite the opposite. I've shown nothing but politure. Politure?

Yes, sir. I don't run the risk of offending him further by defining the word although I want to. I simply wish to understand this breach of protocol.

It's *my prison*, Alfreth. That's the only sort of protocol you need to know. Do you understand me?

It's at this point that I think it's his arse that's going to rise from the seat.

I understand you, perfectly, sir, I say. I turn to Kate Wollington. Please say hello to Kate Thistle, I ask her. (Yeah, I know *her* forename too.)

Will do, is Miss Wollington's only contribution to the conversation.

Thank you, sir.

And I am led back to my temporary pad in the Seg. It smells like a tramp's beard in there, but already still the officers have ceased to remark on it. I've heard them all—the insults.

Smells like a rat crawled into this shit-hole and died, Alfreth.

Yes, sir.

Smells like a scabby whore's Mound of Venus, Alfreth.

Yes, sir.

Insults don't matter here, at Dellacotte Young Offenders. Why not? Because insults are the air you breathe and you get used to them quickly.

There's a note from Reception. It's been pushed under my cell door, and I unwrap it immediately. It's about the books I've ordered via Julie. Bless her, Julie has tried her best. For whatever reason. The books have gone straight into my Personal Belongings in Reception. All three of them. Rationale: *Material not suited to a prisoner.* Allow it and fuck it. I don't need the motherfuckers anymore. Where has she got the money? That's sixty sheets.

Eight.

Five things.

He asks two questions, but without question words, does Dott. *Prometheus?* he asks. *Hair shirt?* he asks. And then he asks a question, in blood, with a question mark. It doesn't take a genius of memory. He insults me, bruv. Prometheus is the Titan chiefly honored for stealing fire from the gods in the stalk of a fennel plant and giving it to mortals for their use. I can read, you know, Dott. He is depicted as an intelligent and cunning figure who has sympathy for humanity. *Promethean* refers to events or people of great creativity, intellect and boldness. Allow it. But we're not done. Next comes the real question, and it makes me sit down on my mattress.

What is your earliest memory of fear? he wants to know.

If he thinks I don't know what Prometheus and a hair-shirt is, he's playing me for a div-kid cunt. The question, on the other hand, will need further thought. So I think about it now. I have no choice.

My earliest memory of fear stems back to when I was seven years old. It's my earliest memory of anything at all. It's my garden—or rather the communal garden, round the back of the flats where I grew up. I'm playing off-ground tag with my sisters and I'm stung. A bee lands on my right forearm and sperms me his worst. My muscle is inflamed for a week. It is not until this moment that I know I'm allergic to bee stings.

The second-to-last thing Dott has written is this: *A million* *years of bee stings, Billy. Think about i*t. And I do. I think about it and I read these words for a good half an hour, careful to listen out for footfalls. Obsessive compulsive. He knows, I'm thinking. But how? I am stranded on an alien island. Don't like it. Cunt knows. But *how* does the cunt know?

The last thing on Dott's pillowcase is elementary. *Read your visitor's message*, it says, *and take heed*. I am allowed out for exercise. I do my pull-ups. I don't get the reference to Prometheus or to the hair shirt. I await my so-called visitor's message. And eventually it comes. It comes on the day after the Adjudication. I'm asleep. My time down block has offered me a chance to catch up on my sleep if nothing else. Most of all I miss my job in the Library. Christ alone knows what my reception will be like if I'm ever allowed back there: my reception, I mean, from Miss Patterson and Miss Thistle. For I feel that I've let them down. A silly sensation, maybe, but it persists.

Screw Wells is taking up my doorframe. If you imagine your stereotypical montage of what a prison officer looks like, you're thinking of a hench hard body like Screw Wells. Who tells me now:

Slag wash, Alfreth. On your feet. You've got a visitor at ten.

I'm not expecting anyone, I reply, but I know that this isn't true. I've been expecting someone since I took possession of Dott's pillowcase. Who is it, sir? I ask Wells.

Even his shrug is seismic. How the fuck would I know? he tells me. And while you're at it, empty your slops box, would you? It smells in here.

Yes, sir. By now the pillowcase is good and stained with faecal matter. Although I'm sweating like an athlete, my passing of the shit and the fabric into the chute elicits nothing more than a sneer of professional good conduct.

Bet that's a relief, Alfreth, innit?

Oh yes, sir. More than you can imagine.

His dumbfuddled frown burning into my spine, I return to my cell with the bucket and wash my bits and pits in cold water and prison issue lubricant. The stuff is as slimy as spawn. Satisfied not to know all, Wells closes and locks my cell door. My pulse is racing and I can't resist it any longer.

Dott! I shout out through the window slits. Dott, are you listening?

I'm listening! he calls back. Could it be that he's been waiting to hear this question? The reply is just about loud enough for me to hear.

Who's my visitor, waste?

There is no reply to this one. So I shout it louder—only to get a complaint from Jacob in the intervening cell. I tell him to mind his manners and make it clear that if he doesn't do so there will be repercussions. He shuts up, but that doesn't help me with Dott's silence.

Dott! Who the fuck is it? Show me your hand! Show me your motherfucking currency, blood! You want me to believe you show me!

Who said I wanted you to believe anything? Dott shouts. *WHO IS IT, CUNT?*

The answer is among the last things I expect. It chills the piss in my bladder and makes me tingly and numb at the extremities.

It's your Mumsy, Billy, Dott shouts.

There can't be any more doubt in my mind: Dott is in touch with some of the boys I roll with on road. Or worse, he's linking with Julie. Man doesn't even want to think about that noise.

Who is it, Dott? I'm calling now. Who you chatting?

I'm not chatting dick, Billy-Boy. I asked her to visit you.

Is it better or worse to know that Dott has got something

going with my mum or with my ting? Frankly, both notions make me feel sick; for a man who wants to know so much about everything that goes on, I am suddenly doing an impression of a guy who prefers to be wilfully ignorant. I am reminded of what Dott is in for.

So much as touch her, Dott, and I swear I'll make your life not worth living. Are you listening?

Yeah, I'm listening, Billy, he replies. And what makes you think it is?

Is what?

Worth living. Dott does not wait for an answer. That question I asked, he continues immediately. When you were stung by the bee.

How do you know about that? I demand to know.

I was there, Bill. I was the one who poured water on the sting.

It's not often it happens, but right at this moment I am utterly speechless. I back away from the window slits and lean against the cool metal of the door. But my legs aren't the equal of the task for long. My knees are drained of juice; as my body goes down, my gorge goes up. I vomit. Not another word passes between me and Dott. I treat myself to another slut wash at the sink. I freshen my breath on a swallow of toothpaste. No amount of rationalisation will chase from my head what Dott has told me.

And it's summer again; I'm a boy. I have to view the pictures through the veil of pain that struck my body after the bee stung my arm. The pain is the overwhelming sense, and it takes me a few seconds to bite and kick my way back to the real memories of the event. I'm going nuts, I start to think. This can't be right. There was a man there. There was an application of water to the afflicted area. He was a man who lived alone in one of the ground floor flats. He was in his early twenties then. I was in the communal garden and I remember his face at his flat's kitchen window. He brought me two blue plastic beakers of chilled water. Through the residual pain I try to remember his face with more clarity, his voice with more clarity. In those pre-prison/pre-regime days it was first names we rolled with. His name was Ronald. And Dott's first name is also Ronald. Wait. There has to be a sensible explanation. My brain can't have distorted Dott's age so badly, can it? That was thirteen years ago. That makes Dott in his mid-thirties at the youngest. But he looks like a twelve year-old.

Screw Wells arrives to escort me to Visits. You look like you've seen a ghost, Alfreth, he tells me.

I don't know how seriously to treat the accusation.

Nine.

How the fuck do you know Ronald Dott, Mum? I demand.

Mumsy appears shocked. Well, that's a fine way to greet me, she retorts. You're not too old to be slapped, you know. Ask Julie.

Christ. She told you?

Yes; and I'm glad she did as well, William, Mumsy tells me. What possessed you, young man? I didn't bring you up like that.

Mum. Have you forgotten where you're visiting me? I see it in her eyes—that look of disappointment I have inspired on so many occasions—and immediately I regret the sarcasm.

Don't take that shirty tone with me, young man, Mumsy says.

I am only referred to as *young man* when disdain is on the menu. It's her way of refraining from saying something more apt and more bitter.

Sorry.

Now. Who's this Reginald Dott? she wants to know.

Ronald. You know when I had that bee sting when I was seven or eight? There was a guy downstairs.

You were seven.

Seven then. There was a guy downstairs.

Put water on it. I remember, boy. Why you ask?

What was his name?

It's not often you hear laughter in the Visits Room. The job of the visitor is to shuffle and deal out some memories for the inmates; but most of them, well-intentioned or not, arrive carrying a card reading: *This is what you ain't got no more, Jack. Lick the plate clean because it's all you're getting.*

My mother laughs with one of the good, rare ones. It's genuine. And she adds to it: Billy. Have you any idea how many people have been there?

Like I'm some sort of prick.

A lot, I know. But I thought you might remember something like that.

Mumsy frowns. If you recall, young man, I was more worried at the time about your eyesight, and how you might need spectacles.

Spectacles?

The problem was, I couldn't get good enough evidence of how you saw the whiteboard at school.

I was never there. I know, Mum, I'm sorry.

My point exactly, she adds—not without a shirtiness of her own, I might say. She knows the best way to make me feel worse about myself and my surroundings is to ignore an apology—especially one that's been repeated to the nth degree.

Cooling my temper, I ask: Could it have been Ronald?

She waits for a second or two. It could have. Relieved by the appearance of a quiz, her favourite, her tone is softening. She seems to shuffle her own hands. She strokes her own hair. What up?

But was it? I push.

Her appearance is anguished. I don't know, baby boy! she tells me in response.

I nod my head. I breathe out loud for a few seconds. What's the name at the bottom of the letter you've been asked to bring here today? I ask.

The sentence takes her by surprise. She has yet to produce the article. She is not sure how I know there's correspondence to be handed over.

It's unnamed. But it's not exactly a letter, she adds.

I call out to a screw called Rapattas: Permission to take a letter from Mumsy, Gov!

Ordinarily he's all right. He can beat me at ping pong and he knows it. This gives him an unworthy and worthless point over me and I enjoy him enjoying it. You learn quickly to give in to the little things, with screws. Sod's Law that this is one morning when he's bored (the Visits Room is very quiet) and/or he has been asked to keep an extra-special eye on the visitors of anyone currently in the Segregation Unit. Usually calm and collected, this morning Rapattas wants to know the colour of your tears, your stools, and everything else in between, so he approaches like a polar bear preying on quarry. Holding out his right arm, he wants to know what I want to read.

Me first, he says pedantically—and Mumsy, good as gold, hands the squidgy dollop of dough the sheets of paper she has produced from her bag.

I would like to point out to the Governor that there are members of staff who would do worse than to visit an optician's office or the diagnosis studio of a first class teacher of dyslexics. Screw browses the writing as though it's *Finnegans Wake*. The anticipation as he studies is like a toothache. What has Dott written? I want to go back to my cell to read it.

Pardon me, Rapattas says to my mum, but what's this?

A letter, I'm about to say.

It's a work of fiction, my mum interrupts. Rapattas accepts the information with a nod of the head. A work of fiction? The screw's brow is furrowed and twitching. I'm about to find out why but for the moment I am ignorant. Mum adds: It's from his sister. It's a story for her GCSE English.

Rapattas nods again. Big-minded literary critic that he obviously is, he replies, She's got talent. But love stories aren't really my thing.

A love story? I'm thinking as he hands the two sheets of paper to me. *I can remember the first time he held me in his arms,* I read quickly.

The handwriting is tidy, tight and discreet. It occurs to me that I have never seen Dott's own handwriting but since learning that I'm to receive the message I've imagined the script to be the chaotic cloud formations and heroin scratches of a mid-career mass-market rapist. Yeah. I've expected the writing to be a scream. I've even expected the writing to look like Dott himself. I'll come back to that so-called 'letter'—this Mills and Boon romantic fantasy—in a moment. Why? Because I only glance briefly at it for a couple of seconds and I don't know the full score. It's an empty moment. It shouldn't be, but it is. The thought strikes me once again. Whoever sent what's been sent knows Mum's address. How can this not add weight to Dott's argument?

There are two letters, actually, Mum tells me. Or two things. She's out of her depth somewhat, and she knows it.

Ashamed of myself—just acting up, really, and putting on a show, playing the giddy goat—I'm getting bolshy. In my mind I'm going *Jesus, let me have them then!*

The first 'letter' is on standard issue lined A4, with the blue ink scoured deeply into the weft; but the second has been typed.

It's full of typographical errors. But as Dott has not been allowed into the Education block, I am wondering how he's had access to a computer and a printer.

The last line of the fourth paragraph of the handwritten letter—after a lot of waffle, breeze and guff about a moonlit night, a clinch on a beach, the scent of his aftershave and the bristles on his chin—reads as follows: *Please go to a search engine and enter 'Prometheus' and 'Hair Shirt'.*

I printed the results out for you, Willy, says Mum, busting proud. That's as far as I read. Promise.

I see what Dott has done: he's covered his arse. That's what the cunt has done: he's covered his rapist arse. He has assumed (correctly) that no one will want to read more than a few paragraphs of pseudo-erotic bullshit, and he's started his message proper from that point on. The instruction to seek out Prometheus and Hair Shirt—it's not directed at me. It's Mum's. It's Mumsy's property.

Thanks. Have you any news to bring me, Ma?

I'm jealous to be sharing these facts. Plus, I don't want her involved. I can't help but believe that knowledge—sniffing its rim—is a dangerous ting.

Not really.

Allow it.

The second piece of writing is a printout—or a copy-type of a printout: as I say, full of typos and that. The instruction, it seems to me, to consult websites was for Mum's benefit and not mine. She confirms this theory.

I typed directly from the screen, she says. And I knew I was part of your game, Willy. Rightly or wrongly. I knew.

There's no game.

I didn't read any further, I swear, she tells me. I knew the first bit was disguise. I'm not stupid.

She's not. I stuff the pages into my tracky bottoms. Confined as I have been down block, I am keen to receive a second opinion about what I have done to Julie. For the moment I want to forget the letters and I want to know how the outside world is viewing my behaviour.

Do you blame me? I ask Mum, knowing that with a mother's innate fifth-gear drive towards intuition, she will understand what I'm getting at.

I don't approve, Willy, she says, after a pause.

That not what man ask.

Talk properly.

That's not what I said, I try again.

Mum disagrees with my verdict. She invested your money, William; that's hardly worth a slap.

She invest it with another man as my motherfucking banker!

Don't use that language in front of your mother. I deplore violence.

Envy drives my next question. What's he like? I ask.

Who's, Bailey? No, the Pope, I think. Yes, Bailey, I say to Mumsy.

I've never met him. Why do you ask?

Nothing.

What a grave disgrace I must truly be, I have seconds to consider. In for what I did, and not for what they comprehend nothing about whatever.

That was always your father's answer as well, she adds, all uppity.

No further comment is necessary, I feel. I don't even ask after my sisters as I can't see the point. As grim as it is, I want to get back to my cell. I know that Mum must have sat for nearly four hours on a train to get here, up in the hills, and then the taxi from the tumbleweed station, but I don't want to speak to anyone anymore. Apart from Ronald Dott. Allow it the cunt wins.

I remember my manners. Thank you, Mumsy, I say.

There's nothing more to add, really, is there? Except this.

Ten.

Billy.

Forgive the four paras of gobshite. Necessary work. Boring but you know how it goes. I'm sure you've guessed the reason yet. Now listen. Prometheus was a cunning, deceitful piece of work. No awe for the gods, ridiculed Zeus, although he was favored by him for assisting him in his fight against his father Cronus. The Ancient Greek means 'forethought'. Got that? Thinking about it before the act, until. In Ovid's Metamorphoses, P is credited with the creation of man 'in godlike image' from clay. Some say Zeus. But it was P who hit Z on the head with a rock. As a result, from Z's head popped the Goddess Athena. Some say. Others say Zeus demanded a sacrifice from Man to the Gods—to show willing and that. P would've earned your scribble of approval, Billy. Slashed an ox and counted it out into two piles. One with meat and most of the fat; the other, the bones covered with fat. Choose, Zeus, choose! Zeus knew that if he claimed to be duped he'd have an excuse to vent his anger on mortal man. He chose the bones. Denied men the secret of fire. Prometheus felt sorry and took fire from the hearth of the gods. Taught us to cook. And this really pissed Z off. P is taken to Mount Caucasus, where an eagle pecks at his liver. Forever, Billy. Imagine that. What's the nearest you've got? Fuck incarceration. Imagine a million years of bee stings. That was P's sentence. We've got off lightly. Or you have, anyway. Even the Greeks back then understood that the liver is one of the few bits of the body that can regenerate itself spontaneously. That's creative cruelty, that is. That's World War Two cruelty. It's what I need but I can't find, Billy Alfreth. By the time I'm freed, there will be nothing more left than cockroaches, army ants and wasps - which sounds impossible, right? You need an ecosystem, right? I'm not sure. Prometheus got 30,000 years, the poor bastard. My sentence isn't so far away from that, I fear. Same as that poor bastard.

I experience a shiver of remorse, knowing that Mum might have read this too, despite her claim to the contrary.

And then I read:

Save me, Billy.

I am sitting in my cell in the Segregation Unit, wondering how or why I should save a man who has mutilated fourteen women. I clean my windowsills with my fingertips. There has to be more to life than this, ho ho. So he's suffering? Join the club, Dott, I want to holler. He goes on to inform me of what I already know about a Hair Shirt: 'An adornment worn at various times in the history of the Christian faith, for the purposes of the mortification of the flesh rough cloth, generally woven from goats' hair, worn close to the skin, itchy a breeding-ground for lice, which would have increased the discomfort worn by ascetics, saints, monks, and lay persons.'

What's he getting at? A self-realised sensation of victim-hood?

The next bit is what gets me to the gut.

I was there, Billy. It was me. No one else. I used to think kindness was the way, but I was wrong. I was travelling the wrong way with kindness. I'd be closer to the end if I'd slit your throat. The water was useless. Some people make their way through time; some people make their way through people. It's my only shot. I'm sorry I've hurt who I've hurt. So sorry. But I really wish I'd smashed you up a bit when I had the chance. You have no idea how much kindness has hindered me so far.

He kissed her and she melted in his arms. The moon was an uncommon sight of cheesy blue.

I am starting to get a feel for what's going on.

Part Four:
Grow Your Own Kings

One.

Returning from the Segregation Unit is like returning home from another country. I arrive back to certain pieces of extraordinary news. Carewith is gone. Carewith has been shipped out—to Big Man Jail, Lincolnshire. While I can't imagine a place with more hills than this, I hear the news with a rigorous sensation of misplaced nostalgia, as I've been there. It's not just a case of the grass being greener; it's the case of injustice that I share with Ostrich—that someone has earned his promotion before me.

Ostrich is incensed. What man have to do? he asks me.

I am trying to keep him sweet when I say: It just a jail, blood.

Wrong response by a big fucking yard.

It Big Main Jail! He's irate that I don't take part in cutting up and distributing his cake of impotent rage. I fear the worst. I have seen Ostrich livid at losing a gramme of Golden Virginia tobacco at chess or draughts. I have seen what he's capable of with a melted-down CD case.

Whatever the weather, I tell him. Do you want a burn?

He regards the question with no small amount of suspicion. Indeed the question is foolhardy and misplaced on my behalf.

For what? he wants to know.

We are sitting on the steps that lead up to the next landing.

To smoke, bruv, I reply.

What's the price?

He's got a point: kindness and generosity is as conspicuous as bacon in our chocolate mousses. Tastes funny. Looks even iller.

No price. *Gratis*, cuz.

Ostrich gives me one of them ones where you don't know if he understands he's been a victim of a piss-take. Right now, in the din, it's touch and go. He wants and wants not to take it all broadside.

Here. I hand him a smoke. Lovingly rolled. And I do mean lovingly. Fact barges into my brain with the force of a shank through skin—I will miss Ostrich deeply if he goes to Big Man Jail. I'm glad it's Carewith on the one-man train south, back to a normal life of smoke in the air and dust.

Fuck this healthy oxygen shit.

You've seen the wildlife documentaries: the fox on the railway line, night-time, eyes burning the sick colour of virulent pus. He's out there cautious, blood. Wary. That's how Ostrich accepts his burn.

Allow it, he tells me.

I nod my head in agreement.

When man back in Library? he asks.

Tomorrow.

I have work to do before then. Desperation as my whip—whip as in whip and not as in car—I start to compose a list of questions for Kate Thistle. I'm going to start flirting with her again, in a fresh style.

We go back and I realise I don't have any writing paper left. Screw Nickels is an old-hand but he knows the ropes. I ask him for paper.

Use your bumwad allocation, he informs me.

So I do. Microscopic script on absorbant loo roll. Ready.

Two.

Good things come to he who waits. Granted access to the Library, I am informed by Miss Thistle that Miss Patterson has called in sick. In the absence of an authorised member of prison staff, the Library will not open for visits today. Miss Patterson has left a phone message detailing my administrative duties for the next six hours. For three hours in the morning and three in the afternoon it's going to be just me and Kate. Result. I can scarcely believe my fucking luck. After a welcome that is as warm as it is wary, Miss Thistle invites me to put the kettle on—to 'brew up' as she puts it. In order to squash any thoughts in her mind that I am taking her presence here as anything other than ordinary, I pretend I can't remember how she takes her tea.

Milky. Two sugars, she tells me.

I spoon three heaped teaspoons of coffee granules into my usual cup. The coffee is better than the prison issue crap I get in my cell and I'm not one to look a gifthorse in the mouth. The black coffee has me buzzing, and I need it, fam. I have been up half the night learning my questions and script for Kate.

You look well, Billy, she says, two hands curled round her cup. The steam rises up into her face as she lifts it, blurring the beauty of her eyes.

Do I, Miss? I reply. I feel awful.

She nods her head. Was the Segregation Unit so bad? Like a million years of bee stings, I give her.

The simile almost floors her. She has not expected me to know that she's read Dott's letter. Don't know where she's read it, but she has. It deals an opponent an important blow—to realise that the other person is closer than imagined. Less elegantly, it does me good to know that I can still shit her up peculiar. Some-times the relationship between predator and prey is more complex than it looks from the outside. I'm the wasp. Kate Thistle is the skin I want to land on.

What a funny way to put it, she tells me eventually.

I keep her gaze. Is it?

Yes, I would think so. She is sifting through the information.

I tell her I can make it all so much easier and she looks at me with a quizzical expression.

Let me help you, I offer.

And what makes you think you can help me? she asks.

I know Dott. Or I'm getting to know him.

Maybe it's not much of a hand but it's the only one I've got. I haven't been able to research the full range of my themes but I'm on a roll. Or so I believe. Evidently Kate isn't as impressed as I've thought she might be.

She shrugs now and says, So?

So you want to know him better. (Which brings me to some of what I have spent the wee, itchy-eye hours rehearsing. Firming my grip around my drink, I plough on.) I might believe, I say, you're some sort of psychologist, Kate, but you've got nothing to do with education.

Then what am I? she demands.

I've touched a nerve. Getting nearer.

You're investigating the fact that Dott doesn't age, I say to Kate. You're talking to people who knew him. People who've been affected by him.

She takes her time replying. She sips. And that's you.

That's me. As you know. The bee-sting.

Have I gained an advantage—any advantage at all? I'm not sure. Miss Thistle is proving as impossible to get inside as ever and just when I thought I had an in. Man think she penetrable, not im-. Man wrong.But I can't give up now, surely to God. And Kate thinks the same.

While she waits, I ask her: And how come, by the way? How come you're allowed to be a non-prison employee with sole charge of an inmate?

I don't follow, Kate tells me, picture of innocence yat.

Question simple enough innit. How come? I say for the third time. Not like I'm in for fucking money laundering or bullshit. I'm a violent YP.

Kate places down her cup. Your records, she replies, are exemplars.

Which you've read.

Which I wrote, Billy. Grow up! Or helped to write anyway.

I'm lost, I confess. Hereby I lose any mastery I've gained. Comes a point when it simply doesn't matter anymore. You slug a brew, say fuck it.

You're halfway there, says Kate.

It's a bit like raking leaves. Allow it taking the piss, I've had my jobs. I know what it's like to scoop half a broomful and then lose it in the breeze. Keep most of what you've got together in one place.

You're shaking, Kate informs me.

I'm scared, I confess, losing every point I've scored up till now.

Don't be.

I can help you, I say.

I know, she replies. I'm just not sure how to use you.

I wait for another word—another insult. Finally I say, You can use me to brew up again. We've got no one coming.

Brew up again, Kate instructs me with a nod of the head.

I aim to please. Do I say this or only think of saying it? Not sure. There are bare things I think I say, sometimes, and I never do. Bare things I never say but imagine otherwise. I wish I could be a doctor, to look at my own head.

Miss Thistle? You've got power.

I'm not sure I would go that far, Billy, she replies.

I'm not like some of the other lads in this nick, I've come to realise. Some of the other lads reach their most eloquent and dramatic turns of phrase at the point of maximum vulnerability: when their backs are against the wall. Me, I'm different. In the possession of price-raised information, I've realised, I'm a veritable Camus or Sartre. I know my shit. So I say:

I think you are, Miss. Either Governor Glazer or Governor Manners has okayed you to be in sole charge of a perpetrator of a violent crime. I stabbed-

I know. You stabbed someone in the arm.

So what's the arrangement? I want to know.

I'm not sure I follow you, Billy, Kate replies—and I like her style.

What do I get for helping you out? I ask slowly.

What do you think I can give you?

My pace is calm; my tone pure buttermilk and whipped yoghurt. Temperament-wise, I'm a fucking dessert. I want to be bruleed. Toasted in brandy, innit.

A meeting with Dott, I reply.

Swiftly on the defensive, Kate informs me she's not certain she can swing that one around. I tell her she can, if she wants to. It's my only hope.

I'll see what I can do, she tells me after a longish pause. Would this do in the meantime? A visit.

To where?

To his cell in the Seg. His TV magazine.

Has he ordered one? I ask.

Yes. It would normally go to his cell on the Puppydog Wing—he paid in advance for the month—but it's worth a Try. Why are you smiling?'

I like it, I confess. Like rubbing salt in the wound.

I don't follow, Billy.

We'll be giving him a TV mag in a place where he's explicitly forbidden to watch TV, I tell her. It's beautiful.

It's not quite what I had in mind.

I'm still smiling. But then again, Miss, I say, you don't have my mind.

Which point, the scary thing happens. Kate Thistle responds with:

No. No, I don't. Not yet.

Three.

What was that nonsense I heard about you slapping your bird? I am asked.

His name is Screw Oates. I have mentioned him before but the names don't really matter. We're deaf to prison officers' names, half the time. (Maybe you are as well.) They're not deaf to ours but we're deaf to theirs. And it's not just the yoots who are immune to the charms of screws' monikers. In the past I have overheard the occasional conversation between members of the Education Department, in which one will admit to another that he or she doesn't know the name of the screw on the landing corridor with them. Consider that. You're in a room of convicted killers, say, and your guard's your best shot if something kicks off. And you don't even possess the civil and self-preservative courtesy of learning the cunt's name.

Anyway. Oates is my unofficial guide around the Dellacotte grounds as I hump my day-glo sack of reading goodies to the wankers and the nice guys. Don't usually qualify for a chaperone, but after the slapping incident, they're covering their arses so thickly it looks like pork rind.

She stole my money, sir, I reply accurately.

How much?

We've reached the Segregation Unit. It's ugly how the feelings from such a recent encounter with the god-forsaken place rear up in me now.

Eighteen grand, sir.

Oates turns to me as he uses the first of his two keys to get us in there, out of the murmuring rain.

Eighteen grand. He even whistles.

Yes, Gov.

I would've killed her, Alfreth. Get in there. Do what you need to do.

Thank you, Gov.

My mind is pinching back together every thumbnail-sized scrap of memory that it can find—about the bee-sting day, back then. I want to call Julie tonight to tell her that she has wasted her money buying me books about mass hysteria and that bait: because she hasn't. She's wasted my fucking peas. My paper, my sheets, my work, fuck's sake allow it. We'll be talking again, she and I, but not about this subject specifically.

The hall still smells the same, not surprisingly: rinsed rat and garage oil and badly spent hope. Screw Oates introduces me. I think his name is Goodman, the one who nods his head in the little office.

Don't worry, he tells me, I haven't forgotten your ugly mug yet.

And then it's me, with my sack. Half of the contents have already been distributed; it's as light as mild push-ups in the Gym. I approach Dott's cell. Some people disagree about the existence of déjà vu, but if you are in my head at this moment there is no doubt the cunt exists. It's as though I'm approaching the cell on Puppydog Wing for the first time again.

Have you come back to see me, Billy Boy? Dott shouts.

I say nothing. I push his TV guide under the door.

How thoughtful! he shouts once more—and I turn my back. There are eyes and cameras on my every move and I can't afford to waste this chance. I head back to the office and announce that I'm ready for D Wing.

Hours later, and I'm losing a game of pool with Shelley—my heart isn't in it—and Ostrich is linking a yoot name of Gardener—I'm not listening—and nothing is making sense— the food in my belly like a tank of piranhas—and I'm wondering if I'll manage to sleep tonight—and I suddenly feel queasy.

I run for the sink in my open cell. I pass the parcel. Head jerking to either side, worst cocaine headache I've ever had and I ain't touched the shit, and I'm coughing and spluttering like the village idiot pisshead, shaking. The mirror shows me a frightening picture. I look dead. Gripping the side of the basin, I close my eyes. The image is still there, burned on like illegal pirate copies on a CD. Can't get rid of the fucker.

Are you there, Dott? I ask in my head.

When he answers I'm always there, Billy Boy I fall down.

Because it's not possible, innit? Mind control. Messaging. So how do I explain the fact that I hear his ghastly voice? One of the female screws is present. Her name is Blake, I think; I can hardly hear her talking as she asks me if I'm all right and if I need a visit from Health Care. All I want to do is sit still on my bed, with my hands warmly holding my head, not thinking. And the last bit's the important bit: not thinking.

I explain that I don't need Health Care and make it clear that I've just had some bad food. (That so-called lasagne was rough, to be honest.) Look of relief on Screw Blake's face; the relaxing. She knows it will come to nothing more than I threw up prison food; she won't have to write it up. It happens every day, with the mud and pond-life we're expected to digest.

Couple of minutes later, here's Ostrich. Wogwun? he asks.

I'm all right, fam, I lie. I had the lasagne. Taste like upholstery, blood.

Understandably and understandingly he nods his head.

Man need a favour, cuz, he says. Man just lose at draughts innit.

I copy his gesticulation. How much you need? I ask him.

Two burn.

On the windowsill.

Safe? You sure as rain'll fall, blood?

Take it all, I answer (recklessly in hindsight—he might have taken me up on the invitation). His eyes are all jumpy and sad. I know why. It's nothing to do with me, swear down. He's been sipping the blackadder hooch that Woodward on the threes has been brewing behind his radiator. Lethal gear. You don't so much get drunk as go straight from a position of sobriety to one of partial liver failure and temporary brain damage. It cuts out your days.

My thoughts return to Dott. I have nowhere to go to escape from them.

Bending the rules slightly, Ostrich takes a seat on the bed next to me. He's supposed to sit on the plastic chair or on the dressing table. Not speaking dick—not speaking a single word—he uses my papers and my burn to roll one up. He licks it closed with the finesse and the frown of a true friend—or at least of someone who wants to be.

Burn, he explains unnecessarily. We go twos, he offers—equally as unnecessarily.

There are tears—no, not tears, but the stings of tears *en route*—in my eyes as I watch him flare the cigarette and exhale against my poster of J Lo.

I nod my head and accept. I follow the blood's lead. What

be going on? he asks.

Complicated.

Man nods his head and rinses his mouth with a yawn that he loop-spits into my sullied and browning basin. Why me? I have time to argue with myself. All I done ain't no one's business. But I suppose it is. Everyone's business is some cunt's business. Or it's not business. We smoke our burn. Sosh time is coming to an end. Ostrich knows it although he doesn't wear a watch—and I fucking know it because I can feel it. Because you learn it. Or because you learn to feel it. Blood times it perfectly. Saying this:

We trade, yeah? You win pool, man spill his bake beans. Now it the other way round: you offer me burn. No question. Man asking why. So man tinking, how can man help man out in return? No money. Shirt on man back? Allow it that noise. *Fuck* that noise. Man can creep man some rumour.

Some rumour, I repeat.

Allow it.

I'm nodding my head. Be my go-ahead guest, blood, I tell him.

And I repeat: coming back from the Seg is like returning from a foreign country. I feel like I've been stalled at Customs for half a week. I'm about to feel more so.

You were away, yeah, man talk about Dott and his control over time.

Somewhat jealously I agree with this. It's part of what I've discussed with Kate Thistle.

There's no such thing, I state staunchly. It's a bit like feeling that Kate is having an affair: I wanted it to be between her and me.

Allow it. Man's dramatically cut down on man's reality in-take, blood.

That's one way of putting it, I tell Ostrich. What do you mean, brere?

He can mess with mandem's head. He can take away some *time*.

So the secret's out—even if it's a bitter pill of a secret and one that I remain surprised with myself that I want to keep to myself. Then Ostrich snuffs out the burn in my toothmug; he straightens his back—it goes *click*—and summons up a summary of sorts. He's a road man still, even inside the walls: a dreamer, a disbeliever—so while his road vocabulary is always fresh, up-to-date, he is about to bring to bear a collection of words to explain a phenomenon that we're all not used to. It causes him a great deal of effort ('Sosh Time over!' someone shouts) and he knows he has only a few seconds.

Back to your cell, mate, Screw Blake announces from my door.

Yes, Miss, Ostrich replies. At the door jamb he turns and says: A time-vampire, blood. Suck out your time. He doesn't wait for a reaction.

Allow it, I call back, suddenly absurdly grateful—a complete change of my emotions—to have a confidante. I'm about to find out, cuz. No. Not just a confidante: a witness before the act. Ostrich is my safety shot, I realise; my alibi, almost. And I need to tell him quickly.

What, man? he shouts when I can no longer see him from my bed.

Cookery Class back on for tomorrow! Dott's on the Labour List!

And so am I.

Four.

They recruit you to do bare dirt for them, man! Then they spray you up with nine em-em! Shit's not right, blood!

But a contrary contention is swiftly offered. Ah, says the

other, whisking his cake-mix with a furious and a genuine passion, but he took his chance, bruv. Thirty grand is a big change!

Not big enough to get sprayed!

The noise is outlandish, the violent subject of the conversation—usually banned inside the classroom— permitted here in the heat of the Cookery Room only because the two speakers happen to be reflecting on the implications of a film seen last night.

Believe it or not, the two speakers are Roller and Meaney. The Cookery Class is packed full. This is a test. Every one of the ten cookers is being used—oven roaring, hotplate blazing—and as I say, the noise is nearly unbearable. But the heat! O my days! The heat! The sweat! And this is a test. Some will pass and some will fail. Not a test of our cooking, of course: it's a test of our stamina (parched air, building-site din) and it's a test of our trust. This test is the last chance for a Cookery Class in the future; it's a chance to get Roller and Meaney together—with Dott. And with me. No pun intended, it's a pressure cooker. We are the ingredients the scene needs. Ten students means this: at least five (loud) conversations going on at one time. Often more. Some yoots can one-man- band it, innit, holding three or more chats simultaneously—to the backdrop noise of scraping knives and banging pots.

So I'm listening to a review of a film called *Mad Filth*—

bottled him with a perfume bottle still, blood, yat—

and I'm listening to a preview of an expected sexual liaison—

since I come in here she's got nice bums and nice plums; I'll move to her, blood— even though he's a lifer.

And then I'm listening to so much shit being chatted that I'm busting vex and I want to take the butter knife I'm holding and ram it right into Meaney's arm. Twist it good; grind it hard.

Really put it on the cunt— although he's done nothing wrong to me.

There's a high squeak of pain—remarkable that it can half silence the noise; more remarkable yet when I understand it's my own. Thoughts tumble through my head. I've been burnt on my arm. The burn's too high up. I've been bitten by an insect.

I've been stung by a bee.

I've been stung by a bee.

The notion overwhelms me. Pain exactly at the point where the fuzzy little fucker stung me when I was seven. I shake my arm and let go of the butter knife by mistake. Thank the Lord!—the bastard thing rattles against the saucepan in which I'm cooking bolognese sauce.

Alfreth! the Gov shouts.

If that knife was anywhere else but on a stove right now, I'd be looking at at least two months down block.

Just an insect bite, sir, I call back. Sorry, sir.

But I got you for a second there, didn't I, Billy Boy?

That's the voice at the back of my head. Dott's voice. When I turn to him—Dott—over there in the corner, where he's been since the start of the class, he is smiling. He mouths it—no noise—but I hear him in my skull.

Nearly made you do it, Billy. Could've made you if I'd wanted.

I concentrate on his face; I concentrate on his voice. Though it ripples through me like revulsion I even think of his crimes—or what I know of them. I must get closer, I tell myself, getting stressed. But Dott—Dott can't hear me. I can't do it, any more than I can ride a unicycle or cure myopia. I start to take out my frustration on my sauce, compulsively stirring in shake after shake of chilli powder. Dott's on my mind but he's not in my head. Left the building; hung up the line. Drops me one lousy communiqué and then dumps me. I remember him shaving his chest in my presence.

What the hell are you doing, Alfreth?

It's the Cookery Gov's voice, in my ear. Makes me jump.

When I blink my way back, two lively tears spring from my eyes into my bolognese.

I could nick you for that, he informs me.

For what, sir?

Misuse of prison property.

I'm still not quite certain what he means. What, the chilli, sir? I ask.

Yes, the chilli, sir. You got a deathwish or something?

I just like it spicy, sir, I improvise.

You'd better had, Alfreth: you're eating the fucking lot.

The walk from the Education block to the Wing will be a race with the Devil, as I struggle to hold into my intestine what desperately wishes to crash out. The noise inside my cell will be like a tractor dropped into a duckpond. But first there is another ordeal. First I have to eat the fucker. Twin agonies, in fact. I can't bear Ronald Dott's indifference to me as he works on his cheesey pasta bake. Is he taunting me? Indirectly, maybe, but not full on. He's in his own little world, and no one's invited. No one's speaking to him. When the dish is done he sits down with the rest of us to eat what he has prepared. Eating in the Cookery Room is the only quiet time of the session. We are no more likely to speak than lions around a fallen zebra are to flirt or play. We guard our prey avidly.

I spoon in the first forkful of lava. Towards the end of our meals we take it in turns to claim the attention of the Cookery Gov—asking dumb questions, usually—so that some of us can stuff what we're too full to eat into our boxer shorts for later on—either to eat or to sell. I won't be doing the same (I imagine the feel of solid fire and it turns my stomach) but I'm not surprised to notice Dott fisting the last portion of his bake beneath the waistband of his tracksuit bottoms. It is better to conceal your food quite close to your scrotum. When we leave the room and the screws pat us down for hidden tools, they are not allowed to touch our bollocks. But other methods are used. I know of at least one inmate whose chosen style is to cook curry to a ripe old density and then smear it all over his upper thighs on a visit to the toilet before the end of the lesson. I have never favoured this approach myself, but each to his own.

It is time to go back to our cells. Bowels screaming and lassooing, I hobble alongside Dott, simply hoping for something—some exchange, a raise of the eyebrow even still.

He leaves it till the very last instant. Just before our paths have to part in order for us to aim for our Wings, Dott moves slightly closer and says, Hold out your hand, Billy. And I do so.

I can't look down—but I identify what he has placed in my right palm anyway. I close my fist on it and reposition my hand inside my pants—the fashion statement is so widespread that the screws don't give it a second glance. It's not until I get back to my cell that I can comprehend why Dott has squidged some of his pasta bake into my grip. Does he think I'm hungry?

My position is secure on the toilet, but my body doesn't care about comfort or convenience right now. I will be there some time. Plenty of time to read the letter that Dott has stuffed inside his meal.

Five.

Darkness has fallen by the time my lower body has recovered. It is one of those feverish evenings that sometimes shatter the monotony; one of those evenings when bizarre but unquestioned matters arise. For no reason at all a yoot on G Wing starts singing 'I Want to Break Free' at the top of his voice. It is spooky that no one seems to have a TV blaring or a bass-line tumping. The sound carries. It's an anthem for us, of course; and before long the lone voice—which I can just about hear at first—is joined. One yoot, two yoots, seven yoots more. It's like an epidemic the way it spreads from Wing to Wing. From A to H, via Puppydog F Wing: eight Wings and four hundred versions of Freddie Mercury. Singing our lungs to bursting. Mindless. I can even imagine the dead rising from their graves, in the cemetery yonder, rattling their long brown bones on the headstones, keeping time and keeping rhythm.

The boys on C Wing take the guitar solo.

Though it's happened before—this kind of spontaneous singalong—it has not happened for a while, and now, with Dott present, the singularity of the exercise assumes an eerie new implication. I sing anyway. The last time it happened it was 'Jailhouse Rock'; the time before that, 'Folsom Prison Blues': old songs that somehow (it's on the wind, it's in our food) we all know the lyrics to. I sing along to 'I Want to Break Free' for, I don't know, the first thirty or so repetitions, into the night. The chant is still going strong when I decide to call it an evening and re-read what Dott has handed me—stopping reading only when a screw whose eyes I don't know (he or she must be short) opens my flap and regards me and my silence with brief suspicion. Not wishing to cause trouble, I start to sing again.

I can't get used to living my life, living my life, living my life without you, by my side.

It's two sheets of A4 lined paper, both sides covered, the script miniscule; in some places Dott has even written two lines of print between a set of lines, the words on top of one another like motoring wrecks.

I start to read again.

Entr'acte:
The Prison Ship and the Oasis

Oil trapped on water is what I remember most clearly. The slicked rainbows and the water-bound constellations. The dreams that the smears seemed to incorporate. I was there—and I recall it all vividly.

In the distance we could sometimes hear bombs detonate. We didn't care. The oil and the water—they were what we lived for.

Something pretty. Something pretty in the relentless gloom.

I was thirsty. We all were. All two hundred of us.

You think you know about cramped, Billy Boy?

Fuck double bang-up. *Fuck* bunks and shared privileges.

You don't know how lucky you've been, son.

We were there on that ship, all two hundred of us, fighting for a place to sleep, and dreaming of the water in the oasis. Imagine that: every day. A fight—a physical fist-fight— for somewhere to lay your head when you got weary.

Some tried to vault the barriers. Granted access to the upper deck—the equivalent of an Enhanced—some abandoned their mops, climbed the rails, and belly-flopped into the stagnant tide. To escape.

They died.

The oil was a treat and a curse.

It was smeared across the water like marmalade. It stank of offal and aftershave. But it was my guiding inspiration.

They drowned. Or they took a bullet in the shoulderblades. Either way.

The Prison Ship was called *The Oasis*. And we were moored in the Oasis. Rumour ran that the rowboats surrounding our ship were manned by robots and electronic personnel. I have nothing to prove it either way. There was a rumour that when one of our jailers spontaneously exploded in his rowboat it was because of water in his circuitry. But I can't *prove* that.

The Oasis is two miles wide. Skinny ghost that it is, it's about a half of that long. And no one has ever asked me where I came from.

I made certain of that. I chose my crimes carefully.

What is more likely to eclipse an interest in a past than a present that is so repulsive and abhorrent? I chose rape and mutilation.

You'll ask me why. You'll ask me many things, Billy.

And I will try to explain.

Just like I did, you came to Dellacotte in the back of a padded van. In the desert there are no padded vans. My crime was theft. Prometheus stole fire and was punished for eternity. But me, I stole water—and was sentenced to a lifetime on top of it, in the hold of a ship. My equivalent of a padded van was a pre-programmed boat. To cheers and boos I was manhandled into my rowboat but I had no need of oars. The boat knew which way to go: towards the hulk in the distance, looking liquid under the noonday sun.

I climbed a wriggling rope ladder and was hauled aboard.

Among the first things that I was told was not to take personally the savage kicking I received when I landed on the deck like an asphyxiated trout. All new arrivals got their guts and livers kicked blue. It was a way of establishing routine, normality—and hierarchy.

Above everything else, violence establishes a hierarchy— a chain of command, if you will. But you know that already, don't you, Billy?

Why else are you here? Because you lost the race.

And I will always have more answers than you have questions.

Raging is too grand a term, but a war was certainly ongoing. You could hear the pilots overhead; you could hear the pock-marking detonations.

A war was ongoing and I didn't wish to be a part of it.

My crime was theft. Bombs meant nothing to me, blood. And to tell you the truth, blood meant nothing much to me either.

I stole water. I stole water more than once, but I was thirsty. Dying of thirst. I didn't know what else I could do to maintain my equilibrium. I *needed* water.

Is that clear enough?

I needed water as much as I needed air. It wasn't free and I couldn't afford to buy it. So I did what others did: I stole it.

The oasis was feared and revered. To the inhabitants of the shanties and the slums it was where a stereotypical Heaven and a stereotypical Hell met comfortably. It was home. It was life. The oasis meant a break from the heat.

There were makeshift establishments, scattered here and there. Little pockets of civilisation. Freckles on the arm of a country.

But *which* country?

I'm astonished, Billy-Boy, that you've been so slow in the asking. You disappoint me, cuz.

You'll ask me where. You're not a moron: you'll ask me where.

And I'll say: desert.

…Barry Manilow wrote the songs the whole world sang.

I commited the crimes the whole world watched. And subsequently, I was able to brilliance a total re-focusing away from my past, from my history.

Given what I'd done, who *cared* where I'd lived.

Dott? What sort of fucking name is Dott?

I stole it from a Neasden Town snooker player.

My name—my real name—you will never know. You don't need to.

Not twice in your life would you be able to spell it, and not once would you be able to say it aloud. Imagine the car- crash of letters.

The only important thing is where I lived.

Places shape us; places build us.

I was a desert child and no one has ever thought to check me out. To dry me out to bare the desert: *the* desert. The Sahara.

Made from sand and dust, I was a man before I was a boy. I have never been a boy. I don't remember anything but the sand, the dust…

Wearing a scarf and a pair of goggles was the norm. It was a necessity, to protect your eyes against the white light and the smotes. You started your day fully clothed—stepping out into the raging heat—and you finished it by stripping to the knackers. In other countries you dress for the chill of the night- time hours, but we—we couldn't wait for it.

Night-time was like having the cuffs unshackled.

I remember the time when Morjardahid discovered grass.

It can't be explained. But Morjardahid found grass in the sand—and grass doesn't grow in the sand—and he brought it back to The Wethouse for inspection and praise. His lips were baboon-bum red with excitement.

The Wethouse. The Wethouse was what we called the hospital. The sick went in and did not return. The negatives— the not-yet-borns—went in and stayed a long time. The wetnurse's name was Saira el Door.

That name, and the taste of her left nipple, I remember fondly.

Me? I had the ageing disease.

Generating electricity was part of the punishment, for some lags.

You've seen the films, Billy.

Row! Row! Row your boat! Gently down the stream! But there *was* no boat. And there *was* no stream.

There was a ship and there was an oasis.

Why a ship? No rain, and yet the oasis thrived. Allow it.

But why a *ship?* Why not drown us and burn the bones? We meant next to nothing. So why the consideration?

Why a ship?

The Leper Island is the answer.

We were held in the grip of fear by the Leper Island. It might have been no more than the size of five prisons, but it didn't matter.

We felt the breath. *That* was the real punishment.

Blackened breath on a stale, hot breeze.

…I've changed my mind: my name is Noor Aljarhalifaro. (I've changed my name too - but you already knew that.) You can call me Dott. That's a joke.

If it had one—or one that was widely accredited—the township was called, variably, *Umma*—meaning 'community of believers'—or *Mostashifa*—meaning 'hospital'. A town called Hospital.

There were two other terms.

The first was *Mostashifa Tamaninat.* 'Hospital.' 'To be motionless.'

The second was more complex. *Ana mabsout beshughlak*, it

ran. I am happy with your work. A town called 'I Am Happy With Your Work'.

You know those cartons of fruit drink that we get every day? The breakfast slops. You've probably got one in front of you right now. Study it.

There's a picture on the front. There's a picture of a halved mango, a halved apple, a chopped banana, diced pear; there's a picture of a mangled kiwi and a decimated nectarine.

In the same picture is a whole—an entire—peach.

Why? Why did the peach survive bowdlerisation and viciousness? I'll tell you why. Because the peach is the only fruit to resemble the human body.

The peach looks like a woman's arse. Pure and simple.

Even ad campaign designers recognised this fact.

I am happy with *your* work, Billy Alfreth.

I have no choice but to be so. No one else has ever made the effort.

Apart from Kate.

One last thing—or 'ting' as you would say.

I've got all the time in the world—literally—but *you* haven't. Rinse me clean of this disease and I'll follow you to the ends of the earth.

I'll talk to you about time.

I love you.

Ronald Dott x

Part Four:
Grow Your Own Kings (continued)

Six.

Bollocks, I say as I finish reading. The door opens.

You look like death warmed up, Screw Jones informs me.

Thank you, sir, I reply. And a very good morning to you as well.

Don't get sarky.

I'm not, sir.

His left brow stabs northwards. What's that you've got? Jones asks. The paperwork.

Short story, sir, I explain. Creative writing.

I need to read the fucker, sunbeam.

The missive is held over and I pull on my tracksuit bottoms and get ready for the day. Confident in the knowledge that I have spent the better part of the night copying up what Dott has written—on toilet paper, no less, using biro—I will enter the day with a spring in my step. Original, been digested. You can get drunk on another's bad words. Get drunk on mine. Check it. I go to the Library and I ferret my way through my daily chores. Pay Dott no mind. Do my business.

Aldhouse on C wants a change to his TV mag. Perkins on G wants something different with which to bash. These things I can deal with. But the fear builds up—again—like a physical presence. Like a wall: brick by brick. But a strange wall: a wall that not only obstructs, but also embraces. Crumbly embraces, no matter where you are. Check it sideways, cuz. A wall that knows your own heart rhythm. Tell me a better definition of the word *fear*.

So this is where we are. Miss Patterson is still off sick with menopausal complications. It's me and Kate Thistle. Not exactly standing on ceremony, I wait for the officer to leave and then I say:

I know all about the prison ship and the oasis. I haven't even taken my seat at the microfiche machine. However, if I expected to make her flinch I have failed.

Do you now? she replies.

Yeah. And I know that his real name is Noor.

Unforgivably she gives me an identical response: Do you now?

I do. And now I'm going to get on with my work while you decide, Kate, how much you want to tell me and how much you don't.

I'm used to hours, but these ones pull on the dead. The hours that follow—the prolonged silences and the elongated torture of the same—feel like an excavation. We're tying the dead in the cemetery together; we're dragging them from their graves, united in a mission. It is half past eleven, and nearly time for Movements, when Kate eventually opens up. The sigh that accompanies her leap of faith is fulsome.

I was telling you the truth, Billy, she says, when I said I was a student.

She won't look at me. I'm standing by the little table, idly leafing through the *Inside Times*: I'm attempting to comprehend why they thought—the editors, the teams—that printing the joke about the six criminals around the breakfast table was a good idea. It's an old one. But why a good idea?

And suddenly I can't stand it: the noise of the silence.

I've got one for you, Miss, I tell her—but tell her too quickly. Gabbling.

Got one what? she asks.

Six prisoners at breakfast. Another bleak day. A murderer, a sadist, a masochist, a rapist.

You're not making any sense, Billy, she tells me. Slow down.

They're at breakfast, Miss Thistle.

She switches the side. Tell me about Noor, she continues.

No. You tell me about Noor. We've got fifteen minutes still.

That's no time at all, Kate informs me.

It's a start.

Nodding her head, she repeats, It's a start, and then goes on to talk about the 1940s. But first she says: I am a student of criminal psychology.

Seven.

They were found in the 1940s, the tribes of the Hola Etta-luun… Nomads. Warlords, Innocents. Perverters, Creators. Call them what you will, Bill. All human life is here, as they say. They came from everywhere.

I don't interrupt.

Do you know what a lurry is?

I confess not.

It's a repeated, monotonically, by rote, boilerplate speech. It's a hubbub, babble, it's a jumble of voices; it's a throng.

Then it's right at home here, innit.

And it was right at home there, as well.

Bully for it; for the lurry. And how do you know about it all anyway?

Because I was *there*, Billy.

Eight.

Ostrich wants to tell me about an extraordinary achievement in the Gym. He has bested his previous top score on the bicep-fucker. He is glowing.

Man bust four. Man bust it *blind*, blood.

You should be proud.

Allow it, bruv. Allow it twice. Your own day how it go? he adds, remembering his manners in a rare show of politure.

I had a long, long chat about Dott.

With the Library ting?

Allow it.

Ostrich starts to laugh. You and she, he says, you and she—man, yous using on that shit, blood. Yous man bringing it forth, blood.

I don't see it that way, Ostrich-cuz.

Man sure you don't.

I'm frustrated by the accusation. But I don't have the words to rebut the thought. I'm subject to the facts, as I've been told them: that Kate Thistle, looking no more than an old girl of thirty-four or thirty-seven, claims to have been in the desert in the 1940s, there to witness the tribe of good workers.

Say it isn't so, fam. But we've read 'em: the stories of the frogs falling from the sky. The babies born, forehead to heel, with a duvet of sharpish hair all over their tiny bodies. Tings happen, blood, and I'm starting to buy the merchandise. I'm getting ready to accept my stings.

What's the earliest thing man can remember? I want to know.

Man's forearm on man's neck: holding man down, he tells me.

Rape?

Nar nar nar. Punishment blood innit yat.

For what?

Early violence, Alfreth, Ostrich confesses with a shrug.

Boys'll be boys. Cuz there's nothing else to say. Boys will be boys, man. Girls don't seem to understand this fact. But Kate does.

Can you hear me, Billy Boy? I hear suddenly. *Are you listening?*

I don't want to talk. I'm too full of pus. My missing money is like a vacuum—it's like a Black Hole. Sucking everything in. I know I am capable of accentuated retribution. I know I can take in that Bailey cunt and show him the time. It won't help anything but I know I can do it. Likewise Dott.

The end of Association Time is looming and I am not ready to disassociate; I am not ready, check it, to un-associate. The food is heavy in my stomach, and I hear it again, I swear down.

Dott calling Alfreth. Come in, Alfreth.

Just fucking like leave me alone, I say out loud.

Ostrich gives me the look: the one I've seen before. More than once. Long-since-gone Skelton—a risky transfer from Puppydog to our Wing—once cheated Ostrich out of a promised blancmange pudding. Well, let me tell you—and check it—Ostrich waited for his moment. Ostrich waited for his moment and then paid a yoot called Mbombo to set his bed linen alight at a specified moment (memory serves: eight- fifteen, an autumn evening) while simultaneously, or at least proximately, taking a slash on his own desk. Mbombo's desk. Oh, and faking an epileptic fit. And do you know what? My sympathy—for once—goes out to the screws of Dellacotte. Or of any Young Offenders Institution. How would *you* deal with that? Arson, prisoner's health and damage to prison property. That's a tough one to call, priority-wise. And Christ knows what Ostrich must have paid. Of course the bells go off, the screws dash it. To bust it. Leaving the gateway open. Well. Skelton's transferred to a nearby secured hospital the next day. One nostril, they say, will never heal but the left one looks okay. The cartilage that the screws found on the draughts board was unfixable, but Skelton will breathe for a good few more years.

Motive: no blancmange. Method: laboriously prepared, sharpened mouthwash bottle, the original plastic melted down to the consistency of road bitumen. And the act? An attempted nose removal.

Point being when Ostrich expressed—to Skelton, but in my presence—his abject disappointment at being cheated out of a plastic carton of blancmange and then gave the bruv the chance to repair the wounding—I saw the look. Ostrich's look. The one that says: don't dick with me, Charlie.

I get the same look at this moment.

Quick to reconfirm the status quo, I say: Not you, Ostrich-fam.

Then who, blood?

I don't want to make too big a deal out of it, so I reply, with a shrug: Voices, rudeboy. I'm hearing voices, innit.

Voices?

And I'm expecting one thing—I'm expecting Ostrich to say something like, Get you to the Health Care block, blood; or, You going nuts, cuz?

What he says instead is truly frightening. He says:

Me too.

Nine.

What I've said about my conversation with Kate Thistle: that didn't take up the full fifteen minutes that we had available before Movements—which were five minutes late as it happened anyway.

How do you mean, you were there? I ask.

The statement is pretty unequivocal, Billy, Kate tells me, and then adds, changing the subject: That extractor fan, over the computers?

Yeah?

Does it work?

Yeah it works, I tell her, confused. The PCs get hot innit. They're old shit. They used to set off the fire alarm.

Turn it on for me, would you?

As I'm leaving to cross the room to do so, Kate takes the cassettes from an audio recording of a popular loan: the abbreviated, divved-down version of (of all things) *Bleak House*. Yeah! The one with the prison ship.

Carrying the case only, Kate follows me across the Library.

Well, let's see how well the bloody thing works, shall we? she asks me.

Why do you need a cassette box? I want to know.

We can use it for our ashtray, she replies.

Can't smoke in here!

We can take our chances.

No, Kate. *You* can take your chances, I say. What's it be? A bollocking? Well, me, I'm looking at a week down block. We can't do it.

She delivers it—stabs it: the one that I want. I have a packet of twenty Marlboro Light cigarettes in my trouser pocket. Carried like a man, she says. And I've only smoked four. That's sixteen left.

Marlboro Lights are like crystal meth is on the out.

One to smoke now—with me—and the rest of the packet as you so choose, Kate says, now reaching into the pockets of her black slacks and freeing the box. It's a bit like observing a master magician at the slice-through box: the victim smiling. Can't say it's the best thing you have ever watched. But you can't stop watching either.

Have a burn with me, Billy?

Can't, I'll lose me Redband.

And then she says it, twisting the knife so to speak. The thing I haven't heard her say and the one that gulps me up to her level. A trust ting yat.

Fuck the Redband, Kate Thistle informs me.

Seconds pass.

I haven't got a lighter, I eventually mumble.

The Zippo is in my handbag, Kate says. Now fetch it.

But let's not forget our positions, I am thinking.

The nicotine reaches my brain's nerve sensors with the surety of a Tube train. There are only two directions to travel in, and one is barred.

What was on the water? I ask as we smoke.

The cigarette is like smoking a chair-leg. We are used to thins.

I don't follow, Billy Alfreth.

She exhales like a 1930s Hollywood star. (I have, over the years, become an interested and utterly undiscerning consumer of 1930s Hollywood. Yeah: I'll watch any old shit.)

Yes you do, Kate. There was something on the water.

And she wastes no further time in telling me what it was.

Oil.

Oil on the water, I elaborate. Where from?

There are bigger questions that you need to ask, she tells me.

No, Kate—no, Kate, I disagree. And I can't fucking wait to dump the butt. I am jumpy for my position. I am jumpy for a lot of things. I spend my life jumpy.

And where were you?

She doesn't hesitate. The Sahara Desert, she informs me.

I am still mid-swim through my Marlboro Light.

You're winding me sideways. Where was the oil from, Kate?

Tapping a dreadlock of ash into the cassette box, she does a sick impression of someone with no real clue of what she's being asked. Sick as in good.

I'm afraid I have no idea. From ships? she asks me.

Possibly.

I am suddenly aware that she has been right to question the weight of the inquiry. I mean, who cares?

Do you like the ducks? I say. I am desperate. I am struggling for balance, I want a breather. The ducks are neither here nor there.

There were ducks at the Oasis, too, Kate says. Do you know what a duck was in ancient times?

No.

Stability. Constancy.

You're not giving me madness about a duck, right?

No, Kate replies. I'm giving you the truth about ducks.

Suddenly I want another cigarette.

Supernatural powers, she adds. The weather prophet. Also sacred to the Greek God Poseidon and to the Egyptians, the Great Goddess Isis.

Who gives a duck? I say, aiming witty.

Kate is on a roll. She doesn't hear me. To the Hebrews, she says, the duck was regarded as clean food. It represented immortality. To the Native Americans, Billy, it's a go-between, between the sky and the water. It was a duck that dived down to collect mud from the floodwaters to make the Earth.

Bully for the duck, I mutter. Man don't wanna talk ducks, Miss.

Talk Dott is what you're saying, Kate replies. Bait. Okay. Straight in?

Straight in, Miss.

There was a rumour that kings could be grown in the desert, she says.

And suddenly I'm looking forward to the next Cookery class.

Ten.

We're in the exercise yard, and believe me, I'm of the opinion that I could *ride* some of that Oasis heat. It's freezing, blood; there's water in the air that's rawing up my nostrils. Through the wire-mesh fence, the rubbish bags are heaped up outside the Recycling Workshop. Ducks are ripping open the black plastic, sniffing out bacon rind, potato peelings.

Health hazard innit, says a yoot named Sarson.

Check it, I agree.

There'll be rats and whatnot in there. He chuckles. The heavyweight championship, rudeboy: the rat versus the duck.

Rat bust it, blood, I reply.

Ah, I'm not so sure, blood. Seen a babymamma duck one time. She's there with, like, fucking, nine little kitten ducks.

Ducklings.

Ducklings, rah. And there's a fox, yeah? he says. A lady fox, right?

How could you tell? I ask.

Sarson gives me the look like I've just spread marmalade on a CD and started to eat it. No dick, blood, he replies. That's usually quite reliable.

Joker! I reply. You can't see it, blood. Fox hung like them Puppydog raper boys, blood!

All right, Sarson tells me patiently. It was a man-fox. Man happy?

That's not the point, blood.

Fuck it. Fox was a neutered, motherfucking androgynous hermaphrodite fox, blood. That tick all your boxes, Alfie?

You're in a bad mood, Sars.

Yeah I know. Sorry, man. The point is, the duck and the fox go toe-to-toe, blood, to protect her little fluffs.

Sarson leaves quite a long pause, which I feel obliged to fill.

What, you mean the duck won?

No, man. You on crack? Fox mashed her up good. But the babymamma duck put up a damn good fight innit.

Mothering instinct, fam. Nothing stronger.

Don't know if it's the sudden whisk of dirt-carrying breeze or the thought of my Mumsy saying *Don't take my boy. He's a good boy*, that brings out the only hot thing available tonight: a pinprick of a tear, burning in my left eye.

Nothing stronger, Sarson agrees. Where *is* everyone tonight?

They've gone to London to meet the Queen. They've gone to the pictures. The fuck do you think?

He makes the 'dickhead' sign: fist moving sideways across the mouth, tongue moving in the cheek to simulate a penile presence. And then we bust chuckles. There's another long pause. The only sounds I hear are from the rubbish bags that weren't collected because of the Bank Holiday Monday. But they weren't collected the week before that either, or the week before that.

People are in a strange mood, Sarson mutters.

There's no music. There's no shouting. There's not even a fight to restore some sense of normality.

You're telling *me*, blood.

Part Five:
Declensions (The Sadness of Roses)

One.

No one kicks off in the Cookery class. But violently worded debates are the order of the day. By means of a little barging I have managed to secure the stove next to Dott's. It is usually Chellow's place of work, and the man gives me a boysing about it, but I explain the breach of protocol in a manner that all us inmates comprehend:

Man and I've got beef, bruv.

Chellow nods. You wouldn't be doing nothing stoopid now, Alfreth, would you? he warns me in his sternest-but- wouldn't-scare-a-sparrow-type tones.

Need to link man, is all, I reply.

The Cookery Gov wants to demo. Ordinarily I enjoy this part of the lesson—as a rule I like to learn—but this time it's all but unendurable. I can't wait to chat to Dott. We're doing chick fricassee. I already know how to make it. Gov understands this and wants to elicit responses from me in the way that a good teacher does. I play along. Perhaps because the class is still on a sort of probationary period, the first part of the lesson is conducted in verbal silence. And this is no use to me. I can't stand it. So, as I say. No one kicks off in the Cookery class, but disagreements are the order of the day.

Yo, Meaney!

Wogwun, blood?

Your team play shit at the weekend, cuz, I taunt him—not only completely ignorant about his team's performance but by no means even vaguely aware of what his team even is, or if he has one.

You on smack, Alfreth? he replies in the sky-high cadences of utter disbelief. We fucking cream 'em, blood!

The debate is slow to get going—it's like those shows where the hench man pulls the lorry with the rope, with the harness around his torso. Once it's in motion it's hard to stop.

You're chatting waffles!

As soon as the argument is good and going, I can talk to Dott. Or rather, he can talk to me.

Heard the life story then? he says. How does it work as a narrative?

Every day's a school day, Dott.

Very philosophical.

You're telling *me*, blood, I say. But who can *I* tell?

I'm reminded of a conversation with Kate Wollington, a few months earlier. The hour is stoned o'clock, but when you've got psychological problems you talk to a psychologist, right? But not a Criminal Psychologist: a Psychologist Psychologist.

Gov, I'm whining that night, can I go to Health Care, please?

When? In the morning? asks Screw Oates.

No, sir. Now please, sir.

It's two o'clock in the bloody morning, Alfreth. You wet the bed?

I've got stomach cramps, sir.

His eyes are working mine something fierce; he's thinking—well, actually, Alfreth isn't known for pushing the night bell or clowning around. Maybe it's real. There's been a short epidemic of food poisoning, after all.

Get dressed, Billy, he says.

I happen to know it's Kate Wollington's turn to work nights. And she's from a therapeutic background. She's not like the Education Govs, who always play their cards close to their chests. Kate reveals—from time to time—little pieces of information. She's got a cat named Sooty. Favourite colour is mauve. And when she does the night shift she leaves her office door open; she doesn't like the silence or the confined space. (I could tell her her fortune, cuz. Don't talk to a YO about confined spaces.) So she will hear us approach.

That's the plan. But will she?

She's playing Mahler at a discreet volume as we enter the corridor. This isn't helpful. I do my best to make my footfalls louder; I even clutch my stomach and indulge in a pregnant moan.

Nearly there, Alfreth, I'm told.

Kate Wollington appears at her door. Workhorse that she is, she has been applying nightcream to a nasty-looking delta of eczema on her left earlobe. What's going on? she asks.

Gut rot, Miss, the screw replies.

I catch her eye. Whether or not I have learned anything from Dott about mind control is questionable, but it's a technique that I pray I'm at least a novice at right now as I will Kate to want to speak to me.

We're almost past her. Then she says: If you're feeling a bit better in a little while, Billy, I need you to pop in and sign your Psych Report from a few months back. I don't know how I missed it.

Yes, Miss, I tell her. Thank you, Miss.

You're welcome.

And so it is that I enter the Health Care Surgery. Salty- eyed and with a brisk moustache, sallowed by nicotine and what looks like tomato sauce from his midnight snack, the doctor's name is Peregrine or Montgomery or something old school like that. If it's not, it should be: he's got a Bertram appearance about him. He's also got a sleep-deprived appearance about him— and the sort of breath that suggests he might have stopped at the local for a few whiskies before he started his shift.

What are you thinking about? Dott asks me. You're miles away.

Did you put it there? I reply immediately, suddenly flaky with new panic.

Put what there? Put what *where?*

Me and the doctor. In my head. Me and the Psychologist.

Working lazily, Dott smiles. Bless you for the compliment, he says, but I'm not sure I'm *that* good.

You've done it before.

Not a memory, Billy! Dott replies. An impulse, a thought.

Get on with your work, the Cookery Gov tells us.

We have to get back to our dishes. But the class will be nearly three hours, like all of them. I'll have time to re-connect, to re-link.

What else did she say? Dott asks.

My first reaction is that he's on about Kate Wollington, but of course he means Kate Thistle. All the same, I decide to keep him waiting. I have been kept waiting for long enough by him.

Clutching my midriff, I stop at Kate Wollington's door in the middle of the early hours. I have been given an aspirin; I've had my mouth checked to make sure that I've swallowed it. My performance has not been good enough to get me sent outside the gates to go to hospital. Instead I am holding a teacup-sized bottle of water with a second aspirin dissolved in it. The con-sultation has taken quite a few minutes because the doctor has needed to check my medical records for notes of any allergies.

Come in, Alfreth, Kate Wollington says.

From the door I see that what she has in front of her is a standard black text-on-white paper form, and the few strides I take towards her do nothing to make me change my mind. The screw waits in the corridor.

Just check what I've written and sign at the bottom if you would, Kate says, issuing me with a ballpoint.

Instead of picking up the form I lean over and read it on her desk, not understanding the game at all. It is quickly obvious. In the space under NAME she has written the words *I can* and under PRISON NUMBER she has written *help you*. In the box left for today's date is her handwritten *with*. The rest of her message follows in the larger boxes for PSYCH HISTORY and REPORT. And it reads: *your problems on the outside—with Julie, with your mother—but only if you decide to talk to me. To help me. I want to know why what you remember of the night of your crime is different from what was seen on CCTV. Was there more than one crime that night? Were you more coked up than you have told me? Help me. And I will help you.*

It just needs you to sign to agree, Kate Wollington tells me.

I sign my name in a badly-shaking a scrawl as I now continue with my meal in the Cookery Class. Dott is still waiting for me to answer his question.

We were still in the Library, I reply, and I say *Kings?*

Two.

Kings? I repeat. Did you say kings could be grown in the desert?

That's exactly what I said.

I don't understand. Ducks now kings, this is insane.

Kate is appearing somewhat dreamy now. She's reminiscing; she's lost the hardness of fact and is soft with a different

DAVID MATHEW   133

focus—the lens of memory.

Everyone there was obsessed with time. And time meant something slightly different for all of us. Time is strange in the Hola Ettaluun... She giggles naughtily. Bloody understatement of the year! Another cigarette?

The craving of a few seconds ago has already left me in its dust. We'll get caught, I tell Kate Thistle.

You're already in prison. What's the worst that can happen?

Seg? Loss of earnings?

But she's not listening. Besides, I'll take the rap, she says, lighting up again. I decline the polite offer nonetheless.

So what did it mean for you? I ask. Time, I mean. I am struggling to hold all of the pieces in my head; it's like holding onto pieces of a storm.

It meant needing to change my life every few years— *completely* change my life... I could murder a gin and tonic.

Allow it.

Would you like one? she asks me.

You're getting it twisted. You'll get fired, Miss.

You're right. I'm not supposed to know where it's hidden anyway.

This takes a second to filter through. You mean it's the Librarian's gin?

Oh yes. Quite the Liz Taylor, she is. Little bar behind the DVD Returns trolley. I found it by accident, says Kate. She sometimes has a little evening party with the guards—sorry, *officers*—on B Wing. She exhales.

Angela?

Kate laughs. Well, she probably won't thank you for using her first name, she tells me, but yes—Angela.

So much has rattled around in my head for the last little while that I cannot tell anymore when someone is lying to me.

Surely Kate Thistle isn't being serious. Or has she had one already?

All right, I'll have one. I call her bluff.

No, you're right. Too risky. I wouldn't want to get you in trouble.

She has smoked less than half of her burn. She doesn't want it. Making a sort of *yech* sound that you might more commonly associate with a child refusing its dinner, she crushes out the butt. Let's sit down over there.

I don't care how she intends to dispose of the remains of these smokes—my head is ringing. My voice is whiney when I say: Please make me make sense of all of this. Don't help me. Make me.

Okay. But she takes bare time to breathe in deeply through her nose—like she's sniffing the bouquet of a well buff burgundy, blood.

And then we're interrupted. The door is opened and in walks an officer, his face the physical equivalent of a fart. Everything okay, Miss, he asks.

Fine, officer.

But he doesn't leave us alone immediately. The smell of smoke must be in the air, as much a giveaway as dirt on your boots. I can see his frown pose the question that his mouth fails to release.

Anything wrong? Kate Thistle calls.

We're left alone—but it doesn't take a genius to work out that he'll be back, doing his rounds, much sooner from now on than he is required to do. Why? Because he'll want to catch us. Because that's what screws are like.

Could you give me a job to do, please? I ask.

Why's that?

For a prop. For when he comes back.

Kate gives a brisk little nod of the head. I think that pile of books there need new issuing stickers inside them, she says. And could you report any damage to the pages on the slip at the back.

It feels good to be given something to do. Despite everything—or maybe because of it—I do not feel comfortable looking at Kate's face while she speaks. It is as though I have developed some sort of phobia. I start working as Kate starts speaking.

I had Usher's Syndrome, right from when I was a girl, she says. It's a condition that meant my eyes were getting worse—getting worse quickly. It was frightening. Imagine: there I was, still in school, and some days it was darker than others, even at the height of summer. I was a miserable child.

I'm not surprised.

It got worse. By the time I was entering puberty it was starting to affect my hearing as well—sometimes my balance. There were good days and bad days but the darkness—the internal darkness—really scared me. On a good day I could go to school and do maybe half the timetabled lessons. Then the page might start to darken, the words swim. Or I wouldn't be able to hear my name being called and I'd be accused of being naughty. So it was easier to say nothing at all. On a really bad day I couldn't hear my own voice.

You ain't been diagnosed, Miss, not at this point?

No. That didn't happen until I was nearly sixteen, says Kate.

And the air is charged dry—not only as a result of the extractor fans. There is promise in the air, I think—something that is about to be said. It can't be any longer than a second that I close my eyes, but man, it feels like a whole bunch of hours. It feels like I've gone to sleep. Because I dream. Burning as with a fever, I am skimming over broken, bony land—cracked and parched. My feet are not touching the ground. I have no feet. I am mind and consciousness only; my one point of view is what I should by rights be treading on. But I am six feet up, and moving at a remarkable speed towards what? Towards water. I can smell it. Not the fresh, salty smell of the sea—or at least not what I can remember from my one and only visit to the shore, when I was a boy. Or more of a boy, anyway. No. This is ripe with repugnance; the stench is that of an animal's body torn open and left to rot. There is fear on the wind. Decay and rotted promises. My motion slows. And now I am swimming through the air, doing breaststroke: surge and glide, surge and glide, I top a rise crowned with coffee-coloured sand and the small bleached bones of the unfortunate, and there it is, down at the far, far bowl of this particular dune: the Oasis. Waves of stinking oxygen. The water gently lapping in its riparian way, leaving curves of dark grey oil with every tonguing. I want to bathe. In order to get closer I need to scratch my way through an invisible membrane barrier. I am swimming as hard as I can, my limbs pumping. I am running out of air, and I know that I cannot sink to the hot dry desert floor. It feels like drowning and I am panicking. There is nothing to breathe. For the first time I am aware of a terrible sun on my back; I've become flesh. Proximity to the Oasis has watered me whole: from desiccation to solidity. Dusty ash to skin and bone, like the process of death in reverse. Living backwards. Like Dott.

Kate is shaking me back to the living.

Billy!

Cool air floods my lungs and I cringe with a sudden graze of heartburn. I clutch my chest. The bellyache I never had—the one that I fabricated in order to get a meeting with Kate Wollington— strikes up its big band now. Still seated, I bend over so that my elbows are on my knees. My piece has shrivelled back into my pubic bone, a frightened rodent.

Fuck that, I'm saying to no one at all. What happened? I say to Kate.

You stopped breathing, Kate tells me. You were going blue.

Catching my breath, I look up—at Kate's breasts—but keep looking up until I find the underside of her chin; she is leaning over me, her left hand still on my right shoulder from where she's been pulling and pushing me back to consciousness. I focus on a tiny birthmark on the right side of her jaw. I don't want to meet her eyes—not directly, not so soon.

You do that? I ask.

Do what? she wants to know. Nicotine breath: reassuring. But I can still smell the brackish stench of the Oasis—the water, the oil in it, or maybe it's the smell of the animals I haven't seen, or of the dead I haven't seen.

Take me there, I clarify.

Take you where? she asks, now backing away from me, sitting down.

To the Oasis.

No. Is that what happened? She sounds excited.

Fuck. Man feel like man run a sprint, blood.

You were *there*.

Yes, Kate. Miss. I was there.

My breathing has returned to normal; if anything, in the silence that ensues, it sounds too quiet in the no-chat. I picture the scene again. I rummage through my memory. It's like putting on costumes, or fancy dress plucked from a trunk. There they are: some filthy ducks on the water, some ducking their heads for polluted fare; a lady duck grooming her guy. Babies—chicks—in the murk, black tennis balls. More than ever I want a slug of Angela's gin. *I was there*: Kate has told me so—as if I don't know it. What's she waiting for? Why the moon-eyes? Why the thin-lipped smile? *You were there*. The idea is enough to knock me sideways if I let it. She must see something on my face—that *eureka!* moment— because now she nods her head.

I was there, wasn't I? I ask her.

Be clear, Billy, she tells me slowly. What exactly do you want to mean? Be as clear as you've wanted me to be with you.

I was there… with you. Wasn't I?

Kate says, Yes. Yes, Billy. We first met at the Oasis.

Too much. I want to go home, Kate.

Well you can't.

To my pad, I mean. I want to go back to my cell.

No you don't, Billy, says Kate. You told me to make you understand.

It's not worth the brain cells, I protest.

You'll lose more brain cells worrying about what you can't get. Get?

Understand, I mean. We might not have another chance like this, Billy. Think of it like an affair. I can be the scratch to your itch. I already am.

You already are, I confirmed. If I was there. . .

Why don't you remember?

Yeah. Why don't I remember? *When* was I there?

Kate shrugs her shoulders. My guess? she says. My guess is you were there in the future, she tells me.

I grasp my head in my hands. Tell me about your blindness, I say.

Three.

Association Time. Sosh. Six p.m.

It being Tuesday, it is my Wing's—E Wing's— turn for evening Gym. Bucking a trend, I don my sports shorts and a too-tight T-shirt, awaiting the question at my door flap. When it comes to exercise I prefer to go it alone in my cell. Gyms are demeaning. Man has no business watching another man perspire. Plus there's the ego ting: the boys who watch, the boys who judge. So what? So what if I can't bench eighty kilos? Don't I have more important things to worry about? The flap is flipped open.

Gym, Alfreth? asks Screw Jones.

Yes please, sir, I reply.

Well bugger me.

In the freezing cold I cross the yard, side by side with Shelley. He has already remarked on how unusual it is to see me going to the Gym.

Getting flabby innit, I tell him. Need a workout buddy.

As predicted, Shelley takes this as a compliment. Shelley has biceps like coconuts. Pretty soon we're in the warm (scent of bodies and shower gel), and you can feel the competition in the air; it's as noticeable as the clanks of weights dropping, as the whirr of the rowing machine wire. I'm here to do myself an injury. I'm here to overdo it. I'm here to pull a muscle—all the better to get a visit to the outside. I want to go to hospital.

Take it easy, cuz, Shelley warns me shortly after I've started.

I have not worked up to the workout; my body will ache in the morning, but I don't care. I want it out. I want to sweat out all of the badness, the memories.

Did you hear about Ostrich, blood? he asks later.

Ain't seen him today. Wogwun?

Man going, blood. Big Man Jail.

Shut. Up!

It's true, rudeboy. Told him before dinner, says Shelley.

Is that why he's not out of his cell for Sosh?

Probably.

Shelley is on the machine next to where I'm benching. Shelley is overacting on his thighs. With every closed-leg action he's emitting a tennis player's grunt or a childbirthing howl. He's overdoing it too.

Wish man told me, I say to my partner.

Probably packing his see-through sack.

Even so.

You'll still get to say goodbye at breakfast, says Shelley.

But I don't just want to say goodbye. Opportunity knocks but once, and all that; if Ostrich is going out, albeit in cuffs, albeit in the wagon, then at least there's a chance that he can be used in some way.

A letter?

Pumping the weights, I think on. I hurt my brain and not my back; and the thoughts lead me back to Kate Wollington. She is willing to help me as long as I help her. She has seen the CCTV footage of me and others attacking a helpless victim, but it hasn't happened. It didn't happen. Not like that. I don't think so.

Was I really attacked? That's the story I have told all along. What I remember is stabbing that yoot's arm, but is that the truth? If not, what is? For a second or two I disappear into my memories. No. 'Thoughts' is probably better than 'memories'. How can something be a memory if it hasn't yet occurred?

By now I am punishing those weights: *clank*. Whirr and then clank: over and over again. My heart is a stressed-out motor. Eyes now opened, I am easily able to see what has got the Gym Govs so spooked. There are three of them watching us. One is puzzled, one looks fearful, the last one angry. I don't know how it has happened but all of us yoots—all twenty or so of us—have fallen into a workout rhythm. The sound of synchronicity is nothing but chilling. My weights are banging down at the same time as Shelley's; that alone might be seen as peculiar. But twenty-five in-mates? How has *this* come about? A revving hum as the wires are stretched—on bench, on seat, on bike, on rower—and then the sound of weights bumping down. It's like a rally of some sort; we are in this together, comrades. And it's frightening. When I cease my exercising it's like I've hit a bum note, singing at the back of the choir. Savage but brief are the looks the yoots throw me. Relieved are the same from the screws. A hench sadistic bastard name of Pequod takes the lead as the rest of the yoots stop their own exertions.

Showers, lads! he calls.

Even the boys down below, beneath the balcony, playing shirts-and-skins, three man-a-side basketball—even they have been playing in time with the exercises up above: bouncing the ball in good time and in contrapunt. What the hell is going on? I want to know, acting the innocent.

What's going on, Alfreth, says Pequod, is the shower tap. Get stripping. And don't forget to wash underneath the arches. Go.

In the showers I am still next to Shelley. He has forgotten to bring his shampoo, and asks to borrow mine.

You ain't got no hair, bruv, I tell him.

Got a goatee and knob-brush, though, innaye? he retorts.

Fair dues. I hand him my Head and Shoulders, thinking: I'm about due for a haircut myself.

Cheers.

The water is warm; my heartrate remains fast; too much fear, too much fear. This is going to kill me, I think, closing my eyes. I saw the water; I flew towards it. The smel —I can smell it now, in the showers—something putrid, vile and offensive. I can see the Oasis. Low sun a dream-blade, a mere metre from my eyes; patches of white ground, bald of dark sand smoothed else-where hereabouts by a combing wind. And the water is mauve where oil has spoilt it; black in other places; there are octopi eyes of the purest blue—the sky above pulses with perfect azure. Fist-sized in the distance, the Prison Ship, a rectangular brick of black. A rowboat is ten metres from where I now stand. The captain of this modest vessel has skin stretched like plastic (he resembles a burns victim)—plastic pulled tight across a face with no nose or mouth. The eyes are silver. He or it—she for all I know—waves me forward. *It's your turn, Alfreth*. Voice like something automated, gadgetry; I'm afraid of my journey to the Prison Ship.

It's your turn, Alfreth, the mouthless one says again. But how? The voice is in my head—I can feel it behind my eyebrows—*It's your turn*.

With a jump and a cough I return to the showers in the changing room at the Gym. The cough, in fact, is more of a choke; falling water has filled my mouth, and though it has left it late enough, my gag reflex has probably saved my life. I might have drowned, there and then. I spit out hot water. Shelley is holding out my shampoo bottle for me to take.

It's your turn, Alfreth, he says again. How many times has he said it? You okay?

Just dreaming. I take the bottle.

I know the feeling, Shelley goes on.

He turns away from me, wanting to talk but not wanting to see my penis. This is mandatory good behaviour, as iron-bound a law on the inside as it is on the out.

I think they're putting something in the water.

This causes me to start.

What's that stink, man? shouts Sarson, a few heads down to my left.

It'll give some indication into my sleep- deprived, wired-up, wankered state of mind to say that my first instinct, on hearing this demand, is to think I have drawn back into reality the stench of the Oasis from my trance-life.

It's the butter beans, blood! Jaakko is protesting. Too much fibre!

Do you smell *me*, cuz? Sarson continues. Do you think I

had a motherfucking steak instead? I ate the same food, boy!

Audibly this time, Jaakko lets another one rip; then he laughs.

Fucking hell, Shelley calls out, turning away from me and also laughing, anybody injured? He has shampoo running down the crease of his spine.

Two minutes, lads! Pequod shouts above the din of water sprinklers. Then it's up the hill to Bedfordshire! Nighty- night time.

Wanker, I mutter. How old are we again?

Did you hear about Bachelor, Alfreth? Shelley asks me.

No. Puppydog yoot? I ask.

The very same.

Shelley turns off his water and reaches for the towel that he has draped over the rusting shower head; the towel is already wet, but Shelley doesn't seem to pay this fact any mind.

Got twisted up on the gardening detail. I was tempted to join in, the dirty bastard.

Why, what's he done?

He raped that woman in Truro, Shelley answers.

No, what did he do today? To get twisted up.

Oh.

Shelley has started to dry himself off. I decide to do the same.

Well, he was acting weird, cuz. Talking all about hearing voices. Seeing things. And talking about that Ronald Dott yoot.

I am rubbing my chest dry. What *about* Dott? I ask.

Yoot's saying, like, fucking, Dott's got this mind control voo-doo shit going on. You know? Like he made the yoot scratch up his own fucking arm.

Yeah, right.

Yeah right, Shelley agrees, frowning; but the funny thing is,

Alfreth, you know, in all the time he's been doing gardens with us, man's never shown himself to be a self-harmer. You notice shit like that, don'tcha, specially with a Pup. Not a mark, blood. Yet here he is this morning, left arm like a roadmap, cuz. Sliced to ribbons. And then, right? We're doing some weeding in the bed by the swimming pool? Fucker plucks one of them yellow roses and starts to cut himself up again on the thorns. One right across the wrist.

Fuck.

Right there! In front of everyone!

Ready, lads? Let's go! Shorts on. Cold out there! Pequod yells.

Like we were gonna go back to the Wing with our pieces swinging. Silly bastard.

So who, I ask, twisted him up?

The screws, blood! Who else? Shelley seems to wonder genuinely.

I thought you meant someone hit him with a shovel or something.

Nah! But let's face it, shit coulda got scrappy, right? Screws bundling Bachelor, so what's to stop us doing the screws? They don't think, that's their problem, Shelley tells me in a tone of the profoundest disgust.

We are getting into our sweaty Gym kit for the journey back. I can't wait to get into bed: for the warmth. Not the sleep (I won't sleep, I'm certain of that) and definitely not the dreams. It's a fact, I reckon, that I'm going to get dreams that I don't want and can't afford, emotionally speaking.

Thing is, Alfreth, Shelley pauses. Promise you won't tell no one.

Promise.

Mumsy's life?

Mumsy's life, I repeat.

I think I kinda know what he was talking about: the voices. His eyes give my face the once over, but I'm not giving anything away, as far as I am aware. He pushes his lips together and pushes them out, a fat kiss. You don't believe me. I can't say I blame you.

I believe you, I tell him. O *my days* I believe you, Shell. We're all having strange feelings, blood.

Well, what is it? Shelley rolls up his towel. His skin is still damp; he will freeze in the air outside. Do you know what I think? Something in the water.

I stole water, Dott's long message to me read. *I was thirsty. Dying of thirst.*

How do you mean? I ask Shelley. I know what Dott meant.

Shelley shrugs. What better way of keeping us all under control?

Than what? Psychotropic drugs? Come on, Shell—don't make sense. Think of the cost, apart from anything else.

What cost? Fuck it's cold! What cost, really? I was shotting on road, don't forget; I know how cheap you can get brown, or a bag of sugar—as long as you buy in bulk. Now me: that sort of thing's a risk, cuz. I'll be the first to admit it, bruv: I'm small potatoes when it comes to shotting. Bit of zoot: that's usually my max. Get Judas? Slap on the arse, rudeboy. Nuttin. But *these* cunts? Government endorsement innit. Wouldn't surprise me. Nothing would.

Sounds like bollocks but I give him: It's an interesting theory.

He shrugs again. Whatever the weather, he remarks.

We are halfway back to E Wing, our passage swift on account of the chill, before Shelley speaks again.

Can't believe how fast that hour went, he says.

Allow it.

This whole month has gone full-pelt, bruv.

Allow it, I say again.

Are you listening?

Yeah.

Are you sleeping a lot more these days, Alfie? Shelley asks.

Nah man, the opposite. Can't keep down, I tell him.

And I am having *bare* twisted dreams, rudeboy. Even during the day. Even today! Finish gardens, have a poxy baguette, what the fuck was that meat, by the way? Something dug up from the cemetery tasted like.

I haven't thought about the cemetery for some days.

Then I'm dropping off. Nigh got this dream, blood, I'm standing beside this big fucking lake, right?—but I don't want to be there. And I'm trying to make these guys understand, I'm in the wrong fucking place, blood. They want me to get into this little rowing boat but I keep saying: *no, ninguna.*

What does *that* mean?

It means no. In Spanish. And then one of the guys there, he's talking to another guy, and they're dressed up in those long dresses that desert blokes wear. And they shout out to this little kid holding a horse. He brings the horse to me.

We are entering the Wing.

They're offering me the chance to get away from the water, on horseback. But I can't move. They start laughing at me; and one says, *No sabe montar a caballo.*

And what does *that* mean? I ask at the foot of the metal steps.

He doesn't know how to ride. Then I wake up sweating like a rapist.

I didn't know you speak Spanish.

I don't.

We are standing outside his cell.

Es una de pérdida tiempo.

Move on, Alfreth, says Pequod.

It's a waste of time, Shelley translates for my benefit.

Four.

There were people there from all over the world, she says wistfully.

You've said that. Tell me about your blindness.

Well, I'm saying it again! My blindness. I was twenty. Mere slip of a thing, as we would have said in those days.

What days? When was this?

Late Fifties, early Sixties. I got a job working as a secretary for a law firm. Which I hated.

Wait a minute.

We haven't *got* a minute. You said as much yourself.

This is important, Kate.

So's the guard coming back. *Officer*. Just a second then.

If you were twenty in the late 1950s…

I must be a dry old bird by now, is that what you mean? How old do you think I am?

Late thirties, I would have said.

Close enough.

You're chatting breeze, Kate! You can't be twenty in '59 and only forty in the twenty-first C. It don't make sense!

For the record, I never admitted to forty.

Whatever the weather, Miss. It's impossible!

Who says?

Fucking nature says, Kate! That's not how it works!

It's how it works in the Hola Ettaluun, Billy; and believe me, mine is by no means the weirdest of the time stories you could have found there.

I've never been there! I'd have remembered.

You've changed your tune from a few minutes ago!

Well, what a difference a minute makes! This is twisted.

Maybe so; but you wanted it point blank, as you guys say. That's just how I'm giving it to you. Both barrels, nine-mm, rude-boy. Allow it.

Have you been at Angela's gin, Miss?

No. Drunk on excitement and nothing more, Billy. I should be serious, you're right. I can imagine—I can remember—how difficult this must be for you. But ask yourself this: what possible advantage have I got in lying?

None. None whatever.

So shall I resume?

Resume.

Okay. The law firm's name is not important. It was office junior stuff at first, and bear in mind the time we're talking about. Grey suits and attitudes. Could you make us all a nice cup of tea, dear? Those moustaches. Jesus. Could you run out for a bottle of milk, my angel? Could you pick up the birthday pressie for the wife or girlfriend, or both; it's all paid for. Actually, there was one guy there who bought exactly the same present for his spouse and his tart, just so he didn't get confused.

You're drifting, Kate.

Right. I need a nap. So where was I?

Law firm.

Yes. Law firm, first six months a living hell; but it was a living. I couldn't afford a place of my own and no human male was taking any interest in me so I stuck it out, me and my dou-ble-glazing specs. Picture that! What a fox I must've appeared, staring down at each piece of paper, like a giraffe, you know, bending down to chew up some grass. But little by little, I earned a modicum of respect; I picked up speed in my work, got in early, stayed late more often than not. I could type. I could file. Less and less often I was asked to go outside on some silly errand. I knew Pitman's shorthand; I learned it from a book and some cassettes. Cost a fortune, but it meant I could sit in on meetings and take minutes, or take notes from consultations with clients. You wouldn't believe some of what I heard, Billy—the divorce cases, the arguments with the neighbours, the violence. Really not much has changed between then and now. It's just reported differently now. There was one guy, Gerald Barter, I'll never forget, he used to get his kicks by having a dump in the swimming pool in Swiss Cottage. Five times before he got.

Kate, please.

Sorry. Sorry, I just feel…

Drunk?

No, of course not. I feel…

Kate. Am I making you nervous?

I'll tell you the truth, Billy. You've made me nervous from day one.

But I'm harmless! *Ish*. Certainly in this shit-hole I'm harmless. What have you got to be nervous about? What happened?

(*I stole water*, Dott says.)

I heard a particular story, Billy, that's what happened. Me in that office, with my pen and my spiral notepad, writing *nightmare music* as fast as I could, according to one of the partners.

Nightmare music?

Oh, it was nothing—a silly joke. His name was Patterson, funnily enough—the partner, not the client. Just like our good lady of the gin bottle. He used to say that my shorthand symbols looked like musical notes, I was writing a symphony, but it was nightmare music. I've always remembered that.

I get nightmare music, Kate. The singing of the dead, sometimes.

The Dead were a good live band. Dylan and the Dead.

I'm being serious: ever since Dott arrived. Nightmare music is right.

Anyway. The client's name was Brian O'Farrell, and he was giving his deposition, pushed into it by his grown-up daughters. And as I'm listening I'm thinking, this isn't for us. This isn't law. You don't need a solicitor, Charlie, you need a headshrinker; you're nuts. 'Cause he was talking about a— what do you call it?—a pilgrimage he'd made. To the desert. To the Oasis.

What was he?

A journalist. Travel writing... I think it was February, and the heating was on in the office, but it wasn't that warm. He was sweating like a racehorse, fidgeting in his seat, wanting to talk about a lawsuit. So he comes to us—to Patterson, be precise— asking if it's possible to sue a *place*.

As you would. Sue a hotel, sue a restaurant.

But you can't sue a body of water, Billy. You can't sue a *township*. So he says to his editor at his rag: okay if I go a bit further afield for my next piece? I've had it with Venice and Vienna, and so have the readers. What about somewhere a bit further from the beaten track? The Sahara Desert, to be exact. Well, the editor's not exactly champing at the bit, so O'Farrell volunteers to fund the trip himself and not claim on expenses; all he's asking for is the usual cheque on publication or a half-rate kill-fee if the piece is spiked; and to cut a long story short, he travels east. Trying to find something he's only heard about in gossip and rumour.

But what did he want to do there?

Find out if it's true. Find out if there really *is* a place on earth—if you'll forgive the cliché—where time has stood still. Not metaphorically: *literally*.

And what did he find out?

There isn't. Or if there is, it's not the Oasis. Time doesn't stand still there; that's way too simplistic. Time there is—it's like an unfelt storm. You think you're in the eye of the hurricane but in fact the quiet part is where the forces are raging and infecting worst of all.

Infecting?

Yeah; and everyone in a different way.

Don't cry, Miss.

Sorry. It's. Sod it, I'm having another gin; this is hard. Do you want one?

The screw will smell it on my breath, Miss.

Say it's mouthwash.

Gin-flavoured mouthwash? Anyway, we're not allowed to have mouthwash: it's got alcohol in it.

Then I drink alone, Billy? There were children there— babies even!—who were shrivelled up like walnuts. They looked eighty. There were teenagers, their own bodies growing at different speeds, at different times—torsos twice as long as their legs, girls of ten who appeared pregnant with children they weren't carrying or hadn't even conceived. . . great bulky pregnant tummies. Christ, that's better. Are you sure I can't tempt you?

You can tempt me. Then I'm piss-tested and fucked.

You get the picture, though?

Sure. It was a freakshow. Any radiation thereabouts?

No. And don't belittle this, Billy. I think you are. When you've seen a ninety year old woman gaining weight to take on her middle-aged spread, mate, it's no laughing matter. She looked about forty but she was ninety.

Bit like you.

Similar. But more like Dott, Billy: moving backwards through time. Born at whatever age, like he was when he soothed your bee-stings, and getting younger. Younger as *we* would see it. Disappearing back to the egg. Me, I'm different: I'm going in the right direction. Only slowly. My years are longer—longer than yours. I was twenty in 1960, you think I'm late thirties now. You do the sums!

. . .Why was O'Farrell suing?

Because he was frozen! In time, Billy! He wasn't ageing!

Then where do I come in, innit?

You don't come in. You go out.

Suddenly a screw pops the door open. Come on, Alfreth, he orders.

Officer! I didn't hear you come in!

No, I bet you didn't. Miss Thistle. Toe-rag here needs his sustenance.

Of course. Off you go, Billy. Speak soon. Tomorrow?

If there's time.

Five.

That's what Kate Thistle told me, Dott.

So now you know, he replies. The question is, what are you going to do about it? Knowledge is one thing. . .

The Cookery Gov is approaching. What's this? he asks. Fucking sewing circle, lads? You couldn't stand each other half an hour ago. Now you're bending each other's ears.

Dott is slow to reply. But then he asks: Who says we couldn't stand each other, sir? I don't remember saying that.

The Cookery Gov snorts. Word goes round, Dorothy. I hear tings.

I don't talk like that, sir, Dott adds quietly.

You won't talk like anything if you don't get a pissing move on, son. I want you to do your pots in the next ten minutes. Lesson's nearly over.

The lesson is nearly over, I repeat in my head.

Dott is about to bust a chuckle. Maybe I should slug the fucker with a rolling pin, Gov, he says.

Just try it, wasteman, I say, no humour in my voice.

Hey, Meaney! Roller! Dott calls. Shall I repeat your panto-mime here with Alfreth?

Fuck you, rape-boy! Meaney replies.

Or I could, Gov, I could kiss him—like those screws did.

The Cookery Gov is confused. The fuck are you on, boy? he asks.

We're just chatting shit. We'll get the washing-up done. Stand on me.

I fucking will, son.

The Cookery Gov walks away.

Silly fat cunt, mumbles Dott. Has no idea, has he, Billy-Boy?

Of what?

Of what I could make him do. And what's with the *Dorothy* shit?

I shrug my shoulders. It's a game he plays sometimes. Like he'll call Meaney Maggie, I tell him. Or me Wilhema. Feminiz-ing us.

Why Maggie?

First name Magnus. Not much else he can do with that.

Magnus Meaney? Dott laughs. What did they do for an encore?

Who?

His parents.

Yo, Dott! Meaney calls. You boysing me, blood?

No, you're blessed, mate, Dott answers.

Thought I heard my name being mentioned, cuz.

Dott fixes him with a stare. You're mistaken, my friend, he says. *Now drink from the hot water tap, you waste of time. No hands. Do it!*

The command is in my head, every bit as loud as it must be in Meaney's, I reckon; but it's like an echo. Sometimes, unexpect-edly at night, there's a fault in the TV transmission in the pads. If I watch the box late at night, there is a slight delay between what

I hear coming from my own set and what I hear from the cells in which sets are tuned to the same channel, beside, above and below me. Electronic stammer. I can hear it second-hand.

Sweat beading on his skin, Meaney turns on the hot tap.

He tests the temperature with his left knuckles. Then he bends at the waist and drops his mouth to the flow, gulping greedily.

The Cookery Gov is not impressed. He shouts the yoot's name.

O my days! says Tweed, a skinny boy with bad speed-teeth.

Fucking stop that! the Gov calls. A few strides and he's minimised the distance between his beer gut and Meaney's protruding backside.

Allow him, I say to Dott.

He's thirsty, Dott tells me. You don't know what thirst is. He does.

So you say. Pick on someone else. What's he done to you?

Oh, call me Mr Compassion, he adds, letting go of Meaney.

The yoot's knees bend and he drops to the floor. In the mêlée that follows I say to Dott: Have I met you there, blood? What's my place?

Your place in the world, he sighs. Wouldn't we *all* like to know?

I bite my lip; let the surge of anger simmer and cool.

You're scared, Dott, aren't you? You don't look it, cuz, granted that, but you are. You're getting younger, you're disappearing.

I'm getting fatter, Billy-Boy, I don't know about disappearing.

But you said it yourself. You thought you could stop the flow back to being an infant, I explain with as much patience as I can muster; you thought you could do it by being kind, being generous. You soothed my sting—because you didn't want to reverse, you didn't want to be a baby.

It was *you* who was being a baby!

I *was* a baby!

You were seven years old! And frightened of a bee! Man or a mouse?

Whatever, Dott. Am I right? Then you realised it's not about *kind* things that'll keep you anchored. You need to exercise the black muscles in your warped little rapist's soul. To stop you rotting. To keep your numbers—to keep your age—going north instead of south. Am I fucking right?

Spot on with sugar and cream, is Dott's reply.

And you're something to do with the silences, aren't you? I ask. Be honest, Dott; this place has got too quiet sometimes. And it's you.

His smile doesn't falter, doesn't gutter; it stays put. So ugly and unrefined is it that I shudder with the sudden notion that it will never go away. It's as though he's been frozen—the wind has changed while he's pulling faces—and now the rictus will linger.

You got that bit right at least, he says. I'm helping some of you wacky kids to pass the time faster. I'm *taking time*.

Total immersion, I'm told, is the best way to learn a new language and to get to grips with the nuances of a foreign culture. But how long have I been totally immersed in this one? Every time I think I understand the meaning of a word I'm thrown a boomerang I fail to catch; I'm tossed a banana skin to slip on. Who was it? Who was it who told me? My brain—it must be in part down due to the heat in the Cookery Room— but my brain is slow. I cannot recall who it was who told me that Dott has been making these generous offers. But like Mumsy says, a bargain's only a bargain if you really want it.

What's in it for you? I ask.

It's a hobby, Dott replies.

Don't boys me, Dott!

Alfreth! the Cookery Gov shouts from the other side of the room.

Meaney is back on his feet, resembling, it seems to me, a newborn calf; he is not at all steady on his pins.

If you two start creating it's the fucking block.

We're cool, Gov, I tell the guy.

Good. Do your pots. Now.

Unless it was *me* that Dott gave that information to. It's worse than amnesia, this thought I know something I can't reach. It blunders around my body in the form of a concentrated squirt of anxiety; it follows my bloodlines, capillaries and veins. Who am I to Dott, right now, as I flinch the dead blubber and skin from the flat of a saucepan, using a washing-up wand whose hair is threadbare.

Are you listening, Dott? I say.

Can't remember how many of these stains were here in the first place.

Fuck the stains. Are you listening?

He sounds as petulant as a schoolboy as he continues: If that fat bugger thinks I'm cleaning up earlier deposits he's having a bubble bath.

O my days! Dott? Will you fuck the stains, please? I've got a punchline.

Go on.

By now I don't much care who is eavesdropping. Full comprehension comes only to the totally immersed; and these guys around me—my contemporaries—have only toes in the water.

You're saving up, aren't you? I half-ask and half-dictate.

Dott favours me with a new-bike-at-Christmas expression.

That's a nice way of putting it, he replies. Let me ask you, though, to clarify yourself.

If it's true, I go on slowly—if it's true you can steal time from us, as a so-called favour—and I gotta say, Dott, we've a lot of us been sleeping a lot late—then you're not doing it to be nice, are you? Nice don't work. Not for you. With nice you're still going backward. With nice you're *dying*, blood. You're selling something, cuz; you're getting something back, I lie?

You don't lie.

But whatever it is, you're saving it all up. Collecting it.

The fuck are you two gassing at? Chellow interrupts.

Allow it, Chells, I say to the man, barely turning to murmur over my left shoulder. Back to Dott I state: You're building up a stockpile of juice.

Dott wipes his hands with a now-smudged tea towel. Asks me: What does Kate think about kings?

Admitting it is like a paper cut. Breath—hot breath, oven breath, desert breath—is a lump at the core of my torso. They can be grown, I tell him. Are *you* one, Dott?

He shakes his head.

Not me, Billy Boy, he answers, still grinning. It's *you*.

I feel sick, but he's not finished.

Me, I was no more than your gardener, he says, and turns away.

Six.

So why the secrecy, Ostrich-man?

I was hoping to leave without the agony of a goodbye, he answers, rather elegantly. Take that as a compliment.

Nevertheless, I'm still cross with Ostrich. Sure, I say. And I hope I never fucking see you again either.

You got it wrong, blood. He doesn't elaborate on the point.

What time you leaving? I ask him.

Whatever the weather, blood. I'm ready.

Ready to meet Carewith again, I say.

Ostrich laughs. *Creo que las cosas, poco a poco, van cambiando*, he replies, translating it immediately afterwards. I think that, bit by bit, things are changing. Yeah. All the way to Lincolnshire, rudeboy, and I'll probably end up pad-buds with Carewith waste. I'm in the pink, blood. Ostrich snorts derisively. Thought man would never see that wasteman ever again.

Carewith? I ask. Carewith bless, blood.

Ostrich sniffs away the very suggestion.

I know this non- verbal utterance of old: he doesn't wish to pursue the matter. Sour scores, maybe; it's not important to me. Ostrich wants to talk hills.

True says in Big Man Jail, blood, man can see hills innit.

Swear down fact, I tell him.

Point blank?

Sure, blood. Not like this rat-infested khazi, rudeboy.

O my days! Allow that, says Ostrich. God's poetry, fam. Hills innit.

God's poetry, I repeat. From our own pads we see walls.

There is a silence, an interlude.

Then: There's suttin I wanna say, Ostrich tells me, the expression on his face succeeding to change the subject as effectively as the alteration in his tone of voice does, about last year. Bout this time last year, rudeboy. Evidently he's tired already of God's poetry.

What is it?

Moby Dick, blood.

Excuse me?

The CDs, rudeboy, he explains patiently. D'you remember that yoot, Emma Hutt? Fat as the ace of spades, blood.

Sure. Emma Hutt. Benjamin Hutt in reality—an early example, looking back, of the tendency to gainsex a prisoner's given forename. The difference is, with Hutt's pear-shaped figure, childbearing hips and F-cup breasts—the yoot *asks* for the comparison to be made. In the end, after a list of questionable decisions regarding the guy's personal hygiene, his attitude to authority, his hunger strikes, bed-wetting, bed- soiling, arson, violence to prisoners physically larger than himself, and eventual spiral down into the hearing of voices, the speaking in tongues, and the sighting of ghosts and man-sized insects dressing up in his clothes, he is captured on a Psych Form and assigned a weekly appointment with a therapist. Final straw is when Hutt spies the face of Jesus in his porridge one weekend morning, and he's carted off to a secured Psychiatric Hospital on the Isle of Man.

What about him?

The *Moby Dick* CDs went missing. Recall it, Alfreth? We all have our cells spun, couldn't find 'em. Hutt borrows 'em from the Library.

I remember. Boy does block for it, I say. Three weeks.

Allow it, says Ostrich. Class as damage to prison property. It was me.

What was?

Stole 'em from his pad innit. Door's open to collect our dinner. Man goes in, licks a twelve-point-five of G.V., some green Rizlas and this box of CDs with, um, fucking, whale fucking thing on the box.

Why? I ask.

Ostrich thins his lips; his eyes are bright with the memory, the conquest. Man puts the box under me dinner plate, blood.

It's a big box.

Check it, Ostrich agrees, smirking. Tray's like a wedding cake, cuz. Like la *Tour Eiffel*. Screws don't see dick.

If you been caught, I begin.

To which he shrugs. I was borrowing it, forgot the rules.

Give it back. Let the fat bug snitch and sneeze. Tomorrow morning, head's in the khazi innit. Why? Well, one to show the youngers who's boss. And two. Shottin', blood, shottin'. Can't shot brown or sniff, so. Shottin's what I do. It's like when that Psychology Squaw says why don't you don't do shottin'. Don't do shottin? he wails incredulously. Mean, why not I don't breev, blood? Ya-nar?

Nodding. But Ostrich-man, I argue, who's gonna buy an eighteen-CD box set of *Moby Dick*? What's you hoping to get for it?

Pack-a burn? Nay-way, man starts to listen, blood: that night. And it's good, Bill. Decide I don't want to sell it on; wanna hear it all out. Wannit be first book I ever finish. Like a project.

Why is he telling me his war stories? I wonder at this moment.

I'm up all night listening, volume down low, continues Ostrich. Couple time, screw breaks my concentration. What's that? This is before the cell-spins, rudeboy, no one knows it's missing yet, not even Emma Hutt. Radio, gov. Educating my mind, gov. And yeah, so what if it's four in the a.m? What have I got's so important I need my beauty sleep?

Fair enough. How you get rid of it?

Didn't, Alfie: simplicity itself, blood. Man save his Canteen. Stead ordering them fucking pick-a-chews and Mars Bars and noodles and shit, man buys what? Check it. Man buy postage stamps from me spends. Ostrich snaps his fingers and laughs like a rattle of machine gun fire. Send the CDs to Mumsy and set fire to the box. Saves on weight.

I'm baffled.

Then she can burn 'em onto fresh CDs and send 'em back. Now they're mine. Hey presto, blood! Man's play it six, seven time.

Your point being? I ask.

One line: *The path to my fixed purpose is laid with iron rails, whereon my soul is grooved to run.* Think about it, Alfreth.

It is a question of now or never.

The desert, I tell him. Why not say you were there, cunt?

I wunt. But he does not question which desert, or what I'm trying to say, or any of that time-wasting nonsense.

Yeah you were, Charlie. Grow up and stroke your bruises. I know you were there, Giggles, so don't shit me, right, soldier?

Man got wrong man, blood, Ostrich gives me, turning his gaze to the left.

Just that: a flat denial. Nothing to talk about. Nothing along the lines of questioning my sanity, which would have been fair enough in most situations. The only thing that occurs to me, in Ostrich's defence—something I might as well get ready for—is him saying something like: I thought you was talking about a club or a pub: the Desert. Where something happened. I'm prepared, internally, for something like this now.

I reply: Bollocks. Kate told me.

Ostrich gives me it straight barrel. I need to get out of this, he says.

He looks into my eyes; they are grainy with silver-red hair's-breadths of bad sleep and weeping. He grips my arm.

Still me daddums, blood.

With which he releases his hold on me as abruptly as he took it up, and he begins to pull on his fingers. Is Ostrich losing his mind? I'm wondering. Has he lost it already? Where do you find a lost mind? Where could he have put it?

What daddums? I ask. You were there, blood.

I have no idea why, at this point, he has mentioned his father. The only time he has ever mentioned his father, to my mind, was when he was talking about killing him. And even that guy wasn't a real father. Has Ostrich received a letter from his old man? A letter from a missing father is enough to splinter the strongest mind; to shatter the most robust of souls. I cannot tell you anything about my own daddums.

There summing what, cuz? Ostrich asks.

He is jumpy. We are having three or four conversations at this point—and none of them makes sense.

Fucking THERE. Don't stripe me, blood, I add—wary of advice that I've given to plenty of yoots myself.

I'm leaving.

Yeah I know, I tell him.

Gibberish-mode is taking over. Things are sliding and I can't stop them. The pains I faked to get me into Kate Wollington's room in Health Care—they come on for real. I start to sweat like a rapist in a schoolyard. My eyes mirror the redness and rawness of Ostrich's own; I can feel the capillaries pop like champagne corks. I'm trying not to notice, Ostrich-man, I remark—but that doesn't make much sense either. Gather your thoughts. It occurs to me that just at this moment my neurons are being polished by Dott. I have to concentrate. We don't have much time.

I say: But listen to this. Are you listening? I'm a king in the desert.

Thank God it happens: a questioning after my own sanity. The impotence makes me feel stronger, like I do have some truth to tell.

Fuck are you talking about, Alfster-blood? Ostrich asks.

You were there. In the desert. Tell me if I can make it any clearer.

We are having *five* conversations now, or so it seems to me, and none of them makes any more sense than a few minutes earlier. But all of them—present in our predicament—are— What am I trying to say?

Fuck off out of my head, Dott! I scream silently. There is no response.

O my days! says Ostrich.

We are numb with a powerlessness, thoughtlessness and silence that has become less rare than it should be. We don't know
how to carry on.

So why the secrecy, Ostrich-man? I ask again—softer now.

Every argument follows a code of explosion, eye of the
hurricane, then dust. Every argument is chatting breeze, in one
sense; as serious as cancer, the next.

No secrecy, blood. Only just find out.

Seven.

So who you hitting these days? she asks me.

This is not blood slang. This is sarcasm.

No one, Julie, I answer. Thanks for coming. How's Patrice?

She's had the fucking oopy cough, innit.

She's had the what?

The oopy cough. It was a real awful couple days, says Julie.

Whooping cough? I ask.

That's what I said! she protests. Coughing its little lungs out,
weren't she? But she's better now. Thanks for your concern, Billy.

I didn't know! Are you sure?

Already we are going wrong; I can sense her getting angry.
When she asks me, What do you mean, are you sure? that little
vein pulses in her temple. It's still a thing I find cute about her.

Sure it's whooping cough? I add. Did you take her to the
doctor?

No, Billy, I took her to B&Q. What sort of question is that?
Vein pulsing harder now. I'm a good mother to our daughter, Billy, you know.

I'm not saying you're not!

It occurs to me right now that Julie has arrived intent on

achieving a disagreement. Spoiling for a fight, they say in some of the crappy books I borrow from the Library when my brain is too tired to focus on anything more substantial. She is leaving me, I realise suddenly. Paternal concern battles with lovelorn pride.

What I mean is, I begin.

Oh I know what you mean, William! she interrupts. You mean I can't look after our daughter without setting fire to your bank account—or so you think. And don't pretend you weren't gonna bring that subject up either.

It is not the case that we must place our hands palms down on the reinforced plastic tables in the Visits Room, but the common word is that it's a good idea to do so. It keeps the screws happy and relaxed. Especially when matters start getting a tad frayed between con and visitor—as is clearly the case right now. A screw named Southern is not far from my table. I place my hands palm down on the surface. I have a reputation as a hitter, after all.

I try to be reasonable, saying Julie, Julie, please. What I'm getting at is, whooping cough takes more than a couple of days, usually.

She laughs like a seal. So you're getting a medical degree now, are you? Tell me what my symptoms are, Billy. Why don't you do that?

Your symptoms?

That's what I said. What's wrong with me?

And God I'm struggling, now. I want to hit her again; I really do. Not in a moment of red mist, as I did before. I am thinking about it. I want to do it. The hands on the table—they are balling into fists.

Julie notices. Is that for my benefit? she asks coolly.

The vein in her temple isn't moving anymore; she has calmed down. My impending violence has soothed her. She has been waiting for this to happen. Provoking it. The significance of what she has said is now clear crystal.

You're pregnant, I tell her. So what are we saying? Morning sickness?

My delivery is so offhand that it makes Julie blink. The disgust I feel—not disgust that some other guy has slept with her, which is bad enough, and will need dealing with, but my disgust with myself that I can feel good by making the mother of my child feel bad—is whelming. How has it come to this? Pot-shots and name-calling.

Who is it, may I ask? Bailey, I suppose.

You don't know him, Julie replies, a little closer, I suspect, to tears than she is letting on. The remark is ambiguous.

I don't know who? Know Bailey, or your new squeeze?

Oh, you definitely know my new squeeze, Billy.

I'm confused.

Bailey's gone.

She is finding this difficult. Adrenalin is washing through my system as I decode the latest in a long line of riddles—all of them leading back to the arrival of Ronald Dott.

Wait a second, Julie. When you say *Bailey's gone*.

I am pacing myself, the fists clenching a little bit once again.

Do you mean gone. As in, gone with my money?

I'm sorry, Billy.

It seems as though Julie has only been here for a few minutes—but it also seems as though she hasn't left since the last time she was here. We haven't moved an inch from this very table. In fact, it is the same table.

Slowly. Gone with my eighty grand? I say, searching for clarity.

I trusted him. He said he'd make it an investment, Julie tells me.

Utilising screw-antenna, screw-logic and screw-anti-wit,

the screw approaches on his screw-issue screw-shoes, in his screw-blacks and his screw-tie, and looms screwishly close, anticipating screw-response. There will be none required. Instead I enlist his assistance.

Sir. Is it possible for man to see his daughter if she sick bad sick?

The screw affords me screw-shortshrift and screw- advance-denial. He says, plucking at his black tie, You know the channels, son.

Screw plods off.

What you getting at, Billy? Julie asks.

Am I smiling? I don't know. I reply: You can't bring her here, right? Or am I wrong?

What? Coz I think you're gonna bray her?

Julie definitely *does* smile. It is not a pleasant smile, not this time; it translates like a foreign language. It's an anti-smile, proffered in an atmosphere of garlicky disgrace.

No.

Then what are you getting at, William? Julie wants to know. She was sick. Now she's not. But I'm not scared of bringing her to see her father.

I'm shaking my head.

Contamination, I say. Whooping cough. Listen. You got a ticket from the doctor saying whooping cough, right? Well say she's still sick. Might get permission for compassionate leave.

Julie is stunned by the notion. Talk about that fucking vein pulsing!

You would do that? she asks. Use your daughter.

I'm eyeballing her.

Not a man in here wouldn't do the same, I tell her. You'll use anything, Julie, and it don't usually work. So you wait. You wait for a good one, I say, fingers relaxed on the helmet-plastic.

And this is a good one? Julie hisses. Your daughter being sick. It might work.

For what purpose? Julie says—and it occurs to me that nearly everything she has said today has contained some form of questioning. What are you intending to do if they let you out for a day?

See Patrice.

But what else? Forgetting the fact she's actually getting better.

She don't need to be, I say to Julie.

You want me to make her *ill* again?

Julie is leaning closer to me when you might think she would lean further away—but she hasn't yet heard all I have to say. I have yet to think it.

It's a chance, Julie. And by the way, I say, leaving a pause. You say I know your new boy.

You stabbed him.

This narrows it down to nine or ten possibilities, but I don't have a watch and I don't know how close we are to the curtain call of Visits.

Julie, please.

It comes to something, I know—it comes to impending doom, let's be honest—when a fair-sized proportion of your sentences with your ting begin with: *INSERT NAME*, and then the word *please*. What it means, in gut-born essence, is that no fucking thing is being said. Am I losing my mind? Is my mind losing me?—There it goes, the old cunt, with its off-to-London spotted hanky of essential belongings, at the end of a pole or stick. Yeah, Charlie? Well I *come* from London. Go back, cat—go back, Dick—your money won't be worth horseshit on a shovel when you arrive. It's like something I overhear when I'm doing the Library run to one nameless classroom to another—and some yoot, long since left for Big Man Jail, says something like, *In Gha-*

na, blood, five pound and you're a rich man. Well, you're not *in* Ghana anymore, are you, I tell the man. Next three weeks he's spitting me evils. Fuck him.

There'll be feds all over you, says Julie, after a pause, returning to the theme of my application for a day's compassionate release on the grounds of serious illness of a loved one.

I'm a Redband. Perhaps I've earned something. Who I stab? One of the boys?

No, Julie answers, and then reconsiders immediately. Well, maybe. I don't know, Billy. Maybe he was. He says he weren't.

Who says?

Billy.

But *I'm* Billy, I protest.

Julie slouches back into her chair. He's Billy too.

What—and then you meet Billy Three? Fuck this, Julie!

That's enough, Alfreth, warns a different screw—I think the name is Vincent—but instead of apologising to her, as I might have done, a month earlier, I offer her, in her screw-identicals, her screw-neuterings, an anti-smile.

I don't have time for this bullshit, I say to Julie quietly. Who?

Screw Vincent lingers. Julie tries to smile her away but the effort does little to reassure her, so Julie gives up, returning her attention to me—eager with something to say. So she says it.

Billy. His name is Billy. Billy Cardman.

The shock is enough, not to make me bellow, but to make me silent. Screw Vincent doesn't like for one moment this sudden cessation of the row. It makes her nervous. As Ostrich himself once said to me: *Blood. Sometimes my threats are silences and sometimes my threats are stones.* This silence is clearly a threat.

Billy Cardman is the name of the man who put me in this nick. Not saying most victims want to be victims. Not saying he's the exception either. He's the one I plug in the arm with my knife.

I say:

Sorry.

I'm sorry to Billy Cardman (but the man wouldn't give me what I was asking for).

I got involved in a victim support group, Billy.

This is too much, I tell her. Now you're supporting the enemy. It's not bad enough I'm in here because of him.

Because of yourself, Billy.

But now I've got to picture him fucking you? Too much, ting!

Julie is getting upset again—if she ever stopped being upset in the first place. Actually, come to think of it, if she ever stopped being upset from the moment I was sentenced.

You don't have to picture him doing that, Billy.

How can man not? You know what he's got? He's got revenge, I tell her. Like I'm going to find revenge when I get granted day release to see my sick little girl. You wait and see if I don't.

I'll refuse you access. I'll say you're dangerous.

I snort. You get one thing right at least.

Julie smiles: this one seems sincere. You're a cuddly bear and you know it, lover. Or should I keep my voice down, blood?

She waits until Screw Vincent has moved away.

But things have changed, Billy. You know they have. *You've* changed. So have I. I didn't expect it to happen with Billy.

I'll be a laughing stock, Julie!

Why? Who's gonna know?

My boys!

Oh, please. Your boys, Bill? Where are they? While I'm here, where are they? Seriously. Do you think they still care about you?

This hurts. This hurts because I've known it to be true for some time. I lean forwards now, my hands still in the right place.

Do you know something? I ask Julie. I was like a king once,

me. I was growing like a king.

What are you talking about? You been brewing hooch?

In the desert, Julie. In a place you can only dream about.

She backs away from me, saying: Well, you're in no doubt they're gonna let you out for a while, Bill. Problem is, it'll be to a Psych Ward.

You don't know anything about my past, Julie.

Her eyebrows beetle. Shut up, now, honestly. You're scaring me.

One last favour, I say to her.

I owe you that, she admits, sounding a jot relieved if you wanna know.

Just a visit, I begin.

Okay, no worries. If they'll let you out you can visit.

No. Julie, listen. Just a visit I want *you* to make.

Oh, Billy—of course I'll visit. I wasn't on the straight when I said you can't see Patrice. Maybe it was my hormones jabbering.

No. Not to me. I don't care if you don't see *me* anymore. You've broken my heart, Julie.

She is baffled. Then to who? she asks.

Another D. Another Defendant. His name is Ronald Dott. Ask him one question, I say to Julie.

Eight.

What's the hullabaloo this morning? asks Kate Thistle, once we've earned a moment to ourselves.

Miss Patterson is unexpectedly back at work, but she's taking a piss-break. Female staff are obliged to go downstairs to the other toilets owing to a plumbing fuck-up in the Ladies' shitter on the ones. We've got at least five minutes, what with all the doors she'll have to lock and unlock. With a bit of good fortune, I think to myself, the staff toilets are akin to ours: always out of bumwad and with honky flushes that mean you have to pull on the chain for about an hour like a demented campanologist. You don't want the next yoot along to see what you've left behind. I always make sure I have my movement before Movements— not that I've had much to expel, not of late. I've been off my feed for some time.

I answer Kate Thistle's question with a shrug and a tilt of my head. Four yoots on A Wing, I tell her, started a riot.

Oh, how exciting, she replies in a sarky, ironic tone that implies she is anything but impressed. About anything in particular?

I *could* say random cuntishness, Miss. That's what it normally is, innit. Random cuntishness from the screws to us, leading to random cuntishness back. Or just us: playing up, as Mumsy used to say.

But not this time? she asks. No bad food, no cell spins?

You're learning the lingo, Miss. But no. It's Dott. He's taking.

Taking what?

Taking back part of his investment.

Predictably enough, we're in the Library. We're not alone. The prisoners from the Spanish class— learning Spanish—have their turn to visit, and there are eight of them present, with their teacher. Don't know her name; she's new, I think. Throughout what we're trying to say—Kate and I—we are hassled by these Ds and Co-Ds, re-issuing True Crime, horror-lite, some Spanish textbooks and dictionaries. Only one of the guys—by gigglingly asking me what Julie is gonna make of my new friendship with Kate—actually acknowledges the fact that I am having a conversation. You often become almost invisible when you achieve a Redband. There is more concern about borrowing a pen to fill in a magazine requisition.

Investment?

I nod my head. He's put quite a lot in the kitty. Thank you,

blood. Next Tuesday, all being. For Dott it's payback time. Literally. Pay, back, time.

Whereas mine nods, Kate's shakes—her head, that is.

I was beginning to think I understood all of this, she tells me.

Hard lines. He's buying time, Kate. In the sense you know
about. He's trading. What he gives with one hand—like taking
away yoots' spare time, to make time go quick time—he just
fucking, takes back with the other, Miss. He causes damage, like
you say. It keeps him anchored at the right age. He don't wanna
slip backwards so he needs to trade some damage.

What happened in the riot? Kate wants to know.

One ear-split; one nose-split; one hospitalisation: a left eye.

Great. That should keep him going.

He wants to die, Kate.

Who? This voice belongs to a weasel named Peel, who is
standing in front of me with a yellow English-Spanish dictionary
in his hands. I can help.

Wash your mouth out, young man, Kate tells him.

Sorry, Miss. Seriously, Alfie—who?

There is no point in lying. Half the population of Puppydog Wing and a good number on the normal Wings, too—they
want to die. From time to time. The impulse grows. I've had it
myself, way back when. The future being black, and all that. You
can either ping yourself with the elastic band around your wrist—
get that tiny spark of discomfort that constitutes a replacement
for self-harming—or you can bang your head on the pad wall
and get a Self-Harm report written out on you. Or you can properly self-harm, of course—there's always that option. There's all
the fun of the fair, rudeboy! For some yoots, the phrase 'the CD's
scratched' has a completely different interpretation: that yoot
will have forearms like city road maps. That yoot will go through
cigarette lighters faster than packets of burn itself. For that yoot,

it's a case of tortures for courses; torture, torture, everywhere, and not a qualified shrink.

Dott.

Uncharacteristically, but not unexpectedly, Peel is quickly irate. I'd pull the switch on that wasteman myself. Fucking dreaming about the cunt now.

Do you want that renewed? I ask.

Yeah, mate. He brightens suddenly, pointing a finger. And do you know what else I want, geez? *Deseamos un régimen democrático.* We want a democratic regime. See, Miss? Clearly pleased with himself, he taps his temple with the same forefinger. All going in nice. Good teacher, that Kate.

Miss Thistle to you, please, Kate replies.

Peel's face is a squashed meringue of confusion. Nah, Miss. *Teacher Kate* is a good teacher, is what I'm saying. Cheers, Alfie. *Ándale!*

I have stamped his book. Miss Patterson has returned.

And at first I'm disappointed not to have enough time to remark on the coincidence of forenames—a third Kate, me still smiting from being a displaced Billy—but then I realise that it hardly needs mentioning. Everything else is fucked. We do not speak—we do not have the chance to speak— for nearly another hour, and even then it is as part of my tea- making duties. I am afraid that Movements will take me back to my pad before I can talk properly. Fortunately, when the guys from the I.T. class are in for their browsing session, one of them—whose name I don't know—somehow manages to discredit the honour of another yoot's country of origin. Additionally fortunately, they both had pens in their hands at the time—to order their softcore bash— and so the resulting conflict is as bad as I need it to be.

Miss Patterson thumbs the green button and the radios whistle and whine.

In come the desperados! The fight is eventfully dispersed (one of the screws gets a new biro tattoo above the wide left wing of his ridiculous moustache) and when the reinforcements arrive, the other yoots are escorted back to their Computer Literacy textbooks and flickering screens. Miss Patterson—it seems—could do with a nice lie down. Well, it seems as though she might go for a swig of her own hidden hooch, but as that is not an option she repairs once again for the Ladies Room downstairs.

Kate Thistle and I are alone at last. It almost feels romantic. She looks me in the eyes. She places one hand on my thigh.

We don't have long, she tells me.

Nine.

I went there to heal my eyesight, Billy. Cause you know what they say: time healing everything and all that. So what? It's a cliché. I buy that. And I bought it then as well, after that visit from the guy who wanted to sue the Oasis. I went out there. I was desperate, Billy, you have to understand that. But time heals everything, and I wanted the healing that time's supposed to bring.

My family and friends thought I'd gone insane. Trust me: these weren't the days when it was normal for a single young woman to bugger off to the desert, with no plans that didn't revolve around getting a suntan. I ignored them all; I was hooked.

Have you ever been addicted to anything, Alfreth? It's nasty—but that's what I had: an addiction. When you're miserable without something and then getting that something makes you feel happy, then I reckon you're an addict. I was addicted—to the idea of time being my healer.

I couldn't believe some of the things I saw! I mean, Billy, what would *you* expect if someone said she was going to the desert? Sand? Well, of course sand. And the fact that I was there to witness—to be influenced by—a *storm of time*, not to mention a body of water in the middle of the dry land, well, this suggests that I would have had my eyes open, right? But nothing could have prepared me for some of the things that were there.

There were computerised river taxis—though the Oasis obviously wasn't a river. What else? Robot bartenders!—in these shacks—and even the word *shacks* is over-selling those dumps to be honest—ramshackle dumps selling rose-wine and fermented camel milk.

And the politics you wouldn't believe! I remember a war between two rival groups of bus drivers. Two *groups*. You wouldn't have thought that *one bus* was needed in the. . . sorry, I shouldn't laugh; this isn't a laughing matter, is it? In the town called Hospital, was what I was trying to say. The Healing Town.

Yeah, right. Take a look at the walnut-faced poor bastards who live there and tell me how much they've been healed. So I suppose the people searched for distractions, like in any other community. Violence is one key to that particular lock, isn't it, Billy? You should know that as well as I do. If not, better. But there were bus trips around the township for the elderly and the infirm—and occasional trips away, for supplies and so on. And these two different companies set up against one another. It was bloody.

There was no sure way of knowing whereabouts to go in the Oasis to be affected by a particular influence of time. If you wanted to go back, for example—back two years to say goodbye to your father before he passed away—you didn't just form an orderly queue at Point A. It wasn't a scenic tour or anything like that. It seemed random.

And as I think I said before, we mustn't forget that the Oasis, for most people, was their *home*. They weren't pilgrims searching for a Messiah. This wasn't *Mecca*. This wasn't *Lourdes*. Generations—sometimes—had grown up there, though not always at the speed we would know it. Three score years and ten, Billy? Forget it. I heard about a clan that lived in two adjacent fenestrated huts, with blankets on the roofs. The patriarch, the matriarch, seven siblings, all of them married with children of their own. Three generations, Billy—and the oldest and the youngest had been born within eight years of each other. Rumour had it they looked like raisins with limbs. It had fallen to the wives and husbands who had married into the family to look after the entire brood. A sixteen year-old, for example, taking care of her twelve year-old grandfather. Again, it's only rumour—but this one went that neither the grandmother nor the grandfather could remember their parents; that they hadn't actually had any—it's not as though they'd died or anything. The family was born in *and of* the dirt and rocks surrounding *Umma*—or *Mostashifa Tamaninat*, if you prefer.

So where should I go? Where would *you* have gone, Billy? You ask around, right? Well, I did—and that got me little more than blank looks, until I heard the story of Noor Aljarhalifaro— the old man, the gentleman thief. *The one who stole the water.* Yeah, that's Ronald Dott to you and me. And I've been obsessed with him ever since, or until then, depending on your point of view.

He was older then, as you know. And he was something of a legend in the town, let's put it politely. One old woman, her body was changing ages at different speeds, divided at the waist. She was treating some wounds I had one day when I fell down and gouged my knee on a bleached cow's skull. She was something of a local G.P. Didn't think much of her bedside manner, mind you. For the stitches the needle was sterilised at the end of a lit cigarette. There was no anaesthetic. As I was being stitched up, in fucking agony by the way, she was like a hairdresser asking me if I was going anywhere nice on my holidays. It didn't matter much, not to her at least, that she couldn't speak English very well. She knew some basics. And I guess she was trying to keep me occupied while she savaged me with her surgery. In hindsight I should have known better, seeing's she had a needle in one hand and my knee in another, but I was intrigued by the story of the geriatric burglar. In *this* country we've got Care in the Community programmes to help the elderly into suitable employment. But to tell you the truth, Alfreth, I would find it rather cute, if I *had* to be robbed, if it was some old guy who did it. Shows there's life in the old dog yet, and all that. What I found out, getting my knee stitched up, is that Noor—or Dott—how should I refer to him here? Okay, Dott. Dott was by no means considered a quaint old duffer with a magpie penchant for valuables. 'Cause there *were* no valuables, or at least not as we would know them. No doubt some family heirloom, or family importance stuff; but nothing like rubies or gems. The valuable commodity was water itself. And Dott nicked some.

So it was a bit foolhardy of me to mention the recent incarceration of this thief, out there on the prison ship. If I understood my surgeon's Pidgin English correctly, the message was along the lines of: I hope they release him quickly so I can kick him to death before my legs get too old to do so. Her lower body was ageing faster than her torso. Of course, this sort of reaction could only make me more determined to learn his story—or even to meet him. I mean, what else was I going to do in Umma while I waited for time forces to have their way with me? Get a job? I had money to last me a while—a month or so—because while I might not have been earning well in England, in the desert I was a rich woman. A white-skinned princess, no less, as one dirty old man who was actually five told me.

I swear I saw more spittle sizzling on hot ground in the following week than I have ever seen since—and certainly had ever seen before. Because that was the reaction from some that the

story of Noor provoked: *spontaneous spitting*. The name acted like
an emetic, especially among the citizens of Umma who really
were older and not just looked like it. It was felt, sort of, that he'd
let the side down a bit. Elders—even if they were elders like Noor,
a bit wayward, rootless, a bit maverick—really should know better. They should—don't laugh—they should act their age.

That said, *some* were willing to talk to me—as long as I kind
of crept up on the question. As long as I wasn't too full on. How
do you boys put it? As long as I wasn't *point blank*. No one could
tell me where Dott, or Noor, had come from. And I don't mean
geographically, necessarily—as I say, there were people who'd
been at the Oasis for generations— but no one knew anyone who
knew anyone who had been there before Dott. But this sparked
me up. I mean, think about it, Billy. If Dott is moving backwards,
living his life from old back to young, where did it start? How old
is old? Was he another one borne of the desert? Okay; it's weird
as hell to us but it happens there. But where did he start? Aged
what we would call two hundred? Aged what we would call *two
thousand*?

There were even stories about him, Billy—not like stories
in books but more like fairy tales, I suppose. Myths. The story
of the old man who got younger was told to children at bedtime,
although God knows why. There's no message to it. No moral.
Not as far as I can see. His daring life of crime—joke!—began,
as far as anyone could estimate, and after I'd sort of collated the
answers, his life of crime began when he was about a hundred
and one. The crime was public indecency, Billy—repeated public
indecency. If he'd been in this country at the time, oh and eighty
years younger, he might have got the very cell on the Puppydog
Wing that he actually *has* got.

What I learned from the whispers behind hands, when people didn't wish to be seen mouthing such filthy ideas—but at the

same time couldn't resist a gossip—was he would go down to the water. A hundred and one, this was! He was learning how to walk, shuffle, crawl. He was a baby, after all. Townsfolk used to look after him with soup and potatoes, but the story goes that there was a great, great sense of relief when he started to work out how to put one foot in front of the other.

How can I put this politely? Okay I won't. He was wanking in the Oasis. Just for fun, as far as anyone could tell. Maybe, in his world, in his skin, he was a teenager; he was going through puberty, learning how to satisfy himself. It's impossible to say: there's no logic there. That's the beauty of it.

How long do you think we've got left? Angela could be back any second so I'll speed up a bit—just like I slowed down a bit in my time there, in Umma.

What I went there for I got: a slowing down in the deterioration of my eyesight—and even an improvement, over the course of the months I was able to eke out my earnings. See? My eyes got better—or at least time stopped them getting any worse. The effects slowed my body down. You know I'm older than I look; I'm an old bird, Billy—an *old ting*. But my eyesight is so-so. The Oasis healed me. Time healed—or as I say, stopped me getting any worse. Nothing's perfect. I've had laser treatment and you wouldn't believe the strength of these lenses, but there you go. I wasn't supposed to be talking about me. I was talking about Dott. Damn it. We'll have to wait for her next piss-break.

Part Six:
Sleeping Among the Amnesia Trees

One.

Ask him one question, is what I say to Julie, back in the Visits Room.

I return to my pad—this is when the shakes and twitches kick in. After about an hour of praying with my beads, I hit the night alarm, although it's far from being night. I'm in fear of night arriving.

Screw Oates comes to my flap. What is it, Alfreth? he asks.

Permission to get under my covers, sir.

Why, what's wrong with you?

Gut rot again, sir. I know everyone will be aware of my visit to Health Care and my complaint will carry weight. Besides, I'm not exactly lying. A lie-down and maybe even that rarest of beasts, a sleep, will do me some good. But we're not allowed to get under the covers without permission.

He takes a second before he says, Granted, Alfreth. Need a visit?

Just had one, sir.

From Health Care, I mean.

Oh. No, sir. Paracetamol won't do it, sir. Need to rest properly.

Okay. I'll check on you in a while.

My bed is warm as toast and exactly as scratchy as the same. It dawns on me I can't remember the last time our linen was changed. *Rest?* The very concept feels alien to me. I am tired to the point of distraction and even sickness. *Relax.* I let my thoughts float and chatter. This is fever sleep: the thoughts choose *me.* They bang and clatter and din. My thoughts play with me, not the other way around. And I go to that place, I go to that place I often find when I am dropping off to sleep: that state of mind that's like a magic spell. A bit like when I'm having sex (if memory serves) and I'm trying to hold back, to make Julie come first, that emotional mantra I repeat inside my skull, to stop me busting a nut too early. Try to explain it and the spell is ruined and warped. Same with sleep. I travel into a dry, warm place be-fore I know I can close more than my eyes—I can close my mind. I can shut down for the night and re-boot. Dry, warm place: like a desert.

The connection is enough to wake me up again; it frightens me. Lying still beneath my Redband-enhanced prison duvet, I try to imagine Ulla. I try to imagine a town called Hospital. Or rather, the Oasis is trying to imagine *me.* I can feel its pull as sleep gets closer.

Inevitably, the face of Ronald Dott enters my head. He is getting younger—he is disappearing, little by little, towards what we call birth. For him it's death. Or is it? He needs to perpetrate evil deeds in order to keep him at the age he is, roughly speaking, give or take a year or two. He has what Kate Wollington would call 'serious sexual concerns'. He uses us. He uses anyone. He wants to get older, older—much older. And he needs us, as well as uses us. He takes our time. We sleep and sleep. He induces mad actions. Screws kiss each other in the Cookery Room and Ds erupt into spontaneous acts of violence.

But what does he want with *me?* If he fouls and fouls he will manoeuvre in the direction that we all do, one year plus one year equals two years. He wants to go back to his beginning. To find what? To start again? What good will he be as an old man, commencing the journey for the second time? Or maybe not the second time. The third? The fourth?

Dott? I call to him. *Can you hear me?*

There is of course no answer. I can't sleep. Can't as in mustn't. I kick off the duvet and pull on my tracky bottoms. I light a burn from my emergency stash. I start a short routine of sit-ups, roundhouse kicks and push-ups.

You recovered quickly enough, you lazy cunt. . .The voice is from the flap on my door. Screw Oates' eyes, scrutinizing my workout. Pull a fast one on me like that again, son, and you'll be tripping down some stairs.

He thinks I've lied to him. He thinks I've used my aches and pains as an excuse for a crafty kip. But what can I tell him? The evidence is right before his eyes.

I tell him: I can't sleep, sir. Need to wear myself out.

When he disappears I notice how quiet the Wing is again. Can it be everyone is asleep? I overhear, once, two screws talking together, after the Prison Officers' strike, when hardly any uniforms come to work and there is no one to wake us up in the morning. Everything cancelled for the day. Fucking eerie, one screw says to another. And I feel, at that time, as though I'm on a desert island—or in the desert—on my own. Awake and red-eyed: staring out my barred window. Same now. Same now, too, the conversation between two screws, outside my door—or near it.

Fucking eerie, I think it's Herman says.

And then I hear Oates agree with him: What're they planning?

No music is blaring. No one is shouting. But we're not planning anything either. I could tell the screws this but I won't. They think they're whispering—maybe they are—but I can hear them perfectly.

Me, I was no more than your gardener, are Dott's words.

They echo inside me—and not just in my head. They make my stomach lurch, and my dick grow tumid. Dott. Dott is saving up favours. He is taking away yoots' time to make the days and weeks go faster for the inmates, but they will owe him, and more than a packet of burn or a bash mag. It will take a great, a creative act of wrongdoing to get him back to the age he wants to be—wrinkled, weak-bladdered, diabetic possibly, and ailing. Why not stay at the age he is now? I don't know. But he talks about Prometheus. He wants to die, I am sure of it; and I think he is striving to wriggle and leap back to where he started—to a point before he started, in order to end the whole game.

Ask him one question, is what I say to Julie, back in the Visits Room.

Two.

Miss Patterson's next piss-break doesn't arrive; it seems for the moment that her bladder has been adequately evacuated. So I face the stark understanding that it's going to be another twenty-four before I speak to Kate Thistle again. But I am desperate—desperate to hear my own side of the story. I want to know what Dott meant about gardening for me. I'm baffled. The day is like chewing gum—pulling chewing gum off your shoe, stretching it until it breaks, only to find that some's been left there on the sole. Dinner is a lonely affair, with Ostrich shipped out to Big Man Jail, following Carewith along their time-lines. I talk to Sarson a bit, but my heart's not in it. We stand outside for a while when we're allowed to, during Sosh—in the chipping-away, dust-carrying wind. The air is freezing. Stinking, too. We talk about the rubbish bins again. They are piling higher and higher, as if they're reproducing and not just being added to; no one is collecting them.

The outside world, on the out, is on strike, it seems. Between us we spy three rats and I'm certain I see, over by the perimeter wall to my left, a solitary squirrel, blown off course somehow on its crumb-trail for a nut or two.

Health hazard innit, says Sarson, bored—and I know we are about to embark on the same discussion as before.

There's no choice. Nothing changes. I share a burn and consider provoking a fight. In the evening I take my thoughts for a walk. I sit on the can with the seat down, leaning forward to help ease the pain in my stomach, and I close my eyes, for something to do, tracing every step I know of Dellacotte Young Offenders, up here in the hills. In my mind's eye I stroll back and forth to the Gym, to the Education Block, to the Segregation Unit. Nothing's satisfying. I feel like I felt when I came in, drying out from alcohol for a few days. I am nervy, jumpy, tired. I visit, not in any way in the order of geographical convenience, but rather the opposite—to make the operation longer and more drawn out—the Wings, from A to H, backtracking on myself, crossing courtyards, following the yellow lines on the ground, inside which the delivery trucks and food trolleys must remain. And it's still only nine. Nine o'clock, tick tock. Come on, life.

Come on, Dott. Show me.

Eventually it is morning. I must have slept because I can see and taste the dream that lingered longest, lingered hardest. In it I am flying again—flying towards the oily water of the Oasis. When I get there I pay with coins into a slot, once I've seated myself on the hard wooden bench on board the rowboat. The computer only knows two directions: to the Prison Ship—also called *Oasis*, as Dott reminds me in my sleep—and back again. The ship holds two hundred prisoners. It does not move. Looming quickly in my dream, the black walls of the ship, as high it seems as the walls of the nick in which I'm locked. There is no way to climb the bulwarks or the gunwales. I am stranded here, unless someone throws me down a rope. And if someone throws me down a rope it must mean I am a prisoner. Someone throws me down a rope.

Rise and shine, Alfreth, calls Screw Jones. My door is open. Not like you to need a wake up call, son.

Sick, sir.

Well you'll be needing your Coco Pops then, won't you, for energy.

Yes, sir.

In our batches of ten at a time we fall in line at the canteen door, near the Prison Officers' main office on the Wing. I collect my cereal, my cube of juice (straw removed), and my carton of milk. I return to my pad. Immediately after eating I am sick into my sink. I clean the mess up and wash my hands, oxters and groin.

I am ready for work, but Screw Jones says: Are you sure you want to go back to duties today, Alfreth?

That's twice now in the space of half an hour I haven't heard him approaching my door. The first time he even gets as far as opening it without my noticing him in the vicinity; the second time the door has been left wide.

You look peaky, son.

Not sleeping well, sir, I tell him.

You could have fooled me, son. Jones laughs. We could hear you snoring from the Staff Mess. Kicking and grunting, you were.

Someone throws me down a rope. I start to climb, and with many a kick and with many a grunt I make progress. I can now smell more than the oil on the water; I can smell the confined aromas of two hundred lags in close quarters. The smell is nauseating. My powers of flight having abandoned me, I continue to climb. I reach the bulwark. There is no one to help me board ship. No one on deck either. The ship has spat out its inhabitants like the vile, wretched commodities they are. Deathly silence. No, not silence—I can hear the contaminated water lapping against the prison; I can hear the gentle swish and low hum of a motor as the computerised rowboat moves back to its points of origin. I am alone. Utterly on my tod. Until a yowling crosses the sky. The noise, so sudden, so loud, makes me start; instinctively I duck my head. It's an aircraft speeding overhead, through the priceless blue. Dott's words about the war raging return—as soon as I see the full stop dropping from the sky. I know what this is. The full stop swells into an inkblot; the inkblot puddings into a golf ball, even though it's going to drop a long way from where I'm stand-ing. Explosion is enormous. Water climbs high into the scorched air, dampening it down; a series of waves rocks the ship, as large and sturdy and apparently unmoveable as it is. Blades of fire chop along through these new currents, attracted by the oil. Fire sniffing at the oil pools and smears like an animal going about hunting business; fire eating water, like a parasite eating its host. Slow motion. Then fast.

For God's sake, boy!

Someone is screaming and yelling at me.

Get below deck! They're fighting again!

The face I see, contorted with anger and misplaced concern. A hand waving me towards its owner. It's a door leading down below deck. Someone has risked his own health, maybe sanity, to knock some sense into me. He is beckoning me towards safety. I take the advice—slide on the oily water that has splashed over onto the planks; tumble headfirst down the stairs, nearly knock-ing my rescuer onto his arse as I go. He breaks my fall. Pain is like frost up and down my arms; it takes me a few seconds to recover, to take stock. Stifling heat. Reptile house stench. I straighten up; pick my bones up off the floor, fully conscious of eyes on me.

There is no conversation; no murmurs, no reproof. Silent men in gangs, some standing, some sitting, all staring at me. A hundred men? Some craning for a better view. *Two* hundred? Now jostling: want to see me. Outside, closer than the first, a second bomb detonates. The ship is rocked, but down below decks the imprint on our reality is not so strong. A few people are knocked a metre or so to the side; nothing serious. Absurdly, there now comes the consternated quacking of a duck, from above.

Welcome back, says the man who called me down.

Welcome back.

It's a peculiar way, I think, of addressing me. The sentence belongs to Kate Thistle; I have arrived in the Library, shop Movements having begun.

Feeling better? she asks.

Than what?

She appears confused. Than you have been?

Yeah, I'm fine. Where's Angela?

Miss Patterson has just popped to the Cookery Class to beg, steal or borrow some teabags, Kate replies. We've gulped our way through a box in the last day or two. It's been boring without you, Billy. She smiles.

Kate, what are you talking about? Miss Patterson's only been back at work a day. She was ill, remember?

No, Billy, you were ill. Miss Patterson's been back all week.

What day is it, Kate? I ask.

Friday.

I've lost two days. I remember Cookery on Tuesday.

You were ill, Kate replies, a little bit hesitantly.

He's got to me, Kate, I say to her. The bastard.

Language, Alfreth. Miss Patterson has entered her domain; the door is open, always, until the first class or Wing visit of the day. In her left hand she carries the kettle she has filled in the

Cookery Gov's place of work; in her right, a brown clutch of prison issue economy teabags.

You know I don't like language like that in this room.

Sorry, Miss.

Could you make the tea, please, Alfreth?

Of course, Miss. What else would you like me to do today, Miss?

I have to confess: I am desperate to do some work—to do anything to rid my brain of the thought that Dott has paid me a visit, first footed me no less (Happy New Year to you too, cunt!) as the first one over the threshold. I am not a victim. I am not a victim in the way that the women he assaulted are his victims— not even close to the same thing—but I feel violated nonetheless.

Miss Patterson's over-zealous bladder seems to have righted itself. I keep offering to brew up more tea, in order to make her want to go—even though in my unremembered absence the Staff Ladies toilet on this floor has been repaired and a quick trip to drop her knickers won't give us half as much time to talk as we require. But every second counts. I wanted a run-up. Man need a run-up: to Fridays. Friday is the day F Wing visits the Library. Puppydog Wing. Therefore, maybe Dott. As the morning pro- gresses I realise that I both do and don't want to see him. Choice isn't mine to make, anyway. He doesn't arrive.

He got twisted up innit, says a yoot called I don't know. Pressing the night bell all night. Sounded like panic attacks.

Don't sound like him, I answer, making a show of returning the *Prison Poetry* books back to the shelf.

Why, you know him then? I'm asked.

Well as I know any cunt on Puppydog Wing.

That's fighting talk, Redband.

I shrug again. Start it up. See who does Seg: me or you.

We both will, and you know it. Loss of TV.

I don't watch TV, four-eyes.

What am I doing? I wonder, picking a scrap with a dilapidated granny batterer and handbag thief. And no one's gonna see me throw the first punch.

I dare you.

For a second I think he's going to cry. I am certain of what he's about to say, before he says it. We're not all rapists on that Wing, you know?

I didn't say you were.

We are Vulnerable Prisoners.

I know that.

So why would you say something like that?

Like what? Like I know Dott as well as anyone on your Wing?

That's not how you put it, Redband.

Pardon my manners. Excuse my gutter tongue. Now get away from me, you dirty oaf. Stop trying to make friends with normal criminals.

To my surprise he moves away, feigning a spontaneous interest in the atlases and *Who's Who?* I don't know why I've done what I've just done. I am angry and frustrated, and these things don't help. So Dott's been beaten up, has he? *Good.* Tired to the core, I execute the remainder of my morning duties in all but total silence, confidently not bringing up further antagonistic utterances, and in fact only speaking when I'm directly spoken to. I make the tea. Miss Patterson is sitting pretty, not moving an inch. Maybe she's got a piss-bag, a wet-bag. What do you call them? When you just go down your leg, in a tube. I'm tempted to offer her one of her own gins, just to speed up the process a little.

At eleven-forty, the screws' radios start to bleat and whistle. The morning session is coming to a close, Movements are about to begin.

Papa Alpha to Charlie Two. . . and Charlie Two answers in the tiffany-thin code it's assumed we're all too pigshit-thick to decipher.

There's no time. In another couple of minutes it'll all be over until Monday. I can't wait that long. The Library door is anchored open with a small table on which sit what remains of a pile of *Inside Times* newspapers— free to any con fast enough to get a copy. Charlie Two today is a young female screw. She leans into the room.

Ready, Redband? she asks. We're off.

Dejected I say, See you next week, Miss—the singular form of the noun intended to embrace both members of the staff I'm leaving behind.

Billy, don't forget your book! Kate calls when I'm at the door.

Holding it out in front of her, she takes the few necessary strides in my direction. I have not issued out a book. I have plenty to read in my pad that I do not read without having another addition to the pile stamped.

With a smile I accept it and say quietly, Call me Alfreth in front of Angela.

Kate nods. I take the book.

And call her Miss Patterson, she responds.

Safe, I tell Kate, thereby thanking her for reminding me not to leave the book behind. I don't even dare read the title in case Miss Patterson sees me doing so and starts to wonder whatever an old girl starts to wonder when she finds her career stalled in a rat-infested shit- hole such as Dellacotte Young Offenders. It's only outside I dare glance at the cover.

I've been given a copy of Agatha Christie's *The Murder of Roger Ackroyd.*

Blood quickens. While acknowledging the *Wogwuns* and

occasional hand-slaps of inside-friends, I make a beeline for my pad. Because you know what? I got a memory, rudeboy. Got a memory, cuz. Since I've been Library Redband I must have seen the list of available titles a thousand times or more. Not once— not once in my memory—have I ever seen a copy of an Agatha Christie novel on the shelves, or even on the screen of availables. Not once. So where has this come from? From on the out.

It's a relief when the screw locks me in. It's a hassle to wait for my call to collect lunch—so much do I want to open the book. I don't dare. Trembling slightly, I claim ownership of my Friday-treat baguette (extra filling). *Fuck*. It's Friday, I keep forgetting—this means there'll be Canteen, where those who have paid for them from their spends are able to get chocolate, sweets, crisps and noodles. I myself have a collection to make. Last week I ordered extra packets of cup-a-soup, back when I used to get hungry on a regular basis. This means Kate's book will have to wait even longer to be opened.

A door being locked never sounded so sweet. Outside my open window—open despite the nip in the air—a couple of ducks seem to sound pleased on my behalf. Their quacks are the same as applause.

Three.

Ask him one question.

Card in hand, I queue for the telephone. It's Saturday, just after lunch. I intend, at my own undoubtedly exorbitant cost, to call Julie. Mobile phone, naturally; it's hard to think of Julie actually having an address because she's never at home. She lives on the street. Maybe literally. Who knows? Now that that Bailey waste has done a hop, skip and jump with my money, what's Julie living on? There'll be benefits of course, the usual handouts, but still.

The D in the booth is called Finer. He seems to have accumulated about an eon's worth of phone credit. Through the plexiglass I can hear him in a mumbled fashion going on about what food he's been eating. I want to bang on the door and say *It's not important, save your money*. Or *say I only need a minute or two, could you call her back?*, for I'm assuming he's talking to his Mumsy. Who else would want to know details like that?

Yes, he's getting plenty of exercise. Yes, he's keeping himself out of fights (an out-and-out lie, by the way). And yes, his chances of parole look solid. Which is bullshit: no one ever gets paroled from Dellacotte YOI.

Even the ducks outside, dropping black messages wherever they waddle, are serving life sentences: either Mandatory, Discretionary, Automatic, or Imprisonment for Public Protection—the old IPP, bless it, and save all those who sail in it. All I want to know is if Julie has booked her visit with Dott. After time out of mind I get to ask. One thing about Julie is, she never turns her mobile off. Never. She always takes the call. In the cinema, in the shower—more than once she's spoken to someone when she and I have been having sex. The first time this happens is offensive; the second time onwards you realise, ah, well we all have our quirks. There she was, riding me on top and discussing her sister-in-law's hen night. It's possible she's having sex right now, I suppose, as she answers. I don't bother to identify myself—she knows my voice.

Did you book it? I ask.

Booked it and done it.

Pardon?

I've been in already. Yesterday, Julie tells me. I didn't have to wait long for a visit appointment because no one's been to see him yet.

You travelled all the way up yesterday? I ask.

Yeah. It's what you wanted me to!

Well, yeah I did. Didn't think it get done so fast.

You sound disappointed, she says in a disappointed tone of her own; and I know that she is trying to please me—to make amends. She must have driven through the very early hours. Visits start at ten.

It's stupid, I admit. I wish I'd known you were coming.

You weren't answering your phone, she tells me with sarcasm.

Okay. Do you ask the question?

Yes. How do you spend your time? I have to say, Billy, if it wasn't you I might have thought you were going a bit stir crazy in there.

I *am*.

But then again, if it wasn't you I wouldn't have agreed in the first place. That's a compliment, by the way.

Thank you.

Oh, and Patrice is fully recovered, thanks for asking.

Not now, Julie. What does he have to say?

Not coming to see us then? she taunts.

Julie, please, I have about two minutes of credit on this fucking thing. The phone just eats it up. If you really want a row, wait till next time, eh?

She waits for a second or two. The second piece of telephone etiquette that Julie religiously observes is this: she will never put the phone down in anger or disgust. Quite correctly, she sees this as a vilely rude thing to do.

Okay, she says. I had to make some notes. How long have you got?

I told you! A couple of minutes!

Keep your hair on, Billy! Fucking hell—I'm doing this for you!

I apologise. Please tell me, Julie, what he said. I can't speak to him and I would really, really like to know what he said.

He talked about energy. She leaves a huge pause.

Still maintaining the status quo, temper-wise, I urge her to continue.

First of all he congratulated you on a good question. At this point I'm like *lost?* What's good about it? But anyway, I don't really wanna know. So he says: I'm saving my time—and other people's time—what does that mean?'

Slang, I lie. It's new code, Julie. Carry on.

Oh Billy, you're not planning something for when you hit road, are you? she asks with a definite moan of worry running through her words.

Don't be concerned, I try to reassure her. Nothing illegal.

Then why's it in code?

Please.

All right, all right, don't throw your rattle out of the pram, Billy. He's saving his time and yours and other people's, like Prometheus did with fire. I won't ask. Then he laughed—he found the whole bloody thing hilarious, to be honest—he's quite a happy-go-lucky bloke, really, innee? What's he in for?

Rape, is what I want to say—the truth. Death by dangerous driving.

Someone die? Julie asks.

Yeah, someone he had beef with. No one innocent. What else does he have to say? Saving time, Prometheus fire, what else?

He's had it with stealing water. Whatever *that* means. So he's going to steal as much time as he can, till he's full like a tick full of blood. He's going to—wait a minute, let me turn over the paper—he's going to save it then kill it. Does that make any sense to you, Billy?

Not much, I admit.

I kept asking him if you'd know what he was talking about but he just smiled, says Julie. Said—he couldn't keep going on the way he was, smaller and smaller—whatever *that* means—because it's a circle he starts again.

Didn't think of that.

Think of what?

Why he might be frightened of getting younger as we see it, older as he sees it, Julie. Because it doesn't stop for him, you see? A million years of bee-stings. Prometheus on the rock. Eternal punishment, Julie! *That's* why he wants to go back to being young. Well, old; but young for him. Well, he's still old—but his years on the planet are less, at that end.

Billy, *what* end?

I'm right—what I say to Kate. If he does enough damage, he'll get older and older to the point where there must be a start! The only way to kill himself, Julie, is if he takes himself past the point where he started!

You're not making any sense!

It's not Julie putting the phone down that kills the call. I've run out of credit. But it doesn't really matter as I think I know what needs to be done.

Four.

The Murder of Roger Ackroyd bears on its inside back cover no adhesive ticket on which to stamp a return date, but it has been sheathed in protective plastic: Kate's own work, I reckon. This is a book she's brought into the jail. This is a message to me, but nothing subtextual. I mean, I happen to know that the narrator done it—whodunit? The narrator done it—and if there is anything to go on by her choice of book, it's beyond me. We all know I done it. Although I pleaded not guilty in court, I know damn well I stabbed the very man who has since got my Julie pregnant.

And grudgingly I sigh through it, this televised memory, thinking with candour two things, namely one: why do I always remember being attacked by three men on that night, and two: well, if you can't call that a good example of tit for tat then what can you? Billy Cardman banging up my bird, I mean; not the three guys setting on me, although for all I can recall, so coked-up was I in those days, this might be true as well. As I've said, I don't know where the memory comes from.

There is a letter inside the book. The paper is as thin as toilet tissue—presumably so it's easier to conceal. It is headed: *The Heartbreak Diaries*. Then it is written: *Chapter 1: Nightmare Music*. I get it. If the thing is discovered, it's more creative writing from my sister. She is writing her first novel, I'll say. So be it:

Chapter 1: Nightmare Music

Noor showed early talents for pain—for inflicting pain. They were few and far between—and usually against animals. Given the ability to walk, he walked into conflict. Given the mindset that encompassed choice, he chose to hurt. He would stub out cigarettes on the hides of oxen. Punch camels in the face. Throw stones at the feral cats and dogs. And only slowly, over a period of years and years, would he graduate upwards—to human be-ings. Very often the damage was limited, paltry—and very often as the result of imbibed fermented products. Fights in the bars were commonplace, occasionally legendary. He had a knack for goading people, for egging them on. He started fights, sometimes, in which he didn't even take part. He was happy to watch. Why wasn't he exiled from Umma? This was something I was desper-ate to learn; but the answer—if there is one—had been long since lost in the dust by the time I came to ask questions. Possibly? Possibly because he recanted his earlier ways. After a while—a long while—a period of decades—Noor was calm. Like a prizefighter settling into retirement. He got along well, the word goes, with the citizens of Hospital; but if he'd stayed that way of course there would be no story for him. No clothes to wear. And figuratively speaking, during that time, he had no clothes to wear. He was poor. Days and weeks he spent, like many others, trying to scratch a living by working for a filling meal. There wasn't enough work. Noor started stealing. Years earlier, when Noor was older, he had gained daily sustenance from a wetnurse named Saira el Door. The image might seem disgusting, even frightening, but this old man as we would see him was no more capable of his own self- managed salvation than a baby would be, and *the Wethouse* was how the word *hospital* translated. Noor would crawl in for his wassail at this old matron's saintly dugs. She gave suckle to the infantile and the senile alike, given the circumstances. With Noor she even waived direct payment for her services. She and Noor had become friends. It was frequent that Noor would spend hours in her company, at the Wethouse and in her shack. She fed him, legitimate food by this point, or he fed her, depending on whether or not he'd been able to thieve any vegetables, or a chicken, or had been able to sell his muscle in return for a few handfuls of rice. It was common knowledge that Saira was a wisewoman of the township. And it was believed it was Saira who put the idea of a pilgrimage back into the desert into Noor's head. The claim was that in the sands, far away but no one knew in which direction, there were other, smaller oases. There were kings that could be grown from the parched earth. All they needed for cultivation was special water and faith. Saira could provide the water—she could bless a carrying skin of water—if Noor had faith enough to venture to the sun, endure the bitter nightfalls, and return with a king on his side. Who knows? Perhaps it was all fallacy. It's occurred to me that this might have been a convenient way for Saira to be rid of the albatross around her neck that Noor had become. But that is not how the towns-people told it. If desperation has an eye—a central point of calm—it might be constructed in the shape of a town surrounding a vast body of water that has no right to exist in the wilds of a desert. It might look instead like a prison. Go outside of that eye and what might one find? Maybe hope? Maybe joy. Something positive—who knows?— on the face of the desert. It was a common belief. Such pilgrimages were commonplace. No one—it seemed—was precisely sure of what the concept of growing a king actually meant, but I took it to refer metaphorically to an act of faith and devotion. Finding God. Finding the Devil. Finding oneself, perhaps. Bringing good fortune back to the tribe, and the knack of bringing food to the table and water to the cup. But it was a boy called Morjardahid who was finally Noor's spur to go off in search of a king. The boy—it was said— was beatific in appearance; angelic, almost. A dark-hued seraphim from the scalp and then the brow of the desert's face, as seen from above. It was a cobbler called Siam who told me the tale. Siam was mending espadrilles but was happy to talk to this strange Western woman with her inquisitve nose for a good myth or yarn. Morjardahid arrived in Mostashifa in a condition of great excitement. Even his own parents had disregarded any hope of seeing their runaway son alive again. But not only was the boy alive, he had been energised by his travels. 'The hair is grass!' he repeated, over and over. When I asked what the boy might have meant, Siam told me of how a desert, viewed down-upon from above, was the shape and had the features of a face. Dunes for cheek-bones; the troughs between for dents at the temples, for lines on a forehead. Plump rows of sand-hillocks delineating the lips of the Allbeing. And when the wind moved the sand, the face changed. The Allbeing was eating, his lips and jaw moving, when a storm kicked the sand about into different and swiftly changing regular patterns. The Allbeing was angry; the Allbeing was sad. When the Allbeing was contented, the temperature dropped. It was night. I asked Siam: 'If the desert is a higher being's face, what part of that façade is Mostashifa?' He stopped his shoe repairs. 'A birth mark,' he replied. Morjardahid had discovered grass. God's hair was grass. It would have been far from prudent to inquire after the hairstyle, so I waited for Siam to continue. The story still baffled him—and even puffed him out. As he told what he intended to finish, he was breathing as though he'd run from the desert himself—a surrogate to the child, experiencing the same sense of revelation. Morjardahid was one of Saira's errand boys; but she was also his teacher. She taught him scripture, morals, and Spanish, bizarrely enough. Comparatively wealthy by local standards as she was, and unbeknownst to anyone in the township (although tongues wagged and rumours abounded), Saira had paid the boy's impoverished parents for the right to send Morjardahid on his expedition to find sources of food and water. He'd come back with a boast about grass! How he showed it off in the Wethouse, proud and seemingly still amazed: a tuft of grass. A muted interest, and no more than that, was abroad—apart from in the mind of Noor. It was Noor who consulted with Saira on the theoretical subject of where there is grass there might be soil for cultivation. Of course the logic was flawed. Did they not live beside a vast watering hole where there shouldn't be one? But all the same, sensing change and possibility, Noor took hold of his fear for the future—his terror of growing younger—and enlisted Morjardahid's assistance in returning to the other form of distant oasis, more or less before the boy's boots had cooled. He told Saira that he wanted to find the green grass, to grow a king; and he wanted the king to stop him travelling backwards. When Saira refused, however, to bless the water he'd need to carry, Noor committed the unthinkable, and desecrating their bond and friendship, stole water in sheepskins from the Wethouse, along with as much money as he could find after breaking into the building one evening and knocking Saira unconscious, underpaid the boy's parents, and set off into the wilds with the child. What happened, months and months into the wayfair, was even more speculative than what has been written up to this point. How could it not be? With the stories of Noor's life in Umma, there were at least witnesses—witnesses being storytellers, co-defendants, accessories—or the offspring of witnesses, however corrupted and curdled the tales might have become. Do echoes ever really die down to nothing at all? Perhaps the township is still talking about the old man who became a younger man, who rode into the lap of a heartless son, with a boy at his side. But how did they live? What food did they take? What water, other than that sterilised in processes that are vital to the welfare of a shanty medical centre, did they sip as they plodded and gasped through the sand? As they crested one dune after another, what did they discuss? What demons assailed them as they prayed for a god? Four months after they'd left, the boy arrived back in Umma for the second time. He was alone. He was also in a state of high fever and prone to a virulent strain of epilepsy from which he had never suffered before. He kept talking about sad roses. The answer to any question, for the first few days after he lay down his head in his parents' home, was 'sad roses'. In accordance with one belief that anything the human body sheds can be recycled, his mother wrung the sweat from his sheets and pillowcase and distilled the salt from it to feed it back to her son's parched lips. His father butchered one of his valued and valuable hens, to make broth. Together they nursed the child back to something resembling good health. Physical health, anyway: it was feared that Morjardahid's mind was gone—fried to nothing. A robot drew a beam along his legs and torso, diagnosing any-

thing erroneous in the boy's human make-up. The printout sug-
gested that limbs and organs were in working order. However,
when the brain was scanned the robot could find nothing to print
out. There was no diagnosis, and it was feared there was nothing
left working inside the skull. 'What happened to the old man?' he
was asked. 'He's still there.' 'What's he doing?' 'Growing roses.'
'Roses?' 'Roses. They are knitting together to grow a king.' After
a further two weeks, during which Morjardahid changed his story by not one jot, but when in every other sense he seemed to be
of generally good mental health, it was assumed that Noor had
put some kind of spell on him. Assumed he'd managed to condition him into his beliefs. Nearly a year had passed since his de-
parture—when Noor returned to the Oasis. More sprightly than
he had been when he left, he hobbled into a town larger than the
one of a year before—more bustling, more chaotic, irrefutably
louder—fully expecting the flags and trumpets of a hero's welcome. What self-delusion, the passage of time, and sheer hubris
had erased from his memory, however, was the fact that not only
had he violently attacked Saira el Door, which might have been
forgiven, seeing that she had passed away in the intervening span,
a victim of brain contusion and heartbreak, but he had also stolen water from the Wethouse, the crime of water theft being re-
garded as heinous. So, no celebrations; quite the reverse. As soon
as he'd been identified and tracked down—he was frequenting
the same bar he had patronised for several years—he was stunned
with an electric cattle prod, stripped of what remained of his
clothing, and shackled in a set of wooden stocks by the water,
there to be tried by a hangman jury the following morning, if the
chickenhawks failed to peck the skin from his bones and the liver
from his torso in the meantime. His neck was saved. Despite his
protestations that he might well have saved the township with his
derring-do, Noor was sentenced to an indeterminate tariff on

board the prison ship. All the while he was dressing in his off-white prison fatigues, he continued to say the king could help them all. The computerised rowboat was programmed and waiting. But things get hazy after this. That Noor was dragged on board the prison ship is not in doubt; nor is the reality that he toiled and struggled thereon. What I find intriguing, though, is what he is said to have screamed from the rowboat as it was taking him away—and screamed till his lungs must have itched: 'My king told me he would find me, or I must find him!' And: 'My king told me he'd be everywhere!'

Five.

Fortunately for me, I have all but burnt the strips of paper into which I've torn Kate's letter when the door is unlocked and opened. The toilet cistern is still refilling from the most recent batch of washed-away cinders.

Screw Jarvis is on the threshold. What're you doing, Alfreth?

Burning, sir, I answer.

I can see that, numb nuts. What are you burning?

Letter, sir. My missus has dumped me. Don't wanna read it again.

Hard lines, son. But I'm afraid it's about to get worse. Cell spin.

Okay, sir, I sigh wearily, standing up from the side of my bed. May I ask what you're looking for, sir? My only unaccounted-for item is *Roger Ackroyd*.

You may not. Wait in the Sosh Room with Sarson. Door's open.

He moves to the side as I walk closer. Anything to declare? he asks me.

No, sir. I'm a reliable Y.O. You said so yourself in my last report.

Indeed I did. He seems to relent a little. Just routine, Alfreth, he goes on. Let the dog see the rabbit.

I imagine Jarvis is simply trotting out a withered piece of verbal garbage, but there's some truth in the order. Stepping outside into the corridor, I see one of the drugs dogs, tail wagging like a helicopter blade, being held by its master. I know the drill. I keep my feet apart slightly in order to make it easier for the dog to sniff my crotch. I have nothing to hide. Why then do I feel so suddenly nervous when I glance down and notice that the dog's playful tail has stopped moving? It's dropped like post-coital dick. The drugs dog sniffs again; it makes a tiny whine, a whimper.

What's your name, mate? the handler asks me.

Alfreth, sir.

You changed your tobacco recently, son?

No, sir. We only get G.V.

Stopped or started smoking?

No, sir. Has the dog identified something out of order? I ask politely.

He doesn't know what he's identified, do you, boy?

I haven't done anything wrong, sir, I say—both to the handler and to Jarvis, who has remained standing stock still on the border of my cell. I'm nervous; I shouldn't be— nervousness will enflame their curiosity.

I'm a Redband, I add; I've got too much to lose, sir.

Jarvis speaks. You're friends with Ostrich, aren't you, Alfreth?

Well, I was, sir. He's been shipped out.

I'm perfectly aware of what's happened to the twat.

Point being? asks the handler.

Point being, adds Jarvis, that that twat was always on the hooch or worse. He get some down you, did he, Alfreth?

No, sir! I protest. I don't touch anything!

Piss test, I'm afraid, son, says the handler.

Go to the Association Room, says Jarvis. I'll be along when I've finished ransacking your belongings.

Perfectly candid at least, I think to myself, mooching off.

Sarson is livid—he is fizzing with rage. Refusing to acknowledge the presence of the officer assigned to watch us for the next few minutes—a screw I recognise but can't place.

Sarson says: They think I'm on drugs!

Me too.

Do you have to do a piss test?

Allow it.

O my days! he continues, more in sorrow than anger now. He slams a hand down on the surface of the ping pong table. This could fuck me.

Not if you're innocent, the screw says from the first of the two doors—the one that is open, as Jarvis said it would be. The metal door with bars has now been locked—we're locked in with the screw while they spin our cells.

Why just us, sir? I ask.

It's not just you, mate. It's the whole Wing. Some brown was found behind the water pipes of a YO who's been shipped out to adult prison.

Some brown? The hell does he get that? I want to know, but my question is no more than rhetorical.

Does *who* get that, mate? asks the screw.

You're talking about Ostrich, aren't you?

I didn't say that, son. Know something I don't?

I don't know dick. Sir.

What the fuck has that got to do with us? Sarson demands. I've got an interview on Monday to see if I get me Enhanced! This ain't gonna help!

The screw is stoic—offensively so. If you've got nothing to hide then what's the problem? We're asking you to pee in a bottle, not give blood.

I'd rather give blood, Sarson huffs.

The screw shrugs his shoulders. Then you'll get your blood tested instead. Easy peasy. Relax, son.

Don't call me son. Ain't your son!

How do you know? Maybe I made your mum squeal.

There are some screws who do like a joke with the yoots, and there are plenty of yoots who, from time to time, appreciate a giggle with the screws. But there are limits, unless the two strata know one another essentially well, blood. And if you're new to a Wing, as a screw, quite fresh, and if you happen to be locked in a room with two YOs who are already pissed-off at being targeted for random drugs and alcohol testing, then as a piece of advice I might say that it's best to lay off the *I-raped-your-mother* insinuations.

O my days! I echo Sarson—as Sarson makes a lunge.

It takes all the strength and speed I possess—a diminishing supply—to stop the yoot before he can get to the screw. Why do I bother? Because, despite everything, I think I'm deep down a good boy, as my Mumsy would say, and I don't want to see him fucking up his chances to become Enhanced. Seeing Sarson struggle in my arms is a source of amusement for the screw. I could hit the bastard myself, but instead I spend my energy on telling Sarson to calm down and I walk with him in a kind of headlock to the window.

Out of earshot I say to Sarson: You okay straight, bruv?

Reluctantly he replies: Yeah, blood.

Tell me something. You been sleeping a lot, right?

More than usual, yeah. Why do you ask?

Can you remember any of your dreams?

His left eyebrow arches upwards. My dreams?

Yes. Can you remember any of them? Recently I mean.

He thinks about the poser for a couple of seconds and then answers. I'm in a kind of wasteland, he says. Just sand and bones. Weird pony shit.

I think I'm thinking it but in fact I'm saying it: It can smell the desert.

What?

I realise I've spoken aloud. Nothing.

Did you say the dog can smell the *desert?* he asks with incredulity.

Yeah I did. Aiming to make light of everything, I bust a chuckle. Maybe Ostrich did leave something in my drink, I add.

What are you two yobs whispering about? the screw calls over.

The pleasure of your company, sir, I call back.

Careful, mate. I'm not renowned for my good humour.

It shows, sir. Can we please have our piss tests?

When they've spun your cells.

And then the others will come in, is that right, sir?

Sarson is looking at the side of my head; he's trying to suss me out. So is the screw, safely over there by the door with his pouch of keys.

What others?

The others Dott's got to, is what I'm saying inside my mind. *How many is that?*

Rest of the Wing, sir, is what I actually say.

But I know it won't be the rest of the Wing. Know the dog has already been up and down the landings— along the ones, the twos and threes—and sniffed out the candidates for the embarrass-a-thon we call a piss test. *It can smell the desert.*

That's *our* business and not yours, son, says the screw.

Sir, my name is Alfreth. I'd be really grateful if you don't call me son.

I'll call you fucking Sally-Anne if I feel like it, he retorts.

I ignore the insult. And what's *your* name, sir? I ask.

Officer Oxford.

He's been wrongfooted by my courtesy.

When you're ready, sir, only I'd like to enjoy my weekend if possible.

Why? Oxford grunts. Are you going somewhere nice?

Six.

What do I have to do around here to get beaten up properly? Those pansies hardly scratched me, Dott complains after we've been shown the practical.

This Tuesday it is baked chicken with courgettes, aubergine and tomato *ragout*. I've had it with fucking chicken, but as ever I'm delighted to be called across to the Cookery class. Even when your name's on the list there's no guarantee a class will run or, I don't know, someone might set fire to a bed. Because the dish takes longer than we might have— because anything might happen: a fire alarm, a fight—the Cookery Gov has already heated all the ovens to one-ninety C. The classroom is excruciatingly hot—especially after the chill of the air between the Wing and the Education Block. As with last week, I have managed (with Chellow's permission) to secure the oven and workspace next to Dott's. I am eager to talk. Should I start an argument about football again, just to get the volume up? No. I can wait; I can bide my time. I season my chicken breast with salt and pepper and sear in the flavour in a frying pan smeared with olive oil. The smell is fantastic. The smell is gagging. My breakfast worms around in my stomach and gut; the food is alive inside me—a parasite. I transfer the chicken to a plate, add more oil, and toss in my trimmed and topped aubergines and a diced shallot. I can wait. I've waited this long. Sweat is on everyone's brow, even Dott's—in particular Dott's: sweat running down his face and seeming to avoid the fresh bruises on his cheekbones, like strollers poodling around the shore of a lake. Or an oasis.

Why does man want to get beat? I ask him.

Dott says, Exercise.

I won't let it go. Seriously, why? I press him.

Dott eyeballs me point blank. I'm serious, too. *Exercise*. Keep in shape. I made them do it, in case you're wondering.

This comes as something of a surprise. As I'm stirring my mixture—the onions softening, losing their opaqueness—I say: Why do that? Immediately I believe I have the answer. Does it count towards your bad shit quota?

It certainly does, Billy, says Dott. I might have earned myself a few minutes, nothing more. It's hard to say. They weren't as vicious as I hoped.

That's not what *I* heard.

Are you two old birds squawking again? asks the Cookery Gov, an amused but tired grin on his face. Why don't you just propose to him, Alfreth?

Just chatting shit, sir, I reply.

You are that. Add your courgettes.

Yes, sir.

I wait until the Cookery Gov has lumbered away to supervise someone else.

So what is this? I ask Dott. Is this blind devotion? And if it ain't, what *is* it? What do you expect me to *do?*

Dott's response is simple but it doesn't answer my question. I gave you life, he says. I grew you in the desert, against every odd there is.

If you say so, Dott, I tell him.

Don't make fun, Billy. His tone is as dry as the air inside the room. Don't forget, I saved you from the bee-stings as well.

Which you've since admitted was a mistake, but okay—if you say so.

What do you mean, *if I say so?* Don't you *believe* me yet?

The confession is like chicken skin in my throat—a dog's-tongue-sized length of the stuff, trying to choke me and stop me speaking.

But in the end I say it. I say, Yes, Dott, I believe you—because I don't have any choice now. But why don't I remember? I almost beg.

Why do you think? Dott teases. Because you were dead, Billy. Dead.

There is nothing I can say for what feels like a minute or two. My mouth tightly closed, I stir tinned tomatoes into my frying pan until everything is good and drenched. My pan resembles a full-scale nuclear meltdown. As we've been shown how to do, I tip the resultant mixture into a roasting pan, clearing a space for the chicken I've seared. I thrust the roasting pan into the oven, which roars the dirty heat of unwashed griddles into my face. Drips of perspiration roll between my lips.

Dead? The Hola Ettaluun are the tribes of the *dead?* Don't make sense, I say to Dott, relieved now that other people are talking. Chellow is even humming a song under his breath: *Release Me* by Engelbert Humperdinck. Two other yoots chatting breeze about poom-poom.

Tell me about it, Dott answers with a snigger.

What do you *want* from me? I ask.

To help me get back there, is Dott's answer.

Sure—sarcastically—I'll lend you my passport.

You can go and I can follow.

I'm in the same prison as you, cunt!

You were dead then, he tells me. You can be dead again.

Is that a threat?

Quite the opposite. I'm offering you a gift, Billy-Boy.

Inside the space of a couple of minutes, the whole class has finished its preparation for the best meal of the week. The Cookery Gov instructs us to do our washing-up while we're waiting for the meals to heat through. The hot tap has been disabled for a long time now, and so we clean the utensils and receptacles we don't need any more today in water so cold it is like a nice dream compared to the room's torridity. Conversations continue, but not between me and Dott. I have too much in my brain; once I've finished doing my pots I sit at the central table to write up a bit of my theory—my coursework I mean—while the ovens chug on like steam trains. Soon I've been joined by most of the group; no one, by this point, has much more to say. The temperature has dried out the shit we chat. As I write today's date and underline the word *Ingredients* with the handle of a ladle, Chellow (being all but illiterate and reluctant to write anything) volunteers to do the sweeping up, and Meaney (a lazy arse) asks if he can swab the sinks.

Dead? What does he mean by dead?

What do you think I mean by dead? I can hear him say, in my head. Is he speaking? Am I listening? Or am I making the whole caper up? I don't know any longer.

Can you see that the end is in sight, Billy-Boy? Dott whispers in my ear.

No, I tell him.

You came to see me on the ship.

No I didn't.

Don't be naïve, Billy. It's too late for that.

I don't remember.

You were sleeping among the amnesia trees, that's why?

I was *what?*

My voice is too loud. My classmates turn to me; the Cookery Gov turns to me, asking in a bored tone, You got a problem there, son? and I shake my head, commenting that I have nothing of the kind. He leaves me alone. He has something of a rarity—an oddity even—in the shape of a near- silent class. He doesn't want a bogey like me to spoil the magic. The ovens moan and mumble. I try my best to recall the ship. Knowing Dott must be speaking the truth, I try my best to recall the ship—my time on the ship. *Welcome back*, I am told. But it's a dream, surely to God.

I will find you or you will find me, Dott whispers again, but when I twist my neck slightly to face him he has turned away. The words I've just heard—they are not words shared with or eavesdropped on by anyone else. Dott has spoken directly into my head. *I will find you or you will find me*: that's what you said. *And I have found you*. Give me a sign. Concentrating as hard as I can, I stare at my page—at the single word I've managed to write—the word *Ingredients*—and I leave half a side of A4 and write the word *Method*, under which I will report on what I cooked and how, for my NVQ portfolio. The third heading—*Results*—as it turns out will never be written. *I'm trying as hard as I can, Dott*, I think, attempting to aim the thought to my side so that only the recipient will read the message, if that makes any sense at all. I reach for the box of tissues in front of me and mop my face; I am leaking vital fluids, vital salts. I need some fresh air.

Okay, Dott says under his breath.

Roper is chosen. The yoot stands up from the table, pen in hand. I hope Dott isn't going to make him stab someone; that wouldn't be fair—everyone is getting along famously these days and I feel like a chump even to admit it. No. With a haunted look on his face Roper does something else. In full view of everyone including the Cookery Gov, he staggers over to the walk-in storage cupboard, inside which is the chest freezer, the washing machine for our pinnies and towels and the fire alarm. We don't see him do it, of course, but I hear the click of a cigarette lighter's barrel turning.

The Cookery Gov asks, What you doing, son? Get out of there. And he follows the yoot inside.

Seconds later, if that, the fire alarm has been activated. Clamorous and sharp, the sound bounces through the ovens' misty exhalations.

You've got some fucking explaining to do, son! shouts the Cookery Gov.

I stand up. We all stand up. There will have to be an evacuation of the entire building. But we are in a workshop and things aren't so simple as walking away. It doesn't matter if the fire has reached our toenails, the equipment will still need to be checked before we can taste freedom. Or comparative freedom anyway.

Tools away—*now!* the Cookery Gov shouts; and we are all bounce and action as we replace our ladles, spoons and chopping knives to the shadow boards on the wall, where they'll be locked behind glass for easy inspection against the threat of theft. With most of us up to scratch with our washing-up anyway, this performance doesn't last long. The Cookery Gov moves from oven to oven, almost gracefully, like a ballerina, secure in his position in a time of trouble, turning off the ovens in case we're out of the Education Block for some time and the food burns.

Charlie One—Screw Vincent—she comes to the door and unlocks it; swings it open. Tools secure, sir? she asks the Cookery Gov.

Secure. It was Roper. It's a false alarm.

We still have to get you out, sir, she tells him.

We file and bustle past, all nine of us bar poor old Roper, who looks solemn and dejected, confused and utterly drained.

He looks like he's pissed his pants—literally. There's a dark stain at his crotch, which might be sweat (my own grey clothes are similarly stained), but is more likely to be the consequences of abject fear.

I'll fucking have you, son! the Cookery Gov scolds the poor weak-minded little gibbon. See you before Number One Governor, any day soon. You're off the course.

Down the stairs, wriggling like worms in salt with the learners from the other classrooms, and then, in the stairwell, joining the other landing's human cargo and contributions to the melee. Through the holding area, with both sets of metal- barred doors open wide—a clutch of screws at either portal— and blissfully, thankfully, into the daylight chill. I walk with Dott. We will head back to our respective Wings. We have minutes.

You helped me escape from the ship, Dott says. I'll always be grateful to you for that. I can help you escape from this prison.

No you can't, Dott. I've done my history, bruv, a long time afore you got here. *No cunt has ever escaped.* Not even in the really old days, when it's a women's prison and they still hang people. No one gets out those gates.

Who said anything about gates? Stop being so literal.

Why? You got a trampoline in your cell, have you, Dott? Bounce me over the walls? You're chatting shit, cuz! As usual.

For the first time in a while Dott appears rattled. I would have thought, he says, by now you'd stop this silly charade of blokeyness. *Open your mind!*

Why? So you can steal a couple of days away from me again?

A mere demonstration, Billy-Boy. But you saw it, didn't you? You saw the desert.

In a dream—yes I did. It was a *dream*. But I decide to stop pretending, and galling as it is, I know once again Dott is not chatting shit. The desert is real. And I am real. And Kate went there, and Dott was there. I was there too.

A screw barks his orders: Move along, lads! Quick as you like!

We are strolling at the speed of old men on unimportant errands: stretching the time at hand as stringy as it will go.

Takes courage, but I say it: How did I help you off the ship?

You repaid my gift of life.

The rose? You grow me, you say.

Right. A drop of water, a second drop, a drop by day for God knows how many days. I was starving. Delirious. There on that second oasis—just grass.

What did you drink?

Nothing. A drop of water every second or third day, with your permission, but those were moments that tested my faith. Walk slower.

Impossible, I tell him; and I'm saying this word in response to both the claim and to the command that Dott's made. No one survives without water.

I did. I thought I was gonna die out there, Billy; but I was determined. I caught a scavenger bird once—it came for me in the night, probably thinking I was dead. I wrung its neck and that alone made me strong. Just the killing of it. Should've taken that as a sign, shouldn't I? Kindness was never going to work for me, Billy. I killed the bird and I ate it over days; maybe a month. I had no way of tracking time while I was waiting for you to grow. I licked the feathers clean for you, Billy—to stay alive. To wish you alive, too. It was faith.

I know that, Dott. Faith but not reason. You were over-dosing on the sun; you were delirious—you said it yourself. You weren't thinking straight.

You know who you are, Billy, he replies. You just can't see

the whole picture yet. You will. I built you from clay, dust and grass. You're like me. And you told me you'd find me or I'd find you. And you found me.

Wait, Dott. You came here, I tell him. That means you found me.

No. You were born, Billy—on your estate. You think you can't remember but you can, if you try hard enough.

Being born? Of course I can't remember!

You *can*. And I was waiting for you to arrive, kicking and screaming into the world, Billy. I even prayed for you and for your mum, the night she went into labour. I watched you grow up on that estate. It was me who convinced your dad to leave you. You didn't need him.

I stop walking. You did *what?* I demand.

He was violent. I didn't want to risk him hurting you, so I thought I'd do the right thing for you by getting him to leave. To tell you the truth, he didn't need much persuasion. He all but had his coat and hat on anyway.

To my astonishment there are tears in my eyes. What you do? I ask Dott. Mind control? Beat him up? Threaten him?

Money.

You paid him? And he went?

Move along back to your Wings, lads!

Dott and I start walking again—shuffling rather—and Dott's saying, attempting philosophy, I think, Every man has his price.

I don't ask what that price was; I don't want to know.

Dott is continuing: You see, I thought if I was kind and good I'd be able to get older again. I was scared of getting younger again; going through that horror again.

Again? I ask.

This isn't my first time round the block, Dott tells me. Every time I go around it's different, but it's still full of terror and angst.

So how old how old are you?

Who knows?

Come on, please, Dott.

I don't know! Dott protests. Maybe I was there for two thousand years before I was dragged out of the desert. Two thousand years has a nice ring.

We have spoken quickly, like speeded-up records—we have lived the last few minutes in FF. Double arrow, pointing east. But I want to go double arrow pointing west: I want to Rewind. Let's start again.

Two thousand years. Can it be Dott's simply plucked that number from the air? It has such weight, that number; it tinkles bells inside my skull. Talk of faith, implications of devotion, a desert, it all sounds Biblical. And although I know I'm probably going to regret it, I say it anyway.

Are you the Second Coming? Are you Christ?

As predicted, Dott snorts laughter. What do you think, you daft bastard? he asks me. Did Christ rape joggers by the side of canals? If he did, it would certainly put a different spin on things, wouldn't it? Me at the head of the table, and the rest of the Wing as my disciples. You make me laugh, Billy!

I'm not trying to, I reply, but Dott is on his horse.

Talk about a Last Supper, he's saying now. Macaroni cheese and Um Bongo fruit drink. Brill, I must say. What's for pudding?

Don't boys me, Dott, I tell him; I'm getting vex.

Well, pardon *me*.

Back to your Wings, lads. I won't tell you again, I'll nick you, okay? I've been reasonable, says the courtyard screw, and he has a point.

Behind us the fire alarm is still blaring. Won't be long before it's discovered the evacuation is a falsey, but I ask the screw anyway:

Are we going back to class, sir? It was just some waste with a lighter.

This waste have a name?

The Cookery Gov see it all, sir.

Then probably, yes.

I'll see you back in class, Dott! I call to the scrawny half-dead bird, splay-footing his way heavily from my stationary position.

Missing you already! he shouts back, over his shoulder.

Seven.

The cell spin comes back negative, of course—negative for all concerned. Unfortunately for me, so does my application for an outside visit to Patrice. INSUFFICIENT GROUNDS FOR PERMISSION is stamped diagonally across a photocopy of my original letter. Disappointed but not surprised, I take charge of the mop and bucket from Jarvis, my next-door, and start to clean the floor of my cell. Killing time. No more and no less. There is time to kill. While mopping, and taking my time about it, I remember something harvested from one of my few rare appearances in school, back on road: something in Physics. About energy. Energy can't be created or destroyed, only translated into a different form of energy. Is that how it goes? And if so (or if not), is *time* a kind of energy? Dott is taking it from some of us, whether we like it or not, and he wants to use it to go backwards, to get older by getting younger; to return to the grass, to the dirt—to before he was anything in the scanty breezes and stink of desert. If I'm right I can help him die. And I want to help him die—I think. As long as it doesn't mean I have to do so too. But how can I survive if my creator is scattered into atoms for the sand beetles to crawl over and mate upon? He says I came from there but I have a Mumsy, I have sisters; I was born in London. Up here in the hills, in Dellacotte YOI, is as exotic a place as I've ever seen, blood. Or *not* seen, as it is. I helped him escape from the prison ship, he says. He was trying to repay my kindness by protecting me. So what better way of Dott ensuring he gets what he wants than by reversing the entire lifelong process? By *destroying* me. But I'm his energy. He can't destroy me. Only *translate* me.

Yo, Alfie! says my next-door Jarvis (as opposed to Screw Jarvis). You wanna play X-Box for a hot minute?

Sure, I say.

Using heavy duty laser fire, we obliterate each other's rag-tag and bobtail brigades; heads purple open like cantaloupes. There is a quest for treasure and a quest for immortality. Give me the treasure every time, if Dott's miserable reaction to the latter is anything to go by. Jarvis's cell stinks of Golden Virginia by the time we've finished. When, days later, the fire alarm is raised by Roper and we are returned, first to the exercise yards outside our respective Wings, and then when the shouts come out—*Everyone back to their cells!*—I am so generally pissed off at not being allowed to continue with my lesson and more importantly, my discourse with Dott, that I challenge Jarvis to a re-match, the stake being two burns I don't care if I win or lose. Feeling sick, I play badly; he engulfs my character in a well-aimed trumpet of acidic spray. Poor old Alfie falls, like Troy. As a result, on the screen, the rest of my troops wilt and wither, die screaming in molten pools of their own selves and essences.

How many times can you think a thought without wearing it out? Then again, a thought is like a muscle, perhaps, exercised, pumped up and strengthened by regular use. Whatever way, the thought returns—the one that runs like this. *If Dott dies, what happens to me?* And then: if *I* die, what happens to Dott? I don't remember it yet but I will.

Being divorced from the meals we have prepared and half-cooked—this does not go down well with the ten lads in Cookery. Once we know we're not going back to the Education Block, there's a sour taste in the mouth. It tastes like I've licked a rat or the wings of a bird. Back in my cell, bored with playing computer games and with the door wide open, I take hold of my beads and settle down on to my knees to pray. I don't know what to pray for. That's disgusting. If I pray for my time to go faster, all I'm doing, quite likely, is getting Dott involved. I wouldn't be surprised if that's how he has found those yoots he's worked with in the first place: by answering their prayers, of whatever denomination. Reaching out; swinging the radar. How else has he stolen people's time? If he's not careful, by executing the very deeds that are asked of him, he'll be in danger of doing something helpful and nice; and we can't have that, can we? But what's the alternative? I can pray for my time to drag and go slower—it's a madness, it's a beef with your own logic, such a numb idea. Playing safe in the end, I pray for my Mumsy and my sisters. I pray for Patrice. Very carefully, using my mental scissors, I cut Julie out of my prayers. Whether it makes me look a cunt or not, I don't wish for anything good for that girl. She has someone else to wish her well tonight and from now on. My job is done. Seeking privacy, I close the cell door, use the lavatory, nurse the nasty pain in my stomach with a soothing palm of cold water, and make tea. More than ever I am antsy, dissatisfied, longing for something to do, to say.

I thought I was close this afternoon. It's *my* fault, really, we had to leave; and because of the class being today, I deliberately declined my lunch. I am starving now. Thirsty too. I want a break; I want a holiday. That trip to see Patrice, that would have done nicely. But it scares me somewhat, the depth of my feeling of utter passivity; what I mean is, I get the notification I've been unsuccessful with my application. Do I fight? Appeal? No; I say, *fuck it.* I'm not bothered. I'm disappearing into lethargy, I swear I am. Endeavouring to do something positive, I pray again—this time kneeling more comfortably on my bed. Beads in hand; hands together. It is sacrilegious to recapitulate the exact words—and the covenant, anyway, is shattered by such an action—but I can tell you I drift far. I float through distances— great distances. Using only what material I have managed to locate in the Library, I picture a desert—the combed dunes, a token camel. But something tells me I'm not being authentic. Or rather, someone does: Dott is with me. How long has he been here?

You're thinking in clichés, Billy, he tells me. *Don't create it—it doesn't need creation; it's already there. Just remember it.*

That's easy for you to say, Dott!

You can do it. Kill off everyone else. Kill off everything. It's only you and me. Jigsaw pieces of land; vast; separated by cracks. Can you see them?

Yeah, I can!

Can you smell it?

The aroma is as large as the eye can see. In any direction—I am flying now, over the baked void—I can sense the desert's smell tickling my nostrils.

Noor? Why did you want to get beaten up? I ask as I move.

To get to hospital, he says.

The voice is close enough for the yoot to be in the same cell as me. It's not like it's in my head anymore.

I don't see the connection, I tell him. How's getting twisted up gonna get you back to the desert?

Not the town of Hospital: the *hospital.* Accident and Emergency.

He is not in my head, but he's not talking to me either. This is something new. It's an awareness of Dott's comportment; it's his energy, present, transferred into sound for my ears—but I'm reading his mood and not listening to words.

Why? That powerful word: why?

An outside view? A change of scene? he replies, rhetorically. *But most of all because I knew you would have to follow me. There's no choice now, Billy-Boy. You would follow anywhere. To the ends of the earth if necessary.*

Am I following you now?

Or I'm following you. It doesn't much matter which, does it, Billy?

I suppose not. Where are we going?

Where do you think?

The oasis the boy found, of course! Where you grew me.

Indeed. Where I grew you. Where I was dead. Until I grew you—yes.

So is everything dead until nature in some form takes hold?

I was only your nature, Billy. There's nothing offhand about it.

Whizzing now! Faster and faster! God's speed! There are words on the wind but I cannot make them out, I am travelling too swiftly. I'm losing focus; I'm getting hot—I'm hearing Dott's voice, but I don't know if the words are coming now or if they were in my ears from before, or from the future or from where they are.

But it was my mistake, he is saying— repeating? *I needed bad things to do. Bad things.*

I know.

Very briefly he pauses. *I helped you with the bee-stings*, he says.

I'm twisting the air behind me in a corkscrew trail; I feel like I'm going to burst.

I shouldn't have. I should've smeared raspberry jam all over your face, Billy, to give them a feast.

That's no way to talk to your king, Dott, I sort of joke.

Why do you think I lived so close to you for so long? Dott is saying now. *Why do you think I got myself sent here to* this *dump? I thought a trip to the hospital might excite.*

Like you had a choice, you mean? I ask.

I had a choice not to hurt those women.

But you need to do bad things to keep getting older, don't you?

Bad things. How cute. I could have killed any one of them.

But you didn't.

I should have.

Loops of discussion; are all of them real and true? Am I inventing any of them? The big question looms of course, and I ask it to the wind.

Dott sniggers and the air in my cell ripples like heat haze; the walls deliquesce, albeit briefly. He is scorning me and he is scorning my query.

You don't think I've tried that, Alfreth? he shouts into my face. *You don't think I might just have bought enough headache tablets to floor a pissing elephant and swallowed them all at once with two bottles of vodka? Give me some fucking credit. It didn't work! All that happened was I started again.*

From the beginning?

From the very beginning, Billy! Dott replies.

There below! I see it! The patch of grass, as out of place as a squashed fly on a sheet of blank paper. It shouldn't be there, but it is. Either with Dott or flying solo (I'm not positive which) I swoop lower, towards it.

If I see the desert, must I be dead? I wonder. Am I losing this time? Is it being sucked from bones, like meat off a chicken? Where will I be when I wake up? Call it illusion; call it reality. Call it something slipped into my drink. What I observe induces the gut reaction of more than a dream. The grass feels familiar; the small patch of roses—this patch feels familiar as well. The roses are climbing and winding around two small trees. Seeing them clearly, as I do right now, atomises any effect they once had upon me. These trees, I am sure, are the Amnesia Trees; by floating down into their orbit, and now—by touching them gently, the suppression in my head is neatly lifted.

When the screw comes to check on me, he finds me sleeping soundly on top of my covers—or so he thinks. I am resting. In an unusual move, he uses his baton to rap on the cell door.

Time to collect your dinner, he says.

I don't even know which screw it is. Legs wobbling, I climb to my feet; I'm aching everywhere, blood. I collect a portion of beef stew that goes straight into my toilet—no middle man required. I feel too weak to lift my plastic utensils to eat. All I want is to relax. All I want is to sleep. Three more times that night I pray. Dreams come creeping.

Eight.

Am I building these thoughts from popular myth—from movies? I don't know. But what I see is this:

The prisoners are working. They are shackled to the benches on which they will spend the remainder of the day. It's a little after midday, but you wouldn't know that, not down here, below decks. The light is all but non-existent; the air is thick, muggy and it stinks of male and female sweat. There is no gender demarcation aboard the ship. Here is Dott. Here is Noor. Callused hands on a long oar. Dott is sitting nearest the small portal, rowing in time with the other three men on his bench—one bench among scores of benches identical to one another. Male or female, torsos are exposed. Dott's back is sliced red from where he's been whipped and struck as part of his penal servitude. Why are they rowing? The ship doesn't move as a result. This is punishment for the sake of punishment: backbreaking physical labour, intended to squash ambition, thoughts of liberty and body energy. He doesn't see me. However, I can't be invisible: other rowers see me, turning to face me as I walk down the aisle between the benches.

Perhaps they think I am one of the jailers, there to whip. Scared of me? Who can blame them? My face is new to them, I'm sure of it. How can they know I mean no harm to anyone? How can they know I mean the opposite?

There is noise behind me, in the gloom. I turn. Descending the wooden stairs I once tripped and fell down is a large man with a face full of hair. The beard is matted and long, the moustache spanned out like seagull wings. Even his eyebrows are thick as adult thumbs, tied one to its partner with no gap between. He asks me what I'm doing. In fact, he asks me what *I think* I'm doing, which is a much more difficult question. Turning on my heels, I walk purposefully back in his direction. Although rowing doesn't stop in this galley, there is a marked deterioration in effort and strength; prisoners want to see what is happening.

Change of leadership, I tell the hirsute slave-driver—he who is also a prisoner on board the ship, one who has risen through the ranks to be able to command the men and women who are newer to life on the water. The man is amused.

Do you think so? he asks me.

I know so, I say.

I remove the small shank I have secreted in my loincloth; I too am topless—pigeon-chested and weak-looking, but the power of my intention can't be in doubt. The nights are long on board the ship. I have managed to fashion a knife of sorts by sharpening a piece of wood I have torn from the one of the walls of one of the living quarters, lower still than the galley, below our feet, in the bowels of the vessel. As with everyone else present, I am a prisoner. Rebel too; or so it seems.

We don't need to do this, I tell the man whose name floats through the air in waves, from his head to mine.

His name is Ayaan. Along with several other stormtroopers (four or five, I think) he helps to run this boot camp. He has wielded authority over me before, I realise; this is my second time aboard the Oasis. I have served a previous sentence—for what I'm not sure. No more certain than I am of what I'm doing here on this occasion—unless my sole purpose is that of liberation.

We don't need to do what? he asks me, eyeballing the shank in my right hand. Stay where you are, he continues nervously.

Let them go, I demand.

You know I can't do that, says Ayaan.

We'll take our chances.

In the oil? Impossible! No one survives the oil.

How many have tried?

A good many. Now enjoy the remainder of your rest period. When it's your turn to row, I assure you you'll have an easy shift.

I don't believe you. My back is stinging, where I was flogged yesterday.

Not by me!

It doesn't matter who by.

Will you stand aside?

No.

Ayaan removes from a loop on his belt the whip that is coiled there like wire. The whip is only three-quarters unfurled when Ayaan flips the weapon with a wristy motion: the business end of the whip strikes out; there's a warning crack of air about a palm's width from my left eye. I'm aware of how accurate Ayaan can be with his weapon of choice; he's a marksman with it. The shot, I know, is merely to frighten me back into submission—and it nearly works. The thin rope is on the floor after the assailment. Taking the force of what needs to be done as my spur, I stamp my bare foot down on to the whip—he tries to pull it back—and I attempt to pace along it like a tightrope walker, climbing up the weapon as I stride closer. The sharp end of the wooden blade—I dash it into Ayaan's left upper arm. He whimpers with the discomfort, the pain lending him strength in his other arm. Pulling harder on the whip, he burns through some of the skin on my feet; I am knocked off balance as he retrieves the whip I'm standing on. A fight begins. Dissimilar to a fight at Dellacotte, there is no noise from the onlookers. Sure enough the rowing stops— that pointless, pointless exercise—which will shortly be noticed, but not one of the prisoners breathes a word of encouragement. They watch as Ayaan and I grip and wrestle, punch and bite. He is the stronger, no doubt about that, and I understand that my knife to the arm is no deterrent. Though I don't wish to hurt Ayaan (as far as I know, he has done nothing wrong to me other than follow orders) a stark reminder of whose dream this is is required. I pluck my shank from his bicep. As we struggle on, it is like being in a waxwork museum: not only does no one speak, no one moves either. Though I don't pay much attention to those around me, what I do see when I get a fraction of a second to glance—what I see are dead eyes, lifeless eyes. And two sudden movements. Ayaan and I are wriggling on the wooden floor; splinters bite at my exposed, rough and raw skin. I notice a woman with dark hair—a woman in her early sixties—make the sign of the cross on her chest. The second movement is Dott standing up. Ayaan is striving to prevent me from stabbing him again. And while I don't want to have to stab him again, I can't see a valid alternative. He has a job to do. His job is bringing his problems upon himself. I can't tell him this. My sharpened piece of wood is aimed for his shoulder. It is my opponent's deflective blow that knocks the point elsewhere: the wood slides effortlessly into the left side of his neck. Ayaan's eyes are wide with horror. I hope what my eyes say is apology enough. As blood starts, first to trickle, leak, then to spurt, I roll away from his writhing body. When he starts to scream I understand that Noor and I will have to move faster than ever.

You're all free! I shout.

Not only a gross exaggeration, but an oversimplification to boot. We remain on a ship in the middle of a vast body of polluted water. There is no way back to shore, other than to swim; and once ashore? There is no home remaining for prisoners, however close to the ends of their sentences some of them might be. I try to read the mood of the gathered slaves. Attempting to rile them to mutiny, it seems, has been as effective as nailing the oil to a wall. If anything, what fills the eyes in those few not stunned to inertia by months and years of pointless physical abuse, is resentment. I have torn the status quo.

Come on! I say to Noor. You can be free!

We ascend the wooden steps, but Ayaan's screams— possibly even the unexpected stench of his blood, as if the wound I hope won't be fatal has unleashed the rotting insects of his soul— have alerted his muchachos. Three more men, similarly hairy as this particular watch's driver, arrive near the crest of the stairs. One of them—the youngest, I would guess—is carrying a strap: a snub-nosed automatic pistol that seems out of place, but I'm confident will be no less convincing for it.

I shout to Noor: Run!

Not one heroic bone in his body does Dott contain, it seems, for he doesn't wait for me to offer the chance of escape a second time. Bewilderingly light on his feet, he makes a sprint for the stern. The three jailers set to: on me. Nobody has taken the chance to overcome the powers that be. For all the lack of noise from below deck, I might be travelling on a ghost ship's maiden voyage. Trying to keep hold of my wooden shank, I lash out, fearing a bullet might pierce my skin and a major organ. I fight with relish, but the hullabaloo is concluded, almost before it begins. No show of concern is shown for Ayaan, bleeding away his life, downstairs. Nor does any one of the three go in pursuit of

Noor, smugly comfortable in the notion that he has no place to run to. Though I've managed to scrape and poke with my shank, I am forced at gunpoint to relinquish my hold on it now. Weapon-free, I am now taught the error of my ways. The beating, still at gunpoint, is savage and enthusiastic. I have heard no splash; no sound of Noor's entry into the water. What can he be doing, the ingrate? I am taking this beating in order to liberate him, and he doesn't have the common decency to flee when he has the chance! Will they beat me and then put a bullet in my head?

They are certainly making sport of the first half of the retribution for my actions. I am rolled up into a ball, the kicks landing thick and fast. The blood in which I wriggled—Ayaan's blood—I smear on the deck, smudging it around like paint. Finally I hear the splash of a body striking water: Noor has jumped for it. Between blows to my system I have a crack at informing my attackers I've given up. Gladly I will take Noor's place on the chain-gang, working his shift after my own. Little by little the assault wanes. I try to imagine him swimming. Oily as a seabird, his arms already weakened from rowing, pumping hard and painfully through the muck.

I am left alone to examine my injuries—or for them to examine me—leaning against a mast that feels cool to my forehead's touch. For the moment I can't remember Noor's voice; it's an effort to remember his face. But what is clear enough, moments later, is the manner in which the prisoner spent his last moments on the ship. The follow-up kicking is as equally severe. I am told it will happen after dinner, so that's a nice dessert to look forward to. Not that I receive any dinner. The upper echelon of the ship's hierarchy dines and rests. When the meals have gone down and the food has been digested, it is time for me to have my chain unlocked so I can cease hugging the mast. And the reason for this second onslaught? On his way to freedom, before he crash-landed into the oasis, he stole more water. He stole a bottle from Ayaan's own supply. In a surrogate fashion, I received the brunt of the jailers' bad tidings.

Dott tells me I helped him escape, and I did. What he omits is the part where I nearly lose my eyesight to do so. Where my testicles are cramped by kicks, pushed up into my torso; where my scrotum is scratched open. But after half an hour, the vicious-ness desists; the attackers have grown bored. Again, I am chained to the mast, there to stay—whatever the weather; weather come what may—for the next seventy-two hours.

What's in it for me? I can't help wondering as I wake up.

Nine.

The days following the aborted Cookery Class are like tor-ture—like a slow-acting poison against my will and resolution. I am crabby. I am jumpy. Repeatedly I turn down Jarvis's offers of an X-Box games competition, or Sarson's attempts to get me chatting during Sosh. As the cliché goes, I'm a shadow of my former self. Perhaps I'm in love, ho ho. Sure as hell, I'm not eat-ing anything much more than the bare essentials to keep alive. On the other hand, I'm drinking water as if the supply's being turned off any day now. Since dreaming of the desert, the Oasis and the ship, I have a thirst on me that's as dry as a camel's hoof. Leaning over my sink, every five or so minutes when I'm in my cell, I scoop up water, eschewing the uses of my plastic mug, and gulp in water and air in equal measures, so that I'm bloated and gassy—the eructations you won't believe—and then, a short time later, I am doing precisely the same thing over again. I can't wait for Friday. Dott is not picking up the psychic phone. Not listening to me. Nor has he ordered any reading matter that will necessi-tate my visiting his cell. I can't even count on that for a chat—for a resumption of what he has to say. In fact, generally speaking,

there's been a marked reduction in yoots ordering much of anything to read in their cells. The only thing to say is, it's in keeping with the air of weirdness circulating around Dellacotte of
late. Even the ducks are acting peculiar. Yet knowing what's to
blame doesn't help me, does it? Doesn't help me get to DottThe
days drag like songs on a melted LP. There's no better way of
putting it. In the meantime, on my arrival in the Library, Kate
Thistle shows me she's trying to be cute by saying Wogwun at
more or less every opportunity, until it starts to become a pain in
the hole. Miss Patterson weaves her way through the day, setting
me tasks and no doubt (now I'm aware of her fondness for the
spirits) fantasising about her first glass of Gordon's Gin when she
gets home. Or before. Until she's of pensionable age, she's killing
time. There is nothing unpredictable in the days, this Wednesday to this Friday. Now I've established that the weary pessimism
that's infected the YOI is here to stay, it's something like observing an army, four hundred strong, of harmless zombies. Shared
thoughts? Perhaps. I don't know. All that's clear is, when Movements started before Dott was around, it would take the screws
on both landings of the Education Block fifteen minutes to get
the motherfuckers settled. And it's piss-easy to sympathise with
the disruptions. Give me a job to do or be a six-wanks-a-day man,
decomposing spiritually in my pad, I choose the former, on every
account. But for others—not Redbands, and without Enhanced
status— the choice is simply not there. They wait and rot; they
rot and wait. An excursion to Computer Literacy or Maths is
like a Greek holiday. Hardly anyone speaks as they enter the Education Block. Murmurs, mumbles—if anything at all. I'm no
different. I take my place in the holding area, climb the stairs to
the twos landing, enter the Library, where I spend the remainder
of the morning, before setting off on my bored expedition back
to the pad for lunch, before returning again in the p.m. Cups

of tea and snatched moments of dialogue with Kate Thistle—
these are the punctuation marks to these slow, slow days. For me,
one who thinks he conjectures slowness quite nicely, quite thank
you. Slow has a new meaning now. Kate Thistle listens patiently.
Aware our time alone is limited, she neither interrupts nor inter-
rogates. She holds her mug of tea with both hands and lets me
babble and spurt. Simultaneously I find myself both liking and
disliking her, day by day. She looks older than when we met. An
actual conversation—as opposed to a gobbet of reportage—has
become a rare-ish beast, but it shows its pretty head, late in the
day during Second Movements on the Thursday afternoon. Miss
Patterson has ventured out on the scrounge for a rubber. It's good
to know, despite everything, old habits die hard and that someone's lifted her eraser like this. So we're not all brain dead, after
all! It will be some time later that evening before, while reaching
into my trackies for a lighter, I find the self-same tool. I have stolen it without even being aware of the theft: a habit I don't want
to get into.

Can I ask you something, Miss?

Course you can, Billy—long as you're brewing up at the
same time. Kate smiles, but she is serious about another cup of tea.

I don't know anyone who can drink tea like Kate and Angela. I struggle to keep up.

How much longer you got?

To do what?

Be here.

The kettle remains half full from the last round of drinks so
I simply flick the kettle and settle down on Angela's twirl around
chair.

I mean, you say you're writing about prison language.

I am writing about prison language, Kate corrects me.

But you won't be allowed to stay here forever, Miss, will you?

I don't want to, thanks!

So what's your cut off point?

My thesis should be ten thousand words long, or thereabouts, she tells me. I think I've got material enough for about eight.

I'm surprisingly touched and proud. So I've really been of use to you?

Without question, Billy. You'll never know how much.

Will you put me in the Acknowledgements?

If I'm allowed to.

Thanks.

But what about the other two thousand words?

Kate shrugs. If I don't find them here, Billy, I'll either make it all up—or I'll use what I know of the Hola Ettaluun.' She laughs. Who'll check?

Glad to know you take your studies seriously. Here's your tea.

Ta. But I do take them seriously, Billy. It's just that I'm more interested in the project you're involved in than dissecting the difference between Allow it and Respect me. Do you see what I mean? she asks.

Suppose I do. Allow it. My stab at a silly little joke.

Kate doesn't answer; deep in thought, she stares into her hot drink. I don't know what to say next, but I know it can't be long before Angela returns from her mission.

Kate spares me the embarrassment of further silence. Not looking up from her inspection of the cup's contents, she says: It was more like a world than a township, for the people who lived there in the desert. Some of them—I've never told you this before—some of them treated me with hostility and suspicion. For them it was hard to believe there were other places to live.

Fact is she has mentioned this before; I don't contradict her. I have spoken enough—I'm pleased she's taking a turn.

A world before ours, perhaps, Billy. What do you think?

I can't answer her question; I ask one of my own. What about Dott saying I was dead before he made me with the rose?

That's what I'm getting at, she says. You were potentia. Dott needed to find you to help himself get back there—even if it's a state of mind.

But wait a minute, Kate. The desert's a real place. You were there!

She nods her head. And there alive and well. Can I say truly that's the same as everyone I met? Everyone who spoke to me? Who can tell how many others are dreaming of existence, there, while they go about their everyday chores? It's something I didn't think to look into.

Waiting to be born, you mean? I ask.

Yes. Somewhere in this world or another.

You're creeping me out, Kate!

Only now? She smirks.

No. Not only now. But including now. It sounds like Hell.

Placing down her half-finished cup of tea, Kate is so good as to look at me again as we talk. While I won't say the expression is unfriendly, I can't claim there's a good deal of warmth there either.

You're being too literal, Billy. There's no Hell. Grow up! The Oasis is half wood and half memory, I think. Half water and half notion.

That's a lot of halves, I remark.

She is not in a punning mood. You may be right.

Kate, what's wrong? I venture. You're in a peculiar mood.

She shakes her head. Something came to me last night, she says. Something I've thought about before but haven't managed to articulate, even to myself. I wonder how many other Dotts there are running around.

God, I hope not!

But there must be others, she answers me excitedly. Surely we can bank on that. It can't be only our Ronald Dott. Others must have got out.

Others moving their way backwards?

Perhaps. No, let's be positive. Undoubtedly. Without doubt. It's just that most of them don't spend nearly so long being a nomad, country to country, trying to find an equivalent of you. They live with their lot.'

With disappointment? I say.

Yes—Like the rest of us.

Ten.

Starved of attention, in addition to being starved of food that my system can't keep down long enough for it to do me any good, I am all but braying at the moon in the early hours of Friday morning. It's all I can do not to hit the night bell: at one point I suffer what experience tells me is a mutually- complementary epileptic fit and asthma attack. In the dark I roll a burn; the smoke hits my chest like a harsh rugby tackle, if not worse: I can feel where the three yoots on the ship, the other night, pounded me, kicked me ragged. It's all real, I tell myself. Even the bits in my head—they're real. Nearly thirty minutes pass, the pains sparking over my body, and with me using my newfound powers of communication, however base and unreliable, before I welcome with my mind's eye the news that Dott, at this moment, right now, is being bent over and twisted up by a couple of screws, batons drawn. There is no show to watch. I cannot see the fight. I cannot view the storming onset. And I have no idea what's prompted it. But Dott is getting fucked up good, blood. He has said or done something bad, something bad. How can I sleep after that? Still my breathing regularises once more—very slowly, but it does—and I can sense the bags under my eyes darkening slightly. So tired. No snoozing! I chide myself. At this early hour the siren the ambulance wears like a flashy gown is all but certainly not required. Up here in the hills, how much traffic's there gonna be in the dead of night? The stretched klaxon noises lap at the edge of my consciousness for a few seconds, before I pull myself back from the grip of a brief wee-hours nap. I hear the vehicle get closer—there it is! Midnight Rambler sheep scamper out of its way! Night birds witness the white and yellow, mechanised beast with head-turning disdain. It arrives at the front gates. The siren is doused. Me, I'm getting cock-heavy ready. Why is this? Have I developed some vile kink for cars? Inside these walls I've heard worse: the Puppydog with his erection in the soapsuds tray of the industrial washer in the Laundry; the yoot soulfully knocking one out in the exercise yard on C Wing, watching the ducks. But no: what I've got here is the thrill of the chase, it's clear as. Dott has managed to get the shit kicked out of himself. He'll be going to hospital.

How do I follow you? I ask him—then again, six, eight, ten times.

A spy is no bloody use without senses. I get out of bed. From my window, rolling my eyeballs as far right in their sockets as they'll go, I can make out maybe the first ten centimetres of the offside front bumper of the ambulance. It's parked at a rakish angle to the mesh surrounding the Puppydog Wing exercise yard. Stay banged up long enough with someone, or in my case—as I never want to share a cell—keep your next-door for long enough, and you start to come alive to one another's rhythms. Like women prisoners, coming on together— beginning their menstrual cycles within a day of each other. Jarvis knows, I believe, I'm already awake, but he hisses and calls my name just to be sure .

Are you listening?

Wogwun, bruv, I call back.

The dialogue won't be allowed to continue for long; nor do I want it to. But I'm thinking—Jarvis might be of some use to me at this point.

You watching the show, blood?

Allow it. What you see?

Just the bandage wagon.

Bait. Can you see it all?

Near enough, blood. Back doors are open. They're taking someone out, he informs me—or wants to inform me.

It's Dott, I tell him.

How do you know?

Rumour has it innit, I tell him, effectively closing the subject.

Jarvis doesn't wish it to be closed. What he do? Snitch? yoot asks.

Your guess, blood. Now I'm concentrating.

It's something like relief courses through me when a baton taps on the metal door. The night screw tells me to shut up and go to sleep, then repeats his orders next door. So now I'm concentrating. On what? On everything Dott has told me so far. Every sentence I can recall; every riddle, every instant I've wanted to paint his nose knuckle red. Every time he's boysed me, annoyed me, stolen from me. Cramming all those thoughts is like Julie (she pops into my head, unwelcome now) packing a suitcase for a couple of days away from London: too much for the space available. Won't all fit in. I rearrange the memories for better packing, hoping as I do so to find some new ones—some uncovered ones. This unveiling is a muted, mixed success. Random—or seemingly random—snippets of conversation, like confetti in the wind. Like trying to catch raindrops. Like climbing the tallest sand dune in the desert.

But you're a king, Dott says to me. You should have the privilege of a shorter life.

What does he mean?

I'm as old as the hills, Billy; as old as the dunes.

I know that, Dott! Something new! Something new!

Now my voice, joking?—I'm not sure. Superficially angry: That's King Billy to you, Dott. And Dott saying something about a thorny crown—he is constructing the very same regal item from pieces pulled loose from a rose bush embracing a small tree. The loop-the-loop of memory, bringing me back to this grass, this rose.

How do you spend your time? I ask Dott. It's the key that's been lost in my overcoat pocket.

Follow me with your heart, he says clearly.

Part Seven:

In the Land of Goodbyes

One.

Dear Alfreth.

Of all things, a letter from Ostrich, which I'll punctuate on his behalf. And capitalise. And re-spell. The rest I'll leave, although in its first draft, raw and unpolished, it took me as long to read as it does my Psych Reports and parole files.

How goes it, blood? Me, I'm shaking it, fam, he writes. You're right, rudeboy—Big Man Jail ain't no paradise, blood. Fucking screws are a bit more chummy but that's it. I been already twisted up like ten time or so, but me, I'm just feeling my way and getting cock of the walk. Same time, I'm trying to go legit. Man have a LONG time to consider his actions, as them Psych bitches give it, blood. Don't talk to me about parole. My actions my hole. We do what we need to do, I lie? If there's another way to go, man will take that other way. But I bust the days. I join some classes, rudeboy. Arts and Crafts on a Tuesday afternoon, a full-time Motor Mechs course for the rest of the week. Big Man Jail get sponsorship from a local car dealership—good for the profile, both ways. So I work on real cars, Alfreth. I've learned the difference between a rotary engine and an internal combustion engine. I know what two-stroke means. I know the difference between a carburettor and a camshaft, rudeboy. I had to get out of there, Alfreth. I don't know what it is but there's a stink about the place. Man use to have dreams about the graveyard at the back exploding and showering us all over with bits of dead bodies. We're in the exercise yard and deconstructed slices of dead men and women, blood, they're raining all around. They're twitching. They start looking for the rest of their bodies. Never home, never whole, just like us, cuz. And another dream too. I'll tell you about it in a minute, but the one I just give—I don't know what a dream like that might say about my state of mind, but the dreams have nearly stopped now. Now? Now I dream of nothing at all. Usually. There are exceptions to the rule, every once in a while. Maybe that's a sign I've grown up, even a bit. Took my time about it, yah—go ahead and bust chuckles, blood. I've asked for it. Fuck knows if I'll even send this. Never say it at the time but you were a good friend to me, Alfreth. There are things we can't say that we are happy to say when we hit road. Why's that? Wogwun? What are we scared of, blood? We scared if we say it, it got no place to go? The emotion's out of our head—and our head is prison enough. It can't escape the walls of a jail. You can't unsay it, rudeboy. And if you start to have beef with man, you already told man you love him. What do you do then? So it's easier to say nothing at all. But you were a friend. I have a new friend now, and I doubt you and I will hear much from each other from now on. When you hit road I'll be thinking of you, blood—course I will. The message will get to me somehow. Prison networks. You know how the gossip goes: I'll find out. And I'll be jealous and I'll be angry, and I'll try to tell myself lies like: I'll see you in another twenty years, maybe still. But I won't, will I, Alfreth? If you've got any sense, you'll go legit—get some shit job you hate but pays regular. Keep your nose clean. Keep the knives in the kitchen drawer. Work hard for your living. But me, I'm gonna be an old man when I get out. If I get out. My new friend is helping me with this. His name is Clarity. I think at first it's because he sees the world with clear vision, but no, Alfreth—it's really his name. Although he does as well see clearly. I don't know his first name. He calls me Younger. I'm not Ostrich anymore—I'm Younger. In a Big Man Jail I'm a little boy. Clarity tells me I've got two addictions and I tell him yeah: hooch and zoot. He says no. Freedom and incarceration. I'm addicted to freedom but I know I won't be able to touch that shit again, not without all but killing myself. I'm addicted to incarceration, though; there's no way round that. Try to take me away and I think I'll have withdrawal *shakes and twitches. You should've seen me in the van, bringing me here, it didn't matter how much I was looking forward to moving—I missed Della-cotte like it was in my cells. The cells of my body. In my blood, blood; in my brain. It's a relief to be banged up again. I felt, at home, Alfreth. Tell me: are you really ready to leave? Think about it seriously. Where will you go? Back to Mumsy? Okay, and then what? That shit job I talk about—maybe it ain't coming round to your yard a couple month. What'll you do for peas in the meanwhile? We do what we need to do. That's all there is to it. Be careful of wishing for freedom, Alfreth—it's a powerful drug with no known cure. That's what Clarity says. When I tell him I have a dream of a hamburger, he says, 'It's a drug.' When I tell him I long for nice bedclothes, he says, 'It's a drug.' He's closer to fifty than forty—Clarity—and I suppose he should know. He's been in and out since the age of fifteen. He has never had a home, a job, a family or a ting. Prison's what he knows. He'll be leaving in a year's time. He's scared to death. Not that he'll let me see he's scared to death, but he is. He enjoys the boredom. Once a month he sits on the Prison-Prisoner Forum Meetings, but other than that he lies around thinking. Doesn't turn on the TV. Doesn't open a book. He claims man can generate all the knowledge man needs, by his age. No help required. Perhaps he's right. I used to think I was intelligent in my way, but compared to Clarity, I'm a novice, a begin-ner—I'm a Younger. All I've got to look forward to is a time when I can be as wise as he is. And I'm looking forward to the journey to that place, Alfreth. I feel it calling me. It's like the moon seen through clouds, some days, and other days it's as close as dinner smells and the bell in the chapel on a Sunday morning. One piece of advice he give me: kill time. I say to him: That's rich, coming from you, lying on your bed all day—it's an attempt at a joke. But he takes it serious. So I ask him what he mean and he tell me: 'Burn your cal-endar. The increments are too small. It's not like the run-up to Christmas— this is your life, Younger.' So I burn my calendar. I get twisted up by a couple screws for that; they think I'm trying to set fire to my pad as a protest over something. I tell them this ain't the case but they don't believe me. Or they do believe me, maybe, but just fancy a fight anyway. So be it. What's another* punch? I stop watching the news. I don't care. It's not important. The day the war breaks out that'll need involuntary volunteers to fight the front line and they come to my door, this is the day I'll start watching again, to see what it is I'm supposed to be fighting for. And who I'm meant to be fighting. Other than that, the news is 'new things'. I don't want new things. I don't want old things. I am happy to be here, even though it's not really different from Della-cotte. Not really different? It must be. I contradict myself, Alfreth—I should have structured this better before I start writing. But would that have helped much? I doubt it. All I know is, the nightmares have stopped, more or less, as I say— the ones where I'm walking through a desert. I'm trying to climb the side of this fucking huge sand dune and I keep falling to the bottom and I have to start again. I'm in a circle, a loop— I can't get out. I only have those dreams rarely now. I don't dream of nothing anymore, but I've said that. What else can be new? I've just said I don't want new things—but you do, Alfreth. You'll welcome this letter and these words, I'm sure of that. Burn it afterwards. What else can I tell you? I'm looking forward to the time I finish my Motor Mechs course. When I'm there I'm gonna follow Clarity's lead: meditate all day. Refuse my meals from time to time, just to show the screws I have been as deeply indoctrinated as I'm sure I really have been, because a protest now and then is a good sign, from their point of view. Just a little one; even a cuss, it's good news as far as screws are concerned. It means you're playing the game; the brainwashing has worked, or is working. Perfect passiv-ity, Clarity say—they don't like that. They lose their sharp edge. But I have another reason, anyway, for not eating every single morsel. It's not that the food is shit—it's better than anything the Dellacotte kitchens ground out—it's more, I feel like keeping hungry is really giving the raised middle finger up to the passing of time. I don't want the daily punctuation. I don't want the markers, the clues; I want the riddle. So I'm whittling away at those markers and clues, slowly but surely—catchee monkey. And already I'm making prog-ress—I can tell you honestly, hand on heart, Mumsy's life, I've no idea, right now, what day of the week we're on. I'm not even sure of the month as I write—I know we're approaching the end of one and the start of another.

Yeah. That's what I want. No days, no months, with luck I get to the point where I'm not a hundred per cent on what year we're in. That'll be bliss, and man will be bless. Until then I'll play the game and keep my head down. Man don't expect man to write back. I won't read it if you do, unless I'm weak and I give in to my addictions. This is possible. Not saying I've got it perfect yet—not by a long chalk, rudeboy, as Clarity says—but I'm stepping in the right direction. I'm declining any visits from now on. I don't want to know the outside world, even the ghetto girls. I only care about the moment. So by and large I'll only do what they want me to do, without further arguments. Clean my cell, I'll clean my cell. Time for Gym, it's time for Gym. They say Education, I'll go to my course—I'll paint my pictures—my pictures of the desert, quite often—or I'll learn about oil filters or I'll pick up my spanner, and whatever it is I'm doing I'll set to it. Soon I'm gonna try not to speak. If any of this, Alfreth, make you think man is broken, think again. Man is liberated by being banged up. When the door is closed at the end of the day, I lie down and think myself into a peaceful world. The night screams at Dellacotte are hardly heard, and that's a relief; but the absence of the silence that was everywhere towards the end of my time there—that's gone too. Cons keep their music down to respectable levels; it's good to hear it. There are occasional shouted conversations from cell to cell, but only for a while—things forgotten to be said that can't wait until morning, because no one has a memory here, and if they're not said straight away they're not said at all. And for some people that's a wasted opportunity—a wasted thought. We need all the thoughts we can express, some might say, I'm usually asleep before midnight and at seven the next morning I exercise, wash, and get ready for my day, like a businessman putting on a suit. And in that respect, blood, I am still hogtied by time. It won't last forever. It might not last past next week. I'm going now, Alfreth. I wish I could remember your first name. I can remember your prison number but not your first name. How stupid is that? Sometimes—swear down—I struggle to recall my own first name. My name is Maxwell, I say to myself, my name is Maxwell. I use it as a call to prayer— or even as my prayer. Don't let go of yourself as you slide towards the other names. I don't even know if this is making any sense.

Goodbye, Alfreth. Think of me a last time, if you will. I should be evacuating your memory anyway; everything else does—your memory and mine. You hit road and you be a good man, you hear me? Don't get vex with nobody and nobody get vex with you. I don't want to see you here. Best wishes for the future.

The letter is not signed.

Two.

Dizzy and sprite-like, I chase the ambulance down the hills, away from the prison; I'm a supersonic moth, in flight to touch the pimple-shaped light that crowns the ambulances roof. The siren has been silenced; the illumination has not been dimmed— casting pockets of shadow like bats' wings from left to right, hurl- ing darkness like sheets of soot. I catch hold. Hills banking to either side of the otherwise unoccupied road: they could, in the darkness, be sand dunes. This could be a desert. The prison, an oasis of life—still life, at least for the time being. Inside my skull I repeat, again, every word I can recall Dott using—every exam- ple, every bookish reference, every scintilla of sarcasm. Think- ing harder—and how the wind punishes my sweat at this mo- ment!—I am able to climb inside the vehicle. Dott is lying down on a gurney. Though I can't see the condition of his body, that of his face is indication enough of the savagery of the hiding he's re- ceived. A newly plump face, in hues of grey and cerise. I ask him if he's all right but he decides not to answer. I repeat the ques- tion—subconscious to subconscious, like twins—and he tells me:

I'll live.

The words take on ugly connotations, given Dott's resolu- tion to die.

Why do you need the hospital? I ask him.

I don't. This is all superficial; I'll be right as rain in a couple of weeks, he tells me. Just thought, better be out of Dellacotte when the shit descends.

What shit?

You'll see. Tonight's the night, Alfreth.

And silent he goes once again. No amount of geeing him up can fire further discourse. He's saving—he's saving his energy. But I'm still there, I think. I'm still in my cell.

Don't worry, Billy-Boy, Dott whispers to me; you're asleep. I'll take this time away from you. You won't need to see a thing.

I want to see a thing! I complained. I've waited so long, Dott!

As you like it. Dott waves wearily at the air.

The paramedic sitting on the other gurney wants to know if Dott's trying to say something.

I'm thirsty, Dott croaks. Can I have some water, please?

The paramedic shakes his head. Not just yet. Very soon. We'll be there in about fifteen minutes, he replies.

Dott's eyelids feather closed. On either side of the ambulance, as we decline to sea level—sea level?—the trees and bushes on the hills melt into the land. The slopes appear more than ever like sand dunes I want to climb. If tonight's the night, as Dott puts it, I want it started tout suite. What's the sense in hanging around? And I can't mistrust what he's told me. If he doesn't intend to call in what he needs to call in, why is he performing the act of goodness and kindness that will protect me from the ugly bombs landing? We know that goodness and kindness are no fucking good to the yoot.

Do it now, Dott, I stress as loudly as I can.

Oh, all right, Dott says aloud, making his carer frown confusion.

As you've asked nicely. Wake up, Billy! The show must go on.

Three.

Dear Julie

It shouldn't happen like this but it has. A great but terrible realisation has come upon me and it's taken me several days to be able to pick up my pen, let alone find the words to express how I'm feeling. But here goes. You need to be without me. I cannot support your decision to start a family with Billy Cardman. It is not right with anyone. But if I hold up my hands and accept defeat, it might be easier for all involved. Still, I need to know. Will he take care of Patrice? Please consider this question honestly. If you think the answer is yes, I will not so much walk away as stand still. It's not as if I can move very far anyway. But I won't interfere. I don't think you should visit me again—and I don't want to see Patrice either. It's too painful. I cannot communicate with her and she cannot communicate with me. In this respect, she and I are like you and I. When she can talk—or better, when she can read—there will be a letter waiting for her. I haven't written it yet; and even if I write it tomorrow, which I doubt I'll be strong enough to do, I won't send it yet. Why not? Because I can't, and because. Cardman will destroy it, I think. Before you get angry, please don't tell me I don't know him. Please don't proffer platitudes. 'His heart's in the right place.' 'He wouldn't harm a fly.' Both of those things are as may be. But I'll ask you this: how much more intimate can you get than knife-craft?—than wounding? Believe me, Julie—an attack is a personal thing, even if the victim is random, as was the case with Cardman. I had nothing against him I do now, mind, but that's my problem; he simply wouldn't give me what I thought I had every right to claim. I think differently now, as you know. So what did I learn about him, by attacking him? I learned a brisk lesson about his stoicism and resolve. He resisted me; he resisted a knife. And now this: I can tell you that he's strong- willed, opinionated, hurt and excited about his new adventure. He won't want me to write to Patrice, any more than he'll want you to come and see me. In his mind, you're his now. And I know that you'll hate a sentence like that, but it's true. You will learn, very quickly, I think, about male pride and male jealousy. He will take care of you and our daughter, I hope. Only if he doesn't will I return to your lives. Please pass this message to Billy. There really is nothing much to add. I have resigned my position as the Library Redband. I needed a change of scene, ho ho. With Christmas approaching, I wanted to begin the new year with a new job; and for once serendipity and bald good fortune were on my side. It was Ostrich who gave me the idea, but it was luck that made it happen. Ostrich—you've never met him, of course, but perhaps you feel you know him a little bit, seeing as I've talked about him often enough when you've come to visit and I had nothing of my own to tell you—well, he's enrolled on the Mechanics course; and I thought—okay, I'll try that. Unfortunately, Motor Mechs already has a Redband who's good at his job. On the other hand, when I looked around a little more, I found out that the Bricks Workshop Redband has been transferred to another prison because of some gang connections on the out that are threatening to brew up a war inside. So the job was vacant. I applied. I am the Bricks Workshop Redband, starting on January 1 . Happy New Year! A new year and a new beginning: that's the plan at least. All I fervently want to do, Julie, is to keep my cerebellum busy. Ride my time. It won't be long before I'm released: this is what I endeavour to teach myself. And at the end of my time—what then? A dead five years. Five years of my transitional period between late teenage-hood and early adulthood—gone, all gone. Dust and breeze. Rain and filth. Five years of mould. So you'll do me this favour, won't you, Julie? Please don't write back; and save your money on train fares or petrol—I don't want to see you again. Not for a long, long time. Let me serve my sentence in peace. It's a favour. And I'll be sending a very similar letter to Mumsy, straight after this one. I am certain, if you ask her—if you really want her to—she will continue to support you with her granddaughter. Patrice is the only one she'll have and mothers, I think, do not ever stop being mothers; they do not wish to cease caring. Irrespective of how she might moan from time to time, she will take Patrice in the pushchair—to the park, to the shop, to the doctor, to JobCentre Plus. If I may, allow me a second favour. Don't cut Mumsy out of Patrice's life. Please. Goodbye, Julie. In this spirit of utter candour, I will go a step further. Truthfully, I don't know if I ever loved you; but I thought the world of you. I don't know what love really means, but if I can convince you of anything, allow me to convince you of this: the photograph of you on Ealing High Street, by the bookshop—that photograph got me through many a tricky night. I would stare at it for hours sometimes. But I don't anymore. And I don't stare at the photo of you bathing Patrice in the kitchen sink either. I loved it then. I'm scared of it now. I'm scared of the outside world. People have told me that this might happen, even though I've still got a good chunk of my tariff left to ride. It's my fault, Julie. It's all my own fault. Don't blame yourself. Kiss Patrice goodbye for me, would you?

With my very best wishes.

Billy

Four.

There is no slow-motion commencement to the atrocities. Like flash fires leaping from one dry shrub to the next, the sounds of all-response alarms moves swiftly from Wing to Wing. The silence is detonated. Panic noise rises, swarms and swells. Then the screaming begins. Screaming and roars: the zoo sounds of squirming, writhing animals noticing the vipers in the grass that

are now making their moves. Takes seconds for me to understand what is happening. It is of course night, and the yoots are
banged up. Fights are not possible—neither fights between prisoners, nor fights between prisoners and screws. The only conflict on the menu is between a yoot and his cell. I am still at my
window. But the concept is meaningless: I am everywhere else
too. I'm with Dott in the ambulance; I am also in the prison
graveyard, where the ground is shivering, though not in response
to the evening's frigidity. No. There are pulses abroad. A single
pulse, rather—a magnified heartbeat, or so it seems at first. It's
probably in keeping that I'm walking the corridors on the ones
on Puppydog Wing: the corridors I have strolled for time as part
of my duties delivering reading matter. There are screws in a
panic, wondering what to do; wondering where to start. Not inside every cell, but inside quite a few, the prisoners are bumping
their heads on the walls, in unison. And it's a highly contagious
disease: the thumps are on the ones, but they are also upstairs, on
the twos—and inside many cells on the other Wings as well.

Bump! Bump! —Like a bass drum keeping time to the wick-
ed techno ghastliness of the sirens.

Radios beep into life— I can hear them on the waistbands
of screws outside my very own cell.

Papa Alpha doesn't know where to dispatch the response
units; everything's happening at once. Not that self-harming is
the extent of the insurrection. As foreheads split against bare
walls, or against nudey posters decorating bare walls, there are
other acts of mutiny inside Dellacotte Young Offenders this
night. Noise rises up, like a rocky sea mounting a wave-break.
Televisions are turned on to full blast; stereos too. In the cells to
my left and right, my next- doors flick on their radios, tuned to
staticky unborn channels. Full force ten transmission. Hot water taps are twisted to the max; steam rises—more steam, surely,

than even a night as chilly as this should encourage.

Bump! Bump! The headbanging continues.

I flit from corridor to corridor, from cell to cell, between one Wing and its neighbour—along familiar paths but now viewing yoots I haven't even clapped eyes on before: the ones Dott has got to and used. There are many more of them than I've had any reason to expect. So enthusiastic is one victim in his endeavours that between every butting of the wall, he takes the time to spread his own blood on the paint thereon. He has broken the front fence of his skull—chipped at it as he might do a wall itself, with a spoon, in an attempt at escape. But this is an escape: for Dott's disciples, it's an escape from themselves. To what? I have no idea. I have to turn away—fly away, rather—when the yoot, with one final collision, causes the flanks of his skull to crumble. Porridge-like brain starts to seep from the rift. At this point, unconvincingly dying, he starts to punch the brick instead. As the trend for mutilating one's forehead against a wall fizzles out as fast as it's sparked up, new acts of auto-terror become fashionable. CD cases are shattered against toilet cisterns; the resulting shards of plastic are used to gouge lines in flesh. Yoot on G Wing slashes himself a Chelsea Smile. Yoot on A Wing attempts a circumcision. More than one prisoner spikes himself up the fundament, blood leaking down into his shorts, running down his calves. It all comes to my senses with the force of a bad dream. Am I holding my breath or is there smoke in the air, making it hard for me to breathe? Both. I skate my eyesight left and right. There! Six cells to my right, and Sarson has managed to set fire to a pillowcase, using the fluid from an obliterated lighter. The flames catch; smoke reaches out of his cell via the only egress possible with the window closed: in the gaps around the door. I watch him for a moment—his expression neutral: this is simply something he needs to do—as he assists the conflagration with a cremation of the food products he hasn't yet eaten. The cup-a-soup packets catch quickly, the paper wrinkling like weather-beaten flesh. The cell is full of smoke, but the same smoke is also inside my own cell; it is difficult to get a good lungful of clean air. Like a man possessed Sarson whirls around the limited confines of his pad, searching for combustible fuel. He finds it in the shape of a book on gang warfare, a book called Solitary Fitness by Charles Bronson (the prisoner, not the actor), and the toilet roll he reels out in gluts of ten sheets at a time. I leave Sarson alone to his bonfire. If being occupied without pain is as close as we get to true happiness, then Sarson is happy. So is everyone. In the collected madness and brew, there is not—as far as I can see or can tell—so much as a hint of dissatisfaction. There are jobs to do. There are fires to light. There are cells to flood by blocking sinks with underpants and socks and leaving the taps running. Before long—within minutes, in fact—the corridors on the ones and the twos are slippery with water. Prisoners are applying their entire month's allocation of shower gel and shaving foam to this tide, the better to create a jacuzzi-like froth on the tiles for the screws to slip in. The flap on my door is whipped open. Eyes peer in to see what? A prisoner at his window, behaving. Why me? Why's he looking at me? Immediately I grasp I'm an easy target, here and now. Depleted and divided as the prison staff is—the resources stretched thin over eight Wings that have combusted into a unilateral forceful riot—the screws nonetheless have to be seen to be doing something. I'm doing nothing wrong; therefore he can bother me with clear conscience, earning his salary while doing fuck all. It pains me to do it. But I have to do something. I have to join in with the beef. Returning my attention to the window and my limited view, I hook my rig out from the slit in my boxers and take a piss up against the cell wall.

I'll see you later, Alfreth! the screw shouts above the noise.

Now the prisoners are shouting—shouting and screaming, roaring; some are laughing.

How long has this been going on? A matter of minutes? Or has a fingernail or two of time been clipped away? For sure, that smoke spread quickly; that water from other cells has appeared in my own cell fast enough. Maybe I've lost a few seconds, a few minutes; maybe I'm not scrutinising this as hard as I should be. The screws are taking action. But what are their alternatives, contradicting this tidal wave? All or nothing. They can either gang up on a prisoner, two or three per yoot, for health and safety purposes no doubt, and thrash the fucker purple until the message gets round that everyone's going to be getting a turn; or they can threaten until the squads arrive from other jails—which could take hours. Who can say what might happen in the next minute? They aquaplane and slide down drenched corridors, banging batons on metal doors and warning of long stretches in the Segregation Unit. But how many can fit in there?— especially, now, as the Seg itself seems to have joined the party. In particular because of my visit there, following my slap to Julie's face, I know that corridor of powerlessness; I can smell it now—a scent all of its own, even here among courtyards and paths of throttled ambition and pent-up testosterone. What is it? A scent of rage; the aroma of the untameable. The Seg holds the most dangerous. They will be our foot soldiers tonight—our front line. With screws like insects drunk on fermented filth, scurrying around, bumping into one another, there is no one calling the shots. Not quite yet. Two boys in the Seg swing a line. I don't know their names. I think they call one of them Jiffy; it's not important. When his next-door swings the twisted-up bedsheet from the window, it takes Jiffy—let's call him Jiffy—three attempts to catch it, with the bars on the window making it possible for only his hand up to the wrist to reach through. The line is weighted with a lasso through the handle of a full and boiling kettle. Logic dictates Jiffy won't be able to pull the kettle through the bars, but he tries to do so anyway. His fingers and wrist are rubbed raw on the flaking paint of the bars. He gives up trying. Instead, he unties the kettle—it falls to the ground with a heavy splat of water spilling out—and he pulls the bedsheet inside. The sheet is barely long enough for both Jiffy and his provider to tie themselves nooses. I leave the scene of their compacted suicide—a kind of tug-of-war—and move towards the court of law at the end of the corridor, and back again. Reinforcements are arriving. Most I hear, but some I see—flatfooting it across the yards between Wings. This is full- scale riot; this is what screws think they want, until it bites them on the face. I've never been there, so I can't see it now, but I believe the Control Room is empty; the night staff have left their posts, I reckon, apart from someone, anyone, who'll be needed to man the phones. The Gate Staff, a similar story. In due course a van will pull up to the front gate and honk its horn; a fire engine or two will show its presence. Given the state of the emergency, even the prison Governors will be woken up at home and will be fiddling with socks and braces, de-icing the windscreen on the car, forming a strategy. Someone will have to be on the Main Gate to let these vehicles and people in; but other than that someone, all available staff are on call to attend the uprising. Problem is, nothing's been prioritised. How can it be? Every act of rebellion looks the same, Wing to Wing. The homogeneity striven for by the prison has finally been attained, I think; all it's taken to achieve it is the effort of spontaneous and simultaneous destruction. The hullaballoo is astonishing. Music is blaring, cross- feeding, distorting the very air—the smoky air. Second, third, fourth, fifth and six fires have been set on my corridor on my Wing alone. I cannot count how many blazes are being fed, but I can tell you a popular source: the physics of lighter plus bogroll. One popular method is to unroll the entire supply; set it up. Watch it burn! Once the flames have caught on, feed it more, feed it your stash of dried rice and desiccated noodles, and the packets they came in. One lad on B Wing seems to have been saving his loo rolls for this very explosion of activity. He has unravelled all four of them in a spiralling circle around his cell, over the hill and dale of his desk, can and bed; when he sets fire to the paper it makes for pretty patterns, in the middle of which he stands, tossing in chunks of stale cheese crackers as though he's feeding birds in the park. The birds that live outside—the ducks—are fighting among themselves, confused by the din, their body clocks shocked, breathing smoke from the cells where windows have been left open—or opened for the occasion. They cackle at one another, laughing at how silly we all are. I must do something myself. In the midst of hysteria such as this, compliance with the general order of things can only be regarded as suspicious. My contribution is lightweight, but it will do: I flood my cell. Hardly original, but I'm in no mood to cast myself to the flames—not yet at least. As I say, who knows what will happen a minute from now? Who knows how I'll feel? So I block the plughole using The Murder of Roger Ackroyd; I turn on the taps—full pelt—and watch the tide rise, thinking back (a genuine memory) to that time in '99 when we had the solar eclipse and I stood outside the Language School on Acton High Street, watching the dogs go mad and chase their tails, whining; when the tramps outside the supermarket were stunned into rare silence and momentary sobriety. How the air dimmed. And how it's dimming now! The paradox is, already it's night, and lights have come on since the troubles began; all the same, it's as though a thin veil has been drawn over my vision. Can't only be the effects of smoke, can it? I don't know. My breathing is fast and heavy. Claustrophobia is something most prisoners lose all comprehension of, oh a week or so into a sentence, but it returns to me now: that pinching feeling at the top of my chest. It's a feeling I know I might experience if my life is suddenly dependent on something. It's similar but sharper to how I feel on being doused with petrol, then threatened with ignition. There are prisoners, prison-wide, now sacrificing their flesh to rising flames, but I'm not about to be one of them. I have too much to do. Too much to do I can't do! That's what's frustrating. I run the length—some length!— of my cell, colliding with metal door, crashing into wall. Before long the same short journey requires skidding, rather than striding; my floor is sopping. The screws have no alternatives—or this is what they'll argue later on. Where personnel is at hand, they form duets and choose cells at random. Hamfisted, they go in; they use what they've got—batons and panic-fuelled indignation—to stop whatever that prisoner happens to be doing. Even if what he's doing is nothing more than shouting and shaking the window bars like a monkey in its cage. In fact, these are the simplest victories. Nothing says Shut up! more effectively than the round end of a baton in sharp concussion with a set of teeth. Where pieces of sharp plastic have failed to pierce skin—where resistance has been high, perhaps, to the waves rolling round the nick—the blood flow is still high. Mouths and gums leaking blood as part of the donation. My door is opened. I've been aware that this will happen for the last few seconds: I'm a Redband, a good boy, and I don't cause trouble. Therefore, in a stampede like this, I'm gonna be an early target, as I say. Two screws looking for something to do while the wilder cats play solo games of self- terrorisation. I try to protest that I don't want no trouble, but the words come out of my mouth in a tongue that's not my own. The air is gluey and harsh with wafting smoke, with mist— with the porky and sweet smell of barbecuing meat. The screws look from my face to my exposed dick. Decide what I've shown them is good enough for a kicking—I will have resisted something in the reports to follow, if they are written—and the air dims again; light is draining. The noise level rising yet higher. Tables overturned, Wing on Wing; they are mercilessly kicked, either for the pleasure inherent in destruction itself, or to produce some kindling to burn. In more than one cell, prisoners are using their desks and tables as launching pads: they are jumping from them—tuck up your knees!—and crashing down onto their sinks, to break them from the wall. After repeated efforts, some sinks succumb to the inevitable— as surely as I must—and they fragment in dirty great chunks, with spears of porcelain garrotting through ankle bones and shins; with water jets shooting off insanely, pipes busted and ruptured. Screw Jones and Screw Oates are my friendly antagonists tonight.

Five.

Dear William,

It breaks my heart that you don't want to see me until you get out, and I have no choice but to respect your wishes—but I wish I could respect your reasons too. Then again, how can I respect reasons when none are offered? I have stuck by you through thick and thicker. You have hurt me more than one boy has ever hurt his mother, I think. You should know this. Not because I want to make you feel bad, although I probably will, and I'll probably regret sending this letter as soon as I've put it in the pillar box; but because I want to make you feel good as well. Are you confused? I am. I suppose what I mean is this: if my staying away helps you in some small fashion then a mother's love for her offspring compels me to act in the way you wish, as stinging to my heart as it is. I know you're a good boy, William, deep down—and I know that one day you'll want to come back to me and to the sisters who love you. I don't know when—I wish I did—but I am confident that you are working your way through some sort of crisis. If my absence is a torch through that darkness then at least I'm still of use. That's the positive statement I can make about my own state of mind. Forgive me if it sounds cold. There is not a lot of heat in my heart right now. You doused it when you called me and told me to stay away. If I am as you say, a reminder of all the things you haven't got anymore, then pardon me for not stabbing someone in the arm. I can't be part of your world, son, because I don't understand it. I tried my best for you. I don't know where I went wrong. I didn't go wrong anywhere, you'll say—you've said it before. But William, I did. I did go wrong with you. Because you were never the same after your father left, when you were tiny. Who else can I blame but myself? And don't tell me not to blame anyone—every action is a result that has someone to blame, like it or lump it. Julie was frightened by your most recent—and it seems, final—letter. She asked me if she was reading something in code. She asked me if there was something she was missing between the lines. She couldn't believe that you could be so uncaring towards her and Patrice, and frankly, son, neither can I, but I told her—all you can do is wait for him to come round. You will come round, won't you? Please don't tell us you're abandoning us. I know you think Julie let you down but surely your daughter hasn't. She's an innocent in all of this. Don't leave her, son. It's not fair on you or her.

Seventy-two hours have elapsed. I couldn't continue right there and then: I was crying. I've been crying for three solid days. Again, I don't want to make you guilty, frustrated, sad or inadequate in any way; but I don't want you to feel mean and powerful either. I am not only crying for you—I'm crying for the fragility of things. One phone call—one single, five-minute phone call and you have knocked over the house of cards I've been building on our behalf since you were sent down. That's all it took. Which means, let's be honest, it was never entirely secure in the first place. If I want you to feel anything, feel love. Feel love for Patrice, feel love for your mother, and feel love for the mother of your child. She has the right to a life. And if your letter set her free in one way to explore her own decisions, it was so empty of the right things to say that it's built her a new type of prison—Category A—one with a crèche. Your daughter is in the next cell along, and she hasn't even learned how to breathe properly. Picture that. I hope it does some good, however harsh I have made it sound. Julie can't help loving who she loves any better than Patrice can and will. Or any better than I can. And I do love you, Willy. I suppose all of that—lecture over—is a kind of preamble to something I wanted very much to talk about, especially if this is going to be our last correspondence—hopefully, though, only our last for a while. There is one more thing to say. I suppose this is a sort of introduction. Yesterday, for the first time, I met Bailey. Or rather, I met a man named Bailey as Bailey. I have of course met him before; so have you. But he had a different name then, and it was a long time ago. The truth is, William, even when I was picking Patrice up one time and Julie sat me down and said she had a new man in her life, I was glad. I'm sorry, but I was. A child needs a father figure as well, and I thought—well, I thought it fit nicely, Bailey showing up when her chips were down. Offering help and a strong arm. But I didn't meet him, and why should the name have meant anything? I've never met anyone called Bailey. I supported Julie's decision, knowing it would hurt you. You were angry when he and Julie emptied your savings account. Naturally you were. I'm too long in the tooth, I think— and this game has lasted for too many years—for me to feel anything but dread at the thought of asking you were you got £85,000 from at your age. So I won't. I don't want to know. But I want to tell you this. He didn't steal it from you, Willy. Don't ask me how he and Julie drained your account, but they did, and Julie was telling the truth: Bailey was using the capital as investment. I had it all back yesterday—a cheque with my name on it, for me to look after it for you. He returned every penny, Bailey did. But I hardly even noticed the cheque when he brought it to the front door. It was like, do you remember when you were a boy? You loved your chocolate. But you didn't eat it in a normal sort of way. Remember? You used to take the bar from the wrapper and put the wrapper in the bin. Then you'd start eating it from the middle—a great big bite, severing the two halves from each other. Then you nibbled at each of the remaining pieces—one bite here, one bite there. It was a bit like that, or it seems that way now. Shock was the only thing calling me when I saw Bailey's face, but something had taken a bite out of my time. Crunch! The last two decades, munched away. Only a before and after left Bye-bye! I didn't even recognise him at first. If you take something out of context, it's difficult to see it for what it is. And I hadn't even thought about your father—not properly—for ten or twelve years. Yet here he was, on the landing outside the flat, pressing the doorbell that doesn't work and then using his knuckles to rap on the wood. He is thinner and takes up less space in real life than he does in my uncommon thoughts of him. Withered. Is that the word? His face had all but caved in on itself and he sucked on a set of false teeth for the few minutes he was with me. Yet no time had passed, it seemed— not once I'd quickly got used to his new appearance. Can I describe the emotions, other than the shock I mentioned above? I don't think I can. I thought of the time he left us, which led to that trouble I got myself—and us—into; my blood thinned. Then I thought of how he used to make me laugh; my heart leaped up. What else could I do? I used sarcasm.

'Did you get lost?' I asked him. 'Or was the shop a long way away?'

'Hello, Sylvia,' he said. 'Good to see you again. I have something.'

'Yeah—a nerve,' I said. 'You have a big fucking nerve.'

Pardon my French, Willy, but I was stunned, distressed, elated, I don't know what else. Here he was, on our doorstep, not carrying a bag—that was one good thing, at least he didn't expect to be invited to stay—but pulling from the back pocket of his jeans a piece of paper. As it turned out, a cheque; but I wasn't finished dishing out the recriminations yet. I'd been storing them for a long time, as you can imagine; providing a piece of paper wasn't about to dampen embers inside me that suddenly had been fanned into flames.

'Where you been?'

'Here and there.'

'What you been doing?'

'This and that.'

He wasn't giving anything away, not at first. What else could I do? I did what the British do in times of crisis: I talked about the kettle.

'I'm just brewing up,' I told him. 'Would you like one?'

The smile he gave me was yellower than it was when he left, but no less charming. Is this too much information? It probably is, but I want you to understand that once you let someone into your heart it's impossible to free them completely. You might think you've let them go, but it's like when you break a glass or a mug by accident: you're forever finding miniscule shards on the linoleum. And on that subject, William, try your best to give Julie away but I bet you can't. And you definitely won't be able to give away Patrice. You're a good boy. And it seems, despite what I thought, I didn't give away your father.

'Come in, Harvey,' I said. 'Welcome back.' I walked away.

He entered the flat, saying, 'Bailey, Sylv. It's Bailey now.'

'Why?' I turned to look over my shoulder.

'Bit of bother,' was how he put it. 'New start and all that.'

I was fairly decided on what he meant. 'How long you been inside?'

I took hold of a dishcloth and removed the old kettle from the gas; the handle was scorching. I poured boiling water into the cup I'd prepared: milk and teabag, two spoonfuls of sugar.

'You can have this one, Bailey.'

'Thanks.'

Standing in the doorway, he seemed awkward, ill-at-ease.

'I like what you've done to the place,' he said.

'You haven't answered my question.'

Frustration—maybe fear—was making me stab his teabag with my spoon, again and again, even though the tea had brewed quickly and the liquid was the brown of shoe polish.

'Okay. Three stretches,' he said. 'Six months. Eighteen months. Three years. Do you want to know for what?'

'We might as well start with your war stories.'

'Nothing serious. Promise. Burglary, burglary, aggravated burglary. The last one I was coerced into it; I owed a man a favour.'

I interrupted him. 'I've changed my mind. I don't want to hear your war stories. What are you doing here, Harvey? Why now? If you haven't been able to find the time to call or write since you left, why now?'

'I'd like to see the kids,' he tells me.

'Well, that ain't gonna happen!'

I started to prepare a cup for myself, and I swear to you, William—even now I hadn't put two and two together. I knew that Julie had a fella called Bailey, and now, here was Bailey. I'm so stupid, I was in a kind of trauma, but I just didn't think of them as being the same person. I did a few minutes later, but first we had a row to get through. I won't bore you with the details, but in a nutshell he wants to see if he can try to be part of your lives again. He's mended his ways. My guess is, he's penniless, possibly homeless, and he needs a permanent address in order to claim benefits; but you'll forgive me for being catty and mean, I hope. I told him I'd speak to your sisters about it first, and I said that when it comes to you—to you, Willy—his timing couldn't possibly be any worse. I showed him the frigid letter you wrote me—you wrote your mother. He was perplexed. He knew you were in prison, of course, but he didn't understand this new resolution of yours, not to see anyone. He said that if he'd been allowed to choose he would have seen us every day. I told him I doubted it. Most likely you'll be angry that I even took place in a conversation like this. Sorry. If you're angry—sorry. I know you don't need advice from your dad at this late stage, but he really has acted to help you. What he says is, he found out stories about you, most of them local (and I didn't even know he was still in the area), but occasionally further afield. It's a bit late in the day for a guilt trip, I told him but he didn't smile. Late or not late, he said to me, that's what I'm wearing. He got in touch with Julie in order to help with the baby. This is what he thought would be the hard part, but after he'd shown her the photographs I didn't realise he would have kept—you know the picture of us all by the Christmas tree that Ronald Dott from downstairs took one Christmas morning when you were still in nappies? that really cute one? Julie believed your father's claims. Even felt sorry for him. She soothed his bleeding heart, the poor lamb and she tells me that he was a good 'father' to Patrice. Julie's family were only too happy to have someone else on board—but Julie was working up to the part where she told them he was actually your dad and a good deal older than she was. Not that there was ever a relationship there. Julie kept it secret from everyone, including me. I can't help feeling disappointed about that but life goes on. I think I can see her point. I would have probably had a few words to say on the subject of your father turning up out of the blue and demanding access—not to you or your sisters, but to your daughter. All things balanced, Julie did the right thing, I am sure of it. What your father needed the money for—what exactly this investment happens to be—I have no idea. To be frank, I doubt any investment exists. Do you know what I think? When we finished our cups of tea, and I was silently willing him to leave because the last hour had been too stressful, that was when he attempted again to palm the cheque off on me. I didn't even need him to explain what it was or where it came from. I'm not sure I said thank you. I was washing around in my theories, William. The overriding one is this: In addition to proving, as I say late in the day, there he does in fact have a modicum of parenting skills, I think your father wanted to prove he could also be trusted with money. The clear implication, of course, is that he believes Julie cannot—cannot be trusted with money. Or not with your money anyway. So he talked her into transferring it to his account. How hard could that have been, these days, with phone banking? Internet banking? She would have provided him with any codes or passwords he needed—say what you think about your skills as a ghetto boy, William, but you always were sloppy when it comes to matters of personal finance. I think your father believed that it was a matter of time before Julie dipped into your account anyway, and he was trying to protect you. That's what I think. He let it get a few bob's worth of interest in his own account—maybe—but he didn't steal it from you. He has given it to me for safe keeping. You can have it upon release—so in spite of what I've written above, you will have to see me after all. Hard lines. I'm your mother and you don't lose me so easily. Bailey drives a van now. He has an income. He is living locally, and swears he is going straight. I think prison shat him up worse than it has for you, Willy—pardon my French again. He's too old, he feels, to lose even more time in a cell. And if I've got my facts right, if he does go away for a crime related to those he was convicted of (let's forget the ones he probably got away with), isn't it a case, these days, of three strikes and you're out? He might go to prison for a long, long time. He's trying not to do that, I believe. Will I see him again? That's impossible to say. He claimed to have no land-line phone number and said he'd forgotten his mobile number too. Should I be so sceptical? It's hard not to be, really it is. Bailey was even shady about where he was living—a mate's settee for now, a deposit down on a bedsit for the new year, was the best explanation I could pluck out of the man—so I didn't push any harder. When he left I looked over the balcony at both ends of the flat, to see if he climbed into a white van. He headed off on foot. Now you know. Your money is safe, unless Bailey has creamed off a few pounds for his expenses. Either way, the numbers on the cheque read: £85,104. You can be the judge who says if anything is missing or not. Just rest assured that when you get released, you have here the sort of nest-egg that most people—definitely round these parts—never see in their lives. This has been a long letter; but I have been a long Mum. What I mean is, I've been a Mum for a long time. Next birthday I will be forty. I'm not looking forward to it: you were still be in prison. What I wouldn't give to have you home for a weekend—that weekend—to cut the cake and kiss me happy birthday, with your sisters nearby in the room. To be a family again. But barring a miracle overturning of justice—an appeal against the verdict of godlike proportions, Willy—I'll be here and you'll be there. I'll be waiting.

Love and God bless you—

Mumsy xxx

Six.

Is this the first time my two consciousnesses have fully merged? Is this the first time my two selves have been aware of the other? Have I mingled as surely as hot soup and cream, or am I still closer to the never-the-twain style of oil and water? Oil and water, at any rate, is what I see. It's what I smell as well as I am lowered, a rope around my waist, by a squad of fellow prisoners, up above me, still serving their time but wishing me well for the future. My sentence has been concluded; in this desert reality I am leaving the ship, my time spent, and in jerky motions I am heading down towards the rowboat. I can't see myself. There is no third person, omniscient pair of eyes I can use to view how badly or well my body appears. I feel strong. I know that much. As I take my seat in the boat, the muscles I've used for years to row a ship that never moves—these muscles sigh and relax. I won't be needing them in the short term. What I need is a drink of water. I'll do anything for water, I think as the computer registers the extra weight, my weight, and sets off back in the direction of the shore and the township. My welcoming committee consists of a single person, dressed in black from head to toe, the hood obscuring his face included. When he looks up from his inspection of the oil- smiles on the sand by his feet, I can see his face, weathered and bruised but not old. He looks about thirty. It is Noor. He sports a largely black beard, in which zigzag filaments of the purest white hair. The beard stretches down to his clavicle.

Welcome back, he bids me.

Bids me warmly? Enthusiastically? Not a bit of it, no. Noor is here on duty, nothing but; to add to this air of non-committal there is something ill-at-ease about the man, the hood serving only to support my contention he doesn't wish to be recognised.

What language are we speaking? It has not crossed my mind to question our mutual understanding in this desert landscape—it's only my memory—yes, memory!—of the screws' faces in my cell when I'm speaking in tongues that makes me ponder now. In the language we speak I say:

I need to drink water.

Don't we all? I have money. But you'll have to buy it yourself and bring it out. There's not a bar I can enter in Umma where someone won't see me.

See you? Anyone can see you! You mean recognise you.

Angrily Noor counters with: I know what I mean! To some people I'm invisible. They know I've been on the Leper Island. That makes me invisible.

Is that where you went? When you got off the ship.

Noor nods his head; the hood wriggles back on his hairless scalp a few centimetres; Noor wastes no time in rearranging his attire.

Come! he says.

Where are we going? I ask him, the muscles that relaxed now tensing up again. The question hangs in the air as Noor turns and walks away.

To get you a drink, first, he replies over his shoulder.

Then to the desert. Where else would we be going?

With my awareness of all that's been said inside the walls of Dellacotte YOI, I am able to frame the next thought with succinctness.

Am I dead again?

But call him Dott or call him Noor, the evasiveness is ever present.

Only if you want to be, he says. Come on, walk faster!

We stop at a ramshackle bar. Outside, a rotund European-looking woman is breastfeeding her son. Or a boy at any rate.

Reminiscences tell me not to take too much for granted, to take anything at face value.

Noor hands me a warped copper coin, the shape of a fifty pence but lighter in the palm.

Get me one as well, he says. Be quick.

I need something to eat.

I have food.

Where?

With the horses.

Which are where?

In the stable.

Christ, Dott. Which is where? I ask, exasperatedly, pulling on a door that feels like it's about to fall off its hinges.

Close by. Don't' worry: I didn't steal them.

How do you get them then?

Worked for them. I'll explain on the way!

This is the extent of my rehabilitation, my integration back into society: a long drink of water in a busy but not packed bar that smells of peanuts, then a walk outside, the shirt I've been given glued with perspiration to my spine, and a terse review of my welcome-home repast:

You took your fucking time.

That's King Billy to you, I want to say. Have I said it somewhere before? I'm not sure. All I know is, there doesn't seem to be much love lost between Dott/Noor and me at this instant. I tell myself he's nervous. He has worked as a blacksmith's apprentice for six months. He has busted toil for no peas, rudeboy. The blacksmith asks if he's a leper; he tells man no—but he's been on the island. Why's he been? Hiding. Wanted. Some blackguards are after his gizzard in a pie. Why, what's he done? He's had sex with a woman and left her pregnant. Not the end of the world, the blacksmith opines. The husband doesn't agree with you, Dott tells him. The horses are on loan—and they're not the most spritely of creatures. Dott has told the blacksmith, who waves us off (cutely) with a red-hot poker in his mittened hand, standing beside an anvil and sweating cobs. Not far out of ear-shot I say to Dott:

These horses'll never make it.

I made it on foot the last time. With a boy to look after.

These horses'll never make it, I repeat. He won't see 'em again.

Dott shrugs his shoulders and flips back his hood. Or us, he says, kicking the sides of his steed with sandaled feet.

The horse bolts. Mine follows suit. The difference is, Dott appears to be a competent rider. Me, apart from a bicycle when I'm young and the occasional stolen motorbike I've crashed while joyriding, me I've never steered anything other than cars I've driven without a licence or insurance. Cars are easier than horses (though not as difficult as motorbikes). Takes some breath-catching lurches and near-falls before I learn to ride the animal's rhythm. Takes skill. The township deliquesces in haze. By looking in glimpses over my shoulder I am able to see it first retreat, then dissolve, then get swallowed up by the yellow and white ground. The patches of sand thicken—stitch together—carpet outwards, the desert proper is what we're in, and it hasn't taken long at all. The horses' hooves pound, their nostrils dilate; the sand is harder to negotiate than the chipped, cracked, lifeless, dry earth. For the riders, too. I for one feel my mount's heart- meant endeavours and tribulations. I am breathing as hard as the stallion is, I reck-on. The sand looks silvery in some directions, from some angles; time is passing, taking its toll on man and beast.

O my days!

The journey takes place in real time, which comes as an unpleasant surprise. What have I been expecting? Spiritual transportation? Well, yeah, I suppose I have. This riding lark's for the birds, that's for sure. Heat from the horse's back is corrosive on my inner thighs, chaffing away at the underhang of my midriff travel bag. My balls are going crazy with jolts of pain.

I need to rest up! I call to Dott.

No time!

What's the hurry fuck's sake? Where's the fire?

Night soon! Dott shouts—he is some ten metres ahead. Rest then!

Soon is no exaggeration—no palliative measure. Desert twilight does not really exist: as with cows sensing rain, the horses' moods change abruptly as they foresee the end of their working day. At first I regard their slowing down as no more than a sign of fatigue, and fair enough; they've charged hard, they've earned their oats. But it's something more instinctive and raw. It's their body clock—it's their telepathy with one another that causes them to kill their strides from gallop to canter to trot. They stop. Dott accepts defeat, dismounts and by flipping open his horse's panniers he wordlessly prepares to camp out for the night. It falls dark and cools down in minutes. Opening my own horse's panniers—it's as close to receiving a birthday or Christmas present as I'm likely to experience anytime soon. Dott has been thorough. There is food in brown paper; there are plastic bottles of water. There's a thick woollen sweater that smells rather too much like its original source for my liking, but which I don gratefully all the same.

Where are you going to tie the horses? I ask Dott.

Any suggestions? he answers me with cool sarcasm.

It doesn't matter that the air is bruising up; I have seen the immediate vistas when the light's good, and I know there are no trees to be used as hitching posts.

What if they run away? I continue.

Then we walk. The exercise'll do us good.

Why is he still behaving in such an offhand fashion? I wonder. I've not said or done anything wrong. I've not said or done much of anything at all. Surely the nervousness he felt back in Umma has dispersed. I check myself. No. This is more than a big deal, I have to remind a portion of my own brain. This is literally a matter of life or death—for him. And for me? The question stings and makes my nose sneeze.

Hope you're not catching a cold, he tells me—the first time he's initiated a snippet of discourse since he met me at the water's edge.

Allergic to wool innit, I lie.

I should've brought you silk.

No, no, I'm not ungrateful, blood. Don't get it twisted.

Forget about it. We've got a few hours. Light the fire, would you?

A test of initiative, no doubt. Brain ticks. I recall what I can of TV survival programmes—celebrities in the wild, trying to kid us there's no film crew around to bail them out of a bind. Collect wood; scrape stones together for a spark to work on something flammable. As I look for suitable fuel and a means to ignite it, Dott asks me with that petulant voice of his:

Where you going?

I explain my actions.

His response is not exactly friendly. Fucking hell, Billy, he says, this ain't The Flintstones. Look in my saddlebag. Lighters and slow coal.

Allow it.

I feel stupid. Brain ticks, but not fast enough, it seems. In fact, brain feels bogged down in a mire that's like jetlag or flu drowse. I can't stand the thought of Dott winning this not-even-argument.

Why we lighting a fire, I ask him, if we're only staying here a couple hours?

You won't need to ask why once your body's cooled down from the ride, he tells me. Forget what you can of the hills around Dellacotte. That's not cold. The desert is where winters come to learn about cold.

Nice image, I give him. Seriously. There's something poetic about that.

I collect rocks anyway, despite the fact Dott's twitted me for so dumb an idea: we need a cradle to put the coal on before I light it. It won't burn properly on the sand, or that's my opinion at least. Collecting rocks for this ad hoc barbecue, I also pick up dried pieces of brush, a few twigs, and the dried-out remains of what I think was a desert fox. If I haven't made up that species. What is left of its skin (the organs are punctured, eaten away—resembling nothing more than sun- dried tomatoes in olive oil) burns adequately. The food Dott's brought is lamb in pitta bread. Neither of us waits to heat up the meal in the flames; we are starving marvin. We are hank. And lamb I haven't tasted in time. I tell him it's good.

You know what I could murder for? I ask him.

He laughs—the first time he's laughed, laughed properly as opposed to sardonically, as I remember, since before the riots kicked off in the nick—and says:

Me! Me I hope, cuz!

Apart from that. Man can kill for a beer.

In the dancing firelight Dott's face comes over straight as apologetic. No can do, he tells me. Couldn't think of everything.

No, you're blessed. Not a criticism, blood. Just an observation.

Dott falls silent as the dunes. We eat our meals.

I wonder what creatures are out there tonight? he thinks aloud, finally.

You should know, cuz.

Why?

You been here before!

So've you! Besides, I don't have any of that—either going there or coming back—in the old memory bank, Dott says.

What happened to it?

Wiped. Too much shit in the intervening years, he answers.

Allow it. How long are we travelling, Dott?

Till we get there.

For fuck's sake, blood, why do you do that? Every time. Man's asking you an honest question. Why can't you just give me the solution point blank?

You're assuming I know things I don't know, Billy.

That's King Billy to you, I tell him, shuddering slightly with the warmth of déjà vu.

I fall silent. Wipe my greasy lips on my sleeve. Watch the horses doing not much of anything—unless you count horsey sniffles and horsey snoozes. I throw the brown paper the food came in onto the dying blaze.

What did you leave behind you? Dott asks quietly.

Chaos. You stuck it to 'em, Dott, I can't take that away from you.

Dott is shaking his head; his shadows stretch like ghosts morphing.

Not at the prison. In your life, he clarifies.

For the second time I say: You should know. You've been hanging off my leg like a lovesick turd for half my life!

I want to hear the words, Dott says, weirdly.

Taking stock in a moment like this is sobering, really. What have I left behind, bar nick existence? (I won't say nick life. That shit's not life. It's breathing and blood moves, but it ain't life.) Mumsy and my sisters, I tell him.

What are their names?

I'm indebted to one of the horses—I don't know which one—for breaking wind at this precise second, the better to grant me an extra second to rifle through the drawers and diaries of my head. It scares me a little—and will do so considerably more, I have no doubt—that the names don't come to me as eagerly as my own does. When you don't use a language, you lose a language; it's like any other skill. Gets rusty.

Their names are, Roberta and Justine.

What do they do? Dott wants to know.

I have to crawl back to one of Mumsy's visits, oh a long time ago—in the past, when I still had interest to show in anything.

Roberta works in a boutique. She gets ten per cent off her clothes, but they cost a fucking fortune in the first place, but she won't be told. Justine's at college: beauty therapy.

Dott nods. Not continuing the family business then? Crime.

That's only me, I say. The girls are good girls. Mum does her best.

Your old man's a one, though, innee, Billy?

Why am I nonplussed and agitated by this? Of course the cunt knows about Bailey. Cunt knows everything. This late in the day, fuck it won't surprise me much if Dott is Bailey. Two miserable, sad little doppelgangers.

He's had a madness or two, I concede, putting my head down.

Okay, I'll watch.

Watch for what? My voice is maybe a little too rattled.

I don't know. Snakes? Scorpions? Fucked if I know or remember. Maybe there are roaming carnivorous anteaters, Billy!

Allow it taking the piss.

Lions and tigers and bears, oh my. Dott's eyes as wide as all else. He smiles. Go on, seriously, Alfreth. Rest up. Three hours enough?

Should be.

Then it's my turn.

Fine.

Long as the sand hedgehogs don't bite my face off first.

I lie down on my hands, which are pressed together as if for prayer. I don't have my beads with me—they are not part of this world. But for the sake of healthy communion, I pray anyway. Pray to reach the end of this donnybrook of the nerves—of the soul, salts and tissues. This last chapter. Symmetrically I guess I dream of the prison. Not the prison ship. I dream of Dellacotte YOI. The fires have melted away the walls between cells; all eight Wings, plus the Seg, are ablaze, people waxing like candles; every Wing resembles a crematory pyre. Air shifts in cow's breath heat; haze warps the picture. Screaming everywhere. Screws on the ends of spears, being heated in the flames like marshmallows, by yoots who are too tough to die. I wake before I'm woken up. Dott doesn't know I've opened my eyes; I see him staring up into a flawlessly black sky. There are no stars. No moon. There's no weather. Other than what hasn't yet burned of the sacrificial lamb I tossed onto the fire—and which won't ignite now in the petering embers—there's no proof of anything else alive in the world. As the song says, it's just the two of us. And we can make it if we try.

Dott? I call out.

Can you feel it, Billy?

Your turn to nap.

I said, can you feel it? grinning broadly. Something's tickled him.

No. Feel what? I want to know.

It's working. I can feel it—I'm getting older again! God,

Billy.

Not God. *King Billy* is sufficient, I say again, not much appreciating for the once the awestruck tone my travelling companion's adopted.

It takes a few shakes of my head to knock the sleepiness from my senses. Not that I don't acknowledge this has probably been the best snooze I've had in a month.

Suddenly Dott is on his feet. Let's go, Billy! It's catching up on us!

My first thought is of desert animals, but up till now Dott has shown no more than an acerbic interest in what lives in the dunes; this isn't about wildlife, instinct tells me. Following Dott to where the horses are lying down, I demand of him the answer to the question of what's catching up on us.

Time, Billy, time! Come on!

You haven't slept!

I might never need to sleep again!

With which he boots his horse in the left flank; the animal whinnies and stretches up to its full height, its own companion copying the action.

We have to get to the roses first!

What about the rest of the food? I ask, pointing back towards the fire.

Fuck the food! Your belly full? Dott inquires brusquely.

For now. It won't be forever.

We won't be riding forever! We're close!

It took you weeks¸ Dott, the first time you went there, I protest.

But then I didn't know where I was going, he answers. I didn't have time chasing me down. I do now.

He mounts his horse in the sort of fluid motion I can only wish for. I clamber aboard my patient steed with all the grace I exhibit when lugging my frame onto a prison ship.

Which way are we going? I ask as Dott's horse takes off.

Which way, Billy? Dott shouts. Towards death, of course!

Seven.

Dear Bailey

If you've as much as half a brain in your head, and I think you must have because I've got my intelligence from somewhere in addition to Mum, you won't be in the least bit surprised to learn I could happily—quite happily—slap you purple, slap you blue. Let me count the reasons; in advance, let me count my excuses. I'll give myself an alibi. I'll plan it carefully. I'll find you one night when you are vulnerable, and I will strike you down for your crimes against the family you helped create. Does that sound irrational? I'm feeling irrational. When I got Mumsy's letter I experienced what I can only describe as a fit. I was dragged off to Health Care. Now I'm not saying categorically that my reaction was entirely the result of what Mum wrote, but to be blunt about it, it didn't help—not on top of the couple months I've just been through. I read it twice. I was halfway, roughly, through my third reading when my vision—it kind of overlapped and I was reading everything twice or not at all. The words did not make sense, and as for the sentences— forget it! No way, Jose! Then I started on a spastic seizure on the floor; I banged my head on the curve of the toilet bowl; I bit my lip open. And though it only lasted less than a minute, it left me exhausted and feeling sick, and next month, apparently, I'll be taken out of the prison to get a brain scan for signs of epilepsy. Define 'irony'. I've been trying to get out—out in physical body as opposed to spirit (don't ask)—for what seems like half a lifetime, and it takes the actions of a wasteman like you to wave the enchanted wand. Indirectly, granted, but it's the behaviour of Bailey that'll set me free for a day. Bailey? Well, I never knew you as Harvey so I'll stick to Bailey, at your request. Why not 'Dad'? You've got to be pulling my leg. That's a word you earn, mate—please don't think you're getting the key to the kingdom just yet. Am I being harsh? I do hope so. I intended to be harsh; if I'm failing in any way, do let me know—seriously. I want you to understand precisely how disgusted I am in your ethics and savoir-faire. Perhaps you'll visit. Why would I want you to visit, you may well ask. Number one reason—obviously!—is to give you that slap. I really will hit you, Bailey, when I see you—for what you did to the mother of your children, and for your cowardice. Don't for a second believe I'm exaggerating. You've had it coming for nearly twenty years so don't pretend you're in any way subjugated by my mysterious words and deeds. If ever you were a man of honour—which is in dispute, but let's give the notion the benefit of the doubt—then you will understand. The knock-on effect will be I'll not be permitted any visits in the immediate future—not after I slapped Julie that time for spending all my money, which I'll come on to shortly if I can sluice the bad taste from my mouth.

But both these things aside, I can't help it—I can't deny it. I would like you to visit me—which I assume means I've just killed any chances of you doing so—because I would sorely enjoy hearing your side of the story. Oh, and watching you squirm, just a little—if you've got a conscience, that is. See, we've met but we've never met. You've held me (presumably) but you've never held me. You've fed me (supposedly) but you've never fed me. Where were you when I didn't think I needed you but really did? Where were you? Inside? Like father like son? Yeah: well, a letter at any point would not have gone amiss. Maybe I'll send you one a day from now on, simply to make up for lost time. And to pester you with some of those pesky inquiries. Namely: I'd imagine it's none of my business to learn how much you were paid to leave

the family you began with my mother. But I'm going to ask anyway. I'm going to ask you because I am curious about the value
of human life, in your opinion. What's the going exchange rate?
What were the markets like back then, when I was scarcely out of
nappies and Mum was scarcely out of post-natal depression? Go
on—tell me. I'm genuinely curious, with no malice aforethought.
Or none that is obvious to me, writing this, at any rate. Look!
I've even got a smile on my face. My mirror hasn't seen one of
them for a while, and I don't expect it will see another one soon.
Shame you couldn't be here to share it with me. Did I ever once
offer you a smile, as a baby? Did you ever once offer one back?
I'm told I have a lovely smile. Very recently I heard tell from
Mumsy that you have a lovely smile too. As I say, like father.

How much was it worth? Describe it. Yes, I'm angry. Of
course I'm angry. At the very least you could have let me know
you were alive—not that I would have made any show of giving
a fuck either way. And by the by, don't give me shit about bad
language. Not at this late stage, mate. I'm a grown man now. I
will speak to you and to anyone else as I see fit. This is my time of
taking no nonsense. All right. If you won't be surprised to learn
I want to slap you, then you won't be surprised either to learn, I
need to thank you. O my days!—that is hard to confess. Thank
you? Thank you? You who drove something worse than a knife
into someone's arm—you who drove a circuit breaker between
the lobes of a good woman's fucking brain. But you have no way
of reminiscing on those days, have you? Because you weren't
there to view them. And I do mean view. Mum was like televi-
sion in the first few years I can go back to in my memory, so I
obviously don't include babyhood. Would you like a leaf through
the pages of that old magazine? Well, here is tonight's program-
ming. Four o'clock, see the kids home from school and start tea.
We do our homework—or rather, I don't do my homework, but I

pretend to do my homework. But what's this? What's this, Dad? Why's Mum given me a cup of hot white water? Silly Mummy! She's forgotten the teabag again! And the first couple of hundred times she did that were quite amusing. The next couple of hundred times she did that were not. Because that was when Mummy started to scream when you mentioned she was a silly Mummy and she had forgotten the teabag again. And that's why, after a while, you didn't mention that silly Mummy had crushed a stock-cube into the cup in place of sugar. Silly Mummy! That's why you simply looked at your sisters and assented with warm brown eyes and shallow nods to drink a quarter pint of gravy instead of a brew of tea. Because silly Mummy wasn't really silly Mummy anymore—silly Mummy was going away. Poorly Mummy was coming to take her place for a while. And poorly Mummy didn't like to wake up some mornings. And poorly Mummy didn't care which of us took the key to the flat on behalf of the three of us kids. And poorly Mummy forgot to boil the kettle and gave us cold tea. Poorly Mummy poured boiling water on our breakfast cereal instead of milk. Poorly Mummy forgot to go to the shops for food. Poorly Mummy got lots of letters that she tore in half without opening. Poorly Mummy was really rather poorly indeed, for a while. Of course, none of this is your fault, Bailey; none of your concern. She might have got sick if you'd stayed. Only this second's it occurred to me that maybe she was getting sick when you left. If that's the case, fuck me!—you really did bottle it, mate, didn't you? At the first sign of trouble, off you went. But I don't know if this is true, to be fair; and to repeat myself, it's none of your fault—not directly—or your concern. Perhaps (I have to accept this rumination) none of your vaguest interest. For which reason, I'll halt.

Bailey, this is the third attempt I've made at this letter. The other two I destroyed, though I've kept the occasional phrase in for good luck. If you think these words are harsh and they're uncomfortable to sit through—fuck me again! You should have been witness to the first two drafts. Make the piss in your bladder go cold, mate. And I'm not self-ignorant either. I've become a fresh master at reflective mores. It's entirely possible I'm simply showing off to get back at you. I admit that. Possible and frankly speaking likely. Realistic. A realistic assessment of current prevailing trends, as someone wise once said to me. He's gone now— dead and gone, or as good as, as far's I'm concerned. His name was Ostrich. I have stopped keeping track of my days, not on his advice exactly but following in his footsteps. It's easier that way. To sum up? My emotions are like horses in a race—a long race. Frustrated Little Nipper takes the lead, but here comes Curiosity Kills the Cat; pulling up fast is Eyeblinding Rage—and the dark horse, Unexpectation. You are truly the jockey on my Unexpectation. I don't know what you'll do next.

Thanking you for returning my money is all but bar the warmest I can be.

Better late than never, I suppose—
Billy

Eight.

There's a certain maniac grace as we put the horses through their paces, their hooves kicking up scatterings of black, then purple, then light grey sand. As swiftly as night descends in the desert, the daylight rears its head; the sand turns a buttery yellow and then white. It's now that I puzzle— clinging on for dear life— whether we're still in real time or not. Are things speeding up? Can the desert have lost patience with darkness so quickly? Has it run out of that cold void? With no better tactic than rough-and-ready sadism at my disposal, I heel the horse's flanks until it's on a parallel line with Dott's own vehicle. There is dust in the air; it enters my mouth as I shout my throat dry and sore.

What do you mean, Dott?

It was enough, Billy! What I did in the prison: it was enough! Enough for what?

To spur us on, Billy! Can't you feel it? Time's behind us! Time's pushing us towards the roses and the Amnesia Trees! Can you imagine these horses going this fast twelve hours ago?

No!

It's shoving us in the right direction, Alfreth! Hold tighter! It's going to be like riding a wave! Do you surf? Dott shouts.

No! I repeat.

Well, it's never too late to learn a new skill, Billy!

What I feel is pressure—pressure on my back—and in the way the horse is leaning forward, I'm certain the animal can feel it too, on its rump. Dott's ploy seems to be working. Though it's hard to believe I'm here, I can't doubt the evidence of my own eyes, ears and taste, can I? The evil Dott's done—the savagery, the senseless disregard for life—this has been his harvest. He's sold it all for a trip back into his past, to get older; but a bonus has materialised, in the shape of a helping hand from time it-self—to get us to the right spot, unerring in our direction, fleet of foot and blank of mind. A journey that should take a week on horseback takes no more than a further fourteen hours, I reck-on—fourteen hours of Dellacotte time, which in itself is not the same as time on road. How many days have we travelled in old money? No more than two by the standards of the desert, but out of dream time?—out of dead time? How long have these horses' hearts pounded on their final tour of duty?

O my days! I whisper when it comes in sight.

But that's as close as we're getting on horseback. Without warning, the animals spook and nag; the halts they draw to are so extreme that Dott is tossed forward, over his animal's head; he executes a perfect ten somersault and even lands on his feet—until the hours of riding remind him he hasn't been using his legs to stand up for a while. His thighs weaken. He wobbles, holds both hands out to hold on to something to stop himself falling—there's nothing to catch—and momentum sends him flying forwards. He ends up a blob of black garments. My own dismount is not much more glorious. I slide and twist off the horse's right side; pull a muscle in the small of my back. I swear the air indigo. I punch the horse's neck; the legs rear up but the animal isn't spoiling for a rumble. The horse runs away, back in the direction we've come from, closely hunted by Dott's own pony. And then, Dott and I—we're alone in the world. I can't think of anything sensible to say. The only thing that might work is a blunt streak of irony I seem to have caught from my co-traveller, like a rash.

You need to get yourself a gardener, I say, half under my breath.

Isn't it stunning? he asks, walking closer.

Well, stunning ain't the word I'd use; but there is no doubting the shock value of what's there before our eyes. What have I actually expected? True it is, no signs of life should be here at all; but I've anticipated something more glamorous than this approximately twenty metre-wide patch of overgrown grass, among which curl spiky ropes of rose stalks; a handful of trees no taller than I am have sprouted randomly here and there. To be frank, it's a mess. If Mumsy sees the communal gardens behind the flat get to this state, she goes bugshit, blood; she's on the phone complaining to the Estates Committee every other day until the scruffy shit's sorted.

Not exactly the Garden of Eden, I say to Dott.

I never said it was the Garden of Eden, Billy-Boy, Dott replies, stepping on to the grass and taking a deep breath.

Is it my imagination? As I follow Dott onto the oasis, I can

smell something—something more than the rare scents of vegetation. Dott's occasion does not last long; the moment passes. He
even goes so far as to snap his fingers, as if to wake himself from
a reverie; all of a sudden he's business again, striding further into
the oasis, his head snapping from left to right. What's he looking
for? The original rose, I assume. The air is thicker as soon as I
join Dott on the grass. To adjust to the shift in pressure, it takes
my lungs a few seconds of heavy toil. When Dott calls to me to
keep up I can't shout what I want to, which is simply a declara-
tion that I can't breathe. It's as though I've been running through
rain. All the same, I chase Dott. As far as vegetation is concerned,
there's not much to slow me down; actually, it's easier than trudg-
ing through sand. He is sitting, facing one of the gnarled trees;
a string of sharp vines is attempting its ascent. A single white
rose—unhealthy-looking—is at the end of the stalk.

This is it, he says.

I can't help but be disenchanted. I come from that? I ask.

Quickly, Billy!

What do you want me to do?

Come closer. Sit down with me.

I do as he asks. Cross-legged, he first and then I lean forward, embracing the tree like a conservationist, and with it the
barbs of the rose's stalk. One of them pricks the skin on my right
shoulder; blood weeps out. This is stupid, I'm telling myself—but
I can sense whatever's been following us, now getting closer. It's
tracked us down. It's followed us from the carnage in the prison,
through the membrane, to the desert (*Am I dead now?* I ask myself for the umpteenth time), and it's besieging the oasis of grass
and stunted flora. I don't need to look back over my shoulder
to see there is no more a vista of sand dunes. The oasis, sur-
rounded by a caul of smoke, is mist and streaks of blood flying
through the curtain like lightning crackling. I'm scared, I'll admit

it. Every month—every minute, every second—of fear I've en-
dured, they come back to me now in one solid and breath-taking
deposit. Doesn't matter what the temperature is like out in the
desert: suddenly I'm sweating like a mule, but I'm freezing cold.
We should have drunk something before this; I feel light-headed
and nauseous. A glance to my right shows me Dott has closed
his eyes. His lips move silently—a prayer or a mantra—and the
only sound I hear is that of our hearts, both pounding as loudly,
it seems, as the headbanging on the cell walls by Dott's victims,
back in the nick. I try to concentrate. I try to join Dott's inner
world, allowing my thoughts to slide any way he wants to take
them. But he appears to have no interest in what I'm thinking.
Does he even really need me at all? I want to ask him. At the
same time I don't want to spoil his fugue. It will come when it
comes, I tell myself—a blind faith that wobbles like a plate spun
on the top of a pole. I can't let my faith fall down to crash apart.

The metamorphosis of Dott commences as briskly as the
horrors he perpetuates in the prison. What his deeds have sum-
moned—the anti-world, the erased existence beyond the bound-
aries of the grass—it surges in closer now. Air is squeezed tighter.
Is this what deep-sea diving is like? My lungs are like I've had the
snorkel to the canisters pulled from my lips. Dott and I are in an
ocean of air, but it's too close; twin wings of agony start flapping
at my temples, my nose erupts with a menstrual cycle's-worth of
greasy blood. Every pain and indignity suffered about my person, my whole life long—every punch I've received, every kick,
every half-hearted stabbing— every pain comes back to revisit
me, unlocking my throat and the vomit I've been holding down.
And Dott seems not to notice a thing. His skin is tightening. Like
those games you play when you're kids, pulling back the flesh
that flanks your eyes to pretend you're Oriental: that's what he
looks like. But this shape doesn't last long. As the grey, bloody

curtain inches closer, compressing what air that's still in here, Dott starts to wrinkle. Slices of laughter lines, deepening now, as if it's revenge time; the execution needs to be swift. I don't know why it takes me so long to figure it out, what is happening; I've been waiting for this a long while. All my life?

Dott is ageing. And ageing rapidly.

The frequency of my inhalations is increasing by the beat; I am too scared to watch Dott's façade get older (while inside he is moving back to his birth) but I am too short of air even to move my gaze away, to turn my head. If I squint I can see beyond the man beside me. The grey curtain, swizzing now like a dead TV channel: transmission bollixed: it is sweeping and lurching, no grace in the movements, here to eat us. Without moving my head—for I'm not sure I can, and the failure will panic me too much—I refocus on what's closer to hand. Dott is shrinking in his garb. I want to say his name, but I don't have to: he knows I can't speak. Indeed, the very action of opening my mouth fills my throat with the stench I smell back from the prison—burning flesh. The blood in the grey curtain has clearly come a long way: briefly altering my attention once more I see more than what the yoots let out of their bodies, back in Dellacotte. I see pieces of the bodies themselves.

What has happened there? Dott? I try again to say. The word is stillborn.

He mouths the words—*Be strong, Billy*—but they do not come out either.

I long for noise; it's too quiet. I prefer the outlandish din of a full-scale riot. This approach from my enemy—this approach from Dott's deity, or so I guess—is too frightening in its wordless potency. Honest dread is what I feel.

Hold tighter, Billy, Dott mouths.

I want to tell him he doesn't need to keep using my name—

to save his breath—but Dott doesn't want to save his breath: he wants to spend his breath, quickly. I can't stop him now—or stop anything else—even if I want to. The effects are brutal in their efficacy. Dott ages in appearance from the twenty year-old I leave behind in the ambulance, to a man of forty, sixty, eighty— the time scale required to do so being puny. Has even a minute elapsed? How much time in real time? He's getting smaller. But so, I notice with a start, regarding my arms for a second, am I. The pains I feel re-surface. I will find him, or he will find me, I remember, understanding in my bones the important message. I am dead before he makes me; I am dead when I unmake him. Dott's my blood.

Don't do it, Dott, I scream, brain to brain.

My eyesight is wavering, blurring; what I see inside the curtain is obviously a contagious image—it is filling my vision. I'm passing out, I realise. It takes all my effort to move my right arm a tiny bit, in order to scratch my skin deeper on the rose thorn—that way to wake myself up. It doesn't work. The last thing Dott's eyes say to me before they cloud over with cataracts long overdue—for Dott by this point must be two hundred years old to look at—is this:

Too late, Billy. Can't you see? It was always too late.

What starts as haze and static, behind us, around us, getting closer, is palpably physical. It is present, pushing down on my curved spine. I'm shrinking. I'm getting slightly older as well (sun spots manifesting) though at nowhere near the rate that Dott is disappearing from me. His outward demeanour is no longer even human. My eyesight fades to black. I am blind. Dott's skin hasn't rotted away, as I have expected will happen, to leave the bones behind. Quite the opposite: the bones that hold him up have dis-integrated under the pressure he feels so much more keenly than I do. He is an abandoned overcoat of flesh, leaking blood into the grass as we hug his stupid tree. He is getting what he always wanted—but what about my wants? All I can see now is what I see with my imagination—and with my memory. I remember being born of the ground; I remember it! The pains, too—I remember them. Literally speaking, it's all coming back to me. As the curtain makes its final leap forward towards us, it folds in over our heads. There is no breath in my lungs. I'm going to die with my maker. Who is now leaking into the grass of the oasis, taking pieces of the rose's stalk and the tree to which it has wedded itself with him. All is dark. All is silent. It's night or day. Dott is dead. But then again, so am I. It has worked. And yet, at the same time, it hasn't worked.

Nine.

Dear Miss Wollington,

Allow me, if you would, a brief moment of disrespect; but shall we cut to the chase? Shall we? You now know everything about me you need to know, and yet I know so very little about you. I have tried my best to be honest throughout, scrabbling around for memories the size of dust particles sometimes; because you asked me nicely and you said I would reap the benefits. With all due respect, Miss—when? Where're them benefits? In your office that night, when you were playing classical music and I was pretending to have a bellyache? Did you know I was coming? You appeared composed—dare I say it, even flattered I'd swing by. Or at least that's how I recall it when I'm here, away from it. How many memories, though still, do we cheat ourselves on? It's like that old philosophical thing about colours, innit? How do we know we all see the same colour? My blue could be your gold, vice versa. But how I remember it is this: you said you'd help me. If I tell you everything, you will help me. We sign a contract, though still. Well, you now know everything I can think of. Your turn. I have referred to you in the third person throughout but there's a reason for this, I'm sure; I can't quite put my finger on what that might be but I know there was one. Easy, it would be easy to ask you—I'm sure you know yourself—if you ever have me over to the Health Care rooms again. When's my next appointment? When do you want to see me? Do you want to see me? Some days, Miss, I am not even certain you exist. Have you left the prison? If so, can someone reading these words please put on file I need a new Psychologist assigned. And if you've left, Miss Wollington—Kate, you said I can call you Kate—I wish you'd said summing. While I'm not claiming I went through this only for you, I did do so a bit.

Hit me back when you get a chance, please?

ALFRETH, WILLIAM.

Ten.

The words I apparently mumble before I wake fully are these: *I live with failure.* Then I'm spluttering—spluttering like that time I drank methylated spirits for a dare. I don't know who might have dared me to do such a thing, but I know it happened, way back when, when the past meant the past and it was something to run from frightened. And then it was something to ignore.

Don't try to sit up, son, I'm told.

The face is kindly, unfamiliar, lightly bearded not through style sensibility but through personal neglect caused by overwork. He is wearing a white lab coat; he's a doctor.

Where am I?

Hospital. You inhaled a lot of smoke, he tells me.

I also took on a lot of physical abuse, as I recall, but I hold my tongue on the subject. I let my pains find me again; they scurry home hard to my bones. Is the riot over? In what shape have I left Dellacotte YOI. I cough again, noting I've been cuffed to a hospital bed.

How's Dott? I ask.

Who's she?

Ronald Dott.

I don't know, mate, the doctor replies. We've had a lot of you guys in here this morning. What started the riot? he asks candidly, wide-eyed.

It's about time. Allow it.

Giving up on me for the moment, the doctor orders me to rest, informing me further I'll be free to go shortly; there's nothing serious wrong. But there is, I want to tell him, closing my eyes again. I don't know if Dott is really dead. I don't know if I helped carry him far enough back, to a place and time that's before his own possibilities for future life. How can I tell? And who else can I tell any of this to either? The answer is Kate. Kate Thistle, of course.

I strike a deal with myself not to cough anymore, whether or not the effort makes my eyes bulge and bleed. I want to show I am fit; I am healthy enough to return to the nick. But is there any nick to go back to? Next time I wake, I'm more aware, not only of my surroundings, but of my senses: the taste of smoke on my tongue; an undeniable shoving sensation against my kidneys; and a body-high, body-wide series of relayed pains and twinges. My gut rot kicks in again, more welcome than any of these later additions, and I treat it as I would an old friend.

Too late, Billy. Can't you see? It was always too late.

I hope I've assisted him to the place he wants to go— which is no place. No place at all; an anti-place. I hope I've been his passport to banality, to emptiness—to the negative. Thinking these thoughts, I sit up. Where am I? Hospital, I've been told, but I've not been given a room and the cupboard in which I've been left resembles nothing like a hospital that I know. A cupboard?

A broom cupboard to boot. If not for the shackles on each wrist, securing me to the metal sidebars of the bed, I might well pick up a broom or a mop and use it as a weapon to get the hell out. The fact the light has been left on—a bare bulb burning above me—is not much of a consolation. Apparently I'm not worth any more than detergent. Hospital? The town of Hospital? Suddenly I'm scared again. Have I not made it back to where I started? Scratch that. Have I not made it back to where I started the previous day? When I shout out for help my throat tells me off; it is raw and aching, and utterly, totally dry. For the sake of continuity—continuity of my mental faculties—it's quite a relief when the same doctor that consulted with me before now opens the door.

Are you all right, young man? he asks.

Apart from being locked in a fucking cupboard? Yeah, I'm peachy, mate, I retaliate. Any of the screws here? The prison officers?

Oh, one or two.

Well, can I speak to one, please?

I think they're all being treated, the ones that're here.

Treated?

In all my years, I've never seen a late shift like this, the doctor continues, shaking his head—even raising one hand to run sausage fingers through his dark, sweaty hair.

Why, what's happened?

Full-scale riot, young man.

Oh, that.

Yes, that. Tell me: how did they get the keys?

Who?

The prisoners.

My mind catches up and joins the dots, but it's not as fast as I want it to be—not as fast as I've been in the past. I say:

Excuse me?

At least one prison officer lost his keys, in a tête-à- tête, shall we say? Went round releasing some of the other prisoners. Never seen anything like it. Several times he shakes his head; then he reacquaints himself with the old bedside manner, and his voice becomes more clipped. All beds are full. So are most of the corridors and waiting rooms. I shouldn't say this, but this could be a time bomb.

Jesus. You mean there are yoots out there without screws to look after them?

The police force's in. The army's in, says the doctor. What I'll do is try to find someone in charge and suggest you're fit to go back, if there's anyone to take you back. We need all the space we can get, to tell you the truth, and you've got nothing that can't wait.Talk about a stretch of resources! What started the riot? he asks me for the second time

I invent a total lie for the doctor to start spreading around on his coffee breaks.

Some of the lads got tired of being raped by the prison officers. That sort of thing can't be allowed to carry on.

The doctor makes a face. He'll be my town crier. For now he doesn't know what to say, but he adds: That's the best I can do for you, right now. I'll be back to check on you in a bit.

Doctor! There's one other thing!

What is it?

Bit embarrassing, doctor, I tell him, but I really, really need a piss.

I'll ask a nurse to bring you a bedpan.

Thanks. And just one more thing before you go. Could you turn off the light, please? I'm getting a suntan in this box: bulb's too bright.

Certainly. Sorry. Will you be okay? Shall I leave the door open?

I'll be fine. I like the noise of activity, I answer candidly.

The doctor sniffs his mild amusement. Well, that's one way of putting it, he tells me. I have to ask you one thing, young man—call it professional curiosity, but I don't see it very often. You're between eighteen and twenty-one, right, to be a prisoner at Dellacotte?

Yeah, I'm twenty, I tell him.

What age were you when your hair turned white? he asks.

There'll be no clues, will there? I'll never know if Dott made it back beyond the starting line, or if he's merely settled once more into the traps, to run the race another time. Poor old Michael Finnegan, begin again. Loathsome old Dott. Where is Kate Thistle when I need her? Where's my visit?

What time is it? I ask one of the three screws in the meat wagon.

Two other yoots and I are on our way back to the dreary walls and the stagnation. We've been assigned an officer each. All three of us are in cuffs—standard—and we've been pronounced fit enough to return to duties; the screws have their batons drawn, even though we are low risk prisoners, otherwise we wouldn't be in the same vehicle at the same time. No one is taking any chances. The screw's name is Vincent: the woman from the Visits Room. She tells me, Two, but I'm so discombobulated I add: Afternoon or morning?

It's light outside, Alfreth. It's the afternoon, she answers, puzzled.

Thanks.

One of the other YOs has a name like Markwell or Maxwell, or something like that. I only know him by sight— he's a regular fixture in the Library on Thursdays, when C Wing gets its trip to borrow books.

Yo, Redband! he says.

Wogwun, blood?

Do you remember much about last night? It's all a blur for me.

Remember bits, I fib. You know how it started?

No idea, cuz. One minute I'm bashing one out.

Thank you, Marwell, says Vincent, nice image for us all.

The next, shit's sticking to the wall, cuz.

Allow it. Miss? Do you think there's any chance of normal duties today, Miss? I've got some important stuff to clear up in the Library.

I very much doubt it, Alfreth. You'll be part of the cleaning detail.

Marwell has an opinion on this verdict. *Fuck* that shit, Miss, he says.

Mind your language, son, says one of the other screws.

I think he's the one who sits in the mosque, looking bored, when we do Friday prayers. Well, not me; when the lads who do Friday prayers do Friday prayers.

I will clean my own cell, sir, Marwell continues, but I am not cleaning up another man's shit. That's unfuckingdignified, man!

And don't call me *man* either! You'll do what we say.

We'll see about that. Sir. There's only so many cells in the Seg, sir.

Your own cells are gonna be worse than the Seg cells for a little while. The screw—is it Simmons?—now smiles. I'm not even certain your cells are safe anymore. Facing facts for a sec, I'm not sure what we're doing is legal.

I can see the future clearly. Twenty-four-seven bang up. No appointments, no visits, no Education, no Library, and no Movements. One unlocked at a time to collect a meal. Cold food. One shower a week. Body odour and a rising sense of compound rage.

They will punish us for what has happened— for what Dott's done. But where is Dott now? Has he also been released from the hospital? Has he vanished from the hospital? If I ask the screws in the butcher's van, here, I'll raise suspicion. I ride the rest of the journey in silence, wishing for a window to look out of. Rather than see the hills we climb, I feel them in the extra efforts of the vehicle itself—as the driver in the cab up front drops down a gear and then another to bust the incline. When we stop at the front gates, I can smell the place. It smells of hatred.

With my newfound trust in the positive aspects of not keeping time, I have no idea how long passes before the YOI is on track to some semblance of normality. My thoughts, in the meanwhile, are proved correct: we are kept locked up. Nothing happens; days die. Scarcely do I notice them go and I don't attend their funerals. I lie on my bed and think of what has occurred. I talk to no one, and no one talks to me. There are no Association sessions; no games to play; no gambling to win at or lose; no hot water. There's no right to a phone call, or an appointment with a Wing representative, or the Prisoner Council; there's no TV. There is no electricity after the fall of darkness. No response to a night bell. There is no Canteen—no extra crisps or choccies at our own expense. There are no shop Movements.

There is bedlam. Protestive acts are commonplace, even boring, and continue unabated and are seldom challenged by the screws. What's the game? What's the intention? That those routinely responsible will burn themselves and burn their anger out? These screws have got a long, long wait; but haven't we all? So I lie down on the bed or on the floor, reading nothing, composing the few letters I must write; and I wait for something from Dott. Meanness makes me feel stronger. I hope he's beginning his journey from old age to youth once again. I hope what happened in the desert failed. I will not need to face him another time in my span on earth. Maybe the next time that I go around, circumstances will paint another picture. But I won't remember any of this, and there's nothing I can do about times to come.

Because I've kept my cell clean since rebounding back to Dellacotte, I am eventually allowed back to my job in the Library, where I promptly resign on my first day of duty, with a smile and a handwritten note. Miss Patterson is displeased: she thinks I'm the best Library Redband she's had working for her in the last decade of her time in the prison. For these words I thank her warmly, and then wish she'll leave the room so I can talk to Kate. It takes till nearly the end of second Movements before I can speak to her alone. I am as certain of what she'll say as I am of my decision to leave this job. She will tell me she doesn't know what I'm talking about. She will tell me I recite a good story, a good yarn; she will ask if I'll put the kettle on. And why do I think this? Because I've made a few points of detection: I have checked the long wooden box in which are kept the borrowing cards of all the yoots who've signed up with the Library. There is no card for 'Dott, Ronald' and when I've mentioned his name a few times, in passing—and only with screws—there's a blankness about the face, a twitch of the shoulders. Perhaps I've killed him before he's born. If I have, he's never been here—been to jail or been to England—if I've got that correct. I'm not sure. I'll wait for signs.

Hit me back, Dott.

I will try to read humour in the eyes of Kate Thistle—when she's quizzing me over, asking me to decode and decipher rougher nuggets of slang she's found within these walls. I will help her. I'm a good boy. But I'm leaving the Library, I tell her. After that she will need a new translator. Or alternatively, she can find me—elsewhere in the prison. I won't be far away. Promise. I've got plenty of time to exhaust.

— THE END —

David Mathew is the author of two previous novels, *Ventriloquists* (Montag Press) and *Creature Feature* with M.F. Korn (Post Mortem Press) and *Paranoid Landscapes*, a volume of short stories. Born in Bedfordshire, England, David has travelled widely, working in a variety of countries. He has since returned and lives in Bedfordshire once again. As a researcher and technical writer, David publishes academic work and focuses on developments in education, health and psychoanalysis.

Printed in Great Britain
by Amazon